SECRET BATTLES

Praise for *Secret Battles*

"Today, when email and message apps make communication virtually instantaneous, it's hard to imagine the agony of waiting weeks or months to read a loved one's heavily-censored words from across the world. Or to fathom the torturous decisions—what secrets to keep, what truths to reveal? Through the letters of Walt and Nora Baran, Geri Throne shares the intimate struggle of two people writing to keep hope and love alive in a war-torn world. *Secret Battles* will have you hoping they succeed."

—Darlyn Finch Kuhn, Author of *Red Wax Rose, Three Houses,*
and *Sewing Holes.*

"*Secret Battles* is an exquisitely written work filled with engaging characters and an authentic and believable story line. Set in the anguish and heartbreak of World War II, *Secret Battles* is aptly named. Nora is a beautiful war bride who struggles with shattered expectations. Her husband, Walt, is a reluctant soldier to whom the idea of slaughtering another human being is repugnant. He goes off to war battling real enemies as well as secret demons left from an unresolved family tragedy. This thought-provoking book engages on many levels and lingers with this reader long after the last word is read."

—Linda Dunlap, Author of *Rail Walking and Other Stories,*
Pushcart Prize nominee

"Set in WWII America, Geri Throne's debut novel chronicles ordinary people whose lives take extraordinary turns in a vividly imagined tale of separation, isolation and the healing power of abiding faith. You won't want to miss this one."

—Anne Mooney, Editor, *The Winter Park Voice*

For Jennifer,

SECRET BATTLES

A Novel

Geri Throne

GERI THRONE

With gratitude for all who served and sacrificed in World War II

ONE

A single golden hair caught his eye the moment his train car rolled into sunlight. Walt pulled it from his khaki coat. Between his fingers the strand of Nora's hair felt strong as cable, sturdy enough to link him to her—her scent, her taste, the swing of her hips, the catch in her laugh.

Her parting words buoyed him: "At least you'll be home again soon."

Not just soon. For good. In one month, his Army hitch would be over, no matter how many rumors of war he'd heard at Fort Bragg. That was the reason he'd enlisted back in January. Serve your one year before trouble starts: That's what the recruiter said and it made sense. If he waited to be drafted, he could end up in the Army a lot longer. Eloping with Nora two months later made sense, too. She was all he needed.

As the train headed south from the Newark station, he pulled a blank piece of paper from his chest pocket and dug out a pencil from deep in his satchel.

> Dec. 7, 1941
>
> Dear Nora,
>
> Leaving you is still the hardest thing I have to do in this darn Army. It was heaven being home on leave. I promise you that next month our life will be—

His pencil skidded across the paper, the victim of a drunken Marine careening down the aisle. The man fell hard against him. Flushed and panting, he screamed into Walt's ear: "Did ya hear the news? Did ya?"

Walt's instinct was to pummel the fool. He started to swing but thought better of it. Too many military police hounded the train cars. He shoved the Marine away. "You're stewed, you idiot," he hissed. "Sit down and leave the rest of us alone."

The marine reeled back, his eyes wide. "*Listen* to me! It's the goddamn dirty Japs. They—they..." He was almost choking on his words now. "They b-bombed us!" His voice grew louder as he stumbled away: "I'm tellin' the truth."

"Get lost, you asshole," another soldier yelled. A chorus of skeptical passengers muttered agreement as the Marine staggered toward the rear door.

Walt winced. Better to ignore the drunk, whose combined stink and noise made him unreliable at best. He pictured the MPs tying a straightjacket on him as soon as the train stopped in D.C., but a nervous silence filled the jammed car after the man lurched out the door. One by one, the passengers—most of them young enlisted men returning to their Army bases—lit cigarettes and shifted in their seats, their tension as thick as the car's smoky air.

Walt noticed such things without trying. He was curious about what made people tick; he had a knack for reading them. "That's the problem with you, boy," his father once told him. "There's two kinds of people in this world—the ones that do and the ones that watch. You're a watcher, that's all you are."

You don't even know me, Pop, Walt thought. The kind of man I am. The things I can do.

As the train barreled south toward North Carolina, tension in the stifling car grew. Everyone in his car was probably thinking the same thing, Walt thought: What if that damn Marine was right?

At the next stop, he jumped off and raced to the nearest newsstand. A wall of customers surrounded the vendor, screaming for late editions. He pushed through until he spotted a headline filling half a front page: "JAPS ATTACK." Goddamn that Marine, he thought as he pulled out a nickel and grabbed a copy. Couldn't he have given us just a few more hours peace?

He scanned a few paragraphs, enough to grasp the larger truth: The United States surely was going to war, just as Franklin D. Roosevelt had wanted.

In the breath that separates reason from panic, he imagined boarding the next train back to New Jersey and running off with Nora. He'd gone AWOL from Fort Bragg twice already to see his wife, hadn't he? And no one ever found out. Surely America was big enough to hide him again. But the thought of Nora made him realize that by now she probably had heard the news, too. He rushed to a phone booth where the line snaked ten-men deep. "Come on, come on. Hurry up, why don't you?" he mumbled under his breath as each soldier picked up the phone. His turn came just as the conductor began to call passengers to board.

She answered on the first ring, her voice small and tight.

"What's going to happen to us, Walt?"

"It'll be all right. Don't worry. We'll get through this." He tried to sound confident. In the long silence that followed, he heard her deep breaths.

"Walt?" she said finally.

"Yes, Nora?"

"I love you." she whispered. She hung up before Walt could tell if she was crying.

***

By the time he was back in his seat, chaos ruled. Everyone in the car knew about Pearl Harbor. High-pitched shouts pierced a low, steady rumble of dismay. For every youthful soldier eager for war, another—often older—man cursed or frowned.

Walt slunk low in his seat. Outside, miles of pale barren fields mirrored his emptiness. His careful planning had amounted to nothing. The Army had him trapped. He couldn't return to Nora any time soon. He jabbed his pencil at his note to her until its tip snapped. "So much for promises," he thought. He crushed the note into a ball and hurled it across the aisle.

War, he was certain, was the invention of politicians and big businesses eager for power and money. He'd heard Father Charles Coughlin preach that message often enough on the radio show his father tuned to every Sunday night. Walt didn't buy everything the fiery Catholic priest said, but he understood why Coughlin called the president "the great liar and betrayer." Walt didn't trust Franklin Roosevelt's pro-war propaganda. Plenty of Americans shared that opinion.

Whenever the men in his infantry company sat around shooting the breeze, Walt tried to explain the truth about FDR. "Can't you tell the guy's every move is calculated to get America into Europe's conflict? Those countries have been going at each other for centuries. What business is it to us?" Walt quoted Father Coughlin until they tired of hearing his name, but wasn't the priest right? Hadn't Europe defaulted on its debts from the last war? And what threat was Nazism to America? He quoted the great aviator Charles Lindbergh: "Over 100 million people in this nation are opposed to entering the war. If the principles of democracy mean anything at all, that is reason enough for us to stay out."

That day's looming truth made all those arguments irrelevant. With Japan's attack, America couldn't avoid war. As an infantryman trained for war, Private First-Class Walt Baran would have but one function: to carry a gun and use it.

He didn't fear death; it was part of life, and his Catholic faith assured him of a next life. Blood didn't bother him either. He'd seen bodies wrecked by wounds when he'd worked at his father's funeral home as a teenager. He'd wiped them clean without a second thought. But causing another person's death—that was different. He frowned, remembering the night his big brother died seven years earlier. His grief still tormented him. So did his guilt.

He stretched and shifted in his seat, careful to avoid nudging the burly soldier next to him. The man's furious scowl warned him to stay clear. Walt lit a cigarette and took deep, calming drags. The car's thick tobacco stench mixed with gusts of coal-fired steam seeping through cracked-open windows.

The train sped across open fields, slowing only to pass through small towns. At big cities like Washington and Richmond, it squealed and lurched to a stop at stations to pick up more passengers. By the time it neared Fayetteville, Walt felt numb. His day had started with hope. Now, one thought possessed him: He had to do something to change his fate.

**

Fayetteville was dark by the time the train wheezed into its station. Walt methodically gathered his things, in no hurry to return to Army life. He joined a ramshackle pack of soldiers hiking to Fort Bragg in the cool night air.

In recent weeks, the base had become jammed with new recruits. In hindsight, Walt realized, their growing numbers signaled war's inevitability. The Ninth Infantry Division was so short of space that Walt's Sixtieth Regiment had to move from wooden barracks to a makeshift tent encampment in a parking lot.

As he approached G Company's area, Walt spotted his two best friends—Tom Lucas and Frank Hatcher, the only men he really trusted in the Army—huddled with their staff sergeant. They spoke so quietly Walt couldn't make out their words until he was almost upon them. The sergeant was saying another regiment in the Ninth Division—the Thirty-Ninth—had already been ordered out, probably to North Carolina's big cities to guard factories and bridges against sabotage. "It won't go too far because the Army never splits a division," the sergeant said. "When the Ninth moves out, it will go as one."

Hatcher turned to Walt after the sergeant moved on. "That's good news, right?" His voice cracked at the last word.

Walt nodded. Hatch, as everyone called him, often had to ask his friends to interpret things outside the logic of his orderly inner universe. Although older than Walt by two years, his upbringing in a rural Jersey town hadn't prepared him for the Army's unpredictable ways. "Sure, pal," Walt said, shading the truth, just as he had for Nora earlier that day. "As long as the

Thirty-Ninth is busy nearby, the rest of the Ninth won't go anywhere."

Tom Lucas shook his head. "I'm not so sure. We never unpacked from our field exercises. The Sixtieth is ripe to leave soon."

Tom wore the intense expression he always assumed when problems arose. Although the youngest of the three men, he was the oldest of five siblings back home in Maryland. Much was expected of him, Tom often said. His parents, strict Methodists who never spared the rod, trained him to be both prepared and obedient.

Walt's upbringing, though no less strict, yielded no similar effect. His busy mind questioned and prodded and analyzed compulsively as he pulled one cigarette after the next from his chest pocket. Lighting a fresh smoke with the still burning butt of his last, he peered back and forth from Hatch to Tom as he pondered the puzzle facing them. When he finally spoke, his tone was firm. "Sarge is right, Tom. It makes more sense for us to stay put. Besides, this war is in the Pacific. The Air Force and Navy will go long before us." He bent down to brush dusty soil from his pant legs. He couldn't bear seeing even a wisp of doubt in their faces.

***

The next day, word spread through camp like an SOS: President Roosevelt was to address Congress at three o'clock. Someone balanced a radio in an open window and turned up the volume. The men of G Company gathered close, but no one pushed or jostled. Tension wrapped them in a careful circle.

Walt positioned himself next to the window and tried not to think of the determined headache that woke him that morning. Touching his temple, he felt a vein throb with quiet fury–his own private warning signal of an explosive inner restlessness. Hatch squatted nearby, twisting his cap in his hands. Tom concentrated so hard on the radio he looked as if he could see FDR speak: "Yesterday, December 7, 1941—a date which will live in infamy—the United States of America was suddenly and deliberately attacked…"

Roosevelt's confident tone didn't fool Walt. It reeked of the same forced bravado he'd used the day before with Nora and his friends.

When the speech shifted to the country's next move, the Congressmen's roars almost drowned out the president's call to take "all measures" for the nation's defense. No one in G Company made a sound, not even when FDR's closing words won robust applause in Washington: "I ask that the Congress declare a state of war between the United States and the Japanese Empire."

All around Walt, an intense mood ironed the faces of the men into smooth, unreadable planes. Was it fear or resignation? The soldiers walked off in small, hushed groups, speaking in flat tones. Then, one by one, they returned to routine duties—straightening their barracks, KP assignments, cleaning their rifles. Walt couldn't fathom how they acted so calm on a day that changed everything.

He cursed his decision to enlist. He had been so sure of his strategy. He thought he was too smart to be hoodwinked, but by now he understood that a military enlistment was unlike any other contract. He was the only one making an iron-clad vow. That recruiter—the one who guaranteed him a one-year hitch, tops—that guy was like a used-car salesman trying to sell a car that "never left the garage." Before his signature had dried on his enlistment papers, Walt had relinquished any right to back out. The Army, on the other hand, could change its terms any time; it could send him wherever it wanted as long as it wanted.

He needed a plan. Without it, he would face the fate awaiting his two best friends and every other infantryman. He pulled out paper, uncapped his pen and took a deep breath.

December 8, 1941

Dear Nora,

The first thing you need to know is that I love you with all my being. Today's news will never change that. Please don't worry. I promise you we will be all right. Whatever time I have yet in the service, even if it is years, just love me as you always have. If you keep telling me you love me, I can take anything they give…

TWO

From the moment I heard about Pearl Harbor, I paced my parents' cramped apartment like a prisoner. The radio reports had to be wrong. Why would Japan bomb some tiny, unknown Pacific island?

The newsmen kept saying war was inevitable. They sounded eager for it. Only hours earlier Walt and I had been planning our life together after his discharge. We would find an apartment in New Jersey. He would work for his father until he found something better. I would keep my job as a secretary; the pay was decent enough. So many dreams. Now all I had were questions: Where would Walt end up? Would he be safe? How could God let this happen?

By the time Walt called, I could hardly speak. He tried to reassure me, but fear made it hard to listen. I had to hang up on him before he heard me cry.

I sat at my father's battered upright piano, my one source of comfort. For as long as I could remember, it took up precious space in our home, its dulled veneer marred by the scratches, stains and dents of earlier owners. My mother touched it only to dust. I treasured it as much as my father did.

Resting my fingers on its yellowed keys, I waited for inspiration. From the moment I pressed the C-sharp start to "You Made Me Love You," my tears wouldn't stop. The bluesy popular tune reminded me of my husband. Its simple melody, so easy to tease out on the keyboard, overwhelmed me with longing.

Halfway through the song, the phone jangled again. I steeled myself. The receiver felt impossibly heavy. "Walt?"

"Hi, Cuzz! Are you okay? It's Milly. Oh my God, can you believe it? Hawaii of all places! My husband says it means we're going to war. At least against Japan. Who knows about Germany…?"

My cousin's chatter rattled me. Older than I by three years, Milly often acted like my big sister, eager to give advice. I could have used it then, but she just wanted to talk about the war. She didn't sound worried. Why should she? Thanks to a lucky high number in the draft lottery, her husband was still home earning good money as a barkeep.

"What do you think? It could take your mind off things."

"Uh, I'm sorry, Milly. What?"

"Margaret Baran, are you all right?" She always called me by my full name when she turned serious. "I asked you to come and play cards with me and Stan tonight. Be good for you."

"I don't think I should. Walt might call again." How could I play games when my husband was headed to some faraway land to fight?

"Since when does he call you late at night? Come on. You can eat dinner here, too. Stan'll pick you up."

"I don't—"

"Yes, you do!" She kept at me, acting as if she knew best, until I abandoned my plans to hide at home that night—"home" being my parents' apartment, the only place I could afford while Walt was in the Army.

As I changed clothes, I realized my bossy cousin was doing me a favor. If I stayed home with my parents, their raw emotions might add to my fears.

Ever since Germany invaded their native Poland three years earlier, my parents both worried constantly about family members still there. Benedyk and Janka Kuczynski migrated to America when they were children, but they clung to their roots. Our country's entry into the war might give them hope, but it also might add to their worries about Poland's future. My mother would pull out her rosary beads, more from habit than faith—she treated her Catholicism like a distant relative, easy to forget until a major holiday or a crisis. My father, a stubborn non-believer, wouldn't pray at all. He'd just turn the radio louder.

My father's lack of faith made sense that day. How could an all-powerful, loving God allow another massive war?

I'd never admit such heresy to Walt, whose own faith seemed bottomless. Even now, he probably was making excuses for God. His mother inspired him that way. Ruth Baran was a passionate Catholic devoted to the church's every ritual. I shot a quick prayer heavenward. "I'm sorry, Lord. I don't mean to be sacrilegious." I wasn't sure what prayers meant in my life just then, but I didn't dare take a chance.

I hurried to brush my hair and put on fresh lipstick before my parents and younger brother came home. I wanted to be gone before my mother stormed the kitchen with clanging pots and pans, before my father filled the parlor with cigar smoke and Polish-language news, before Steve crashed through the front door with school books and a roaring appetite.

My parents owned the three-story tenement building in which we lived, no small accomplishment for immigrants. But to make ends meet, they rented out the ground floor to a grocer at the front and tenants at the rear. That left us with the two-bedroom, one-bath flat on the second floor and two unheated spare rooms on the third. Steve, my brother, slept in one of those upstairs rooms. Sometimes a boarder rented the other one. I was jealous of my brother's privacy. I was stuck sleeping with my mother, whose bed my father had abandoned long ago for a tiny room off the parlor.

I glanced at my side of my mother's sagging double mattress. "I know, I know, God. I should be more grateful."

I left a note on the kitchen table, promising I'd be home early. I raced downstairs to wait for Stan, but just as I yanked open our building's front door, my brother pushed hard from the other side. "Hey, sis!" he croaked. "Where you going?"

I looked up apologetically. Though two years younger, Steve already was six inches taller. "Milly's. I left a note."

"Tonight?" His tone made it clear I was abandoning him.

"Milly insisted." I gave him a quick hug. "Thanks, baby brother."

I didn't care if Milly and Stan won every card hand that night. I wanted their company. But my cousin was wrong about one thing—nothing could make me forget how my world was being torn apart.

THREE

Walt and Tom Lucas sat on a narrow bench outside the mess tent, exhaling cigarette smoke and steamy breath into the cold December night. Now that America was at war with Japan, Germany and Italy, too, all he could think about was escaping the infantry. Rumors of shipping out grew every time furloughs were scheduled and then cancelled. The Ninth Infantry Division was destined for the battlefield.

"I'm not a coward. You know that, Tom," Walt confided. "But I worry about leaving Nora. And armed combat—I can't imagine it. I've got to do something."

His friend nodded. He made no argument, asked no questions. "The Army has plenty of jobs behind the front lines. You'll find one."

Walt was grateful Tom didn't press him about his reasoning. He did worry about Nora, and at 23, he no longer relished dangerous risk. But unspoken guilt motivated him, too.

He ground his cigarette stub into the ground. It had been seven years since his only brother had died in his arms. He'd never revealed to anyone, not even his friends or family, everything that happened that night. Not even Nora. All they knew was that Walt was at the wheel. Yet they supported him, sympathized with him, prayed with him.

He shuddered. Nothing could erase the memory of Cliff sprawled on the side of the road, blood oozing from his side. He remembered pressing hard to stem its flow and screaming for help until his throat was raw. He heard his brother's last breath.

If Walt stayed in the infantry, he was destined to fight at the front. His job would be to shoot and kill enemy soldiers, to cause other men's deaths. He couldn't imagine it. He might as well point a rifle at himself.

***

Not until late December was Walt able to get a five-day pass to see Nora. The Kuczynskis welcomed him into their tiny home as if it had bountiful space. His mother-in-law insisted she would sleep on the sofa.

"You be with your wife," she said.

"I can't thank you enough, Janka."

She scoffed. "What you think? I make guest sleep in parlor?"

That night, he and Nora donned heavy coats and walked to a neighborhood tavern two blocks away. A wall of cigarette smoke greeted them at the door. Inside, unshaven old men occupied five of the six barstools. Walt and Nora huddled over mugs of beer at a dimly lit table near the back, laughing and whispering and holding each other's hands.

Nora reached out to stroke his cheek. "You are amazing. You've done so well in the Army, even hating it as much as you do."

"Well, if amazing means I haven't been court-martialed yet, I guess you're right."

"You know what I mean, Walt. You came close to a promotion once. And you're a—what is that called? That name for how well you shoot a rifle?"

"Sharpshooter? Yup, that's me." He tried to disguise his frown. Now was the time to tell her, he thought. "Actually, Nora, I have an idea. A way I might avoid combat."

Her eyes widened. "You do?"

Walt knew how fearful she was, even though she rarely admitted it. "I'm going to apply to the Medical Corps. It's a long shot, but think about it. I could spend the war saving lives instead of taking them."

She leaned forward, her eyes locked on his. "That is a splendid idea, darling." She looked at him with such confidence he began to believe his own dreams.

***

His first full day back at Bragg, he put his plan into action. He shaved close, spit-shined his shoes and put on a freshly pressed uniform. At the Medical Corps' headquarters, he bragged to a sergeant on duty about his "extensive experience" driving ambulances and his detailed knowledge of the human anatomy.

The sergeant listened attentively. When Walt was finished, the man sounded genuinely regretful. "You sound pretty qualified, soldier, but we have one man too many as it is."

"Any chance that will change, Sergeant?"

"I don't know, but..." He frowned, as if I thought had occurred to him.

"Tell you what—come with me. I'll introduce you to the major. We'll see what he says."

Walt didn't know whether to celebrate or bolt. One misstep could expose him. He knew human anatomy all right, as long as the Army didn't care that he acquired his experience sewing up corpses at his father's funeral home. Not quite the same thing as healing the wounded.

Inside the major's office, he rubbed his palms on his pants as the sergeant relayed his embellished resume. He shifted in his seat, encouraged by the sergeant's enthusiasm.

"Well, Private, I'm sorry we can't use you right now," the major said, "but I expect the Army will expand the Medical Corps soon. When that happens, I'll be looking for men like you. Give your name and unit to the sergeant on the way out. And check back."

"Yes, sir. Thank you, sir. I will, sir."

He rushed to the mess tent to tell Lucas and Hatcher his good news. The major's interest was more than he had hoped for. He'd told his friends his plan the night before—exactly what he'd told Nora. If either of them had shown the slightest disapproval, he would have dropped the whole idea. But they'd seemed proud of him, the way Nora had.

Not until he stepped inside the mess tent did reality block his excitement. He pictured Tom and Hatch fighting at the front. He saw himself somewhere safe, far behind. Guilt stopped him cold. He stood unmoving until he heard someone shout his name.

"Hey, Walt! Over here!" Tom's commanding voice cut through the low grumble of the crowded hall's breakfast chatter.

Reluctantly, Walt grabbed a tray and filled his plate with powdered eggs, cold toast and fatty bacon. He forced a smile as he neared his friends' table.

"Hey, buddy," Hatch said, "Another beautiful day, huh?"

Walt shook his head and tried to smile. "You're impossible. Do you ever have a bad day?" He coated his eggs with salt, picked up his fork and silently pushed the dry clumps back and forth, a sight that made Tom grin.

"If you're not going to eat those, I'll be glad to help," Tom said, aiming his fork at Walt's plate.

The two men acted out this game almost every day. Walt would grab at Tom's cold toast as if Army food was worth fighting over. Their banter could go on for an entire meal—whatever it took to make the Army slop seem palatable.

This time, Walt shrugged. "Take all you want."

Tom and Hatch glanced at each other.

"Sorry, guys," Walt said. "I got a lot on my mind. I was over at the Medical Corps this morning."

"You move fast! How'd it go?" Tom said.

"No openings now. But the commanding officer seemed to like me."

Tom frowned. "That's good news, isn't it?"

"I guess so."

"Then why are you moping, pal?"

"Listen, W-Walt," Hatch stuttered, as he often did when excited. "I was thinking this morning. M-maybe the Medics aren't such a good idea, huh?"

Walt stared at his plate. "I know. I understand why you guys would mind if I joined them."

"M-mind? Hell, no. But aid men are p-pretty close to the front lines, right? You could get yourself killed."

Walt winced. That was Hatch, always worried about everyone else.

"Well, I don't agree with our friend here," Tom interrupted. "I hope you do get in. I'd feel a lot safer having someone as smart as you around with a First Aid kit."

"I guarantee you I am no smarter than either of you guys," Walt said. "And I doubt I'd get my head blown off. I could be useful, though. Most important, I wouldn't have to kill."

Hatch and Tom stared at their plates as if they had discovered something important in the food. Walt's face heated. Had he implied his friends didn't mind killing? "I didn't mean—"

"Maybe none of us will ever have to," Hatch blurted. "K-kill, I mean. I really believe that."

Tom grimaced. "We're infantry, Hatch. That's our job."

In the year that they had been friends, the three men often bantered about hypothetical battles. But rarely did they attach reality to their words. Walt wished he had kept his mouth shut.

Tom rose from his seat. "Got to get back to camp," he said, grabbing his tray. Hatch followed at his heels. Walt lingered behind, sipping the dark dregs of his coffee, awash in guilt.

Jan. 6, 1942

Dear Nora,

I stopped at the Ninth Infantry's Medical Corps headquarters this morning.

Told a sergeant an elaborate, fictitious story about my background. Never have I fibbed as I did today, darling, but I know I could do the job. Tom and Hatch are optimistic about my plan. We'll see. I hope I'm doing the right thing...

***

Standing at a sink at dawn, Walt carefully studied his well-worn razor. He wanted to eke as much life as possible from each blade. Every cent saved would help him afford a hoped-for pass to see Nora. As he dragged the dull metal over his stubborn morning beard, an arc of crimson droplets crossed his chin, as perfect as the curve of sun pushing up over the horizon.

With each swipe he pondered what to do if the Medical Corps accepted him, what to do if it refused. He dabbed his cuts with scraps of tissue and trotted to roll call. Every morning he faced another day of drills and marches to nowhere; of slinking across a field on his belly; of climbing hurdles and jumping into ditches, of becoming the warrior the Army felt ready to sacrifice.

Tom was right about one thing: The Ninth Infantry was battle ready. After a year of training, the soldiers knew how to fire rifles, fix bayonets, hit distant targets and throw grenades. They knew every tank and aircraft. They could run double time up a hill, set up camp in minutes and take it down again even more quickly. They were bullets ready to be shot from a chamber.

In the midst of G Company's thick tension, rumors of Walt's interest in the Medics spread. "You're in a big hurry this morning, Baran," a flushed-faced corporal shouted at him.

"Just trying to get an early start," Walt said.

"Don't give me that." For a little guy, Corporal Aidan Leary had a big mouth.

"Excuse me, Corporal?"

"You're off to the Medical Battalion, ain't ya? Can't get out of the infantry quick enough." Leary dropped his voice and hissed, "The Medics, huh? You fuckin' coward."

Walt took a quick step forward, fists clenched. The corporal, known for using his measly two chevrons as shields, glowered.

"Hey, Walt. Coming with me to mess?" Tom Lucas appeared from nowhere, the way he often did when needed most. Walt joined him, his heart pounding. A solid punch to Leary's jaw would have solved the exchange, no matter what the consequences.

"Perfect timing, pal," he whispered. "One more I owe you."

"Don't mention it," Tom said.

As they walked in silence, Walt contemplated the unexpected gift the Army gave every soldier—the loyal friendship of men like Tom and Hatch. Only Nora's devotion surpassed it.

Nora was his cure for everything the Army threw at him.

He first noticed her in their hometown of Elizabeth when she was only nine—two years his junior. Neighborhood kids gathered at a street corner, teasing each other, swapping jokes and telling tales. She sat on the front stoop of an apartment building, reading a library book. Ziggy, one of Walt's cousins, tried to introduce them. He said their families knew each other and lived only blocks apart. Nora glanced up without a word.

Walt thought she was stuck up.

He didn't see her again until almost ten years later, when she sat across from him at a dinner party at his father's house. "Bring your daughter," he'd heard his mother say when she phoned Nora's parents to invite them. "There'll be other young people here. She'll enjoy their company."

Walt couldn't stop watching her that night. She had a face that men coveted and women envied—full lips, smoky gray eyes, high cheekbones, a delicate nose and chin. As she ran her fingers through her wavy golden hair, she looked away, unaware of his attention. Margaret Kuchynski, as she was introduced to him, was nothing like her name, or her nickname, Marg, or her awkward Polish nickname, Gosia. He had to do something about that. She needed an elegant pet name. It took him two dates to work up the nerve to ask her. "I'm going to call you Nora, okay?"

Even today, he wondered if she knew how much he loved her.

FOUR

January quickly turned frigid, the way my circumstances had hardened since war was declared. Buffeted by sharp winds, I gripped the railing on the back porch of my parents' second-floor apartment and surveyed my neighbors' yards below.

If only I possessed my husband's faith. I needed him that day. I had something important to tell him, something a letter couldn't convey. I needed to tell him in person.

When the cold began to numb my fingertips, I shoved my hands into my coat pockets. I studied the three-story row houses encircling the patchwork of tiny backyards. High fences around each yard provided illusions of privacy, but anyone looking down from a second- or third-story apartment could see everything: the broken bicycle in Mr. Dobranowski's yard; the rusty garden tools leaning against Mr. Slaydek's back door; Mrs. Vacek sneaking a cigarette behind her shed.

My life was nothing as I imaged it would be before Pearl Harbor. I'd pictured myself living with Walt by now, in a place that wasn't the city of Elizabeth.

Before I met Walt, I wanted only to escape this crowded, industrial place. Growing up here was like living in a foreign land. Few people in our Polish neighborhood chose to speak English, no matter how well they knew the language. The grocer, the baker, the parish priest, the neighbors— they all spoke mostly Polish, ate Eastern European food, went to the same Polish church and followed the news from across the ocean as closely as America's.

My parents were no different. They never shook their thick accents and preferred their native tongue. I couldn't avoid learning both languages, but my Polish was a shorthand version that ignored important rules and mangled tongue-twisting pronunciations.

If I had an accent when I was little, I lost it in public school. My classmates and teachers were English, Irish, German, Italian; they were Protestant, Catholic, Jewish, or they had no religion at all. Everyone spoke English. Soon, so did I, even at home. "I'm American," I said. My mother huffed. My father ignored me.

As often as I imagined abandoning my parents' cloistered world, I still clung to its edges. My secretarial job after high-school graduation took me away from the neighborhood on work days, but I returned each night and weekend to shop in its stores, move in its social circles, attend its church.

After Walt – well, everything changed. Everything. He rescued me. He pulled me across Elizabeth's invisible boundaries.

"Mom, Pop"—he called my parents that as soon as we started dating— "I'm taking your daughter to a dance in Bloomfield tonight. What time would you like her back?"

They didn't stand a chance. He charmed them into submission. He charmed me, too, from the moment I saw him at his parents' dinner. I tagged along reluctantly that night, expecting boring conversation with my parents' Polish friends. I hadn't expected the Barans to have a handsome, dark-haired son. His eyes grabbed me the moment I saw him look at me. They breathed fire and fun and love and hell.

He told me we'd met before, when we were young, but I didn't remember. It didn't matter. I felt I had known him all my life. I trusted him. That night, my life began.

***

Fresh blasts of cold on the porch pushed me out of my daydreams. I pulled up my collar and covered my chin with my woolen scarf.

For days I had been sure a life was growing inside me. My period was late after I saw Walt at New Year's. I started to daydream about having a child. I could see its face, hear his—her?—laugh. I saw Walt holding our baby, bouncing him in his arms.

But that morning, I'd awoken to spots of blood and a familiar monthly pain. A terrible yearning swept over me. My parents' home felt like foreign territory, a dusty capsule of old habits and ancient traditions.

***

Nothing in my life with Walt was what I expected, even our plans to marry.

"I think we should elope," he'd said, just weeks after he enlisted.

I was sure he was teasing. "Elope? You mean before a justice of the peace?" Was this the man who obeyed every single Catholic Church dictate?

"The Army chaplain told me we have to wait," he said, scowling. "Wait months. Maybe years. Why wait when we can go to any judge or justice of the peace in South Carolina, on any day of the week, and get married, just like that—for a $2 license and a $5 fee? No blood test. No waiting period. A quick train ride will get us there."

I couldn't say no. I wanted it as much as he did. We arrived in Florence, South Carolina, on a chilly March morning in 1941. We stood before a young judge with a deep drawl in an office barely big enough for us and two volunteer witnesses. No altar. No gown. The ceremony was over in a minute.

"Congratulations, Mr. and Mrs. Baran," the judge said.

"Yes, Mrs. Baran, congratulations!" Walt whispered in my ear.

We made love that night in an inexpensive hotel room, caring little what the chaplain or any priest might say. One month later, of course, we did our Catholic duty. We said our vows before my hometown priest, but that ceremony meant little. Hearing the young judge declare us husband and wife remained the most joyous moment of my life.

I closed my eyes, savoring the memory—that moment of endless possibilities.

When I opened them again, Mrs. Slaydek was crushing her cigarette butt under her heel. Glancing about quickly, she bent down and shoved it into the soil.

She acts as if her husband can see her, I thought, but he's still at his factory job. I longed for the day my own husband would return to me from work each day. I'd seen him so rarely in our ten months of marriage. After our church ceremony, we didn't see each other again for a whole month.

When Walt finally was granted a three-day pass last summer, he arrived home while my parents were at work. I remembered throwing my arms around him and kissing him hungrily. He kissed me back, but his embrace felt distracted. He led me to the sofa. "I have something important to tell you," he said. He sounded so serious I expected bad news.

"What? Are you in trouble? Did you yell at that corporal again?"

A smile flickered on his lips. "No, nothing like that. I—it's just something the priest said."

"The priest?" I was confused. What did it matter what a priest at Fort Bragg said?

"I went to confession last week. I hope you understand. I had to tell the priest I've been using contraceptives."

"You told the *priest* that?" I flushed, embarrassed. My husband had told the priest *everything*, and the priest—a man who never loved any woman but his mother, for goodness sake—had made Walt promise never to use a condom again. I was horrified. Walt—foolish, obedient Catholic that he was—was determined to keep his vow.

18

"What if I get pregnant?" I said after we made love that afternoon. Back then, the thought terrified me. "We don't know how long you'll be in the Army. How will I care for a baby?"

Walt pressed his body against mine and held me tight. "Don't worry, Nora. I'll take care of you and Junior." He spoke of our baby as if it had already been conceived.

Throughout that summer and fall, we had the same conversation every time we made love. Finally, I gave up. I was powerless to erase the careful obedience to church doctrine my husband had learned in four years at a Catholic boarding school. Even though he'd gladly disobeyed the Catholic chaplain to elope, he clearly was incapable of violating a foolish promise made in the confessional booth.

I didn't understand why Walt took his religion so seriously. I'd been baptized and confirmed in the Catholic Church, too, and I went to Mass now and then. Wasn't that enough? I wouldn't dream of telling my deepest secrets to some nosy priest in a darkened booth.

***

Over the last few months, Walt, not God or the Church, gradually helped me believe. He assured me the odds of getting pregnant were slight because we saw each other so infrequently. "If it does happen, dear, it will be what God wants for us, right?" he said.

God better not want me pregnant, I thought then. I wasn't ready. I panicked almost every month because my cycles were so irregular.

Gradually, though, my thinking shifted, with no conscious effort on my part, the way flowers shoot from still-cold earth after a spring thaw. I loved Walt so much, I reasoned, that God surely wanted me to have his baby.

The more I thought about it, the more I wanted a baby, too. The war made me even more determined. No one knew what the war would bring. But a child—no one could take that from me. Walt's child would always be with me.

Another blast of cold air startled me. I grasped the porch railing again. Below me, Mrs. Vacek was back behind her shed, tapping another cigarette from her pack. I wondered how the old woman kept her secret from her husband, why she bothered. Keeping secrets made no sense.

I studied the barren frozen soil. In a few months it would burst miraculously with the fruit of each neighbor's careful plantings—with lettuce, carrots, radishes and tomatoes; with roses, hydrangeas, chrysanthemums and daisies. Closing my eyes, I imagined their abundant scent. Life would blossom again.

Jan. 25, 1942

Dear Walt,

We need to take advantage of every chance we have to see each other. There's so much we need to talk about. Letters don't let us do that easily. Besides, I need your arms around me, and your kisses! How quickly do you think you can get a pass? We can meet at that hotel in Richmond, Virginia. You know the one. Let me know as soon as you can. I miss you terribly...

***

The best part about the William Byrd Hotel was its location directly across from the train station. The 11-story limestone building had affordable rooms as well. Given that Walt had only a one-night pass, I had little time to share my plan. He had to agree with me. I rested a palm on my flat stomach. "Please, God, I'm sorry for defying you. Let there be a next time. Give me a child."

When I stepped off the train in Richmond, he was on the platform waiting for me. "You're here," he murmured, gathering me in his arms.

We spent the afternoon and dinner hour talking about everything except what was on my mind. I talked about my cranky father and nosy mother, about Milly and her husband, about neighbors Walt and I both knew. Walt talked about his Army maneuvers, his staff sergeant's demands, his plans to become a medic, and a loudmouth corporal named Leary who always tried to pick a fight.

I didn't tell him about my dashed hopes for a pregnancy. The future was more important. We made love until after midnight.

The next morning, I awoke to Walt sitting shirtless at the edge of our bed, staring at me intently. I stretched and smiled. "Ummm. What are you doing up so early?"

He leaned over and kissed me gently, the glint in his eyes reflecting our night together. I kissed him again. Sunlight streamed through the thin curtains, a meager shaft of warmth in the chill morning air. It made no difference that our hotel room was cramped and cold. We had all the covers and space we needed in our double bed.

He moved back under the blanket with me, as I knew he would, and we cuddled and joked until he glanced at his watch. "It's late! Your train comes in an hour!"

I was running out of time. "I have an idea," I said.

"Anything you say, my dear."

"Anything? My goodness you are an easy one."

He laughed and stroked my cheek. "You haven't steered me wrong yet,

20

Nora," he said, "not from the moment you proposed."

I shook his arm in mock annoyance. Who proposed marriage to whom was our private joke—an argument with no right answer because each of us had wanted it. "I'm serious, Walt. Listen. I've saved enough money to quit my job and move to Fayetteville. We can rent a room. We can share our lives. You can come home to me every night!"

He stared at me silently, eyebrows raised.

"What's the matter?" I said. "Don't you want me living near you?"

He smoothed back a strand of hair from my forehead. "My precious wife, what am I going to do with you? You are such a romantic."

I shrugged his hand away.

He leaned closer. "Be sensible, hon. Who knows how many days or weeks we have before I'm shipped out?"

"Exactly. Who knows? It could be months, days, hours. Why waste a moment of however long it is being apart?"

"Think about it," he said. "Life would be hard for you in Fayetteville— no friends, no family, living in a tiny place with hardly any money."

"I don't care about any of that, don't you see? I just care about being with you."

He lay next to me in silence. Finally, he propped himself up on one elbow.

"We'll see," he said, pulling me close.

FIVE

Walt hitched a ride from Fort Bragg to reach his destination. At the intersection of Murchison Road and Hay Street, he gave the driver a thumbs up. Newspaper in hand, he hurried through downtown Fayetteville's loud, tacky clutter of taverns and shops before turning east into a quiet neighborhood of weary two- and three-story homes needing paint and repairs. Married soldiers were willing to pay high rents for those rooming houses because they were close to the base. Walt wasn't interested.

Feb. 10, 1942

Dear Nora,

I'll find a way to make your idea work. I wouldn't count on any money from my father, but don't worry. I'll do everything in my power to make you comfortable and happy while you're here. I'm going into town this afternoon to look for a room...

He couldn't resist her, even if he wanted to. He never could. They'd have to watch every penny, but they'd find a way.

His soft-spoken wife constantly surprised him. When she applied her iron will to a problem, anything could happen. No matter how often he'd dreamt about her living in Fayetteville, he couldn't imagine those dreams becoming a reality. Nora could. The determined way she spelled out her plan the last time they were together convinced him. He decided not to tell her about his struggles getting into the Medical Corps. He couldn't stand dashing her happiness.

Nora changed him in ways he didn't know he needed. She gave him the gift of connection. He'd possessed it before, when he was very young.

22

Every time he entered a church, he felt God's absolute love, the thrill of belonging. But after Cliff died, and the demands of his father grew heavier, that feeling disappeared. He came to believe that depending on others was a weakness; only the self-sufficient survived.

If depending on Nora was weakness, he thought now, he would gladly claim it. When they embraced, her heart beat in counterpoint to his. He no longer felt alone.

Walt's search for a safe neighborhood took him far from the city's center. He turned east, up a hill overlooking downtown, into tidier neighborhoods where lawns were mowed, weeds pulled, and houses scrubbed and painted. No matter how long Nora was with him—even if the war limited their time together to only days—she would live in a proper home.

Five times he rang the doorbells of houses listed in the classifieds. Each time other soldiers had beaten him to it. Finally, he resorted to his wild card, an address a lieutenant had given him. He climbed a long, steep hill and passed a cluster of shops, diners and a small movie house before turning down a side street.

A small round woman answered his knock with a flourish. "Well, hello, soldier!" she drawled, smiling and blinking. "I bet I know why you're here. You're looking for a room now, aren't you? You just come on in."

After his many rejections, the woman's gushing friendliness and Southern accent—thick even by Fayetteville standards—caught him by surprise. "I'm sorry to bother you so late, ma'am, but Lieutenant Goodwin said you might have a room to let."

"Oh, my, yes. Of course! Lieutenant Goodwin—a fine young man." She tilted her head and studied him carefully as he introduced himself. "My name is Rita Appleby, dear. You just come in and have a seat."

He followed her obediently to her parlor, decorated in floral fabrics and white crocheted doilies, and sat down carefully on a delicate pink chair.

"Your house is very nice, Mrs. Appleby," Walt said. He wasn't just being polite. Outside, the two-story house was freshly painted a pale blue and surrounded by landscaping well-tended even in the barrenness of winter. Inside, the home was a showplace of antique furniture and fine china. He could see Nora here, her beauty well-framed. He imagined the pride in his father's eyes when he came to visit.

Walt cleared his throat. "My wife will be moving to Fayetteville this month. She's a secretary and hopes to find work here."

"Well now, she shouldn't have any trouble. Not a bit. Businesses around here are always hiring people." She and her husband had decided to rent out a room as their patriotic duty, she said. "Let me show it to you. It's nice and clean. You'll see."

She led him upstairs and directed him to his left. The room was modest in size but big enough for a double bed, end table, bureau, card table and two straight-backed chairs. The walls were painted pale yellow. White eyelet curtains softened blackout drapes on three tall windows—the darkened windows a necessity of wartime in homes near military bases. A gold-and-navy-checked oilcloth tablecloth covered the table. A matching curtain hid a "kitchenette"—a tiny nook with a cupboard and single-burner electric stove.

"There's a private bathroom down the hall," Mrs. Appleby said. "Of course, your wife can use our stove and kitchen sink when we don't need them."

"This is nice, ma'am. Very nice. What's the rate?" He was almost afraid to ask.

"Eight dollars a week, paid by the month," she said, blinking.

"Mrs. Appleby, I think we have a deal." He grabbed her hand and pumped it.

She stepped back at his touch, eyebrows raised, but managed a smile as she pulled her hand gently from his grasp. "It is *my* pleasure, soldier."

Walt computed the math in his head—$32 a month for rent would leave $10 a week for food and other expenses. That should be enough if we're careful, he thought, even if Nora can't find a job. Plus, they'd have $20 left after he paid the two months' rent in advance.

Feb. 13, 1942

Dear Nora,

I have good news! I found the perfect room for us. It's a steep hike from downtown and not the biggest, but the home is very nice. I think we'll be comfortable there. I'll tell you more the next time we talk on the phone. My mom and pop were planning to come here next week anyway, so you could ride with them. It wouldn't be any trouble for them to bring your things...

***

"Absolutely not. I can travel by train."

No matter how hard Walt tried to convince her, Nora stood her ground. She didn't want to join his parents. They argued about it on every phone call.

"I don't see the problem with you coming in their car."

"I told you, the train will give me more privacy."

He suspected the real problem was his folks, or more specifically, Max. He knew his father made her uneasy, but the old man seemed to be behaving himself lately.

"Listen, Nora, I can't stay on the phone too long. There's a line growing behind me. My folks really want this. Let's talk about this tomorrow." He hung up. He couldn't tell her Max already assumed she would join them. If Nora backed out now, his father would be furious. Max didn't appreciate people with independent streaks, especially women. He would call his beautiful wife the next morning. She would agree with him eventually. She had to.

SIX

Driving to Fayetteville in Max's 1938 DeSoto sedan would take twelve hours, but taking a train made more sense. Why couldn't Walt understand? He knew how his father was, how he teased and taunted and chose his words so slyly I couldn't challenge him. I dreaded matching wits with him without Walt by my side.

"Don't be ridiculous," Milly said, when I told her my predicament. "Why waste your money on a train when Max'll drive you for free?"

Milly knew Max only from social gatherings, where he usually was on best behavior. I wished I could take her with me. Quick-witted and fearless, Milly could match my father-in-law at his games if anyone could.

When my phone rang early the next morning, I knew it was Walt again. In a voice both calm and insistent, he simply said, "Just accept my folks' offer, okay?" I had to give in. I lacked the will to keep arguing. I wanted my arrival in Fayetteville to be cause for celebration, not a fight.

As soon as I hung up, I dialed Ruth. "Hi, Mom. It's Nora. I hope it's still okay for me to join you on your trip to Fort Bragg."

"Well, of course, dear. We're looking forward to having you along," said my mother-in-law, sounding oddly bewildered.

***

Four days later, just before dawn, I sat shivering on my parents' front stoop. My belongings were heaped at my feet, just as Max had ordered— two suitcases of clothing and three cardboard boxes filled with dishware, pots, utensils and a few household items. I rubbed my hands together to keep them warm, my heart galloping at the thought of finally being with my husband.

Promptly at six o'clock, Max's sedan screeched to a stop before me. He stepped out of the car with authority, his tall, muscular frame demanding obedience. He tossed my bags and boxes into the car's huge trunk and pointed to the back seat.

"Hurry up, Maggie. We gotta long drive."

Max always called me by that nickname for Margaret; he knew how much I hated it. Everyone in my life seemed to have a name for me of their own choosing. In my parents' and grandmother's homes, I was Gosia, or rarely, Malgorzata. My brother just called me Sis. Until I met Walt, almost everyone else—my other relatives, my co-workers and friends—all called me Margaret. But the only name I truly loved was Nora. Walt taught everyone in his family to call me that—except Max.

"You all right back there, Mags?" Max said.

"Fine," I said, hunching out of the way of his rear-view mirror. I knew most of the conversation traps to avoid with my in-laws—the hidden ruts and roots that launched Ruth's left eyebrow or etched Max's scowl. Conversations with Max could turn into a chat with the Mad Hatter if one wasn't careful. Logic and good manners could disappear. No one could escape, even Ruth.

"Max, please be careful," she said at one point as he raced along a twisted road.

His face purpled. "Oh, so you're an expert at driving cars now, are you? And here I thought you didn't even have a driver's license." He slammed on the brakes and started to pull over. "I tell you what—you drive!"

Before he came to a full stop, she murmured, "I'm sorry, Max."

"Then keep your criticism to yourself, okay?" he said, stepping hard on the gas again.

Try as I might, I couldn't puzzle a reason for Max's behavior. Why would a man so wealthy and powerful in his circle act like such a bully? Why did he need to lash out at anyone who dared disagree with him? Maybe only Max knew why.

I wished I had taken the train.

***

Two hundred miles into the trip, Ruth handed out crackers, sandwiches and bottles of soda.

"Goddamn roads," Max bellowed in between bites. "Nobody knows how to do their job anymore."

As the road narrowed and the pavement roughened, he focused his irritation on potholes while Ruth chatted about the weather, the scenery, and Walt's letters to her. Max ignored her. I answered now and then. Ruth and I weren't close, but at least she wasn't always spoiling for a fight.

My mother-in-law cared about Walt. I could tell. At one point she worried aloud about him getting into the Medical Corps. "I heard from a friend in church that soldiers have to take special classes before the Medical Corps will accept them. She said the classes can be very difficult."

"I'm sure he'd do fine," I said. "Remember the grades he earned in high school?"

Max snorted. "Who cares about grades, Mags? What really matters is how a man does in life."

I'd forgotten Max's attitude about schooling. He'd put both his sons to work at cheap wages before they even finished high school. I suspected he measured their value by how much money they saved him. He put his faith in the dollar, and it never let him down.

From that point on, Max hogged the conversation. I let Ruth handle him. No matter what her husband said about business, politics, the traffic or anything, she nodded and said, "You're right, Max. You're so right."

I wondered what my in-laws saw in each other. Ruth's soft voice shuffled in the shadows of her husband's bragging. She scrimped and saved, acting as if she had only pennies to live on, Max acted as if his bank account had no bottom. He knew every angle. When rubber grew scarce, he bought extra tires from a shady guy he knew in Newark. When cigarettes prices climbed, he bought cartons on the black market. He'd stuffed some of them in the trunk that morning, probably to coax favors from strangers along the way.

I studied them closely. Dressed in his trim, tailored black wool suit and vest, Max exuded wealth. His slicked-back, dark brown hair glistened. He didn't look like he belonged with Ruth, whose mane of untamed blond curls billowed around her plain features. Max often bragged about the expensive jewelry and gifts he bought his wife on his travels, but that day she wore dime-store earrings and a fuzzy yellow sweater that clashed with her shapeless purple-checked dress. To my surprise, she still seemed beautiful. She didn't dress to impress anyone but herself.

I closed my eyes and pretended to sleep. The DeSoto rolled along like a large boat. By the time we stopped at a diner in Virginia for a quick, wordless snack, I felt relief. We were almost there.

In our final hours on the road, even Max grew quiet. The rich scent of the car's leather seats and his billowing cigar smoke unexpectedly calmed me. I daydreamed about living with my husband, about our chances of having a baby, of Walt playing with our child.

As we pulled into Fayetteville, I spotted my husband from a block away. He looked poised and calm in his freshly starched uniform, as if his wife arrived in a shiny black sedan every day. Max coasted to a stop in front of him. Before I could reach the car door handle, Walt opened the door wide, a moist glint in his eyes. He held out a hand and pulled me up. He held me so tightly I felt his heart beat.

"Hey, Butchie. You're looking sharp." Max stood next to us, tapping Walt's arm. As far as I knew, Max, and Max alone, called my husband "Butchie."

"Hi, Dad." Walt shook his father's hand before guiding me to the curb, his arm around my waist. He let go only to help his mother out of the car. "You're looking tired, Mom. How was your trip?"

"Fine, fine. You know your father. He doesn't let speed limits stop him. We got here a lot faster than I thought."

"Okay, where to?" Max interrupted. "Anyplace around here serve late dinners?"

"Just up the street, Pop, but we have time before it closes. Let's unload Nora's stuff first." Walt seemed so sure of himself. He was taking charge, something I'd never seen him do when Max was around. This was Walt's home turf, not Max's.

I held Walt's hand as we all climbed back into the car. The DeSoto finally felt safe.

***

The Appleby's home left me speechless. I gaped at its luxurious touches—the brocaded pillows, floor-to-ceiling curtains, elaborate crown molding and thick carpets. All that was missing was a piano.

Walt pulled me aside. "You look so gorgeous, Nora. Everything go okay?"

All twelve hours of my trip flashed through my mind, but all I said was, "Fine. It was fine."

"See? I told you it would work," Walt said, kissing my cheek.

He carried the suitcases and boxes upstairs while Mrs. Appleby showed me, Max and Ruth to the parlor. "You've got a mighty beautiful home," Max said. "It reflects its owner well."

Rita Appleby blushed. "You're too kind, Mr. Baran."

"I'm just being honest," he said, pulling his seat closer to hers. "I've been in many fine homes and this is one of the most impressive. Even finer, I dare say, than Otto Brandt's. Do you know him? Of the Royce and Brandt Funeral Home near downtown here? He's an old friend."

I cringed, embarrassed by Max's fawning and name-dropping. My own father, though only a factory foreman, had many prominent friends in Elizabeth—doctors, lawyers, businessmen. They flocked to our tiny parlor to smoke pipes and cigars and talk of politics, philosophy, science and the day's news. My father never traded their names like currency.

Max cared little about such heady topics, but he was a genius in business, I gave him that. He knew how to sell himself. I watched Mrs.

Appleby lap up his every word, flattered by his attention. I wasn't impressed. I wondered if Max could tell.

SEVEN

The scar over his father's left eye roiled purple as Walt spoke. The crescent-shaped mound warned him to tread carefully.

Walt remembered reaching for the scar as a boy, fascinated by the terrain of his father's face. "Daddy, wassat?" He'd pressed a finger against it and cried out when the hardened skin resisted him. His father choked out wheezy laughter. "This dirty Wop ambushed me on Jersey Street, Butchie. He got in a good hit to my noggin. Blood everywhere." Max glowed as he described the low blow he retaliated with. "I could tell my mom was proud," Max said. "She used her best needle and thread to stitch that cut closed."

How old was Walt when he first heard that tale? Four? Five? He remembered all of it, especially the image of his grandmother happily pulling silk thread through the skin on his father's forehead. He and his brother treated the scar as a barometer. When their father slept or rested after a meal, content and quiet, the mound dissolved like the moon in the morning sky. It glowed ruddy pink when he hiked through forests, a hunting rifle slung over one shoulder, or when business was so good every viewing room in his new funeral home was in use. But when the scar turned purple, it augured howling storms, a rain of words.

Walt braced himself as he sat across from his father in the hotel lobby.

"Whaddya mean you ain't heard nuthin' from the Medics?" Max demanded, slipping into street slang he never used at work. "Didn't I tell ya to talk to that commander again?"

"Let me explain, Pop. I already applied. I check back every day. I can't try any harder." Walt imagined himself standing toe to toe with his father, eyes locked. He pictured himself matching the tone of his father's rant with a sharp, "That's enough, Pop."

"Try? Trying is for losers, didn't I teach you that? You gotta act!" Max's scar throbbed. "What's that CO's name? Give it to me."

Walt handed it over, more out of habit than obedience. His father put him and Cliff on his payroll before they were old enough to drive, pushing them to work as hard as men at boys' wages. He commandeered their lives. Resistance required more than guts. It demanded patience and shrewdness. Loud arguments never worked on Max, nor did begging. He despised people who groveled.

Cliff was always better at handling Max. His brother knew how to sweet-talk their father; he'd act as if he agreed with him completely even as he gradually nudged Max toward a different point of view.

Walt hoped his firm voice disguised his doubts. "I'll get into the Medics, Pop. I'm not worried."

Max ignored him. Slipping on his suit jacket, he turned to Ruth. "Let's get going. Brandt'll be waiting for us."

By the time they all arrived at Otto Brandt's house for brunch, his father seemed to have forgotten the morning's exchange. He'd lectured Walt as he drove. "Men like Brandt are good to know, boy. Don't forget that. He's important here. People look up to him. Act friendly." Walt bit his tongue at Max's obvious instructions.

At Brandt's spacious home near downtown Fayetteville, Max rushed through introductions before quickly pulling the businessman aside. A broad-shouldered, imposing man, Brandt handled it well, smiling politely as Max chatted nonstop about cash flows, bill collecting and difficult customers. By the time they all sat down to eat, Max's scar was pale pink. He and Brandt held the floor, swapping stories about their many trips around the country. Walt didn't bother trying to talk. He could get to know Brandt after his father left town.

Shortly after noon, his father glanced at his watch. "Listen, Butchie, your mother is getting tired and Otto and I have business to discuss. Why don't you and Nora take her back to the hotel to rest up before she and I leave? Mr. Brandt says one of his men can give me a lift back in an hour or so."

Business—that's all the old man cared about.

Walt slid behind the steering wheel of his father's car and turned to his mother. He had an idea. "I'll drop you back at the hotel, Mom. Nora and I have some cleaning up to do in the room. We'll be back in a couple of hours." He met Nora's eyes in the rear-view mirror and winked.

***

Walt and Nora entered the Appleby's house silently and climbed the stairs without a word. As soon as they entered their room, they locked the door.

Walt kissed her softly as he guided her to the bed. He slowly unbuttoned her blouse. He didn't want words. He only wanted her.

Two hours later, when they returned to the hotel, Walt helped his father pack the sedan. His scar still pink, he slapped Walt's back. "Thanks, son. I'll take you and Maggie back to your place and then your mother and I will be on our way. Write and let us know how you're doing."

Walt shook his father's hand carefully, wary of his father's newfound calm. "I will, Pop. I will." Max's practiced smile failed to reach his eyes, but Walt didn't care. He was relieved the old man was leaving on a positive note.

"You take care, son," Ruth said. Walt gathered her in a hug. He never doubted his mother caring, but now he had Nora. He took his wife's hand. Having her with him changed everything.

***

True to his word, Walt called Otto Brandt the next day. Their conversation was polite, if short. "I'd love to have you and your lovely wife over for dinner someday. You must give me a call," Mr. Brandt said. From his experience in Fayetteville, Walt recognized that Brandt's wording wasn't necessarily an invitation, no matter how much it resembled one. North Carolina gentlemen took pride in acting polite. "Thank you, sir," Walt replied, the way local townspeople would do. "That would be nice."

The first week Nora was there, Walt woke early every morning to stop at the Medical Battalion headquarters first thing. The sergeant offered little encouragement. "The major is a busy man, Private," he'd say. Walt lingered longer each time, making small talk with the sergeant about the Army, their families, their hometowns. By Friday, the sergeant greeted him with a friendly hello, but his answer was unchanged: The commander's schedule remained solidly booked.

G Company's obliging commanding officer let Walt go home to Nora most nights and promised him a full day with her most weekends. Walt requested Sundays, the only time he felt comfortable walking with Nora along Fayetteville's main street. Saturdays were out of the question. On that day, the city's sidewalks became a moving organism of frustrated soldiers with nothing to do but drink. Crowds of them spilled into wide boulevards, stopping traffic and launching boozy fistfights. Some soldiers became so rowdy that restaurants and taverns refused to serve them. Downtown was no place for a lady on a Saturday.

Fayetteville was a patriotic place, proud of its country and its Army base, but Walt understood why many of its 15,000 residents had had enough of Fort Bragg's 125,000 soldiers. At least on Sundays, with all the bars closed, Fayetteville became as close to normal as the times allowed. Normal was what Walt craved.

"This is nice," Nora said on her first Sunday outing as she scooped ice cream from a paper cup. A parade of couples and families passed by. "Look at them, Walt. You'd hardly know a war was going on. Have you heard any news about what will happen with the Ninth?"

He pressed a finger to her lips. "Shh. Remember what I said, love. You can't ask me anything about the war or troop movements. Army regs won't let me talk about it."

To his relief, she shrugged and changed the subject. In truth, the Army didn't care one bit what he told her, since he knew nothing about the Ninth Infantry's plans. He just didn't want their conversation to veer toward the Medics. He couldn't bear telling her the truth—that the Medical Battalion wasn't a certainty, that he was likely to end up fighting on the front lines.

***

Undeterred, Walt kept up his daily stops at the Medics. Every morning, he sat in a straight-backed chair next to the sergeant's desk, smiled expectantly and asked, "Any news?"

Every day, the sergeant politely shook his head.

Then, one cool March morning, something shifted in their exchange. Walt spotted a change in the man's expression. Something unpleasant was being left unsaid. "How are you doing, Sarge? Is everything okay?" Walt asked, keeping his tone friendly.

"Look, Baran," the sergeant said, wincing slightly. "You seem like a nice guy. You should know the commander isn't so sure about you. He's heard some negative things."

Before he could check himself, Walt exploded. "What the—? What are you talking about? Who'd he hear that from?"

"Whoa, there. Hang on." The sergeant frowned.

Walt took a deep breath, fearful he'd just undone all his efforts. "I'm really sorry, Sarge. That was uncalled for. It's just that I have a pretty good record. Ask my platoon chief. Ask my company commander. Who would be saying bad stuff about me?"

The sergeant eyed him for what seemed like minutes. He looked around carefully and leaned closer. "I probably shouldn't be telling you this, but it's some little guy. A corporal. Says you're a troublemaker."

"A corporal? You know his name, by any chance, Sergeant?"

"No, I don't, Private. I'd tell you if I did."

Walt wasn't so sure the sergeant would tell him the truth. He suspected Corporal Aiden Leary was involved. The little bully never stopped harassing him. Leary seemed hell-bent on putting him at the front line. Walt wanted to punch the guy, even if it made matters worse.

EIGHT

For weeks I looked in the classified ads for a job as a secretary or receptionist. Every interviewer acted so friendly I was sure I would be hired. Eventually, I realized what Walt had tried to warn me: Their politeness revealed nothing more than a proper Southern upbringing. Local businesses gave local girls preference and those girls needed the work as much as I did.

Fayetteville was nothing like any New Jersey city. Every business operated at an unhurried pace. Clerks and receptionists drifted casually through their chores, unconcerned that a boss might demand immediate action.

The humid climate slowed me down, too. By early April, spring coaxed out colorful blossoms and bold green leaves. Crepe myrtle, magnolia and peach trees shaded yards. Thick beds of pansies, impatiens, hydrangea, and phlox erupted overnight. The air didn't smell of oil refineries and car exhaust, as it did in Elizabeth, but of cherry blossoms, gardenias and jasmine.

I passed my days reading in my room or trying new recipes in Mrs. Appleby's kitchen. I explored the neighborhood, too—anything to escape her four walls. One day, pretending I was going on a job interview, I applied make-up and dressed in my Sunday best so that Mrs. Appleby wouldn't pry.

The pearl button that cinched my dress at the waist grabbed tightly at its loop, no doubt the result of the hard candies Mrs. Appleby left in a crystal bowl by the front door. They filled me up when my own cooking didn't suit me. I need to pay more attention to my diet, I thought.

I slipped into a pair of navy-blue pumps and pinned on a felt hat. Outside my bedroom door, Mrs. Appleby swept the stairs with long, lazy strokes. I waited for her to finish. Her lavish smiles made my teeth hurt, the way they throbbed when I ate too many candies. When I heard pots and pans clanging in the kitchen, I slowly turned my doorknob and tiptoed downstairs.

Mr. Appleby, a quiet, reclusive man, was rarely home in the daytime and ignored us when he was there. But Mrs. Appleby, who'd promised to treat me like family, fussed over my every move. I couldn't leave the house without giving her a full account of where I was going.

That morning I just wanted to be left alone. I snuck out quietly without grabbing a candy.

At the end of the driveway, I fingered pink buds bursting from ancient floribunda bushes. Seeing no movement in the curtained windows behind me, I broke off a blossom just above its fierce thorns and poked the stem into my lapel's buttonhole. Fayetteville was as safe as a churchyard at that hour, with a few young mothers pushing babies in wicker carriages and older women plodding slowly to stores. Soldiers, meanwhile, were at the base and most townspeople were at work.

I walked carefully on Hill Street's thick red bricks. At the corner, the street earned its name, angling hard downward toward the center of town. The steep grade slowed my pace, jamming my toes into my pumps.

Halfway down the hill, I felt something wrong inside me. Tiny bursts of light flashed in my eyes. My skin turned sweaty; my legs grew weak. I grabbed at a wrought-iron rail along a front yard to steady myself. A nearby door slammed.

"What's the matter, dear? Are you all right?"

A plump housewife rushed to my side and put her arm around my waist. "Lucky for you I was looking out the window for the mailman." The woman guided me to her porch and sat me in a hard-backed chair.

"Papa! Bess! Come out here, quick," I heard her call, "This lady doesn't look too good."

A low rumble of a voice responded. "Put her head between her knees. She's fixing to faint."

I gripped the edge of the seat. I wasn't sure if I was seeing double or if more people were crowding around me. A hand guided me forward. I leaned down, skirt hiked high and head held low. Someone pressed a cold washcloth against my neck.

"I don't know what's the matter with me," I said. "I'm sorry to be a bother."

"Don't you worry," the old man said. "You're no bother at all. This ever happen before?"

"No, never. But I'm just not myself lately. Not eating the right foods, probably. A lot of it doesn't seem to taste right lately."

The plump woman flashed a knowing look at the other woman. She smiled gently and invited me to come rest in her parlor.

"Sweetie, you should see your doctor."

"Oh, I'm not sick, really. It's not anything like being sick."

"I know, dear. Believe me. I have three children of my own."

I stared at her. The woman's words made no sense, but the look on her face did.

"Children?" I pressed my belly softly. A smile claimed my face, revealing my shock, my joy, my wonder. "I'm going to have a child?"

NINE

His prayers were answered—Nora's, too. A new life grew inside her, a fragment of hope. He wrote his parents the news: Their first grandchild would arrive by year's end.

Every day seemed reason to celebrate. In the balmy weather, Nora finally could put away her knee-length raccoon coat and unpack her wide-brimmed straw hat. Walt watched her pin the hat in place and check the seams on her stockings. It didn't matter what she wore; she always looked beautiful.

"Let's go downtown after lunch, Walt. I know it's a Saturday, but you're off duty and this day is too lovely to waste. We can check out the latest fashions in the department store windows."

"You don't need new fashions. You're gorgeous whatever you wear."

"Don't worry," she said. "I won't be spending any more money on clothes for a while, not with Junior adding to my waistline." To him, her three months of pregnancy hardly showed, but she groaned as she buttoned her skirt.

To save a dime on bus fare, they walked the mile to downtown instead. They strolled along the main avenue and stopped for drinks at a soda fountain. At the movie house, Walt counted out six nickels—just enough to buy two matinee tickets to *The Maltese Falcon*. A uniformed usher guided them to their seats.

Walt slumped down when a newsreel showed London's bombed ruins and played Winston Churchill's latest speech. "Why do they have to show this stuff?"

Nora slipped her arm in his. "Ignore it, dear. At least the movie isn't about the war."

He avoided her gaze, trying to conceal his growing worry.

***

May 6, 1942

Dear Mom,

Nora and I spent Sunday aboard Mr. Brandt's yacht. My buddy Hatch joined us. We cruised toward the coast on the Cape Fear River. It reminded me of the times we took Dad's boat out in Barnegat Bay. Tell Dad I had a chance to talk to Mr. Brandt. He's been asking me to do that...

He addressed the letter to his mother, knowing she would share it with Max. His father's cabin cruiser was a toy compared to Otto Brandt's *Sea Flower*, with its full galley, lounge, separate toilet and sleeping space for six, but Walt kept that to himself. Instead, he shared some of Brandt's marketing tricks. That's the news Max wanted—that, and how well Walt was cozying up to the businessman.

Ironically, Brandt needed no buttering up to treat any GI well. In the short time Walt had known him, he'd seen the older man befriend dozens of soldiers. He slipped them money, hosted them at elaborate picnics and entertained them on his yacht.

Walt felt privileged to be invited aboard the *Sea Flower*. "Bring your wife, and a friend or two," Brandt said. "I insist."

A cool, damp mist hung over the river the morning of their trip. Walt was glad he'd made Nora wear a jacket. She lifted her collar as the boat slid from its dock near downtown. "We'll set out for the coast," Brandt said, "but we probably won't reach it. It depends how swiftly we can pass through the locks."

Two hours into the ride, Brandt invited Walt to his wheelhouse. They chatted about the boat, of which the businessman was clearly proud, and then about Fort Bragg and how it had changed the city. Brandt, a veteran, was more tolerant than most.

"How do you like the Army, son? Is it treating you well?"

"It's hard work, that's certain," Walt said, adjusting the binoculars Brandt had handed him. He zeroed in on couples strolling along the riverfront, seemingly unaffected by the war. That'll be me and Nora one day, he thought.

The two men swapped stories about target practice, mock combat and other training exercises. Walt confessed his dread of having to kill. "I'd never have to carry a gun if I was in the Medics," Walt said. "But that doesn't look likely now."

"You think so?"

"I've knocked on the Medical Battalion's door every other day for two months, and nothing."

Walt described his recent encounter with Leary. "First, he mouths off to me. Calls me—well, nothing good. Let's just say it reflected his true feelings about me. Then he badmouths me to the Medics' commanding officer."

Brandt uncapped a bottle of cold beer and passed it to Walt. "This war has everyone under great stress, son. A non-com can feel it the worst."

"Respectfully, sir, I doubt stress has much to do with the corporal's point of view."

Brandt chuckled softly. "Perhaps not, but don't let someone else's short fuse get to you."

Just being able to talk about Leary and the Medical Battalion's refusals made Walt feel better. He'd been too embarrassed to open up to Tom and Hatch and didn't want to burden Nora, who was sleeping poorly lately. It had taken all his powers of persuasion to talk her into coming that morning. "It's such a beautiful day, Nora. It will do you good," he'd said.

By the time the boat passed through the river's third lock, a mild breeze replaced the morning chill. As the *Sea Flower* neared the river's juncture with the Black River, a strong gust delivered an odd mix of brisk sea air and heavy welding odors from Wilmington's shipyards miles away. Walt stood with Nora and Hatch at the bow, watching the broad stretch of water and its fast-moving currents. The yacht made a wide circle to turn around.

Hatch, who had never seen anything like the *Sea Flower*, rubbed his hand along its lacquered teak rails. "Some rig, Walt. Think we can we go out on it again?"

"Up to Mr. Brandt. I expect we will though. He acts like he enjoys our company."

"What were you and Brandt talking about for so long?" Hatch asked. "You two were gabbing the whole time Mrs. Brandt was showing me and Nora the yacht."

"Yes! Tell us," Nora teased. "What could possibly be more important than your good friend and your pregnant wife?"

Walt hugged her playfully, ignoring their questions. He didn't want them to think he was doing his father's bidding. Besides, his time with Brandt had yielded unexpected rewards. The older man didn't just treat Walt with respect, he exuded a calming wisdom.

Nora slipped her arm into Walt's. "I missed you, darling. Stay close now, okay?"

Watching her hair billow in the river's breezes, her cheeks pink and eyes bright, Walt was sure he did the right thing bringing her. A day in the sun was what she needed.

***

Nora stopped to catch her breath as she and Walt climbed Fayetteville's steep hills back to the Appleby's. She braced against a giant oak tree and nudged off her pumps, one at a time.

"You okay, Nor?"

"Uh-huh."

"It was fun today, wasn't it? Brandt's boat is spectacular."

"Yes," she said, inhaling deeply, "it was."

"Nora, I've been thinking…"

She shot him a frown. "What?"

He suspected the reason for her edginess. Anxiety about the looming war often held her captive. "You've been struggling with your pregnancy, Nora, and you're alone almost all day. I think you should go back to your parents' house—"

"No! Absolutely not! Don't say that! I have no intention of leaving you."

"Hear me out, Nora. My orders could come any day. I don't know when I'll have to move out or where I'll be assigned. I may not have a moment to spare. I might not be able to help you pack and—"

"Shush, Walt! I mean it! Medics can end up anywhere. I heard someone say that on the radio. You could be sent to an Army base in Florida or California. I could follow you there. Don't talk this way."

He walked the rest of the way in silence, not because of her objections, but because he had kept too much from her.

***

The next morning, back at the Medical Battalion, the sergeant shook his head before Walt could say a word. His message was clear. Walt's efforts were futile.

He couldn't bring himself to return that Tuesday, Wednesday or Thursday, not when his fate seemed set. He'd rather spend those precious hours with Nora. He was getting ready to join her on Thursday afternoon when Corporal Leary stopped him. "Hold it, Baran. We've got a special detail for you."

"Special details" were what the Army called its dirtiest, most demanding jobs. "Just a temporary septic tank that needs re-digging," the corporal said, handing Walt a shovel. Walt was sure he saw a smirk on the lousy runt's face.

Walt unbuttoned his shirt and draped it over a shrub. Objecting was pointless. He imagined Leary's smug face in the latrine's foul, moist soil. Each time he jammed the shovel into it, he muttered a curse.

By the time he was done, it was almost six o'clock. He turned on a spigot and cupped his hands to catch clean water, but without any soap his efforts did little to remove his stench. As he buttoned his shirt, a soldier ran up and called out his name. Walt rolled his eyes and put both hands on his hips, his entire body demanding: "What now?"

"Captain Jones sent me," the soldier said. "Wants to talk to you about the medical battalion."

This is it, Walt thought. The end of all his efforts. He was about to get a final shove-off.

At the Medical Battalion's headquarters, the front-desk sergeant greeted Walt with a silent nod. He led Walt down a long, dark hallway to the officer in charge of screening applicants. "Private Baran is here to see you, sir," the sergeant announced. The captain leaned back, arms crossed, studying Walt intently. Walt shifted nervously, wondering how badly his clothes reeked.

The captain lifted a paper from his desk. "We have an opening, Private, so I took another look at your resume. It seems adequate, but I had to check with your superiors. You understand, don't you?"

"Yes, sir," Walt replied, stifling a groan. The first thing he was going to do when the captain dismissed him was find that bum Leary. They were going to have a little talk.

"You certainly come to us with strong recommendations, Private. Very strong."

Very strong? Those words had to come from his lieutenant or his first sergeant in G Company. Can this actually be good news? He straightened his back.

"I've decided to nominate you for a position as a surgical technician." The captain must have noticed Walt's excited reaction, because the officer spoke his next words sternly. "Let me warn you, Private, it's not guaranteed. You have to master special training at O'Reilly General Hospital in Missouri. We'll see how you do. And no, Private, I don't know when you'll leave. It'll be soon, though, I guarantee that."

"Thank you, sir. I'll do my best—"

"Dismissed, Private."

With a clumsy salute, Walt pivoted on his heel. This was the chance he'd been praying for.

***

Nora hunched over a library book at the card table. A faint burning odor lingered from the pot of hot dogs and beans on the frigid burner. Her quick glance and the swipe of her eyelashes acknowledged Walt's late arrival.

"There you are. I was getting worried." Her eyes darted back to the book.

He pulled a chair next to hers. "You're not going to believe this, honey."

She stared at the pages.

He grabbed her by her shoulders to hold her attention. He was grinning so hard his mouth hurt. "I'm in! They nominated me for the medical corps!"

"But, I thought—weren't you already accepted? I mean—I don't understand..."

"It wasn't official, Nora. I didn't have it in writing. I do now. Well, almost. I just have to pass some courses first, but that should be easy."

Her tears came fast. He wrapped his arms around her and nuzzled his face in her hair. "Hey, don't cry. This is good news."

In the upper register of her cries, he heard a light tinkling of laughter. "I...am happy, you...you...these are...happy tears."

***

They talked late into the night, until sober reality overtook their joy. It made no sense, they agreed, for Nora to stay in Fayetteville while Walt was gone for seven weeks in another state. Their money was running out, and she was in no shape to continue a job search that so far had proven futile.

"You're better off with your parents, Nora. You know you are."

"Not yet. Please don't ask me to leave right away."

"We can't delay long, Nora. I could be sent to Missouri any day. Plus, there's a bright side. This will give us a chance to save money. Your parents will want a lot less than our rent here, and I'll be too busy studying to spend my Army paycheck. We could save enough to bring you back to Bragg when I'm done with training."

She looked at him the way he'd come to know well. She put all her trust in him.

"Let's call our folks," he said, grabbing his coat. Minutes later, at a diner four blocks away, Walt slipped change into a pay phone. "Pop?" Walt yelled into the receiver when he heard Max's voice. "You're never believe what happened today."

TEN

A somber stillness filled Fayetteville's train station the morning I was set to leave. Midweek trains carried few passengers at that hour. I fanned my face with a train schedule in the hot, sticky air. Beside me, Walt shifted from one foot to the other.

My train pulled in with a loud hiss. I leaned close to Walt, my belly nudging his. At three months pregnant, I was just starting to show.

He hugged me tightly. "Have a safe trip," he whispered. Unexpectedly, a cramp grabbed at my womb, a sensation I'd been feeling on and off for two weeks. I hadn't told Walt. I didn't want him to worry, and my Army doctor said it was probably normal. Besides, my own doctor in New Jersey would tell me what to do.

I forced a smile. "Promise me you'll try to see me before you go to Missouri. You'll be able to get a pass, won't you?"

"I will. Of course." He ran the palm of his hand across my belly. "Don't ever forget, you and Junior are all I care about."

***

July 2, 1942

Dear Walt,

It's strange being back in Elizabeth without you. I miss you terribly. Did you apply for that weekend pass? When you are here, maybe my mother will remember I'm an adult. She still treats me like a child. She still calls me by my wretched Polish nickname...

For five months, I had run my own life in Fayetteville. I'd cared for

44

myself and my husband. I'd paid the bills, shopped, cooked, sewed, and did our laundry. In my parents' house, though, I was still a little girl.

Whenever I tried to fix dinner, my mother rushed into the kitchen and pushed me aside. "You sit and rest, Gosia. I cook."

"I'm fine, Mom."

"Do not talk back. Sit!"

I didn't dare tell her about my cramps. She'd coddle me even more.

My mother needed to understand I was no *nunia*, no little Polish girl. I was a modern American woman. "I can help, Mom, and why don't you call me Nora? Walt gave me such a nice nickname."

"*Nie*! Valter is wrong." She grabbed a scrub brush and attacked a pile of potatoes, muttering to herself in Polish. "Malgorzata is your birth name. Mau-go-JA-ta. And Gosia is your pet name. GO-sha!"

She tested my patience. Gosia reminded me of a herd of goats. On our third date, when Walt started calling me Nora, I hugged him gratefully. He alone saw the American girl beneath those foreign syllables.

***

Milly showed up at my door the first week I was home. By a wonderful coincidence, we each expected to deliver our first child in early December. We stood side by side in my parlor, comparing waistlines. I treasured her company.

"Look at us, Marg. We're getting big already."

I shook my head. "People call me Nora now, remember?"

She rolled her eyes. "Okay, Nooor-a," she drawled.

We talked about our symptoms. I told her about my cramps, which still came and went on no particular schedule.

"You haven't made an appointment yet with your doctor?" she demanded. "Why not? Do it right this minute. I'll watch you dial."

That was my cousin, always in charge. This time I was grateful. It was time. I had put off seeing my doctor, hoping the symptoms would go away on their own. I'd kept them secret from my mother, too.

I told my mother the appointment was routine. She frowned. "Maybe my mother check you."

Her mother—my dear grandmother, whom we all called Babcia—was a healer from the old country, known for the magic she worked with her herbal poultices. I held back a laugh. "No, Mom, I think my doctor knows best."

My mother must have believed me, because she said no more about the doctor visit. Instead, the next day, she presented me her latest money-making scheme.

"I have girdles, Gosia," she said. "Very pretty. We go to neighbor ladies' houses and sell. You help."

"You sell girdles door to door?" I burst out laughing. "Where did you get them?" Foundation garments were hard to come by ever since steel and rubber were rationed six months earlier, right after Pearl Harbor. Most of my friends didn't miss them.

She smiled sweetly. So innocent. "A friend tells me where to get. Ladies like them. Ladies my age. Make us feel like girls again."

I suspected her secret. Working in a mattress factory these last few months had tempted my mother and her friends to scavenge their work places for overlooked items. I imagined her raiding some hidden cache of women's undergarments in a factory storage room.

"You help me, Gosia? We stay in neighborhood. Not go far. Not climb many steps. You help measure ladies."

How could I resist? I liked the idea of getting out of the house and paying my keep. I liked that she trusted me to help.

"You tell me if you tired," she said, shaking my arm with each word.

"You worry too much, Mom," I said, pulling free.

The next morning, I tagged behind as Mother approached the front door of a ground-floor apartment. Mrs. Smolski opened the door with a delighted smile. "Come in, come in!"

I watched our plump neighbor's hips jiggle as we followed her down the hall. As soon as she entered her parlor, she peeled off her pale green house dress. I helped lift her slip over her head. "You will love my girdles," my mother said, caressing her waist with the palm of her hand. "Make you slim. Like girl."

Now I knew why mother had me lace her up in her most form-fitting corset that morning. She was posing as a model. Anything to convince Mrs. Smolski we could tame her mounds of doughy flesh.

I wrapped a cloth measuring tape around the woman's waist and hips while Mrs. Smolski patiently stood in place.

"You're in luck," Mother said after I announced her dimensions. "I have your size!" She pulled a lace-trimmed girdle from her satchel and waved it like a flag.

Mrs. Smolski stepped into the garment, which looked barely big enough to go over her ankles. I tugged it up an inch before my mother took over. Moving from one side of Mrs. Smolski to the other, Mother edged the girdle up, inch by stubborn inch, tucking in bulging fat when necessary to get the job done. Finally, it reached her waist.

Grabbing the laces, mother cinched the girdle tight. Mrs. Smolski winced but offered no complaint. She ran her hands along her waistline, closed her eyes and smiled. She saw herself as beautiful.

Mother smiled, too. She saw herself making money.

***

My longing for Walt made my skin hurt. Barely a night passed that I didn't bolt from my mother's lumpy mattress, jarred awake by the dim realization of another body in the bed, thinking for a split second it was Walt. My mother snored mightily next to me, oblivious to my movements.

Walt's frequent phone calls helped. When I answered the phone, his first words were always the same: "I love you, you know."

Three weeks after I left Fayetteville, he received his orders to Missouri. "I have an idea," he said. "How about you take the train here before I leave? I'll get a room in our favorite hotel."

Thank goodness he couldn't see my unease. I'd told him nothing about my cramps or my appointment with Dr. Wenski the next day. "That's a wonderful idea," I lied. "Let's plan the details tomorrow."

***

The next afternoon, waiting in Dr. Wenski's office, I read his medical certificates on the wall. He's well trained, I told myself, even though he'd done little more than grunt during my exam.

He burst in noisily, in a great hurry, and sat on the edge of his high backed chair. "You look fine, Nora, but I see it's not just cramps. You're bleeding, too."

"Just a little, doctor. Like the cramps. Not much."

"Well, such things aren't unexpected early in a pregnancy. It usually means nothing."

"Usually?"

"In rare cases, it could mean something more serious. I wouldn't worry, though." The overpowering odor of disinfectants in his office made my head spin. What did he mean by "more serious?"

"We'll check you next month. But if your symptoms worsen sooner, Mrs. Baran, let me immediately. In the meantime, take precautions and limit your activities."

Each word he spoke sounded ominous. "Activities?"

He looked at me as if I was slow-witted. "The obvious things, Nora. No heavy lifting, no jostling rides in a car, no strenuous activities."

There was that word again. "How about long walks? Climbing stairs?"

He raised an eyebrow. "As long as you don't rush things, such mild actions are fine." He must have seen the worry lingering on my face. "We want to keep baby safe. No running or sports or such." He chuckled softly, apparently amused at the thought of me being athletic. With a deep breath, he rushed through his final instruction: "And no intercourse. But that shouldn't be an issue. Didn't you say your husband is stationed out of state?"

"Uh, yes, he is, but I plan to take the train to see him this weekend."

He pulled off his reading glasses and frowned. "Oh no, no, no, young lady. Not a wise idea. Not at all. No rough train rides. No intercourse. You tell him those are my orders."

He slipped his notes into my folder and stood. "The receptionist will set up your next appointment."

His warnings and my symptoms left me no choice. I had to do what he said. I would do anything to protect my unborn child, even pray to the God Walt believed in so strongly.

***

From the moment I left Wenski's office I didn't stop praying. The Lord better be paying attention, I thought. I need his help.

True to his routine, Walt called that night. "I love you, you know."

"Hello, darling. I'm glad you called. I-I have disappointing news. My doctor—he wants me to rest. He told me—ordered me, actually—not to take the train. He says it would be better for baby."

"What's wrong? Is Junior okay?" His voice grew louder with each word.

"Fine, dear. He's fine." As far as I knew, our baby was indeed fine.

"Then what?" I heard a hint of panic. And anger, too.

"Just some cramping. Nothing to worry about. Really, I would tell you if it were anything more." A small lie, more like an omission.

Walt said nothing, but I heard his deep breaths. "Walt? Are you there? I'll see the doctor again next month. Don't worry. He says there's no reason to."

"Then why doesn't he want you to travel?"

"I told you. It's just a precaution. To make sure baby is safe."

"I'm going to figure out how to get a weekend pass to see you." That was my husband, always trying to fix things.

"You don't have to, Walt. Please, everything is okay."

"I'll call you tomorrow." And he was gone.

I rested my hands on my belly, willing health and safety for my unborn child, knowing I alone lacked such power. "I don't ask for much, God. Surely you can give me this. Keep my baby safe, I beg you."

ELEVEN

Walt stood before his company commander, waiting impatiently for an answer. All he'd asked for was a weekend pass. Why was the officer scowling?

"That's impossible, Private. You're leaving for Missouri in six days."

Every sound outside the tent magnified Walt's discomfort: A drill sergeant barked commands; a platoon stomped by; a truck's tires squealed. Walt chewed the insides of his mouth and saluted his commander. Arguing wouldn't be smart. Better to leave before his temper got the best of him.

He had an idea. He would go AWOL, the way he had when he'd first arrived at Fort Bragg. No one ever found out that he'd spent the weekend with Nora in New Jersey. So what if this time he'd miss a few days of medical training? He'd sacrifice everything for his wife.

"Are you nuts, Walt?" Tom said when he heard the plan. "You know what will happen if you're caught. Did you forget how hard you tried to get in the Medics? Did you forget why you did?"

More than ever, Walt was grateful for his level-headed friend. Even though Tom didn't know all the reasons why Walt wanted to be a medic, his blunt honesty was a gift. The Medical Corps would give him a chance to save lives and to return in one piece to Nora. He was foolish even to think of risking that.

"I don't know why you keep telling me how smart I am," Walt said. "I wish I had an ounce of your common sense."

Tom laughed. "That's why the three of us need each other, Walt. With your brains, Hatcher's good nature and my so-called common sense, we almost add up to one damn fine soldier."

***

A noisy commotion began to overtake Fort Bragg. Everywhere Walt looked, soldiers were cleaning their weapons, sorting their gear, moving supplies. Meanwhile, anxiety built. War alone wasn't the reason. Like Walt, every man knew that each phone call home could be his last. Each call cemented the memory of Nora's voice, her delicate laugh, her sweet sighs. He needed those memories to last. For months. Maybe years.

That night, Nora answered on the first ring. "I can't get a pass, Nor," he blurted. "I'd do almost anything to come home, but I can't."

"It's okay. We'll see each other soon." But her voice betrayed her disappointment.

"How are you? Any new symptoms?"

She hesitated. "I'm fine. No need to worry."

He wondered if she was keeping something from him, but he was no doctor. He wasn't even a surgical tech yet. He had to trust her. On every call, she reassured him, but he couldn't shake his doubts. Tom tried to help by repeating his advice: "Don't forget how hard you worked to get into the Medics. Don't forget why."

When the day came for Walt to board the train to Missouri, he carried a lightly packed duffel bag and a heavy sense of unease. He prayed Nora would be all right.

***

July 2, 1942

Dear Nora,

Springfield looks more like New Jersey than Fayetteville. It has real dirt, not North Carolina's sandy soil, and the plants and flowers look familiar. If you were here with me, it would be perfect, and the Army would finally be to my liking. I am getting to know some of the fellows in my class. It's an interesting group. Let me know how you are. I need to know if your condition changes, okay?...

No matter how much Springfield resembled his home state, Army rules still applied. Walt and his fellow trainees had no privacy, no freedom, no space to call their own. The more self-assured men in his bunkhouse hogged attention by bragging about their impressive pedigrees. Some were Ivy League grads. Others were medical-school students or pharmacists or had master's degrees. All competed for a limited number of surgery-tech slots. They all had one thing in common: No one knew what to expect.

Their first class was a crash course in anatomy. The stocky, bespectacled man who taught it treated every moment like a test.

"Listen up!" Dr. Morris Hanson barked. "In this class you will learn the basics of anatomy and physiology. We'll cover epithelial tissue; connective tissue; the integumentary system; the nervous system, including the central, peripheral, autonomic, sympathetic and parasympathetic nervous system..." Hanson picked up speed as he charged through his list. "Also, hearing, balance, vision, taste and smell; the skeletal system; muscles; the endocrine system; the heart; blood vessels; the respiratory system; the digestive system; the metabolism; the urinary system; the reproductive system, lymphatic and immune systems.

"Does that cover it?" Hanson looked up from his notes.

Walt glanced around. No one spoke. The two dozen soldiers crammed in the small classroom still hunched over their notebooks, scribbling furiously. Walt had jotted down a few key words. He hoped to remember the rest.

His other classes demanded even more. He had to memorize hundreds of detailed pages about medical aid, fractures, general surgery, communicable diseases, inflammations, bacteria, orthopedics, wounds, X-rays, the circulatory system, the administration of drugs, the organization of medical departments, the handling of supplies. His classmates groaned as the lists piled up. Walt's notes grew more detailed.

Part of him was grateful for the heavy work load. Learning so much about the human body made him feel less helpless about Nora's pregnancy. Even though his teachers never discussed the female anatomy, they taught an extensive medical vocabulary. His newfound knowledge gave him confidence. If he had to, he could grill Nora's doctors using their language.

A nervous energy built inside him, a heady anticipation of something too important for words. He had a chance to prove himself in a challenging new universe, to demonstrate that a mortician's son could compete with Ivy Leaguers and medical students.

July 4, 1942

Dear Nora,

These classes are harder than I expected. The guys keep asking me to join them at the local pub, but I can't afford to fall behind in my studies. Your letters this week relieved me. It sounds like you're feeling better. When is your next appointment with the doctor? I want to know everything he says. Take a notebook. Write everything down...

He stayed up late most nights reading his textbooks and reviewing his notes. He prayed every morning to remember it all, especially the content of the dreaded Anatomy class. On the sixth day of class, Dr. Hanson leaned back in his chair, reading glasses perched at the end of his nose. "OK, class, who can tell me which veins empty into the two innominate veins?"

Two dozen soldiers stared at Hanson, dumbstruck—even the arrogant kid the Army had plucked from Harvard's pre-med program. Walt shrugged and slowly raised his hand. He couldn't believe no one knew the answer.

Hanson almost didn't notice him. He didn't seem to anticipate a reply. Walt imagined that the question was intended as a ruler slapped against a desk—a reminder that the person before them was the source of all they needed to know.

"Uh, sir?" Walt said. "The right and left innominate veins are formed where the internal jugular unites with the subclavian vein."

The pre-med kid turned toward Walt and scowled. Dr. Hanson folded his arms across his chest. "Private Baran, have you been reading ahead?"

"No, sir."

"Then where, pray tell, did you learn that?"

"Embalming bodies at a funeral home, sir."

A roar of groans, snickers and disbelief erupted. Dr. Hanson just smiled, as did Walt. Never did he imagine that the hours he spent draining blood from dead bodies and filling veins with embalming fluid would prepare him for medical work.

The moment wasn't a fluke, it turned out. His teachers' dry lectures about the spleen, lungs, liver, arteries, cardiovascular system, muscles and glands all came alive in Walt's mind. An army of bodies he'd prepared for burial at his father's funeral home marched through his memory—the 60-year-old man who'd lost his legs in a fatal accident, the middle-aged woman who accidentally took the wrong dose of medicine, the child whose skull was crushed in a car crash, the young construction worker who'd fallen from his scaffold. The hundreds of dead bodies he'd attended to, the details his curious mind had absorbed—they attended each lecture, three-dimensional renderings as clear as the day he encountered them.

***

Even a thousand miles away, he looked for ways to please his wife. He squirreled away money to afford expensive long-distance phone calls. He let his hair grow into the unruly waves Nora preferred when he saw that the Medical Corps didn't seem to care. She only had to ask him once for a photo. He had a classmate snap one on the front porch of his dorm.

But he had little time for daydreams. The new sets of skills he was learning taxed him to the core. Without good grades, he might not earn his spot as a surgical tech.

By the third week, Walt knew how to tell a fracture from a sprain, set a splint, check for skin diseases, treat infections, identify diseases of the bone, face, head and neck, stabilize patients with brain injuries, and make and apply plaster of Paris casts.

Five afternoons a week, he was assigned to a hospital ward that tended soldiers recovering from injuries, some from Pearl Harbor. He changed sheets, took temperatures, fed those having trouble eating. He cleaned bed pans and urinals and treated bedsores. By the end of each long shift his white uniform bore the stench and stains of sweat and blood, urine and excrement.

He never complained, not after caring for patients who'd lost limbs, gone blind, or suffered other injuries too awful to contemplate. Their wounds reminded him that it was Japan's attack that forced his country into a worldwide war, not FDR.

He never stopped appreciating the Medical Corps, whose very existence was aimed at helping each soldier survive. It trained him well. It also introduced him to its special brand of camaraderie. The doctors who taught at O'Reilly addressed their students more as equals than as dictatorial Army bosses. Brains mattered as much as rank. He could tolerate the military like this.

***

Aug. 26, 1942

Dear Nora,

    I finished my last day of class a few minutes ago. I've kept track of my grades for these past seven weeks and I think I did okay. I'm still awaiting final exam scores, though. They count a lot. If all goes well, tomorrow I'll graduate and earn the title of surgical technician. I'll send you my certificate. Please put it in a safe place. I worked hard for it...

On graduation day, the trainees filed into a packed auditorium filled with large, round tables. The ceremony was a major event in Springfield. Officers gave speeches; a local radio station's orchestra played patriotic songs; local comics, singers and musicians entertained, and a steak dinner was served.

Walt picked at his meal, his nerves crushing his appetite. "I wish they could have told us our fate before all this," he said to the trainee next to him.

"You aced those finals, Baran" his classmate said. "No reason to worry."

Walt thought he passed the exams, but he needed more than that. If his grades weren't high enough, he might not be certified as a surgical technician. Without that title, he could end up dodging bullets on the front lines working as an aid man, a job as dangerous as any in the infantry.

He had no control over so many things—the war, the Army, his final assignment, Nora's health, their child's health. He needed a victory.

Up on stage, the colonel announced the certificates in alphabetical order. At the sound of his name, Walt bounded up, saluted and wordlessly took the rolled sheet. Back in his seat, he quietly opened it. The space for his name was blank. So was the space for his certification level.

This couldn't be a mistake, he thought. Surely his class would have been warned if that might happen. He messed up his finals, he thought. No wonder no one would tell him his grade average. He bolted from the table toward the lobby.

"You okay, Baran?" Dr. Hanson was right behind him.

Walt nodded.

"Too bad you're missing the rest of the ceremony. It's a big moment. You should be proud."

Walt looked away. His voice was low. "My certificate's blank."

"I know," Hanson said. "Isn't it frustrating? They give you guys this big ceremony and can't even put your names on your diplomas."

"Why?"

"You'd think they'd be better organized," Hanson said. "They're still figuring out who's fulfilled all the requirements." He patted Walt's shoulder. "Take it easy. Your name for surgical tech was never in doubt. You're near the top of the class."

"You sure? What was my final average?"

"Sure? You got mostly A's, Baran. Maybe a B or two." Hanson extended his hand. "Good work."

Walt pumped Hanson's hand so hard the teacher had to yank himself free. I made it, he thought. My bad luck is history.

TWELVE

Aug. 20, 1942

Dear Walt,

    The air is so hot here I don't want to move. Opening the windows doesn't help. That just lets in the wretched stench of Elizabeth's oil refineries. It's so thick now I can almost taste it. But I have good news, too. Now that I'm six months pregnant, I'm no longer nauseous. And Dr. Wenski told me yesterday I could be "active" again. I miss you so...

Peering carefully over my belly, I made my way down the steep flight of stairs that led to our building's front door. A pile of letters lay in a heap below the mail slot. I gathered them up, took a deep breath and slowly headed back upstairs. My worries were behind me. I hadn't had a cramp or spotting in more than two weeks.

At the top of the stairs, I opened Walt's letter. A photograph of him dressed in hospital whites slipped out. He was perched on a railing, his smile confident. His left hand rested on his knee, showing off his wedding band. And his hair! Longer than it had been all year and dark, thick and wavy.

I flung open the apartment door. "Mom! Look at this."

"Gosia," she yelled from the kitchen. "I pick radich from garden."

"What?" I called back. "You mean you're going downstairs to pick radishes from the garden?"

Mother stomped into the dining room and glared. "That is what I say."

"What you said?" I corrected.

"Ach!" She brushed at the air to dismiss me.

Milly said I wasted my time correcting my mother's grammar. She was right, of course, but I stood a better chance of fixing my mother's garbled pronunciations and grammar than winning our daily battles over control of our shared space.

Mother ordered me around like an Army drill sergeant. "Shell peas." "Peel potatoes." "Chop apples." If I pulled out the sewing box and dress patterns, she sat next to me with her own mending. If I went to our garden to pick flowers, she crouched beside me. But she never let me do any chore for more than a few minutes. Her favorite command was: "Nap, daughter!" Her excuse for her bossiness was my health. "You must be careful, Gosia. Think of baby!"

Some days I sought refuge at my father's piano with his sheet music. My mother resented that upright so much that she always kept her distance. The first piece I tackled was Chopin's Nocturne in G minor. Its gentle melody both challenged and calmed me.

But Walt's daily letters saved me. His detailed descriptions of his studies transported me to his world. He made me proud. I knew he would succeed. He was the smartest man I knew and the most determined, too.

***

On a hot, muggy day in late August, Milly knocked on my door to lure me outside. No matter what the weather, she knew how to enjoy it, or at least pretend she did.

"Let's walk to a park," she said, grabbing my hand. "We'll pick flowers."

She chatted happily as we strolled to a small patch of greenery three blocks away. My cousin had reason to be upbeat. Her husband's draft number still hadn't been called, letting him keep his bartending job. She and Stan had all the money they needed. Her mom and dad—my Aunt Irenka and Uncle Robert—let them live in a basement apartment in their house. Irenka—my mother's sister—was a gentle soul. She let Milly do whatever she pleased.

Anyone else blessed with such luck might have made me envious, but Milly was more than a cousin. She was a generous friend. She offered help before I had to ask. She kept her sense of humor. I could ignore her advice without hurting her feelings.

"Put your foot down, Marg. Oh, sorry, Nora," she added, when she noticed me frown. "You're not a kid. You don't have to do everything your mom says." That was her favorite advice. She never experienced the full force of my mother's stubbornness.

On one thing we always agreed: our pregnancies. We measured our waistlines. We compared our babies' movements and our symptoms. We stifled laughter when our mothers instructed us on the demands of motherhood. We were both five months pregnant when they sat us on my aunt's back porch and lectured us on how they reared their own children.

"Gosia, you had good lungs. You scream so loud in garden, all neighbors hear."

"You let me cry like that?"

"Oh, daughter," my mother scoffed. "Okay if baby cry. Good for lungs. Make strong."

My aunt nodded as she poured us glasses of lemonade. "You lucky you babies come in winter. Cold air is good for baby. Every morning, put them in backyard in carriage."

I shot a glance at Milly and rolled my eyes. Later, we made fun of their Old-World notions. Our babies would freeze all day and scream all night if they were in charge.

The following day, we took a bus to the library and searched the card catalogue for books on child care. On the third floor, on a bottom shelf, we found a handful of guides, most decades old and written by men. The word "Practical" was in many titles, as if there was any other way to care for a baby. I pulled out a slender, dusty book and opened it to a chapter on newborns. It stopped me cold. "This doctor says some babies are just fretful by nature. What if our babies are fretful, Milly?"

"I guess we'll end up fretful, too!" She giggled at the thought of it.

"It says here they might fret because they're hungry, over-tired or sick. Or because they have a safety pin stuck in them! Goodness!"

Milly opened another book. "Listen to this. It could be worse. 'A fretful baby could be hypertonic.'" She spoke the word slowly—high-per-TON-ic. "It says, 'such a baby is so tense and restless he just can't relax. He may jump out of his skin if the person carrying him moves too suddenly.'"

I grabbed the book from her hands. "How on earth would a mother handle a baby that fussy?"

I read the answer aloud. "Put him in a quiet room with few visitors and handle him with slow movements." I couldn't believe the next line: "The doctor might prescribe the baby sedatives."

"Drug a baby!" I yelled. "That is crazy!"

"We don't have to worry," Milly said. "We take care of ourselves and the babies inside us. We walk almost every day. We get our rest. God knows your mother makes sure you rest, right?"

We laughed the way powerless people with a common bond find humor in the mundane. Our babies would be born in less than four months. We were ready. When Junior kicked me hard in the ribs, I laughed even harder. Impatient, just like his daddy! Joy rushed through me. I carried the promise of life, the certainty that a part of Walt would always be with me. Calling that truth a miracle seemed stingy.

THIRTEEN

Fort Bragg felt unfamiliar. During the time Walt was gone, all the dated uniforms, vehicles and fighting equipment were replaced with new gear. A heavy tension hung in the air. He sought relief at the service club. He found only grim solitude.

In the club's largest room, a clean patch of rectangular flooring marked the spot where soldiers once smashed billiard balls with chalk-tipped cues. The Army had sold the pool table, cues and lounge chairs. Gone, too, were the card tables, checkerboards, baseballs, bats, catcher's mitts and ping-pong table. The club was an empty shell—a hollow reminder the Ninth Infantry was leaving and not coming back.

He struck a wall with his fist, anything to fill the stillness. A dull echo mocked a reply. His restless nightmares often imagined the Ninth in battle, but that was as far into the future as his mind dared travel. The empty, lifeless room taunted him to venture further. What would happen to the Ninth? Who would return from the war? He punched the wall again, refusing to consider the answers.

> Aug. 30, 1942
>
> Dear Nora,
>
> Rumors are thicker than sand about what the Ninth will do next, but nobody knows for certain. Everything at Bragg is geared toward the war now. I'm working in the dispensary, taking care of guys with infections or injuries. I like the work. This morning, I ran into Tom Lucas and Frank Hatcher. They said the Ninth could ship out any day. I hope I'm still here when our baby is born...

He waited in line a half hour that night to use a pay phone. He needed to hear Nora's voice.

"Walt! Where are you?"

"Back at Bragg, but I don't know how long. I need to see you. We could move out any day."

Silence—as full and real as the emptiness at Bragg—answered him, followed by forced cheer. "Of course, darling. Say when."

"As soon as you can. Maybe my folks can drive you. Are you up to the ride?"

"I'll call them right away."

A soldier tapped Walt on the shoulder. "Hey, pal. You about done?"

"I love you, Nora." He lifted the receiver to its cradle. It felt heavy as a rifle.

***

A humid gust of air wafted through the Franklin Hotel's open window. In the street below, an endless stream of Army trucks rumbled to unknown destinations. Walt nudged closer to Nora on their sagging double bed. The modest hotel was all that was available on short notice, but as long as his wife was there, he didn't mind.

They had spent the evening at a restaurant with their parents, the six of them lingering long after they had finished their meal. Their unexpected attention made Walt feel protected, but he couldn't wait to leave them. All he wanted was Nora in his arms. He pulled her closer and measured his words, noun by noun, verb by verb. He had only one night to speak them aloud, and they had to come out right.

"Darling, if I can't come home—"

"You'll be home," she interrupted.

"—when Junior is born—"

"Oh," she said softly.

"—I'll be with you, you know, Nora. Here." He tapped his chest with two fingers.

"I'll be fine, Walt. You don't ever have to worry about me." She sounded sure and confident, but her lips quivered slightly, the way they did when she was close to tears, and under her eyes he saw dark circles. He hated to leave her.

He took a deep breath. "Of course, you'll be fine. You're the bravest girl I know. And Junior is the bravest, strongest boy." He rested his broad hand lightly on her swollen belly. "I know you'll take care of each other."

"We will, dear, until you come home again."

"It could be a long time, a very long time."

"It doesn't matter. I love you. I'll be waiting."

"Always?"

"And ever."

"Tell me again, Nor."

"I'll always love you. I'll always wait for you."

"Again."

She giggled and repeated herself. He begged her again and again until they both laughed and gasped their chant.

Then, in a heartbeat, he turned serious. "Nora, there's one more thing I must ask—it's important."

She nodded.

"Make sure someone telegrams me as soon as the baby is born, wherever I am. I have to know you're all right."

"Of course, darling," she said, stroking his bare arm. "I'll make sure. I promise." She slid off the bed and went to the dresser. She ran her hairbrush through her golden hair, though she needed no help to look more beautiful.

"Now you must promise me something," she said.

"Anything." He moved behind her and wrapped her in both arms.

"Write me every day." She turned to face him. "To let me know you're all right."

Alive, he thought, I'll let you know I'm alive. "Every day," he said. "I promise."

He'd spent an hour that afternoon reassuring her and their parents about his medical training and his duties in the field. He would be in a clearing company, he said, following the men of the Ninth Infantry, including his best friends. But his unit would be miles back, behind two collecting companies closer to the front. He would be safe, he said. "As safe as a nurse in Elizabeth General Hospital."

As he held her, he felt her tension. He tried distracting her with stories about the Army and its stupid rules, bad food, ill-fitting boots and eccentric soldiers. He described his patients in a clinic on base. He focused her on ordinary things, planting flecks of hope in her eyes. Finally, they crawled beneath the thin wool blanket.

She shifted her body to one side, then the other, then back again. Nothing made her comfortable.

"Here," he said, lifting her head and edging his pillow beneath it. "Does that help?"

"Ah, you're a genius, darling. Junior is pushing my lungs into a—oh!" She laughed. "There he goes again."

He touched her belly and stopped with a grin when he thought he felt an elbow nudge. "Calm down, Tiger. You'll get out of there soon enough."

"He can't wait to meet you, Walt."

He longed for that moment. To hold his child in his arms would be a miracle beyond words. "What shall we call him, Nor?"

She stared at him wide-eyed. "How can you even ask? He'll be a Junior—Walter Aleksander Baran, Junior."

He kissed her nose and grinned. "You're the sweetest girl, but I'm serious. He needs his own identity."

"Then we'll figure out a nickname. He should carry your name."

He rested his cheek at the peak of her belly and stroked her neck, her cheeks, her breasts. "You're all I ever needed, Nor. I love you so much." He wrapped one leg over hers and gently caressed her bare belly. When he'd last seen his slender wife in June, her pregnancy barely showed. At almost six months pregnant she was ripe and full. To his surprise, the gentle curve of her belly filled him with desire. He kissed her lips softly. "I want you, Nora. Is it all right?"

She kissed him hard and pulled him closer.

The next morning, they woke in each other's arms. They washed and dressed and ate breakfast in the hotel coffee shop, speaking little. By ten o'clock they waited at the curb for their families, who had stayed in a hotel just outside of town. Exactly on schedule, Max drove up with Ruth at his side and Nora's parents in the back seat. Nora squeezed in between her parents and Walt climbed in front. They sat stiffly on the short ride to the base. Max drove as slowly as the lead car in a funeral procession.

When they reached Fort Bragg, everyone piled out in a jumble of too-casual well wishes, hugs and handshakes. Walt gave Nora a quick hug and kiss before he walked away. He didn't want her to see his anguish.

Later, he wished he'd made that moment last longer—a minute longer, an hour longer, as long as possible. His orders arrived at the end of the week. With no time left for any more visits, all he had was the memory of their rushed last kiss.

Oct. 6, 1942

Dear Nora,

It looks like we'll ship out soon. They're closing our dispensary. My patients told my superiors I was the best tech there and deserved a promotion. I'm just glad to do this kind of work. I must sound like Florence Nightingale herself, right? By the way, dear, the censors may start checking our letters soon, so remember our codes. When we're about to board I'll use the word "Harry." Don't forget—HARRY. After we land, I'll signal where we're going next with our code. Remember to check the first letter of each sentence at the start of my letters, okay?

FOURTEEN

Walt's letter spelled trouble before I read a single word. The three neat rectangular holes in his first page announced everything was different now.

Oct. 12, 1942

Dearest Nora,

It's going to be difficult writing this now that censorship has started, but I'll try. I had hoped I would receive another of your letters by now, but so far I haven't. I _____, but I'm not sure.

I'm not going to write Harry and Ginny _____, but please give them my best when you see them. Neither do I think I'll write my folks. I'll leave it to you _____. Don't forget about Harry, dear…

I spotted Walt's secret message right away but couldn't take my eyes off those gaping holes. What secrets did they hold? Then I noticed the second page of his letter was shorter than the first. Several lines had been cut from the top. No matter how hard I studied what remained, I couldn't decipher what the censors had removed or why.

I dialed Ruth. She answered on the first ring.

"Mom, it's Nora." I usually felt awkward calling Ruth my mother, but in that moment, I couldn't imagine calling her anything else.

"Hello, dear. How are you? Everything all right with the baby?"

My pregnancy was all Ruth worried about lately. Her concern touched me but didn't make my call any easier. "Yes, I'm fine. I'm—I'm calling because I got a letter from Walt today. He used the code."

"The code?"

"You know—'Harry'—the signal Walt said he'd use to tell us he's about to be sent somewhere else." I kept my voice firm. "He probably left days ago."

Ruth let out a muffled cry, but in seconds she was the one reassuring me. "Don't you worry, dear. He'll be all right. I say a special rosary for him every night."

I never knew how to respond to Ruth's passionate faith. I wished I possessed even a thimbleful of it. "I'll let you know if I hear anything else," I said.

***

Walt's letter lay unfolded on my parents' kitchen table, the object of much scrutiny. My parents passed it back and forth, mumbling in Polish.

"Look, Gosia. Valter is okay. He write with strong hand. *Mocny*." My mother turned from the stove to point her wooden ladle at the letter. A drop of sauce dribbled from the spoon to the floor. "He does not worry. See?"

I swiped at a runaway tear. My efforts to appear brave were crumbling. Maybe Walt wasn't worried, but I was. I came from a family of stoics, a people unaccustomed to showy displays of emotion. I inherited little of it. "He wanted to tell me something important, Mom. Look at those censor's holes. What do they mean?"

"Stefan! Talk to you sister. Tell her not to worry." Mother was growing annoyed. No one was allowed to cry in her house—not my father, sullenly nudging his rocking chair in a corner; not my brother, who preferred jokes anyway, and certainly not my mother or I.

Steven, his back toward her, winked slyly at me. "Buck up, sis. He's a medic. It'll be an adventure for him."

I recognized his tactics—sweet words mixed with conspiratorial looks, trying to show he was on my side even as he took our mother's. My brother had no use for sadness either. When I was young, I'd storm from the room when he and my mother ganged up on me like that, trying to make me feel something I didn't. Now I was all out of fight.

"I know he's lucky to be in the medics, Steve, but I'll feel better when he writes me from wherever he's headed."

Unexpectedly, he nodded in sympathy. "I know, sis." His chair legs screeched as he pushed back to stand. At 17, he already was an imposing six feet. He patted my shoulder as he passed behind me to escape to his room, his third-floor sanctuary.

My father rose from his chair with a groan. He limped away slowly, his role as silent spectator in our snug apartment unaltered. My mother slapped the ladle hard against the pot of simmering stew and faced me. "Go to grocer, Gosia. Buy milk. You must drink. Think of baby."

That's how most of my disagreements with my mother ended—with more commands. I sighed. "Fine, Mother."

***

No letters came from Walt in the weeks that followed. Not a single one. It was as if he'd disappeared. All I had to distract me was my pregnancy.

With only six weeks left before my baby was due, I felt every ounce of him. Few of my maternity clothes fit. I couldn't eat large meals. I couldn't take deep breaths. Milly laughed when I told her my symptoms. "I know! My lungs and stomach both battle with baby for room!" She bent forward a little and shouted down at her huge belly, "Come on, kid! Move over a little so I can eat."

I laughed halfheartedly as my mind drifted to dark places. What if the unthinkable happened? What if Walt never returned home? I contemplated trying to raise a child without him, not having enough money, living with my parents for years.

I tried reciting the *Our Father*, the *Hail Mary* and the *Glory Be*—the prayers of the rosary that Walt urged me to recite. When that ritual failed to comfort me, I created my own. Closing my eyes, I conjured up my husband's voice until it echoed inside me. I heard the words he spoke on our last night together: "I'll be with you, you know, Nora. Here." I saw him tap his chest. I inhaled the memory of his scent, as fresh as ocean waves, as pungent as lovemaking. Aloud, I spoke my *Amen*: "I know you will, darling. I love you. I always will." Whenever baby kicked, I stroked the bobbing bumps on my stomach, heard Walt's laugh and felt his fingertips play on my skin. My daily rituals brought a measure of peace. God was free to join me if He wanted.

I clung to hope. He would write again. He always did.

"I wish I could at least write Walt," I told Milly. "But I don't have his address yet."

She shifted on the sofa and braced her belly with a pillow. "Write him anyway. Send it to his old address. They'll probably forward it."

"Walt said to wait until I heard from him. I just can't stand it. Where do you think he is, Milly? Some island in the Pacific? A port in England?"

I remembered the World Atlas my father kept in the attic. We climbed the steep stairs, me first, the both of us stopping every few steps to catch our breath. We found the thick book in the storage room next to Steve's bedroom. It was written in Polish, but the maps were clear enough. I traced a line with my fingertip from the northeast United States, down the coast,

64

into the Caribbean Sea, through the Panama Canal and into the vast Pacific Ocean. I imagined long lines of military vessels heading west, cutting through stormy seas.

"That's thousands of miles," I whispered. "It could take weeks for a ship to get anywhere close to Japan."

I traced another line across the Atlantic, from New York to Great Britain. "Hmm. That's not far at all. He would be there by now." I thought for a few seconds. "That's it. He must be crossing the Pacific. He hasn't reached his destination yet. No wonder he hasn't written."

I tried to sound confident, though I didn't feel that way at all. As soon as my cousin left, I sat at the piano, closed my eyes, and took long, deep breaths. I picked out the melody of "Blues in the Night" and slowed the tempo way down. My moody version lacked the upbeat swing of Woody Herman's orchestra, but it mirrored my longing.

FIFTEEN

Walt's medical unit left Fort Bragg with such alarming speed that for the first time war felt within arms' reach. He was ready for it, no matter his apprehension. The day before, his commanding officer had assigned him to run the company's shock team, supervise an anesthesia team and assist with surgeries. Each assignment in itself was a challenge. Juggling all three well would be daunting. He wasn't worried. Pride buoyed him.

At Norfolk's busy harbor, Walt joined a long line of soldiers slowly boarding a homely transport ship. At least the vessel was large—one-and-a-half football fields long—and relatively new at two years old.

Walt grinned when he spotted the freshly painted name on the ship's side. "Are you kidding me? Leave it to the Army to call a converted banana freighter the *USS Florence Nightingale*."

Despite its new name, the transport ship served little medical purpose. Tons of cargo were loaded aboard, as well as fifteen hundred soldiers and hundreds of sailors—but only a handful of medics. The men all rushed to the top deck to grab spots at the railing. Everyone, including Walt, wanted a last glimpse of home.

"Ain't that gorgeous?" an unshaven infantryman near him whispered, gesturing toward shore.

Walt nodded, even though the harbor oozed a sooty chaos. Beneath a backdrop of belching gray factories, the dock was crowded with crates of supplies and ammunition. Surrounding the *Nightingale* were other bulky transports and numerous smaller boats.

Walt expected to move out as soon as everyone boarded, but the ship anchored in port that night. The next morning, when its engines rumbled to life, he returned to the top deck with an aggravating cold he'd picked up at Bragg. Even though he felt hot and achy, he was determined to watch the shoreline disappear from sight. He wanted to memorize every detail.

Not until the ship inexplicably stopped at the edge of Chesapeake Bay did Walt let a sailor step in front of him.

"Hey, soldier, you okay?" the sailor asked. "Nothin' personal, but you look like hell."

Walt wiped a sheen of sweat from his forehead. He felt hung over.

"I think you better see a doc," the sailor said. He steered Walt below deck to sick bay, where a Navy corpsman took his temperature. "One hundred and two degrees. Probably the flu." The Navy doctor who examined him agreed. "We're checking you in, Private."

Walt didn't object. He shivered violently as the corpsman helped him into a bed and tucked three wool blankets around him.

"What's going on out there?" he asked, his voice a whisper. "Why are we stopped?"

"They're practicing amphibious landings on an island in the bay. For the attack. We'll be staying here a few days."

"Attack?"

"When we get to Africa. Got the word this morning. You're headed to Casablanca for a major invasion."

He nodded as if he understood.

Seven days passed before the *Nightingale* finally restarted its powerful engines. By then, Walt had lost his voice and most of his sense of smell, except for the acrid bloom of rubbing alcohol and antiseptics that permeated sick bay. Eating itself was a chore. Every few hours a corpsman came by with pills and a cold wet compress, but the cloth steamed dry as soon as it touched his searing forehead. One fevered night, he dreamt he was back at his father's funeral home, wiping corpses clean and hooking bodies to bottles of formaldehyde. Another nightmare deposited him atop a porcelain table at the mortuary, watching clear liquid drip into his veins.

All the while, the *USS Florence Nightingale* rocked back and forth in calm seas. The gentle movement should have soothed him, but he tossed and turned in fevered fury.

"No! Don't...uh..."

His own raspy voice startled him awake. He forced open swollen eyes. Nothing looked familiar—not the compartment, the bed, the white metal cabinets, or the glaring lamp dangling overhead. When he tried to roll over, his sweaty body clung to his sheets and soaked his cotton hospital gown.

"What—the—hell?" Walt tugged at the gown's ties. He had no memory of putting it on. His efforts exhausted him. His breath came in desperate gasps, as if something heavy and determined covered his mouth. No matter how hard he tried to stay awake, his eyelids drooped closed. Like a light bulb flickering on and off, his consciousness came and went along with a fear more powerful than his fever.

"I'm dying," he muttered each time his vision faded.

"Oh, God, I'm still alive," he said when consciousness returned.

One day, a male voice exploded above him like a misfired artillery shell. "One hundred and five degrees. Damn. Even the sulfa and aspirin aren't breaking his fever."

Walt swam out of a wave of blackness. The dim light dangling overhead didn't help. A different voice sounded.

"I'm worried more about the pneumonia. This kid's in trouble if he doesn't get oxygen soon."

"Nothing we can do about that. The *Nightingale* doesn't have that kind of equipment."

Walt tried to speak, but his voice sounded like a moan. He tried again. "If Florence Nightingale...were here," he said, struggling for air, "she'd make sure...I had...oxygen."

No one seemed to hear him.

When they bury me at sea, he thought as he slipped back into blackness, I hope the ocean cools this fever.

***

So deep in the vessel was sick bay that daylight couldn't reach it. When Walt finally came to again, he didn't know whether it was night or day. He rubbed gritty eyes.

"Well, look at that," someone said. "Welcome back, Private."

He hadn't noticed the corpsman checking supplies behind him. "Glad to be back," he heard himself say. His voice sounded like a loose violin string, wobbly and out of tune.

"You've had quite a time here."

"How long?"

"Oh, ten days altogether, give or take. Let's check you out." The corpsman took his blood pressure and pulse, checked his lungs and listened to his heartbeat. "Doc'll be pleased."

"Florence won't."

"Florence?"

Walt smiled grimly. He'd cheated death, and he hadn't come close to a bullet or bomb. How many more strikes would fate allow?

The next morning, the corpsman helped brace Walt at a sink so he could wash and shave. Walt stepped on a scale, one palm touching the nearest bulkhead for support. One hundred and thirty pounds. He'd lost thirty pounds in ten days? No wonder he was ravenous, he thought.

"Back into bed," the corpsman ordered.

Walt leaned against the wall. "What's your name, sailor?"

"Corpsman Bill Peterson, at your service, soldier. Now lie down."

Walt grinned as he shuffled toward his bed. He liked the man's spunk. "Where are we?"

"Who knows? I don't think even the captain knows. I hear we've traveled 3,000 miles so far and none of it in a straight line. We're on a huge zigzag course."

"Sounds crazy."

"War crazy, more like it. Changing course every ten miles or so means the enemy can't tell where we're headed. Surprise 'em."

Good plan, Walt thought, even if it was crazy.

***

Each meal made him stronger, but even five-minute walks around sick bay left him breathless and sweaty. He moved slowly, arms stretched out in the narrow passageways to brace himself when the ship pitched and rolled.

He thanked God for sick bay's thick mattresses, hearty meals, quiet quarters and solicitous Navy corpsmen. He was living like a king compared to his fellow medics and the men in G Company, who he learned were crammed in the hold next to crates of flares, shells, grenades and ammunition. Those men showered in cold sea water, slept on hard bunks, and fought for fair portions of peanut butter sandwiches and dehydrated eggs.

Walt had one goal: start a long letter to Nora, though he had no idea how to get it past the censors and to her.

Nov. 1, 1942

Dearest Nora,

I'm writing this somewhere at sea, a thousand miles from our destination. Since I hope to get this letter to you without it going through censors, I'll speak openly. After we medics left Bragg on October 14, we shipped out from Norfolk. We're making our way to French Morocco in Africa by taking a circuitous route. Our objective is the city of Casablanca, which we will attempt to occupy. No one knows if the French will fight us or greet us with open arms...

He added a little to the letter each day, sparing her details of his illness that might frighten her. Every afternoon, he walked as much as he could below deck to recover his strength, slowly increasing his time to ten minutes, then twenty. One day, he tested his stamina on a ladder leading to a higher deck. One step up, one step down. Gradually, he added steps. Two steps up, two steps down, up, down. Then three steps. Then four. When no one was looking, he climbed to the top of the ladder and peered through the hatch to see the next deck up. Daylight streamed through a port window. Sea air trickled down the passageway from an unseen open door. He inhaled a lusty gulp. The effect was more powerful than any drug.

It was his fourteenth day aboard the *Nightingale*.

***

"You can leave sick bay during the day, but you'll still be quartered here, understand?"

"Yes, sir." Walt wanted to hug the doctor. He had no desire to pronounce himself cured. He could wander at will, then return to sick bay for full-course meals, hot showers, quiet naps, clean sheets and pajamas.

When the day finally came that he could climb all the ladders to the top deck, he stood silently in the bright sunshine, greedy for its warmth. Bare-chested soldiers sat in small groups playing cards or throwing dice, as if they were on a ferry to Coney Island or Rye Beach. Morale was high. Small waves gentled the ship's progress. He stood with his legs apart to keep his balance until the rhythm of the waves flowed through him. It felt natural, like blood pumping.

Cloaked in damp sea air, he reached for a railing and looked out over the water. The *Florence Nightingale* was in a huge convoy that spread as far as he could see. He started counting and stopped at sixty—troop transports, oil tankers, cruisers, destroyers, battleships, mine sweepers, aircraft carriers. Larger vessels cut through the water in formation. Destroyers so small they seemed to disappear in passing waves darted about like watchdogs. Overhead, fighter planes from carriers patrolled the sea. As Walt studied the horizon, he suspected an equal number of ships and planes loomed beyond, hidden from view.

The size of the convoy warned of a looming danger. For the first time, he imagined German submarines lurking in the deep. Despite his lingering doubts about the necessity for war, he was certain who America's enemies were. The immensity of the formation made him feel secure.

He joined four men playing poker and crouched down, waiting for a break in the game.

"Anyone know how much longer we'll be stuck at sea?" he asked as a new hand was dealt.

"Hard to say for sure," a soldier replied, his eyes on his cards. "Last I heard we'll reach Casablanca the second week in November."

"What? That's at least one more week at sea!"

"You should join us on top deck more often, soldier," said another soldier, eyeing Walt's pale skin. "Get a little sun on you. Change your attitude. You in a hurry to be in battle or something?"

He considered the sailor's question. As much as Walt wanted to get off the *Nightingale*, he realized that one week was hardly enough time for him to return to full strength.

From that day on, he circled the top deck every day, picking up heavy metal tools and equipment he spotted along the way and lifting them like dumbbell weights. The poker game was his halfway point; the card players never missed a chance to gamble on rain-free days. He eyed them jealously. He yearned to throw money in the pot; he was good at the game. But he didn't trust his luck just yet, and he had more important things to do. This was a time to concentrate on food and exercise. He added ladder-climbing to his exercise regimen and wolfed down as many helpings of his sick bay meals as he could get away with.

He ventured topside every day, even when nasty storms kept almost everyone else below. One day, another tech from his clearing company joined him at the railing—a tall, gangly guy named Buck Lowery from Pittsburgh. Walt let his body sway with the sea, enjoying the slow return of his strength. The sea roiled before them like moving mountain peaks, dark and glistening.

"Whew, it's pretty rough out there," Buck said, gripping the rail with both hands.

A shadowy movement made Walt glance up. In a heartbeat, a monstrous dark mass loomed overhead, a giant wave taller than the sea all around it. It reared back like a python. Before he could react, the massive wave hurled him and Buck across the deck, head over heels.

The wave twisted his body and slapped a watery hand against his mouth, shutting off his breath. No! he thought. Not my lungs! Resisting the urge to gasp for air, he reached for a chain holding down a hatch. The wave reached the chain first. It snapped the thick metal in two and flailed it against Walt's arm. So much water surrounded him, he felt as if he was being carried out to sea. Suddenly, the deck was again beneath his back. His body skidded fast.

A top-deck cabin stopped him cold, a hard crack against his back. As quickly and mysteriously as it had surfaced, the huge wave slipped away. Slowly, Walt checked his limbs for signs of broken bones and found none. Bruised and sore, he scrambled to his feet. Buck was on his knees a few yards away, dazed.

As the ship lurched through still angry seas, the two men congratulated each other for surviving. Amid the howling wind, Walt thought he heard muffled cries for help. "Man overboard!" someone shouted.

But the *USS Florence Nightingale* kept plowing onward. Stumbling as he ran, Walt rushed to a sailor on watch duty. "The bridge didn't hear the call," he screamed above the wind. "There's a man overboard. Get them to stop."

The sailor shook his head impatiently "Look at the size of this convoy, soldier. No way in hell we can stop. If we stop, *all* these ships would have to stop, and trust me, a convoy *never* stops for one man."

It made no sense. Hadn't a crew of doctors and corpsmen worked two weeks steady to pry him from death's grasp? Didn't the soldier out there in the seas deserve as much? Walt shuddered. It could have been him out there screaming fruitlessly.

A new reality sunk in. At the wrong time, in the wrong place, one man was worth nothing in war. His life didn't matter. Walt hurried below to change into dry clothes and collapse on his bed. He closed his eyes to pray, promising himself and God that, even as a lowly medical technician, he would do all he could to better Life's odds.

Sleep never came that night. The sound of the unknown man's screams replayed in his mind. He turned on his flashlight and finished his letter to Nora, omitting the truth of what had happened that day:

> ...Once, when I was outside on deck during a storm, a wave caught me flat-footed. I wasn't hurt, but I learned to stand in safer spots. We should reach Africa soon. I'm interested in seeing the people there and their customs. I'm going to do as much touring as possible after we hit Morocco. Wait until I get home. Dad's army experiences and tales will pale into insignificance when I start relating my adventures.
>
> Love, Walt

Folded in half, the multi-page letter barely fit in its envelope. Walt addressed the bulging packet and sealed it with tape.

"This'll never get past censors," he confided to Peterson. "I wish I had a way to sneak it to my wife." He'd spent enough time with the corpsman to trust him completely.

Peterson folded his arms across his chest, the hint of a grin on his face. "Baran, you know darn well the crew is taking this heap back to the States right after the invasion. And the first thing I'm going to do is get a pass to visit my family in New Jersey."

"Hey, maybe you could drop this off at a post office. I'll give you money for the postage."

"Don't be ridiculous, Baran. I'm gonna deliver it right to your wife's door."

"Really? You'd do that for me?"

"You kidding? You've spent so much time below deck that you're almost one of the crew. Ask and you shall receive."

"Just one more favor, Peterson. Don't say a word to her about how sick I was, okay?"

"Gotcha," Peterson said, tucking the thick envelope in his back pocket.

That afternoon, Walt wrote Nora a new letter, one he knew censors would scrutinize. He filled pages, even though he knew he would not be able to mail the letter for days. Writing felt like talking. In his mind, he imagined her reading each word.

Nov. 7, 1942

Dear Nora,

Only four more weeks until baby is due. I pray every day you both are well. I never stop thinking about you. I wish I could tell you what is happening here now, but the censors check our every word. All I can say is the most important thing – I love you, I love you, I love you....

SIXTEEN

"Mrs. Baran?"

The stranger at the front door must have caught a glimpse of me when I opened it a crack. I'd hurried down to answer his urgent knocking even though my pregnant belly made each step a risk. Wordlessly, I pressed my face against the door jam and studied the slightly built young man before me. He wore a sailor's cap and dark blue pea coat.

"Mrs. Baran?"

"Oh, my God," I whispered. "No, no."

I slammed the door and latched it quickly. I had read about moments like this in newspapers, seen them played out in movies: A uniformed man knocks on a door to deliver horrible news in person.

His repeated knocks and muffled cries added to my panic. "Ma'am? Ma'am?"

I leaned against the foyer wall and closed my eyes, afraid to make a sound.

He kept tapping. "Mrs. Baran? I promise, this won't take long."

There was no getting rid of him. I was sure he would stand outside my parent's house, knocking endlessly, until I let him in. My hand trembled so fiercely I could barely undo the latch.

A slight frown worried the sailor's forehead. His lips were parted. He looked as if he needed to speak but couldn't find the words. Slipping off his cap, he ran a hand through his matted hair. "How do you do, Mrs. Baran. I'm sorry to bother you like this, unannounced and all. I really am."

As hard as I tried, I couldn't look him in the eyes.

"I have something for you."

I nodded silently, holding my breath.

The sailor held out a thick envelope. "This is for you. Private Baran asked me to deliver it."

74

A sound escaped me—part cry, part gasp, the sound of someone underwater finally reaching air. I grabbed the envelope from the man's hand and gaped at its familiar penmanship. Flinging the door wide, I threw both arms around the stranger's neck—an act so impulsive and unlike me that it startled me as much as him.

"Oh, my goodness, I am so sorry," I said, dropping my arms. "Please, come in. What—what's your name?"

"Corpsman Bill Peterson, ma'am." Face flushed, he stepped into the foyer. "Private Baran was one of my patients onboard. He gave me this letter when we landed in Africa. Asked me to look you up when I got back to the states."

"Your patient? Africa? What do you mean? Was he wounded? Is he all right?"

"He's perfectly fine, Mrs. Baran. Just had a slight infection. No need for you to worry."

I stared again at the envelope, at Walt's familiar compact handwriting. "Oh, I can't believe this," I said, resting a hand on my belly. My eyes stung with tears of relief. I didn't want to let the sailor go. "I can't thank you enough, Corpsman...Peterson, is it? Please, can you come upstairs? I'll put on a pot of coffee."

"I'd love to, ma'am, but I'd better be going." He bowed slightly and wished me good luck, though I thought he needed it more. As he walked toward the bus stop, I kept waving and calling out, "Thank you, thank you, thank you," until he was halfway down the block.

Inside, I hugged the envelope to my chest. It had been two months since Walt had left, two months without a letter. I grabbed the railing and slowly pulled myself upstairs. The second I reached the top, I ripped open the envelope and scanned my husband's words. Phrases jumped out: "But I wasn't hurt" and "the coming invasion" made me frown. The letter bore no sign of a censor's scissors, but some words and meaning still seemed to be missing.

At least I knew he was safe, that his only difficulty was a virus that sent him to the infirmary, that he was off the coast of northern Africa and not in the Pacific. I pulled out my father's World Atlas again and studied Africa's northern rim. I found Morocco, a country that hugged both the Atlantic Ocean and the Mediterranean Sea. I fingered its pale blue outline and wondered where Walt was now.

Nov. 25, 1942

Dear Walt,

A kind sailor delivered your letter today, darling. I was so relieved to get it and to know you are okay. I'm busy getting ready for baby. Tiny newborn clothes look like they belong on a doll! I doubt they'll fit him for long because he feels so big in me. Baby is a "he," isn't he?...

"Why you write Valter?" my mother said. "Is late. You need sleep."

"I'm almost done." I kissed the envelope's flap before sealing it. "Now I'm ready."

Scooting to the edge of my seat, I planted my feet wide and pushed down on the chair's handles to launch myself upright. Walking to the bathroom was a slow, clumsy process. I washed and brushed my teeth, pulled on my pastel pink tent of a nightgown and carefully climbed into bed. Mother already was tucked under two layers of wool blankets and a thin quilt, her face to the wall.

Sleep eluded me. Whenever I shifted position, I slid toward my mother's back. It braced me like a bolster. For the last few months, three bodies jockeyed for space on the sagging mattress: my mother, me, and the baby doing double flips inside me. That night, baby was in charge. He squeezed my stomach, my lungs, my bladder, my intestines. I folded my pillow, punched it and turned on my side; I pulled my knees high and put an arm under the pillow.

"Gosia, what is matter?" my mother whispered.

"I can't breathe, *Matka*. What do I do?" Mother could use any grammar she wanted that night. I didn't care. I needed her help.

She rolled over and braced herself on one elbow, frowning slightly. "Maybe you sit in your father's chair in parlor." She scrambled over my legs, slid onto the floor and reached out a hand. I took it obediently and, with her help, put on my bathrobe. Steadying my rocking body, I followed her down the hall and through the dining room, both hands clasped under my belly.

Street lamps below lit the parlor. The sweet scent of my father's cigars clung to the curtains, carpets and furniture. I sunk into his favorite high-backed chair. My mother lifted my legs onto a plump footstool and draped a hand-crocheted blanket on my lap.

"Wait!" she ordered and scurried away. Seconds later, she returned with a small pillow she tucked behind my head. "Rest, Gosia. I go bed now."

I took a deep breath. "Ah, baby," I said, stroking my belly. "Are you happy now?"

From my bathrobe pocket, I pulled out Walt's letter. The room was too dim to make out his writing, but I already knew most of it by heart. Ever since the sailor handed it to me that morning, I'd kept it with me and read it over and over. I fingered the soft paper like a talisman. It felt like fine pima cotton. Each time I tugged the letter from its envelope, I relived the thrill of opening it for the first time.

When I finally crawled back into bed that night, my mother was snoring softly. My breathing had returned to normal, but a vague apprehension lingered. If I had a clear reason for it, I might have chased it away with logic and the memory of Walt's reassurances. But it lingered like a hazy phantom intent on blocking my sleep.

SEVENTEEN

Rumors that landfall was approaching jolted the *Nightingale* to life. The indolence of weeks at sea—the card games, sunbathing, naps and lazy bull sessions—ended abruptly. The men washed and shaved and cut each other's hair as if readying themselves for dates. They cleaned their gear and collected possessions that had been scattered about during the crossing.

Despite his lingering weakness, Walt readied himself, too. Even his father hadn't seen a place as exotic as Africa when he was in the Army. He looked forward to practicing the medical skills he'd learned in Missouri once ashore. He finally could keep the vow he'd made when that rogue wave struck. He would start saving lives.

The night before the ship reached the coast of French Morocco, the soldiers were served a turkey dinner with all the trimmings. The infantrymen joked lightheartedly. They acted as if a grand adventure awaited them.

The morning of November 8, Walt clambered to the top deck. The men in his old infantry company acted as if they were headed for a picnic as they stuffed their packs with sandwiches, candy and cigarettes. Walt searched for Frank Hatcher and Tom Lucas, whom he hadn't seen often on the voyage because of his time in sick bay. He finally found them hunkered down in a secluded corner. "You guys ready?"

"Don't like those rough waves," Hatch said. "Gonna be a b-bumpy ride in." Like most of the men, Hatch wasn't worried about the Vichy French. He was convinced they were allies who would welcome them.

Tom remained silent, a faint frown hinting at his thoughts. Like Walt, he followed the news. He knew the Vichy French were collaborating with the Nazis and that the landing would not be easy.

As soon as the *Nightingale* anchored a half mile from shore, his friends joined their platoon and prepared to board a small landing craft. Walt shook their hands, praying silently for their safety. "See you ashore, guys."

As their landing craft pulled away, Walt cursed his powerlessness. All he could do at that point was watch the small armada of boats and wait. His medical company wouldn't be needed ashore for at least two days. The boats' progress seemed routine until giant breakers a hundred yards out swamped three of them. They lurched back and forth, pitching men loaded with rifles and packs into the water. Enemy planes strafed other boats, muffling the soldiers' cries for help.

"Can't we help them?" Walt screamed at his first sergeant. "They're gonna drown."

Bursts of light flashing from on high ridges onshore answered his plea. Snipers fired at the landing crafts still afloat. "We wait," the sergeant said. "They have life vests. They know what to do."

As the sea calmed, the *Nightingale* launched more landing crafts to rescue men from the sea. Sniper fire continued. The Vichy French and Arabs must have been warned, Walt thought. They had no intention of surrendering. What if this invasion ends up a slaughter?

***

Every man left aboard ship was pressed into service. Cooks manned machine guns. Clerks hauled ammunition and gasoline from the hold. Medics became sentries.

"You're on midnight shift, Baran," said Captain Oliver Penland, his commanding officer.

At the start of his shift, Walt's first sergeant handed him an onboard phone. "Listen up, men," a man on the bridge said into his phone. "Look out for enemy aircraft, submarines, anything that looks or sounds unusual. Watch for moving objects in the water. German subs try to camouflage their periscopes. Call the bridge if you see anything. Anything at all."

Walt stared out at the roiling sea, wondering what business any Army surgical technician had standing guard aboard a ship. But no one had to tell him his assignment was important. An enemy sub could take out the *Nightingale* and everyone in it. Surgical tech or not, he had to do the job right.

At first, he saw only water—miles and miles of it to the west, north and south. Gradually, though, as his eyes grew accustomed to the seascape, he spotted clumps of seaweed and small pieces of debris. He was studying each particle, searching for signs of the enemy, when he saw a frenzied fluttering on the surface. He grabbed his phone before he realized it was a huge school of bait fish. "My eyesight's too damn good," he muttered.

By the time he entered his third hour on watch, every muscle throbbed from being on constant alert. Raising both arms high, he arched slowly back to stretch his spine while keeping his gaze fixed on the water. A second later, he jerked forward. "What the hell," he said. Something on the horizon bobbed on a wave.

He squinted in the object's direction. It looked bigger than the debris he'd seen earlier but waves obscured its shape. He stared hard. Not seaweed or bait fish, he decided. It moved too steadily against the tide. For a split second, the seas flattened. A rounded shape edged up. That was when he saw them: Two objects, not one. Two barrels moved toward the *Nightingale* in unison, a faint foam trail in their wake.

He fumbled for his phone, heart pounding. "Private Baran reporting to bridge. Two barrels portside moving in direction of *Nightingale*. Doesn't look right. Over."

A heartbeat later, horns and whistles blasted. The *Nightingale's* engines churned as it sped back out to sea. In what seemed like seconds, two nimble destroyers rushed to the scene, closed in on the barrels and dropped a flurry of depth charges. Walt flinched, hoping he had been right, wondering what kind of trouble he'd be in if he wasn't. As difficult as the TNT-filled charges must have been to aim, the sheer quantity of them could destroy anything lurking beneath the water's surface.

A huge black spout of destruction erupted a hundred feet into the air. Drops of oil rained down, along with bits of material Walt didn't want to see. The spout settled. A giant oil slick remained—the last sign of an enemy submarine. The man on the bridge called Walt, "That's keeping your eyes open, Private. Good going."

The havoc was over for everyone but Walt, whose stomach rolled and crashed like the waves around him. He thought about the men aboard the sub. Enemies or not, he had vowed to increase life's odds in the war. How many deaths had he just caused?

At shift's end, he collapsed on his bed, his body aching for sleep, his mind filled with images of black, oily water reaching for the sky. He dreamt he was trapped in the submarine, water slowly rising to his knees, hips, neck. He heard the sound of it: the rushing water, the panicked shouts. His lungs tightened the way they had when he had pneumonia.

His gasps jolted him awake. It took minutes to calm himself. You may not be a hero, Baran, he thought, but you're not a murderer either. He told himself he'd saved many American lives that night, including his own, yet his conscience could not escape the belly of the sub.

***

On shore, the din of battle roared nonstop until November 10, when the Vichy French finally signed a truce. The sharp odor of explosives gradually drifted away. The skies cleared. Walt packed his gear, ready to go ashore. His chance didn't come until the evening of November 11th, when a corporal yelled, "Report to top deck, Baran! Captain's orders!"

Up top, a pair of burly sailors loaded heavy metal cans into a net dangling from a huge hook. Walt looked over the railing at a snub-nosed landing barge already crowded with sailors.

"Climb on, Private!" barked a sergeant, pointing at the net packed with high-octane fuel.

Walt stared at the net. "There?"

"You waiting for a limo, Private?"

Walt scrambled atop a gas can. He held on tightly as the hook swung out and slowly lowered the net. "You're in charge, Private," the sergeant yelled down. "Make sure this gasoline gets up river to Port Lyautey."

Under any other circumstances, Walt would have laughed. This assignment was even more ludicrous than his watch duty. An unarmed surgical technician with a rank of private was in command of twenty sailors. On a landing craft. In the dark.

After all the gas cans were loaded, Walt ordered the craft to move out. The small boat pitched up and down in edgy waves, its cargo creaking.

"Goddammit," a sailor shouted when one precariously stacked can fell against him.

"Shut the fuck up," another said. The words provoked a volley of tense cursing from other men: "Jesus Christ, I wish this bathtub would settle down." "Where the hell are we headed, anyway?" "Move the fuck over, would ya?"

"Settle down, guys," Walt said quietly. "We'll be ashore in no time."

The cursing quieted to a low rumble barely audible above the waves. It erupted again when a rough series of waves rocked almost every fuel can's positions.

"Everyone okay?" Walt called out. He knew how the men felt. The creaking and lurching reminded him of stomach-turning roller coasters at Seaside Heights, but without the certainty the ride soon would end safely.

More than halfway to shore, a large wave slapped the boat so hard a pile of cans collapsed. One split as it landed, splashing cold fuel on Walt's feet.

It was too much for a young sailor desperate for a smoke. He struck a match.

"Put that out!" Walt hissed.

"You chicken?" the boy snapped, holding the flame to his cigarette and inhaling deeply.

In one quick swipe, Walt grabbed the cigarette and match and tossed them in the sea, but the flame exposed a second, unexpected danger. A war-hungry sniper—Frenchman? Arab?—must have returned to his abandoned machine gun and seen the flash of light. As gunfire ripped the silent night air, Walt thanked God for the black night and the dead cigarette. The gunner, uncertain of his target's exact position, swept his aim far to their right. "Cut the motor," Walt ordered. No one aboard made a sound. Even the nicotine-hungry sailor froze in place. Walt waited until the sniper shifted to other targets before ordering the engine restarted.

Thirty minutes later, the craft slowly eased into the harbor's narrow river and moved upstream. Port Lyautey's docks were stacked with heaps of rations and ammunition, a hellish version of Walt's last day at Norfolk. He directed the craft to a half-empty dock, where he tossed a rope around a pole and hoisted himself out.

The job of unloading he left to the sailors.

After four weeks at sea, standing on dry land felt like hard work. Walt didn't trust his wobbly legs or sleep-starved body. He ducked inside a nearby building. I just need to rest for a minute, he thought, collapsing on the hard floor. Within seconds, he fell into a deep sleep.

A nightmare jarred him awake: He was trapped in a sinking boat, pinned down by gas cans. He jumped to his feet. His orders had been sketchy beyond delivering the supplies. "Look for your unit," were the sergeant's last words. Walt had no idea where to start. He scanned the building for food or water but found neither.

Outside, hordes of other soldiers seemed to be in the same fix. They wandered in every direction, searching for rations and their units. GI truck drivers sped through the crowds, yelling for directions. Officers commandeered soldiers separated from their units and put them to work loading trucks and hauling gear.

Determined to do his job as a medic, Walt walked with feigned purpose. He spotted three techs from his platoon—Buck Lowery, his fellow survivor of the rogue wave; Ted D'Amico, a boisterous New Yorker, and a giant of a man everyone called Big Al. He motioned them to join him. "If we move quickly as a unit, we can stay out of this chaos. We can set up a temporary station." Soon, four other men from their company fell in step with them.

As they headed toward the beach to set up, Walt heard a weak voice call out. "Walt, that you?"

Walt turned and whooped. "Tom! Hatch!"

"You made it," Tom said, his voice flat.

"You okay?" Walt asked.

Tom grimaced. "We're alive. Better than some. Lost six in G company."

"E c-company l-lost nineteen," Hatch said, his stuttering more exaggerated than ever.

The two men took turns reciting the names of the dead. They described the gunfire G Company endured. "We scrambled for cover. It was hell getting off the beach," Tom said. "We hid in hollows and scrub brush. Dug packed earth with our canteen covers and bare hands."

Walt listened silently, knowing his own landing was uneventful by comparison.

"We-we d-dumped our packs," Hatch said. "Had to leave everything b-but our rifles, ammunition b-belts and canteens."

"Remember all those months of training, Walt?" Tom said. "All that stupid bullshit using fake bullets and bombs? Nothing like what we went through, not even close."

For a moment, Walt wished he had been in the crossfire with them. The war was no intellectual exercise, like his political debates at Bragg. Friends from his old company had died. Too shaken to speak his guilt, he fumbled for his cigarettes. "Smoke?" he said, shaking two out. His friends shrugged him off.

"Gotta go," Tom said, craning his neck to see where his unit had gone. In seconds, he and Hatch were swept up by another crowd of soldiers.

"Take care of yourselves," Walt called as they disappeared from view.

He wanted to follow them, to stay by their side and keep them safe. He knew he couldn't. He vowed to keep checking on them, no matter where they were. If they needed medical care—any kind at all—he'd make sure they'd get the best. The best.

EIGHTEEN

Dec. 8, 1942

Dear Walt,

 Since we last saw each other in Fayetteville, the only letter I've received from you is the one that nice sailor delivered. I was so relieved to know you're safe. Thank you, dear, for sending it. You wouldn't recognize me now. I am BIG. Baby is almost ready. Don't worry about me. My mom is taking good care of me and my brother does, too...

Steve took my letter to the mailbox that morning, as he had all week. Never had he been so willing to run errands for me.

"I don't mind, sis" he said. "No sense you leaving the house looking so ragged."

"Gee, thanks a lot."

Steve's teasing made me laugh. He almost seemed grown up when he tried to take care of me and I loved him for it. He understood how my pregnancy limited me by then. I was too big to do more than shuffle.

My sleep was restless that night. Then, about four a.m., a dull pain grabbed the base of my spine and quickly disappeared. It throbbed on and off like that every half hour, more annoying than alarming. Finally, I struggled from bed and staggered into the kitchen.

"Oh, God," I whimpered when the throbbing returned, this time more fiercely. Planting one hand on my lower back and the other on the wall, I took deep breaths and tried to be quiet. Still, a low moan erupted from deep inside. From the bedroom, I heard the sound of creaking bed coils.

"Gosia! What?" My mother threw open the bedroom door in wide-eyed fear. When I explained what was happening, she smiled. "Aha! Is baby!"

My mother ran to my father's tiny bedroom off the parlor. "Benydyk! Is time! Get up!" She banged on his door until it slowly creaked open. "Get Stefan!" she shouted.

"Mom, stop. It's easing up now. Just help me back to bed."

Ignoring my pleas, my mother barreled into our bedroom and began shoving nightclothes and undergarments into a small suitcase. My father limped into the outer hallway and called upstairs, "Stefan! Come! Your sister is ready!" My brother, half dressed, raced downstairs. Buttoning his shirt with one hand, Steven dialed Ziggy Dobranowski with the other. Ziggy, Walt's second cousin, ran the Baran Funeral Home's ambulance service. My family acted as if they had prepared for this moment with a drill.

"Why...do I...need Ziggy?" I asked.

No one answered.

My father limped back to his bedroom. Three minutes later, he emerged fully dressed, puffing on a cigar. My mother was still in our bedroom, noisily opening and shutting drawers.

Amid the commotion, a fresh pain snuck up on me, this one even more intense. "Oh, God!" I called out. I wanted to sit, but my discomfort wouldn't let me. Bracing against a wall, I gasped for breath. My mother rushed to my side.

"Hold me, Gosia. I help."

Just when I thought I couldn't last another second, the tight vise on my lower back eased. I could breathe again. Tears followed my relief.

"Ah! Mom, it's all right. It's gone. I'm better now."

Waddling to the refrigerator, I pulled out a jug of milk and poured some into a glass. As I lifted it to my lips, my mother held her palm toward me like the traffic cop at Broad and Jersey streets. "*Nie!* No drink!"

I peered over the edge of my glass at her. A single drop of milk dribbled onto my tongue.

"Baby come. *Nie mleko*. Nothing in stomach."

"*O moja matka*." I laughed and beckoned her closer. "Didn't you hear me? I'm okay now. The back pain is gone."

My mother cupped my hands in hers. "Gosia, this is how baby comes. In waves. Like at beach. You know? We go hospital now."

I couldn't help but smile. Beach? Waves? My mother could be so dramatic. Cramps were nothing new to me in my pregnancy. They came and went for months at first. These felt stronger, I had to admit, but my doctor had warned me about false labor pain. "Mom, I don't want Steve and Ziggy to go through so much trouble for nothing. I really think those pains were just a trick my body was playing on me."

With those words, a great gush of liquid poured from me and puddled on the floor. I bunched a dry corner of my nightgown in my hand and wiped my leg. She didn't need to tell me my water had broken.

"I...I'm so sorry, Mom. It happened so fast."

"Sorry? You crazy girl. Come." She grabbed a towel and guided me to the bedroom to help me into a loose dress and coat. She yelled for my brother. "Stefan! Now!"

By the time I reached the bottom of the stairs, Ziggy was waiting at the curb in a Baran Funeral Home ambulance, a carbon copy of vehicles other funeral homes provided for emergencies, but with "Baran" emblazoned on both sides. The boxy four-door sedan resembled a stubby black hearse with flashing red lights and a siren attached to the right front fender.

Ziggy, whose bum left leg kept him out of the military, helped me to climb inside and lie on the stretcher. My mother perched on a jump seat beside me. Steven sat up front. My father stood at the curb, puffing on his cigar, no doubt relieved there was no room for him, too.

Ziggy limped to the driver's door and hoisted himself inside. "Everybody ready?" he yelled. Before anyone could answer, he pressed in the clutch with his bum leg, punched the accelerator with his right, cut off a milk truck and skidded into a lane. The ambulance careened from one lane to another, its red lights bouncing off other cars and ricocheting inside. "We've got plenty of time, Zig," Steven shouted above the pulsating siren. "No need to speed."

"Don't think so, buddy. My wife delivered an hour after her water broke."

I gripped the stretcher each time the ambulance turned sharply. Fresh waves of pain clutched at my back and stomach. All the while, my mother patted my hair and murmured, "Is okay. Is okay." She didn't sound like she believed it.

Suddenly, Ziggy hit the brakes. "Dammit!" I felt a rush of cold air as he rolled down his window and bellowed, "Move outta the way!"

Steven turned to me. "Just a little traffic jam." I had never heard my brother sound so grown-up.

The ambulance rolled forward a few feet and lurched to a stop again. "Move or I'll move ya!" Ziggy bellowed. I heard the unmistakable sound of metal on metal and felt the ambulance jerk as it tapped other cars. I couldn't see what was happening outside but easily could imagine it. Walt's cousin was—as my polite Aunt Irenka often put it—"a determined sort." Seconds later the ambulance was again speeding down Elizabeth Avenue. Only when it slowed in front of the hospital on East Jersey Street did I let loose a scream that rivaled Ziggy's.

***

"Don't push!"

"Not yet!"

The two nurses wheeling my gurney took turns shouting orders at me, but my baby wanted to come out and I didn't know how to stop him. I understood now what my mother had meant. The waves of contractions had become as powerful as the roughest surf at Asbury Park. I had hardly a moment between them to catch my breath.

"Cross your legs! Don't let that baby come. The doctor isn't here yet."

"Uh. I can't. Uh…oh…uh."

"Cross those legs! No noise!"

The gurney flew through long hospital corridors reeking of urine and acrid disinfectants until finally it reached the delivery room. I tried to lift one leg over the other, but the effort made me nauseous and sweaty. A primal, desperate grunt exploded from my lungs. "Shh!" one of the nurses hissed. Other nurses rattled metal instruments and stacked thick towels. None looked at me, except when I released another muffled scream. "Not yet!" another nurse yelled, as if an order could stop my tide.

I didn't know how much time passed before the doctor arrived. When he did, someone injected me with a drug that blocked my pain, or maybe just my memory. The room wreaked of alcohol, bitter medicine, blood and sweat.

NINETEEN

Despite the turmoil ashore, most of the doctors and technicians in Walt's clearing company managed to find each other within hours. They set up wards in a modern building in Mehdia occupied by the French Red Cross. Walt had the easiest job. Little needed to be done to the room to be used for surgeries; its freshly mopped floors and immaculate countertops smelled of antiseptic cleaners and alcohol.

Soon after patients arrived, though, the room began to reek of sweat and the coppery scent of blood. Every surface became sticky and stained with bodily fluids. Soldiers with gunshot and shrapnel injuries filled every operating table.

"Rough day," Ted D'Amico sighed near the end of his shift.

"You got that right," Walt said. He'd barely had a chance to get to know the wiry surgical tech at Bragg. But here in Morocco, after only a few hours of working shoulder to shoulder with the man, he grasped the most important thing he needed to know about him—his character. Off duty, Ted came across as a braggart and wishful womanizer. In surgery, Walt could count on him. Like most of the medic techs in the company, Ted lacked Walt's training, but he picked up his responsibilities quickly. He was dependable. The torrent of patients that day didn't slow him a bit.

Ted swept a hand through his thick black hair. "Hey, did ya hear about the convoy that brought us over?"

Walt shrugged. He'd assumed the huge armada would hang around a while to support the infantrymen it had delivered to Africa's coastline. "What about it?"

"It's gone. Headed back to the States."

"Already?" He tried to hide his dismay. Florence had abandoned him. He consoled himself knowing that his lengthy, censor-free letter was on its way to Nora in the hands of Corpsman Peterson.

"Medic!" two litter bearers suddenly shouted. They cried out the same word with every wounded man, no matter how serious the injuries, but this time, their shouts hinted of panic. The patient was saturated with blood and losing consciousness.

"Hurry!" they screamed.

Walt and Big Al rushed to the soldier's side. He moaned in pain; his sweat mixed with his blood. Walt found the source of the bleeding—a fresh gunshot wound in the torso—and held a sterile gauze against it. "Who the hell shot him?" he asked. "Didn't the fighting stop two days ago?"

"Shot himself," a litter bearer said. "Happened minutes ago. He was cleaning his rifle. Screwed up. Forgot the thing was loaded." He explained how the bullet passed through his chest, to the left of his heart, before it exited and penetrated another man's leg.

Two doctors joined Walt and Al, but no matter how hard they all worked, a thick, red stream gushed from the gaping hole with each heartbeat. "It hurts," the soldier said, his voice a trickle.

"Damn," Walt said. "He's just a boy. I don't care what the Army calls him."

"Am I gonna be all right?" the boy asked.

"Sure, you will," said Big Al, with unexpected tenderness.

"Goddam liar," the boy hissed.

"We'll take care of you," Walt said.

The soldier lurched with unexpected strength, struggling with an unseen enemy. He arched his back. "Don't let me die! Shit!"

After long, tortured seconds, his efforts exhausted him; his movements slowed; he stopped calling out. His gaze met Walt's for a brief moment before it fastened on some distant point. Walt tightened his grip. He thought he felt the boy tighten his.

Walt whispered in his ear, "Do you want to say a prayer with me?" The boy made a low gurgling sound. Thinking he was trying to reply, Walt leaned closer. A harsh breath escaped. Part shout, part exhalation, the ugly sound jarred Walt more than all the screaming and cursing that had preceded it. A warm gust—the last gasp of life—brushed past Walt's cheek and echoed inside him.

A dreadful silence followed. The oppressive quiet that smothered the scene cloaked the boy, the doctor, the techs, the very air they breathed, as if everyone in the room had stopped breathing at once. Walt heard his temples pound. Hours seemed to have passed since the boy was brought in. When Walt finally looked at the clock, it had been barely four minutes.

"Thank God we don't have to listen to that no more," Big Al said, his hands shaking.

His words sounded cruel, but Walt understood. Listening to the boy's pleas had been almost too much to bear. Yet Walt would have given anything to hear them again, anything to escape the harsh silence. He'd become a medic to save lives and escape death. Now death seemed to stalk him—the sailor swept overboard; the Germans in the submarine; the infantrymen killed in the invasion; this boy.

Walt fled to the adjacent recovery room where life still carried on. The soldier who'd been hit by the same bullet was sitting up in bed, blessing his good fortune. Thanks to his minor leg wound, he was slated to board a departing hospital ship. "Let me outta here!" he yelled. "I'm headin' home!"

Buck checked the soldier's wound. Ever since escaping the giant wave that hit the *Nightingale*, Buck moved like a man making his way through a minefield. He winced at the boy's bravado. "Take it easy, kid. You lost a little blood. You're still in mild shock."

"Yeah, I know, but I'll be all right. How's that guy who shot me?" The soldier grinned, without a care.

"I'm sorry, kid," Buck said. "He didn't make it."

A deep silence encased the wounded man, capturing every molecule of oxygen surrounding him. He moaned softly, "Oh God, oh God."

"You idiot," a nearby patient hissed. "That was his best friend."

The soldier collapsed on his pillow, his skin pale and sweaty. Walt recognized the symptoms from training. Severe emotional stress on top of blood loss could send someone into deep shock, even a boy like this who had been doing well seconds before. Walt grabbed a stethoscope. "His heart's racing. Someone get the doc."

Chauncy Bradley, usually the company's most placid doctor, rushed to the patient's side. "Why wasn't an IV set up?" he shouted. Bradley's broad hands trembled slightly as he checked vital signs and elevated the soldier's feet. Walt and Buck took turns with the doctor pumping the boy's chest. Buck's face was so pale that Walt wondered if the doctor should check him, too.

The soldier slipped into unconsciousness. Bradley worked on him for almost an hour, repeating each step, until the boy's face turned a delicate blue and his lips tightened into a grimace.

Walt wished he knew more about medicine. He wished death had more purpose. To himself, he fumed, "What were you thinking, God? Why this boy, too?"

***

Dec. 12, 1942

Dear Nora,

I haven't received any word from you. I worry whether you are okay. Please let me know. Our commanding officer found a building in Port Lyautey where we'll have more room to take care of our patients. I'm putting into practice everything I learned at O'Reilly General Hospital. I can't say more than that. Someday, I'll tell you all about it...

The large windows in their makeshift hospital overlooked the ocean. The building had large airy rooms, tile floors, netting over the cots, flush toilets and showers. If this was war, Walt could tolerate it. Sunny skies. Balmy weather. No gunfire. Work he found both challenging and rewarding.

Under Walt's direction, Buck and Ted helped organize the surgery. The three men inventoried scalpels, lancets, probes, tweezers, clamps and more. They tallied the supply of sulfanilamide powder and tablets, aspirin, morphine syrettes, sodium pentothal, dried plasma, rubbing alcohol and other medicines. They reviewed their procedures for sterilization and treating shock.

He and Buck never talked about the soldier who died of shock their first day in surgery. Nor did they speak of the giant wave that almost took their own lives aboard ship. Words made no sense of those memories.

On sleepless nights, Walt consoled himself with the knowledge he was gaining. By his second week, he already had learned new ways to stop bleeding, prevent shock, stitch a wound, set a bone.

"You're on top of things, aren't you, Baran?" said Jack Hunter, an amiable young doctor from Pennsylvania. "How about you work alongside me for the rest of the week?"

"You bet!" Walt said. Of all the doctors in his company, Hunter had the easiest temperament. Like them, he was a lieutenant, but he never pulled rank or took himself too seriously.

Surgery was quiet the first night the two of them worked together, until three injured soldiers stumbled in. Walt poured rubbing alcohol on a gauze pad and wiped down the examining tables. The soldiers collapsed on them with loud groans. Combat hadn't ripped them apart; a boozy midnight brawl at a whorehouse had. The men were lucky. Dr. Hunter stitched them up well. Walt worked seamlessly with him, handing over instruments before being asked.

Every procedure that week went just as smoothly. The two men seemed destined to be a team. But first thing Monday morning Chauncey Bradley tapped Walt on the shoulder. "You're working with me this week, Baran."

Walt liked Bradley well enough, but the order surprised him. Except for Hunter, most of the other doctors just took whichever tech was available. The doctors are starting to count on me, he thought. "Yes, sir," he said, imagining a promotion soon to corporal or even sergeant.

His patients boosted his morale even more, calling him — and anyone with a red cross on his sleeve — "Medic," though the title technically belonged only to bona fide medical doctors. Some even called him "Doc."

"Bet you'd rather be back in the States than changing bed pans, huh, Doc?" a patient asked one night as Walt checked patients in the recovery room.

Walt shrugged. A year earlier, he might have seen the question as an opportunity to mock America's eagerness to go to war. Pearl Harbor ended that debate. Japan threw the first punch. Just as in a schoolyard brawl, America had no choice but to engage. It had to do the same thing when Germany and Italy declared war on the States, too. Yet still he wondered: Were those two European countries really a direct threat to the United States?

"So, what d'ya think?" the man asked. "Does this war make any sense to you?"

Walt silently checked the soldier's blood pressure, wishing anything made sense now. Something inside him had shifted. His doubts about the war couldn't match his horror hearing Tom and Hatch recite a list of G Company's dead. Even if war with Germany wasn't justified, protecting his fellow soldiers was.

"I'm no doctor," Walt told the patient, "and this war may be crazy, but I'm just glad to be of use to you infantry guys."

He still didn't trust FDR, though, or Congress, or the generals who plotted his fate. Walt knew the truth. Ever since Cain picked up the jawbone of an ass and slew Abel, men had dreamed up ways to justify their weapons and their wars.

***

Walt huddled with Tom Lucas and Frank Hatcher in a tiny, smoky French-owned café located halfway between their two companies. All around them, clusters of GIs sat near clusters of Frenchmen. No one seemed to care that four weeks earlier the two sides had been at war with each other. No Arabs took any tables, though. Walt heard they preferred their own coffee bars. His British patients told tales of knife-wielding Arabs attacking unsuspecting Allied campsites outside city limits. Walt wasn't sure what to believe.

"I made a vow, Tom." Walt took a deep gulp of his cognac. "I became a medic to save lives. But since I've been here, I've watched five men die— and not even from combat wounds."

"You can't save everyone. You know that, right?"

Hatch nodded in agreement. He looked fit, but his pale blue eyes darted back and forth, and he thumped a heel against the floor so fast his leg vibrated.

For most of the evening, his friends looked like the men Walt had always known—healthy, unassuming, good-humored—even if Tom glanced over his shoulder every time a door slammed. "No harm being cautious," he said. "The invasion taught us that."

At the next table, three American soldiers debated how soon the Ninth Infantry would move to the next battlefield. They shouted over each other, placing bets on whether it would be two weeks or two months. Hatch pushed back his shaggy hair, his leg still jumping. "As long as we d-don't see any more action like that invasion." He smiled like he didn't care.

Walt gripped Hatch's shoulder. "Don't pay any attention to those guys. They're blowhards."

"Yeah. Who cares, right?" Hatch planted both elbows on the table and leaned forward, his smile more genuine. "Hey, any w-word from home, Walt?'

Walt winced. Downing his drink, he thought of Nora. Her due date had already passed. He pictured her huge belly, her lopsided smile and smoky eyes. He just wanted to hold her. He'd written her every day since he'd arrived in Africa and still had received no replies.

He told himself Nora was busy getting everything ready for Junior—the diapers, the bottles, the tiny shirts, sweaters and pants.

"Walt? You hear m-me?" Hatch said. "You okay?"

Walt saw Tom shoot Hatch a warning look. Tom was always better at reading his dark moods.

"I wish I knew if I'm a dad yet, Hatch," Walt said. "I can't stand this suspense. Back at Bragg we could talk to our gals whenever a pay phone was available. We could get a letter to them in a day or two. We could tell them everything that was going on and they could write back right away. But this—it feels like we fell off a cliff."

"And our letters along with us," Tom said. "I haven't heard a word from my wife either. Sometimes I wonder if Bernadette has any idea what we're going through. How long do you think it takes a letter to get here? A week? A month? Two months?"

Walt shook his head. "Don't know. The thing is, I should have heard by now. Nora promised she'd get a telegram to me. I need to know she's okay."

"D-don't worry. Someone will let you know if there's any p-p-problem," Hatch said.

"Yeah. Sure." Hatch was right. His father would make sure Nora and his child were all right. But fear latched onto him. He couldn't shake it loose.

A pang of guilt joined the fear. In surgery, sometimes hours passed without a thought of his wife. The wounded took all his attention. He focused on scalpels, stitches, sulfa and doses of Sodium Pentothal; on blood and body parts; on pain killers and putrid flesh. What looked like chaos to an outsider felt to him like an elaborate dance. He knew every step.

He pulled Nora's picture from his pocket and studied it silently, ignoring Tom and Hatch, blocking out the growing buzz of noisy male voices around him. You know I love you, Nora, he thought.

TWENTY

Dec. 11, 1942

Dear Walt,

By now you've heard the wonderful news. Our son was born two days ago, a whole week early. I wish you could see him. He has your curly brown hair and high forehead and my mouth and eyes. If only I could pick up a phone to tell you how perfect he is...

My hand froze over the words I had just written. One thing was true— our baby was beautiful indeed, the most beautiful I had ever seen.

That first night, when a nurse finally brought him to the room I shared with two other mothers, I couldn't stop looking at him. His eyes were vivid blue, his mouth a perfect pout; the downy softness of his skin against mine made me shiver. Yet he was listless and frail, with no energy to suckle. When I asked the nurses if my body was making enough milk, they told me not to worry.

But the second day he still refused to nurse. He felt limp and warm in my arms. I held him tightly, afraid to give him up. The young blond nurse on duty acted calm. "You get some rest," she said, taking him from me. "We'll make him formula for now. You can try again later."

I wasn't about to tell Walt any of that. My first letter about his son needed to be a proper introduction filled with good news. Capping my pen, I put my half-finished letter on my end table.

When the time came for my baby's next feeding, a heavyset nurse arrived with my dinner tray instead. I pushed myself up and strained to see into the hall.

"Where's my baby?"

The nurse, an older woman with unruly salt and pepper hair, lazily pinned back a loose strand. "You first-time mothers are all alike. We're taking good care of your baby, Mrs. Baran. You'll see him after the doctor finishes checking him."

"Checking him? For what?"

She pressed her lips. "The doctor will be by shortly. You can talk to him then. Now eat."

I picked at the food for a minute before setting it aside. The large clock on the far wall ticked off each second.

By the time Dr. Wenski arrived, the late afternoon winter sky was dimming. Standing beside my bed, he shuffled through papers on his clipboard and grunted softly. He seemed to be discovering facts he hadn't known.

"Doctor, my baby—"

Without looking up, he raised a finger in silent reprimand. A minute passed, and then another. "Okay, young lady. Let's go over this."

I held my breath, the way I'd stopped breathing the day my baby struggled to be born. Dr. Wenski sighed. "Your son is having some difficulties. Seems to have developed pneumonia."

"Pneumonia?" I could barely speak the word.

Ignoring my fear, he rushed on. "Not uncommon in newborns. Their little lungs sometimes aren't yet up to the job. We have him on oxygen. Need to get his fever down."

"His fever?" I swiped tears from my eyes. Again, the doctor ignored me. He flipped the papers back down on his clipboard and patted my shoulder. "You need to heal, too. I'll check the boy tomorrow." He turned to leave.

"Wait! How did this happen? Will he be all right? When can I see him?"

From the doorway, Dr. Wenski smiled gently. "So many questions, Mrs. Baran, hmm? First things first. You'll get your answers in due time."

With that he was gone.

I swung my legs off the bed, but when I tried to stand a sharp pain stabbed at my groin. The woman in the next bed frowned. "I'll ring for the nurse to come back, dearie. You best stay put."

Fear and pain pushed me back on the bed. It held me there until the young blond nurse came by ten minutes later. "I need to get up," I told her. "I need to see my son."

"Not tonight, missus." The nurse gently guided my head to my pillow and spread a sheet and wool blanket over me. "Maybe tomorrow. We'll try to get you down the hall then."

"No! I have to see him now." I tried to shout the words, but they came out as muffled sobs. Before I could speak again, she was gone.

***

The next morning, another nurse wheeled me to the nursery and left me at the viewing window while she checked on other patients. Relieved to be alone, I rolled my wheelchair closer.

I pressed my palm against the glass, willing my love to reach my baby's cheek. In a far corner of the nursery, separate from the other infants, he lay silent and still inside a high-sided crib. I tried not to look at the u-shaped metal tubing in his nostrils or the long oxygen tube fastened to it with adhesive tape. I whispered against the glass, "You are your father's son. You are Wladimir Aleksander Baran, Junior." I shook my head, remembering how Walt rejected that Polish version of his name. I forced a smile I pretended my baby could see. "You are Walter Aleksander Baran, Junior, and you will soon be in my arms, my little Alek."

***

Back in my bed, in that place between sleep and wakefulness, I heard a man's shouts outside my room: "Where is he? Take me to the child now."

A flurry of female voices responded like a bevy of fearful doves. They tried to object, but the man would have no part of it. "Now," he demanded again. "Now!"

The heavy hammer of his insistence roused me from my grogginess. *Max.* I had wondered when my father-in-law would come, wondered what I would tell him. After Walt was shipped overseas, Max called every few days to grill me about my health. His grandchild deserved the best, he kept saying.

He'll blame me for my baby's pneumonia, I thought. I just know it.

I pulled on a pink quilted bed jacket and brushed my hair back. More than an hour passed before Max burst into my room, rubbing his hands together and grinning cheerfully.

"You look terrific, Maggie! So does the baby, considering everything the kid's been through."

I ignored Max's determination to call me by that hated nickname and took a deep breath. "The doctor—"

"I know all about it. Doc and I just had a nice, long talk. Don't worry about a thing. I told him to spare no expense. Give the baby private-duty nurses round the clock, the best equipment, the best medicines, whatever it takes to get him well."

I searched my father-in-law's face for a sign of sarcasm or a joke. *Spare no expense?* I'd never known him to be that generous, but his voice and manner seemed sincere.

Gratitude overwhelmed me. "Oh, my. Thank you."

Max raised an eyebrow. "Don't worry about a thing. The kid will be better in no time."

For once, I was glad Max was taking charge. He had a way of getting things done. He didn't stay long, though. Soon after he left, my mother-in-law showed up. I'd wondered when she would. My parents and brother had already visited twice, but I never knew what to expect from Max and Ruth.

Ruth wordlessly handed me a basket of scented lotions and a set of crystal rosary beads in a velvet drawstring bag. When she finally tried to speak, the tip of her nose turned bright pink. "I've been praying for the baby, Nora. So has the whole family."

"I appreciate that, Mom. I do."

"And I made a vow."

"A vow?"

"I told God that if He protects my first grandson, I'll dedicate a special day to Him every week. Every Wednesday, I'll go to Mass, I'll say the rosary five times, and I won't eat any meat. I-I hope He hears me." Her voice trembled slightly.

I placed my hand on Ruth's. Her vow meant a lot, even for someone as pious a Catholic as she was. My mother-in-law hated the very smell of fish; she struggled to obey the church's command to eat no meat on Fridays. I searched for the right words to thank her. As grateful as I was, I couldn't forget Ziggy's warning when Walt and I started dating: "Be careful. Ruth doesn't trust you. She and Max both think you're after the Baran money."

Ruth broke the silence first. "I'm going back to the hospital chapel. Is there anything I can do for you first, Nora?"

Back to the chapel? I wondered how long my mother-in-law had been at the hospital. "Don't bother about me. I'll be fine," I said. "And, Mom, thank you. Thank you so much."

She hugged me gingerly. "And the baby will be fine, too," she whispered, "with God's help."

***

Four days had passed since my son was put on oxygen. I was well enough to be released from the hospital, but no one knew when my son might go home, too. Sitting in a straight-backed chair next to my bed, I pulled out the letter to Walt I'd started days earlier. Slowly, I added more lines.

> ...Today is Dec. 14. I'll try to finish this letter so you have at least a little news about your son. I've named him Walter Aleksander Baran, Junior, just like we decided. I call him Alek. I hope you like that nickname. The nurses all give him a lot of attention, probably because he is so darling. Your parents have been amazingly helpful. I'll tell you more in a future letter. For now, the good news is that

I'm ready to be discharged. I can't wait to have him with
me all the time...

I convinced myself that I wasn't lying, even though my words hid the
truth about Alek's health. Left unsaid were his 103-degree fever, his
vomiting, his convulsions—the reasons the hospital would not release him.
I didn't have the heart to tell Walt all that. The truth seemed more than
unkind; it seemed cruel. As soon as Alek's health improved, I decided, I
would tell my husband everything. I signed the letter and sealed it.

Reluctantly, I began to pack. I was almost finished emptying my
cupboard when Max strolled in. It was the first time he'd been to the
hospital in four days.

"All set to go home, Margaret?"

I tilted my head at his unexpected use of my full American name. Max
sounded casual, even polite.

"I really don't want to go. I want to stay here to keep an eye on Alek."
As was my habit, I spoke to my father-in-law without actually addressing
him. I didn't want to call him *Dad*, the word I used for my own father, but
Max sounded rude and *Pop* too familiar. Even when he smiled at me, the
way he did at that moment, Max never seemed friendly. I wanted to invent
a nickname for him like he did for everyone else.

"He's getting good care, kiddo. Don't worry about him," Max said.

"I can't help it. He's so sick." I concentrated on folding my pale pink
nightgown into careful creases until I could speak without my voice
breaking. "I wrote Walt this morning. Have you heard from him? Has he
answered your telegram?"

"Telegram? Nah, I haven't sent one out yet. I'll do it in a few days, as
soon as Junior gets out of the hospital." Max squinted at me carefully.
"What did you tell Walt, anyway?"

I gaped at him, not believing I heard him right. "I talked to you about
this a week ago!" I almost shouted. "Walt made me promise to get him
word right away! You said you would do it."

He shook his head. "Calm down, Maggie. You're imagining things."

Tears of frustration and anger stung my eyes. Suddenly, I realized what
might be stopping Max. He wanted to make sure my baby would survive
before he sent word. That morning I'd overheard Dr. Wenski lecture Alek's
nurses: "Make sure the boy gets the proper amount of sulfa. Keep an eye
on him."

I'd told myself the doctor was just being cautious, that there was no
need to panic. Now, a wave of nausea gripped me. My son might die, and
there was nothing I could do. I couldn't even stay with him. All I could do
was pray.

If only Walt could be here, I thought. He would know what to ask the doctor—the same general doctor who delivered Alek, for heaven's sake. What did Dr. Wenski know about treating infections in a baby's lungs?

"Maggie? I asked you a question. Tell me what you wrote my son." Max was smiling, but his tone had a hard edge.

"Nothing really. Just that his son is beautiful. I'm going to write another letter when I get home, though. We should let Walt know all this."

Max's smile dissolved like ice in hot water. "You want to tell him everything, do ya? That his son has pneumonia?" His voice grew louder. "That the kid is so sick the doc won't let him outta here? How is that going to help my son in Africa, in the middle of a war?"

"But—"

"But nothin'. Use your head, Maggie." His eyes were bulging. "My son wonders every day if he's gonna get killed. He doesn't need more worries. You understand?"

"I-I guess," I said, unsure if I did. Walt had assured me he would be safe as a medic. I didn't picture him worried or fearful. The war seemed so far away I could hardly imagine it. "But at least I should wire him. To let him know he has a son. I'll do that."

Max's frown purpled his scar. "You like to take charge, don't you, Maggie? I think I can handle things without your help."

I was confused. Now Max wanted to send the telegram? I nodded, all out of fight.

Abruptly, he shifted gears. "You got a ride home?"

"What? I—my Uncle Robert will take me. He's picking me up in an hour." I folded my bed jacket tightly and stuffed it into my suitcase, then wrapped my slippers in tissue paper and placed them on top. Maybe Max was right to protect Walt from the truth. Hadn't I been thinking that, too?

"Okay then. I'll check on Junior."

"All right," I murmured.

"Just remember when you write Butch again." Max put his forefinger to his lips. "Say nothing about your son's health. Okay? It's *our* secret."

I bit my lip.

"You hear me, Maggie?"

I nodded and turned away. Without a word of objection, I had let Max box me into a promise I already regretted. Our shared secret was more than a lie of omission. It kept Walt from learning every important fact he needed to know about his son.

TWENTY-ONE

Dec. 12, 1942

Dear Nora,

Not much new going on, except that I've been very busy in surgery. You may have noticed I don't write much about my work there. Better to leave those details out of my letters. Someday I'll tell you why. Don't forget to have someone telegram me when the baby comes. I hope to hear soon...

Walt mailed the letter before rushing to the operating room. He hated to be late. The surgeon on duty, Captain Hector Abich, was notoriously short-tempered.

Standing over his patient like a guard ready to pull a weapon, Abich glowered. "I see you finally decided to join us, Private."

Abich injected sodium pentothal into the patient's arm. Within seconds, the soldier's breath came in slow deep sighs, the sleep of the drugged. "Why can't these idiots wise up?" the doctor said, pulling back the foreskin on the young man's penis and grabbing a scalpel.

Walt grunted an ambiguous reply. The last thing he wanted was to rile the surgeon during a circumcision. He wondered how an Army doctor could be that naïve. The clearing company handled mostly routine cases, and this patient had the most common wartime condition of all: venereal disease.

VD could level an infantry battalion more effectively than a dozen tanks, but everything the Army tried to prevent it had failed. Soldiers ignored all the warnings that Morocco's resistant strain of gonorrhea couldn't be cured by sulfa drugs; they ignored the Army's offers of free condoms; they shrugged at threats of severe punishment for failure to use protection.

Nothing worked.

Walt witnessed the results when lonely, sex-deprived soldiers hiked unarmed to the town's whorehouses and caught everything from scabies to syphilis. For some, circumcision was the only cure.

Abich sliced away skin as Walt suctioned off blood. The doctor whistled along with a radio broadcast of the Andrew Sisters' "Don't Sit Under the Apple Tree." Army doctors surely found no glory in cutting soldiers' foreskins, Walt thought, but Abich mocked the job. "I had a residency at Columbia-Presbyterian before they drafted me," he told Walt, who, like all the other technicians, pretended to care. "I had an important career ahead of me." He wore a faraway look as he whistled, as if he saw himself back in New York City at the center of his universe.

"Jesus Christ!" the patient on the table screamed.

"Jesus Christ!" Abich echoed, leaping back.

The drug the patient received should have put him under for hours. But he was wide awake.

"Ether!" Walt yelled. "Someone get the ether."

The soldier flailed and kicked until pain made him scream again. Fat drops of blood splattered the surgical team's white gowns. Walt grabbed a leg. Ted and another tech grabbed the soldier's arms. Dr. Hunter, alerted by the commotion, ran in and grabbed the other leg.

Dr. Abich wriggled his arm through the melee and cupped an ether mask on the soldier's face. "Breathe. Breathe slowly," he said. The soldier's body went limp again. Red-faced and sweaty, Abich moved back to his spot at the table, scalpel poised.

"Ready?" he asked Walt. A quavering whistle escaped his pursed lips.

Walt winced as Abich used jagged strokes to slice off the rest of the foreskin. God help the soldiers who get brought to us from battle, he thought.

***

December 24, 1942

Dearest Nora,

Our baby must have been born by now. I can picture the day he arrived. Hurried telephone calls passed the news from house to house. Everyone dashed to the hospital to see the beautiful mother and baby. But by now all that must have calmed down, and you and baby are home with your folks, relaxing and getting ready for Christmas. My imagination tortures me, Nora. Please send word...

"In nomine Patri, et Filii, et Spiritu Sancti," the priest chanted.

"Amen." The roomful of male voices rang strong and clear.

Walt made the sign of the cross and bowed his head as the priest poured wine into a chalice. In the stillness of the makeshift chapel, he could hear the liquid splash in the silver cup. He tried to concentrate on the miracle of Christmas, but all he could think of was Nora's promise to let him know about their own child's birth. How long, Lord, must I wait?

After Mass, the soldiers milled outside, unwilling to return to their quarters. All wore matching forlorn faces except Big Al, who stomped his feet like a race horse at the gate.

"It's Christmas Eve, for Chrissake," Al said. "We should be celebrating, not moping. How about some songs?" Slowly, his big bass voice rumbled to life: "Si-i-lent Night. Ho-o-oly Night..."

Walt stared in wonder at the transformation of a man known for his cursing and brawling. He pictured his child making contented squeaks in Nora's arms. "All is calm," he joined in, his baritone smooth and steady.

"All is bright..." Ted and Buck added their tenors.

The four men began walking as they sang, stepping briefly inside buildings and tents in the neighborhoods near their quarters. One by one, other soldiers joined them until a circle of nine sturdy male voices, a small choir of stubborn hope, spread Christmas through the makeshift Army compound in Mehdea.

"'Round yon Vir-ir-gin, Mother and Child,
Holy infant so tender and mild...'"

***

Days later, chilly morning air forced the medics to wear jackets inside their unheated building. Walt warmed his hands over a mug of hot coffee, brewed so strong its scent alone jolted him alert. The small room on the building's ground floor served as a mess hall, but its size and the chill kept most men from lingering.

In the distance, Gus called out "Mail call!" Every time Walt heard those words, hope lurched inside him.

"There you are, Baran!"

Gus handed him a thick packet of letters, all postmarked in early December: One from Nora, one from Ziggy, two from old friends and two from his parents. But no telegrams.

Walt pulled out a penknife and slit them all open. He saw right away that his wife's, dated December 8, was written before the baby came. A quick glance at the others told him he would get no real news that day. He sank low in his chair.

Gus pulled a chair next to him. "Sorry, buddy. I know you hoped for more."

Walt took a deep gulp of coffee and lit a cigarette. "I don't get it. I've recalculated the days of my wife's pregnancy over and over. I've done the math again and again, in case I made a mistake."

Gus looked at him attentively, making no sound. The clerk was a good listener, a quality Walt appreciated. He explained that each time he calculated Nora's due date, it landed on December 17. His baby might come late, but this late? Why hadn't his parents sent word?

TWENTY-TWO

I looked through the viewing window to the sick infants' room, a mere spectator to Alek's care. A nurse named Eleanor stopped by his bassinette and caressed his cheek. A lamp heated his bassinette, its glow yellowing his sallow skin even more. I stood watch like that almost every day for hours at a time.

Of the three nurses who tended my baby around the clock, Eleanor clearly loved him most. She didn't just move him often to keep his lungs clear, she cradled him and sang him lullabies, too. I'd noticed she arrived early for her shifts, scooping him up first and holding him close. If he struggled to cough, she whispered gentle comfort in his ear and patted his back.

I longed to hold my son, too, to cuddle him and kiss his cheeks. "His doctor won't allow it," Eleanor explained, an apologetic frown on her face. "He's afraid the little one will pick up more germs." I held back tears, telling myself my baby's health was more important than my longing, that my son was in good hands.

***

Dec. 20, 1942

Dear Walt,

Alek looked at me this morning like he recognized me. I hope he'll soon be able to look at you the same way. I'm wrapping your Christmas presents and will mail them this afternoon. Sorry, dear, I'm keeping the contents a secret. You'll have to wait until Santa comes. I hope you like everything...

The week before Christmas, my mother put up a scraggly, three-foot pine tree. I had no energy to decorate it. The very theme of the holiday—a Child is born to great rejoicing!—mocked my misery. I had no idea how long my son would remain in the hospital.

On Christmas Eve, we spoke little as we exchanged gifts—wool socks for Steve, a maroon wool scarf for me, toiletries for my mother, a new shaving brush for my father, plus some candies, fruits and cookies my mother bought on her way home from work the day before. Steve and my mother joined me at St. Adalbert's for midnight Mass. As usual, my father stayed home. I wondered why I hadn't stayed with him. God seemed absent from my life, too.

On Christmas Day, when no buses were running, I talked Ziggy into driving me to the hospital. Alek lay motionless in the newborn ward, his eyes watchful, a trickle of spittle running down his chin.

"He looks well enough to come home," I told the nurse. "Please can I take him?"

She shook her head. "Doctor's orders, Mrs. Baran."

My throat burned with unshed tears. I was his mother. How could Dr. Wenski keep him from me? Why wasn't the doctor telling me the whole truth?

Yet my letter to Walt that afternoon echoed almost every one I'd written since Alek was born, remarkable for all it did not say. I told him about the Christmas package I'd sent him and described my family's holiday rituals. I made it sound like Alek was with us. I said he was getting stronger.

As I slipped the single sheet of paper in an envelope, I pondered my growing list of clever lies. So many of them. I wrote them now without hesitation. How could I have made that promise to Max? Keeping secrets like this felt like a sin, but if the full truth might cause Walt pain, that wouldn't be right, either. I put the letter out for the next morning's mail. One thought plagued me: If Walt discovered my lies, would he lose all trust in me?

***

A week later, I sat unmoving in my parents' quiet apartment, an unfinished letter to Walt in my lap. The telephone's stubborn ring jolted me from my guilty conscience.

"Kuchynski residence."

"Hello? Margaret?"

I froze at the sound of Dr. Wenski's voice. He wouldn't call unless he had news about my baby. "This is she. Is—is Alek all right?"

"Ah, yes, the baby. He is doing better, actually. His fever isn't as high today."

"When can I bring him home?" My yearning for my child consumed me. I felt incomplete without him.

"Home? Well, I don't know about that. It could be quite a while yet."

Quite a while? Panic froze me into silence.

"Margaret? Are you there?"

"Yes. I am." I cleared my throat. "Why are you calling, doctor?"

He coughed lightly. I envisioned him tugging on the herringbone vest fastened snugly around his belly.

"There's the question of the bill."

"The bill?"

"It's getting rather high. Your father-in-law authorized nurses around the clock. He said he wanted to be billed, but he hasn't replied to any of the invoices."

I inhaled sharply. He was making no sense. "Uh, shouldn't you talk to him about it? Do—do you need his number? I've got it right—"

"No. No. I have it. I just—yes, I'll call him. Thank you, Margaret. Good-bye."

I grabbed the arm of the sofa to steady myself. I tried to guess how much was owed to the doctors, the nurses and the hospital. More than I could imagine, I thought. What was Max up to?

***

My father-in-law paced in his office. "That damn doctor. Thinks he can cheat me, does he? Well, *I'm* not his patient. They're all like this. Doctors. Lawyers. Salesmen. Damn parasites! Think they can charge me more because I'm Max Baran? Think they can bleed me dry of my hard-earned money? They can think again." He kept raving without taking a breath.

I'd never seen him that angry. I'd taken two buses that morning to reach his office. I'd hoped that if I talked to him in person, I could get some answers. "But you ordered that extra care. Dad. And Dr. Wenski said you wanted to be billed."

"I cleared up that mistake, believe me. I told him you and Alek were his patients—not me. Send your bill to Margaret, I said. That'll make him think twice about trying to bilk Max Baran."

My cheeks turned hot. What was he implying? Hadn't he told me not to worry, that he would handle things? Surely, he didn't expect me to pay for all that care? Walt sent home only a few dollars a month, and I couldn't get a job with Alek coming home soon and needing special attention. I barely had enough money to pay for Alek's basic care as it was.

"How—how much is it? I can't—"

"Do what you can, Maggie! Just pay a little every month. Am I making myself clear?"

"But—no—I can't—"

"Maggie!" He was yelling now. "Take care of it!"

I rushed from his office, as frightened as I was furious. Nothing he said was clear.

That night, I told my parents what Max said, how he was breaking his promise. "He thinks the doctor is trying to cheat him, but what can I do? I can't afford any more bills."

My mother fumed. I knew that look in her eyes. She already was planning revenge. But her anger latched onto the way Max had treated me, not the money I owed. "He like to torment people, Gosia. It make him happy."

***

My brother was a coward. I had to learn he signed up for the Army Air Force from my mother, whom I found weeping quietly at the kitchen table.

"Your brother join Army, Gosia. He want to fly planes."

"He'll be okay, Mom. You know how smart he is."

Upstairs, Steve was packing his things. "What are you thinking?" I shouted at him. "Men are dying in this war every day. Your parents need you here. *I* need you."

"Come on, sis. You know why I did it. I'm over 18 now. I'm amazed I haven't been drafted already. I could have ended up in the infantry. This way, I may be able to train as a pilot. I'll be good at it and I won't have to fight on the ground."

I wanted to throttle him, the way I did when he misbehaved as a child. Foolish boy. He didn't even know how to drive yet.

"You'll do okay without me, sis," said Steve. "You are an amazingly strong woman."

His words loosened my tears. Usually, when we disagreed, we teased each other with the taunting banter of siblings. His sweet praise was more than I could take.

***

Three weeks after Alek was born, I finally received the call I had yearned for. "Good news, young lady," Dr. Wenski said. "Your baby is ready to go home."

Relief washed over me, casting out every worry and sorrow. Only after I hung up did I realize another reason to smile. Wenski had said nothing about the bill. Maybe Max paid him. Maybe he was finally over his anger at the bill.

The next day, when I went to fetch Alek, I was ready for anything but his dutiful nurse's sad expression. "What's wrong, Eleanor? Is Alek all right?"

She ducked her head and nodded. "I'll miss the sweet boy. I have to be honest."

"Is he ready?"

"Ready enough. But you have to be, too."

"For what?" My stomach tightened.

"The pneumonia has been hard on him. A shock to his nervous system."

Hard on my baby and harder on me, I thought. Were it not for the sulfa drugs the doctor gave him, Alek might never have survived.

Eleanor led me to a bench and clasped my hand. "Your son has a sensitive nature, Mrs. Baran. He needs as much attention as you can give. Do you understand?" The nurse, only a few years older than I, sounded motherly.

"Of course, Eleanor. I can't thank you enough."

"And be careful feeding him. Do it slowly. The poor thing can't seem to keep things down." She patted my knee and stood up. "All right then, let's get him ready."

Standing at the nursery window, I watched her unfasten Alek's soggy cotton diaper, wipe his bottom and pin on a clean cloth. She tucked his arms into a pale blue nightgown and wrapped him in a thick flannel blanket. Lifting him to her chest, she held him tightly.

I pressed my palm on the window, the signal I had been sending Alek for so many weeks, a signal Eleanor must have felt, too. She brought him out and placed him in my arms. Then she stepped back quickly, cutting their cord.

I held him in my arms in disbelief. My baby felt no heavier than the blanket that swaddled him. When he bleated a ragged cry, I pulled him to my face and breathed in his scent.

"Ah, baby. You're mine now."

TWENTY-THREE

"I have a job for you, Baran." Oliver Penland, a major now, shuffled the papers on his desk, his attention in two places.

A new challenge was just what Walt needed. A wave of ornery depression and fear had claimed him. He still had received no word about Nora or their baby, and weeks had passed since her expected delivery date. Only the worst of reasons could have caused her to break her promise to send a telegram.

"I'm ready, sir," He wondered if his company commander was thinking of a promotion and a raise.

Penland cleared his throat. "As you probably have heard, our VD cases are growing to epidemic proportions. We're losing man-hours."

Everyone knows that, Walt thought. What does it have to do with me?

"We need to take drastic action." Penland clasped his hands and leaned forward. "I should just get to the point. It's like this, Private. I need you in a brothel."

"Sir?"

"To run the prophylactic station at a brothel, to be more precise. Starting tomorrow, your platoon will take over the main house in Port Lyautey. You know the one."

Walt didn't know how to answer. Of all the jobs he expected, running a whorehouse wasn't among them. He knew the place the major was talking about. It came up often in soldiers' conversations. Rumor had it that half the soldiers in Port Lyautey stood in line there at least once a week.

"We've tried everything to get a handle on this," Penland said. "If the Army can't stop the men from taking these dumb risks, it might as well go where the problem is. If we don't, there won't be a fit soldier left when the fighting starts. I want you in charge. Immediately"

110

This isn't saving lives, Walt thought. It's more like babysitting.

The major explained the strategy: A doctor would visit the brothel every afternoon to examine the girls, then two or three medics would be on duty at night, with Walt in charge. The medics would make sure every American soldier coming through the door had no signs of gonorrhea or syphilis. If the soldier was clear, he'd be handed a condom. If he wasn't, he'd receive an injection of Protargol, a silver protein drug found to be effective in treating gonorrhea, before being kicked out the back door.

Walt grimaced at the irony. All he imagined day and night was holding Nora in his arms, and here he was, assigned to a whorehouse.

***

Early the next afternoon, Big Al and a military policeman helped Walt load a Jeep with supplies—condoms, microscopes, Protargol, calomel ointment, swabs and notebooks. Midway through the job, Ted D'Amico appeared by their side and heaved a crate into the Jeep.

"What are you doing, D'Amico?" Walt asked. "You're not assigned to this."

"You lucky dog," Ted growled. "How come you get the fun jobs?"

Walt rolled his eyes. "Ted. It's a whorehouse. Not a church social."

Morocco's modest dress standards had severely hampered Ted's eye for shapely females. He complained daily about the local women's long robes and head scarves. With his piercing dark eyes and prominent nose, Ted considered himself handsome. "At least those gals would show off for me," he said. "Good-looking guys like me have a right to see the goods, no?"

"You are amazing, D'Amico," Walt said. "Now clear out."

He climbed into the crowded Jeep with Big Al and the MP. As soon as they settled in, the driver—a surly, scrawny private named Magnus—took off at full speed. At the outskirts of town, he made a sharp right onto an obscure side road. Then he turned left with the certainty of someone heading home. Walt smiled. I might be the last soldier in Morocco who hasn't visited this place, he thought.

The whorehouse occupied half of a large, unremarkable building at the edge of the Arab quarter. As Magnus and the MP unloaded supplies, Walt and Big Al entered through a heavy wooden front door. Walt pushed aside the thick curtain separating the foyer from a roomy parlor. A haze of incense blurred the five naked young women lounging around the madam, who wore more clothing than all the girls together. He tried not to gawk.

The women's nonchalance disarmed him most. All the scantily clad women he'd ever seen in nightclub reviews couldn't match the scene. Removing his cap, he bowed slightly at the older woman. "How do you do, ma'am." How exactly, he wondered, does one greet a whorehouse madam?

Madame L'Amoureux's lop-sided smile told him he amused her, but he wasn't sure why. With a flick of her hand, she dismissed the girls and motioned him to sit in a chair near her red-velvet sofa. She must have been an exotic beauty once, he thought. Her dark amber eyes and thick lashes brightened the fine corduroy of her face, and when she smiled broadly her face lost at least ten of its fifty years.

He felt himself blush when she looked him up and down just as closely.

"Have you been told why we've come here, ma'am?" Walt said.

"Of course. It is expected. It is not the first time I have had interference in my affairs, and I am sure it will not be the last."

"Let me explain what we'll be doing," Walt said. He reviewed the details with her like a doctor with a patient. When he finished, she led him to a room where the five prostitutes waited, sitting as calmly as they might in their own parlors. Walt tried to appear casual as the madam introduced them: a bored-looking Spanish girl wearing only a gold-flecked black shawl; a dark-skinned young Arab girl with hard nipples and a bold stare; and three French women in fishnet stockings and spiked heels who claimed their husbands were Legionnaires on duty somewhere in Africa.

"We have to work," said one, a raven-haired beauty named Marie. "We could not live on our husbands' pay."

Despite his efforts to concentrate, Walt felt himself harden. He distracted his body with conversation. "Do your husbands know what you do?" he asked.

"Of course!" another wife, Helene, said. "How can they complain? We make more money than they do. Five dollars a customer—and we get to keep half."

The fee hit him like a cold shower. Five dollars? A fortune for a GI. How can these guys afford it?

***

The next afternoon, Walt and Big Al arrived early to find a line of men already waiting. At four-thirty sharp, Al pushed open the front door and began the screening. As each healthy soldier received a condom, he bounded upstairs. The men with symptoms Al sent to Walt, who was glad to have the big man in his crew. No one argued with Al. Walt gave those men injections before sending them out the back door.

"Well, what have we got here?" a booming voice exploded two hours into business that first day. "Inspecting dicks. I shoulda known they'd give you that job, Baran."

Corporal Aidan Leary smirked as he wagged his penis in Walt's face. "Your other dick inspector seems to think I gotta problem. You wanna check it out yourself?"

Walt leaned back and glared at the corporal, the one man in G Company he'd have been happy never to see again. The last time Walt had to endure him, just a day before he'd left for medical training in Missouri, the corporal trailed close behind making high-pitched clucking noises. "Chick-en," he sang in sing-song measure, "chick-en."

Leary glowered, hands on his hips. "Come on, come on. You know you wanna give it a feel. They say that's all you cowards really want."

Walt bolted from his seat so fast Leary almost lost his balance avoiding him. But in a second Big Al was standing between them, his huge frame a wall neither could breach. "You ready to switch with me, Walt? I'm getting tired screening these fuckin' guys."

Walt cut a parting look at the corporal. "Yeah, I'm ready. It's getting pretty foul-smelling in this corner anyway."

From his seat at the door, Walt took satisfaction watching Al jab a needle hard into the Leary's buttocks and the corporal sneak out the back door. If he ever ran into the fool again, he promised himself, he would settle things between them for good.

***

Only during dinner hour, when business slowed a bit, did the girls take a break. They paraded naked in front of Walt before moving to a table behind him. Marie slowed as she sauntered by. "Hi, sweetie. How is my handsome medic?" she purred. Avoiding her gaze, Walt cursed a quiver of lust shivering through him.

By night's end, he'd counted one hundred and twenty-two customers.

Back at his quarters, he tried to sleep. His crowded mind raced with desire, doubt and anger. He imagined Nora's lips on his. He saw himself landing a punch on Aidan Leary's jaw. He felt his first-born child in his arms. He badgered himself about joining the Medical Corps. Why did he become a medic if he wasn't helping to save lives?

***

Walt's second night at the brothel went much like the first. By the third night, though, his reactions changed. The endless line of soldiers affected him more than the women's careless nudity. The thought of how the women earned their money stripped him of all desire. He used a few minutes during a break to write Nora.

Dec. 31, 1942

My Dear Wife,

    Still, I wait for word of you and our baby. I can't stand

one more day without news. I do nothing but think of you all day long. I'm of no earthly value when I get this way. I'm like a young lovesick pup. How can one person have such an effect on a fellow? Your hold on my heartstrings is tighter than ever. Don't worry about me. Things are swell here...

He wondered what Nora would think if she saw where he worked that New Year's Eve. A girl like her couldn't imagine such a scene. Would she trust him if she could?

"You are very handsome, soldier."

Walt put down his pen and gave Marie his full attention. If he didn't, the other girls soon would join in the pestering and beg him to come upstairs. It happened every time Walt tried to read a book or write a letter.

"Don't you find me attractive, soldier? Am I so ugly you must keep rejecting me?"

"You're very lovely, Marie, but no. I'm serious. No." He didn't tell her he was happily married. Married men were some of the women's most difficult customers. The worst were those ridden with remorse. As soon as they had sex, they turned their angry regret on the prostitutes and beat them up.

"I will give you a—how do you say? —a dees-count." Marie was persistent.

"I will do it for free," said Bridgette, the third French woman, who was just starting her break. She draped a blue gauze scarf around Walt's neck and breathed in his ear.

He felt his face grow hot. He wondered if he was blushing. It wasn't desire he felt, but embarrassment at this new level of attention. "No, thank you, ma'am."

Bridgette snorted and turned on her heel.

"She is *tres* angry you reject her," Marie said. "She doesn't understand how you are."

"I have a new name for our Private Baran," Helene announced loud enough for all the girls to hear. "He is *The Cure*. Is that not so? There is no VD to be had with stubborn men like him around!"

"Monsieur Cure. Monsieur Cure." The other girls repeated and giggled.

Walt stood and bowed elaborately, one hand swinging high and the other tucked behind his back. His eyes flashed with delight. At last, he had made his point. "Happy to make your acquaintance, ladies. Thank you very much."

***

On Saturday, the sixth day and one of the brothel's busiest nights, three officers burst through the door soon after the medics began their shift. The full-bird colonel in charge wore a chaplain's silver cross on each lapel and an eagle on each shoulder. Two chaplains of lower rank followed close behind.

The medical team jumped to its feet, with Walt the last to stand. His mood had grown reckless in his days at the brothel—emboldened and energized by his new authority and increasingly agitated and edgy as each day passed with no word about Nora.

"I know what's going on here," the colonel shouted. "Don't deny it."

The colonel scanned the room, his left eye twitching at the sight of Walt and Big Al sitting next to two naked women, both of whom sprawled on a sofa, their legs spread apart.

"Who's in charge of this?" the colonel asked, his voice hoarse with outrage.

A half-smile passed over Walt's face. "I am, sir," Walt said slowly. "Under orders from Major Oliver Penland."

Maybe Walt's nonchalance provoked what came next, or maybe it was the amused tittering of Helene and Bridgette. The red-faced colonel fingered the cross on his uniform and pointed at Walt. "Soldier, you are an insolent, immoral man, and you are herewith demoted to private!"

To Walt, still a private first class after eight weeks in Africa, the threat meant so little he couldn't stop himself from taunting the officer, a man he thought more arrogant than smart. "And will you be reducing Major Penland to private, too, sir?"

The colonel's face purpled. "Get that soldier's name and unit," he shouted to one of the chaplains. "The rest of you get ready to return to your outfits immediately!"

Walt tried to appear calm as he gave the information, but he wondered if this time he had gone too far.

"Au revoir, Monsieur Cure!" the women called as he boarded his jeep. He leaned out the window and waved his cap cheerfully. The thought of returning to his old duties buoyed his spirits. "Au revoir, ladies!"

***

That night, the memory of the Colonel's purple face joined Walt's other worries. If he wasn't more careful, he thought, he might never earn a promotion.

Early the next morning, he took the offensive. He found a cluster of medics—both doctors and enlisted men—sipping coffee outside their building. "Boy, did we have fun at the whorehouse last night, huh, Al?" said Walt, hoisting himself atop a low stucco wall.

Al grimaced. "Some fun."

"Who would expect Army chaplains to take such an interest in our operation?" Walt looked around, a glint in his eyes. He had everyone's attention.

"You should've seen that full bird's face," Walt told the laughing crowd. "Here was Helene, naked as a newborn, sitting like this"—he spread his legs wide—"and Bridgette looking just as brazen with her hands on her hips, and here's the colonel"—he paused and twisted his face into an exaggerated scowl—"but I can't make my face that shade of purple. Boy, was he wound up."

Even Lt. Abich and Major Penland seemed amused at the tale, a response that encouraged Walt. He'd heard that his brothel assignment was known to the battalion commander and even to Major General Maton Eddy, the division commander. He hoped they had a sense of humor, too.

None of that mattered the next morning, when the Medical Battalion received new orders. The medics would follow the Ninth Infantry's fighting companies as they moved eastward. Over breakfast, Walt tried to learn more from Gus. "I can't say the order surprised me," Walt said, scooping up watery powdered eggs with a spoon. "Got any idea where we're going next?"

The company clerk shrugged the way he always did when he knew things he wasn't allowed to repeat. Knowing Gus would tell him if he could, Walt changed the subject. "Well, I'm glad to get out of pro station duty at least. Wonder what the top brass thinks of that encounter I had with the chaplains yesterday."

Gus swallowed a bite of toast. "Wonder no more. From what I hear, they got quite a chuckle out of it."

Walt let out a relieved sigh. "So, no one ran a prophylactic station at the Countess's brothel last night?"

"Nope, and I hear the Countess's lines stretched longer than ever."

No surprise, Walt thought as he swallowed his last gulp of coffee. Business is business, and the Countess knows how to make a buck even better than my father.

TWENTY-FOUR

Jan. 5, 1943

Dear Walt,

I pray every day the war will end soon so you can come home to your son and love him as I do. Whenever I look at him, I see your handsome face. Your parents visited today. They have been so generous. They brought two thick sweaters, a flannel sleeping gown and a matching quilt. Just what Alek needs this winter. He loves the attention. Even your father held him for a bit...

I have other news that frightens me a little. Steve enlisted in the Army Air Force. He leaves next week for basic training. He says he'll be safe. What do you think? Is he just trying to make us feel better?...

I didn't tell Walt, but I had dreaded my in-law's visit that day. I wasn't sure what else Max might be scheming, and Ruth cloaked her feelings like a magician hiding a card trick. I needed to have a private talk with Max. The thought of it made my stomach churn, but I needed to find out if he had paid Dr. Wenski.

At first, my in-laws won me over. They seemed genuinely happy to see their grandson. Max kept chucking Alek under his chin, and Ruth's eyes misted as she cuddled him. "God answered my prayers. I knew he would," she whispered.

Halfway through their visit, Max asked my father to join him at the dining room table in the next room. I wasn't surprised he wanted to escape my mother, who kept giving him fierce looks. I strained to catch bits and pieces of their conversation. I heard Dad complain in Polish about the workers he supervised at the factory. Max bragged about his business in equal amounts of Polish and English.

Meanwhile, we women shared our own stories. At one point, my mother laughed as she described my fussiness as a baby. "Gosia suck her thumb when she little. And the crying! Oh my, such crying!"

At that moment, my father-in-law's boisterous voice rang out. "So, when that doctor said…" A rush of hope made me focus on Max's words. Maybe he was having a change of heart. Then I heard, "I told that son of a bitch he'd better take care of my grandson and not expect extra money just for doing his damn job."

Dad muttered approval in his thick Polish accent. "Good, good" he said, exploding his g's in the back of his throat and forcing his d's through his teeth, so his words sounded like *Koot, koot*. Was my father even listening to the liar? Hadn't I told him that Max had broken his promise?

"Ya gotta stand up for yourself, right, Ben? You know that. You're a smart fella."

I studied the worn patch in our Oriental rug, where bare twine barely held the design together. How many other fathers and mothers had paced back and forth over that rug before it came into my parents' possession? Max knew my parents' circumstances. He knew my mother worked in a mattress factory to help pay the bills, that I received precious little from Walt's Army benefits, that my brother couldn't help because he had just enlisted in the Air Force. But there was Max, slapping my father on the back as if my family had no cares.

If Ruth heard a word of her husband's bragging, she gave no sign. She just stroked Alek's cheek and chuckled at my mother's stories. When Mom's chatter slowed, Ruth stood and sighed. "I'd love to stay all day, Janka, but we'd better go. We've kept you and Nora long enough."

I stood to hug her. "Thank you for your lovely gifts. It was thoughtful of you." In spite of Max, I felt real affection for her. Ruth's love of Alek was too sincere to doubt.

"Oh, I meant to tell you, dear," she said as she pulled on her coat. "We plan to write a long letter to Walter tonight telling him about our visit today. And we sent him that telegram about Alek."

I frowned. "A second one?"

Ruth looked confused. "No, remember, dear? We wanted to wait until Alek came home from the hospital."

I glared at Max. He let me think he'd sent Walt word weeks earlier. He was worse than a liar. I could have sent a telegram myself. I could have had my parents send one. Instead, I left the job to the one person I shouldn't have trusted at all. What was the matter with me? Had I lost all common sense?

My father-in-law gripped me by my shoulders to face him. "When you write Walt, Maggie, don't forget to tell him how well his boy is doing."

I swallowed my rage. I was a partner in my father-in-law's ruse. All along, I'd lacked an ounce of courage to tell Walt the truth.

***

My parents' home throbbed in silence after my in-laws left. My fury with Max bled into frustration with my parents, who turned out to be unreliable allies at best. I hid my feelings at first, fearful of what might erupt. But when my father turned toward his bedroom, his nightly escape from the family, I stepped in front of him.

"I don't understand, Dad. Why didn't you say something to Max about the doctor bill? Why didn't you tell the old fox to keep his promises?"

"Ach," he growled. He waved me aside, brushing away my questions.

My mother grabbed my arm. "Hush, girl. I call Ruth. Talk to her. Maybe she help."

I stared at her, unbelieving. Hadn't she noticed how my mother-in-law survived Max? Ruth was a master of silence and flattery. Never had I seen her confront him.

If my husband was home, he could talk to his father, but the problem was all mine now. I finished my letter to Walt. I invented things to say about Alek. I wrote nothing about Max's tricks, or my father's disinterest or my money woes.

> ...Alek is such a funny, clever boy. Even though the doctors say a baby can't see much at his age, he seems to watch me wherever I go. I swear he smiles right at me. He coos and squeals like he's trying to talk and when I rub my nose on his, he scrunches his face and frowns. Stay safe, my darling. I'll write again soon.
>
> Love, Nora

In the next room, Alek's breathed with raspy effort. I knelt and folded my hands the way my husband had taught me. I beseeched the Power I had no choice but to trust. "Please, Lord," I said, "hear the words I wrote tonight. Accept them as the truth and bless them, so they may grow in strength and fill Alek's life. Amen."

TWENTY-FIVE

By the fifth of January, Walt's anxiety had turned into alarm. Every letter from home was more than three weeks old by the time it arrived. None mentioned his child. The medic in him kept asking what could cause the delay; the husband in him imagined only terrible answers. If Nora was well, she surely would contact him.

He had sent his father a telegram the day before. "Send word about baby and Nora. Is all OK?" Worse than the silence that followed was his utter powerlessness. He couldn't simply pick up a phone to call his father or his wife or a friend. All he could do was wait. Patience was not his strength.

He wished he could box the rare mornings when he convinced himself all was well. On those mornings, every whiff of dawn's cool, dry air jolted his senses. The sun coaxed color from dry palmetto patches. The scent of bay laurel trees spiced the sea air. He felt Nora's spirit.

He would have saved those boxed memories for black mornings like this one—when he awoke cursing the Army, his father and God Himself. All had abandoned him. Even his memories of Nora were dimming. He tugged her photograph from his wallet, the one taken on their wedding day almost two years earlier. She wore her pale blue suit and pinned the generous white orchid corsage he'd bought for her near her neckline. He studied the line of her cheekbones, the softness of her lips, the glint of light in her hair. He remembered the absolute certainty he'd felt that day. No darkness existed then.

He trudged silently through his rounds in the recovery ward. A familiar headache pounded at his temples like a prisoner trying to escape. Someone somewhere shouted his name.

"Private Baran? Private Walter Baran?"

"Here," he said, wincing with the effort to speak.

A soldier handed him an envelope with a Red Cross insignia on the front. Walt pulled out a single sheet of paper: "A message from the U.S. awaits you. Call phone number below." No address was provided, just a long string of numbers.

Walt raced to the company clerk's office to use Gus's phone, but each time he dialed, he heard only clicks and dead air.

"What is this, some kind of joke?" he yelled. "Why the hell couldn't they just send me the message?"

Gus shrugged. Walt dialed again. Again, a string of clicks rattled through the line. He smashed the receiver on its cradle as if that would force the phone to comply. On his third dial, when the same sounds greeted him, he slammed down the phone and bolted for the door.

Outside, he collided with Buck.

"Buck!" he gasped, grabbing the stunned man by both shoulders. "Tell the captain I'm hitching a ride to Mehdia to find the Red Cross office. It's about a message I just got."

As he took off down the dusty street, he thought he heard Gus call to him. He wasn't about to stop. An Army supply truck let him hitch a ride on its open bed. The thought of his child as anything less than perfect set his heart racing. The thought of Nora being seriously ill, or worse—that he refused to contemplate.

In Mehdia, he went door to door seeking directions. He was met with frowns and shrugs. Finally, a clerk at a modern French hotel nodded. "*Mais monsieur, this place you want, ce n'est pas dans Mehdia. C'est a Casablanca. Je suis absolument certain.*"

Walt stared at the clerk blankly. He knew French no better than Arabic, but gradually he grasped the man's meaning. The agency he searched for was in Casablanca, and that was a three-hour ride away. "Damn," he muttered. "Damn, damn."

He couldn't get there that day, maybe not even that week. All he could do was return to his unit. He felt dazed, unsteady. The news couldn't be good. Good news didn't require the help of the Red Cross, did it?

***

"You okay, Walt?"

Relieved to find Gus at his desk, Walt told him what he had learned. If anyone could solve his dilemma, Gus could. He had answers to everything. The men all joked that the Army must have issued him a secret handbook, unavailable to the average soldier.

"The Frog at the hotel was right," Gus said. "I tried to stop you. The place you needed to go is in Casablanca. Maybe that's why the company commander wants to see you."

"Major Penland? Wants to see me? When did he ask for me?"

"About a half hour ago. I'll let him know you're back."

Walt was certain now. Something was wrong. A high-ranking officer didn't involve himself in personal matters unless there was trouble. He ran to Penland's office but stopped when he heard loud conversation inside. He opened the door a crack. Every officer in his company stood around the major's desk, laughing and joking, while Walt's heart was ready to explode.

He fumed. These men were officers only because they'd been medical doctors back home. Only Lieutenant Hunter routinely treated him as an equal. Back home, in the civilian world, he and Hunter would probably be friends. They shared the same wry humor and desire to excel. Neither of them was cut out for the military, although Hunter tried harder.

The rest of the doctors were a mixed bag. For every one who treated him well, another chided him like a child for violating some Army protocol.

The sight of so much glib authority—so much unearned power—reminded Walt of every teacher, priest, cop and officer who'd bossed him around. The harder the officers laughed, the tighter Walt's jaw clenched.

He knocked hard.

"Come in!" the commander shouted over the din.

The room turned silent. Every officer turned to stare. "You wanted to see me, sir?"

"I certainly did, Private Baran," the major said, his tone level. "I wanted you to know I reached the Red Cross in Casablanca by phone."

"You—you—what?" Walt watched Penland play with a sheet of paper on his desk. "Come on, Major. Tell me." The edge in his voice violated every rule he knew about addressing an officer.

The major shook his hand. "Congratulations, Baran. You're the father of a baby boy. Mother and baby are doing fine."

Walt's scowl melted into a small, shocked smile. He gripped the major's desk to steady himself. His baby was fine. Nora was fine. He was a father! His fears disappeared, and with them the tension and frustrations that had plagued him for weeks. Joy took their place. He imagined his wife cuddling their child. He could see them clearly—his beautiful wife, his handsome son.

Like old Army buddies, the officers walked up one by one to shake Walt's hand.

"Best wishes, soldier," said Captain Bradley with one firm shake of the hand. Polite to a fault, he stepped aside to let the other officers have their turn.

"Good news, huh, Private?" Captain Abich held out a hand, his smile unfamiliar to his face.

Last in line was Jack Hunter. He tilted back his head and smiled warmly at Walt's perspiring face. "Relax, Baran, before you explode."

***

He had to tell Tom and Hatch. More than anyone else, they knew how he had worried. Squinting at the setting sun, he jogged a mile west in the direction of his friends' infantry company. He found them sitting under a cork tree outside their temporary barracks, passing a bottle of warm beer between them.

"There better be some of that left for me," he said, squatting beside them.

Tom toasted to Walt. "Hello, friend! What are you grinnin' at?"

"Are you ready for this?" Walt tried to make his face look serious, but a smile escaped as he blurted his news. "You're looking at a proud papa! I've got a son!"

The three of them hooted and hollered and slapped each other's backs. "Have a swig," Tom said, passing him the beer bottle. "So, how much does the little champ weigh?"

The question, as innocent and ordinary as any new father might hear, startled him. It reminded him he knew little about his child or the delivery. He could only shrug and tell his friends what had happened that day, about his search for the telegram and how he heard the news, how he couldn't figure out why his father hadn't sent the telegram sooner. As he recounted each officer's handshake, a broad grin reclaimed his face. No bad thoughts tonight. This day marked the beginning of something new and good.

"Nora will send me all the details, but I'm sure everything went great. My father would've let me know if it hadn't." He kept smiling. He couldn't help it. "I'm telling you guys, getting that news was the happiest moment of my life. It cured all my misery."

"You don't have to tell us," Hatch said. "It's written all over your f-face."

"You got that right," Tom chimed in. "Nice to see you lookin' cheerful for a change."

"Here's to you!" Hatch shouted. "Let's p-pretend this swill is champagne, huh?"

They emptied the bottle in three deep gulps and sprawled out on the sandy ground. Walt pulled three cigarettes from his front pocket, held them in his mouth and lit them on a single match. "No cigars, guys. Old Golds will have to do."

Their cigarette tips flickered yellow in the twilight. A comfortable quiet settled over them. "You know what I wish?" Walt said, breaking the silence. "That we could stay in Morocco for the rest of the war. My work here has been easier than I ever imagined."

"Now I know you're on cloud nine," Tom said. "Come back to earth, Walt. We're moving out soon. Didn't you hear?"

Walt lifted himself up on one elbow. "I did, but I keep hoping it doesn't mean we're going far. The Brits are cleaning up Africa. Rommel should collapse any day now."

"Not according to our Sarge," Tom said. "He says the Brits still need help."

Walt ground his cigarette into the sand, refusing to surrender his dreams. He shook his friends' hands and scrambled to his feet. "See you guys later. And check the newspapers. I'm telling you. The news is good."

Back in his pup tent, he smoothed out a sheet of paper to write Nora. Even though their son might be two months old by the time she got it, he wrote as if the birth had just happened. Because for him, it had.

Jan. 10, 1943

Dearest Nora,

At last, I know you and baby are fine. A telegram came yesterday through the Red Cross. The next letters I get surely will tell me all about the delivery, how you fared, what the baby weighed, how he's doing, why it took so long to contact me. If you need anything or ever have any difficulties, let me know and I'll move heaven and earth to help you. I promise you I can and will, even from here. God will look after my two angels. I asked Him to, and He said He would...

TWENTY-SIX

I balanced my pad of paper on my lap as I wrote Walt, rocking the bassinette with my left hand to keep Alek from crying. The first time I held him I believed I was born for mothering. Now, nothing I did seemed right. I refused to share that truth with Walt. It wouldn't be fair to him.

Reading my mind, Alek began to squirm and howl. Mother ran into the room at the first sound. "Let me, daughter." She plucked Alek from his bassinette and walked him in slow, tight circles.

I sank back on the bed. Alek cried so much. Even in sleep he snuffled and whined. I never gave up trying to comfort him, even when he arched his back and whirled his arms and legs. The child-care books Milly and I found in the library haunted me, especially the one that described fussy babies who might need drugs. Their description of those babies— "hypertonic"—made them sound as if they had a disease. Not my Alek, I told myself. No drugs for him. I'd be fussy, too, if I'd just spent three weeks in that wretched hospital.

When she was close at hand like this, my mother was a Godsend. But most days she worked long hours at the mattress factory, and at night, now that Steve was in the Army Air Force, she slept in his bedroom on the third floor. Most of the time, I was alone with Alek.

"Gosia," my mother whispered. She shifted her weight from one hip to the other, a relieved smile on her face. Alek rested a cheek on her neck in glorious, silent sleep. Without the help of my stubborn, bossy mother, this motherhood business would do me in. I watched her place Alek in his bassinette as if he was paper-thin crystal. I inhaled the delicate silence, taking care not to disturb it.

January 25, 1943

Dear Walt,

Your son sleeps sweetly beside me as I write this. I rub his back when I first put him in his bassinette and he seems to like it. The weather is bleak and cold here. Even though he and I don't go outside much, I dress him in long pants, a sweater and booties to make sure he's warm enough inside. Don't worry, darling, your son is receiving the best of care...

***

The first letter Walt sent after he learned he had a son made me cry. He wanted something I couldn't give, which was every detail of our son's birth. I pretended I never saw his request. I focused my letters on Alek's small strides with elaborate and exaggerated descriptions. Even after six weeks, I still censored my letters diligently.

Max's influence over his family and friends equaled that of an Army officer. He told them exactly what to write Walt about Alek. Those who had seen Alek never mentioned his frail health. Those who hadn't seen him yet became positively inventive. They created an infant who was big, strong and robust—all of which Alek surely was not.

Feb. 13, 1943

Dear Walt,

Every one of my letters seem to repeat the ones before. My life is consumed with baby bottles, diapers, feeding times and, of course, Alek. Yes, all the letters you've received from our friends and relatives are right. He is the most darling boy, and so alert, too. On mild days, when I take him for long walks, his big eyes sparkle whenever someone passes by. What a smart lad he is for two months old...

The weeks it took for Walt's and my letters to reach each other threw me off balance. Sometimes I could scarcely remember what I had written earlier, or how I'd had felt at the time. Walt, on the other hand, noted everything. "I'm glad you and Dad are getting along so well now," he wrote in a letter that arrived in mid-February. "He isn't as tough as he appears. He told me about his visit over the holidays and how well you looked. He says you're doing fine and not to worry, and that he would take care of anything that came up."

My poor husband clearly needed to believe in his father. He didn't even complain about waiting so long for the telegram about Alek. I scoffed at Walt's faith that Max would "take care of anything." If that was the old man's promise, I thought, I would hold him to it.

***

Alek's doctor visits became one more secret I kept from Walt. Besides regular checkups to check his weight and development, my son needed his lungs and health checked every time he felt a little warm or had the sniffles.

"You fret about Alek too much, Nor," my cousin said as she bounced her daughter on her knee. She watched with eyebrows raised as I dressed Alek for a walk in his stroller. "You don't need to wrap him up like a mummy!"

Milly laughed in her joking way, but I knew she was saying aloud what many of my relatives thought. They glanced at each other knowingly whenever I piled extra blankets on him or scrubbed clean everything in his reach. Couldn't they see how delicate he was?

At least my cousin was bold enough to be so honest. Four years older than I, she never shied from speaking her mind. When Anna Lee was born just days after Alek, Milly didn't meekly obey nurses' orders to be quiet, as I had. Everyone in the hospital could hear her yell, "Give me something for this pain! Now!"

I nudged my son's thin blond hair into a single curl. At three months, he'd gained just one inch and 25 ounces. He moved his spindly arms and legs cautiously, as if he didn't trust his body. The slightest noise made him shake. Too often, he wore the sad, pensive expression of an old man. I remembered Eleanor's advice: My sensitive son needed all the attention I could give him. But some days I hardly had time for cuddling. His daily routine imprisoned me: change the baby, feed the baby, clean the baby, wash his diapers, his clothes, his bottles.

Milly suggested we take our babies on a long walk that morning. "Hurry up, Nora," she said as Anna Lee cooed contentedly in her arms. "It's a gorgeous day. A light jacket is all Alek needs. Let's go."

Ignoring her pleas, I bundled my son in woolen pants and a long-sleeved shirt, thick sweater, knit hat and knee-high booties. Then I wrapped him in a blanket and picked him up. Even in all those layers he felt light as down.

"There, baby. Isn't that comfy?"

Alek stared back, his searchlight eyes sweeping my face.

"Okay, okay, sweet thing." I jostled him gently on one hip. Every day I learned new tricks to keep him close to happy.

TWENTY-SEVEN

Feb. 13, 1943

Dear Nora,

After a few days of being unable to write, I finally got a chance to dash off a letter. Let me see, where to begin? Gosh, honey, you may wonder what is happening now but censorship prevents me from telling. Every time I write you, I wonder if a censor will cut out my words. Right now, I wonder how this poor letter will sound to you. I have my troubles. After the war, dear, I'll tell you all.

It's been a relief to get your letters, even if it takes them weeks to cross the ocean. Before I got my folk's telegram last month, I was going crazy not hearing from anyone, even you. Now I get a batch of letters a few times a week. I wish I had time to answer every one of them. I'll write more later.

Forever yours, Walt

P.S. Remember our agreement about Harry, etc. I know you'll do the right thing.

Walt checked the first letter of each sentence in the first paragraph. A-L-G-E-R-I-A. The coded message was as clear as he could make it. Putting "Harry" in his postscript would tell Nora to look for it.

If he could, he would tell her how closely his medical company followed behind the fighting men of the Ninth, how they'd rushed eastward in World War I box cars, stopping just long enough for cooks to hand out cans of cold beans, stew and hash. Morocco was far behind them. Rumor had it the infantry wouldn't stop until Tunisia, halfway across North Africa.

Close to the infantry was exactly where Walt wanted to be. If he couldn't carry a gun, at least he could do everything possible to keep Tom and Hatch and all the guys in G Company alive and well.

His company traveled four hundred miles in three days to reach the city of Tlemcen. Miserable with hunger and cold, Walt welcomed the converted stable and pot-bellied stove that served as their temporary quarters. He didn't know why they'd stopped and didn't care.

Walt joined Ted and Big Al at a bar in town that served Spanish sausage omelets and red wine. His first three glasses quenched his thirst; the fourth delivered a mild glow. When he started drinking in high school, he wanted what every guy did—to prove he could drink like a man, hard and fast. He'd surely accomplished that. None of his friends could match him. No matter how much booze he downed, he never looked drunk or felt it much.

On nights he drank heavily, he sometimes lost pieces of what happened—little gaps in memory some called a blackout. If only those gaps could erase the one thing he longed to forget: the night his older brother died. It took more and more booze to numb the agony of that memory now. Tlemcen's red wine was strong, but it produced only a faint effect. He switched to brandy.

By the time Walt was about to order his sixth drink, Ted was picking up a dark-eyed Spanish girl at the bar and Big Al was picking a fight with two burly French Legionnaires. Ted would be fine as long as no jealous boyfriend loomed nearby. Al was another story. Walt quickly paid his tab and rushed to his side. "Let's go," he said, grabbing the big man's arm and leading him out the door. Al lurched and growled like a wounded grizzly bear. "Why ja make me leave?" he said. "I was jus' fine."

"You're not fine at all, buddy. Take my word for it," Walt said. "I was saving your life."

Walt fell asleep easily that night, grateful for the slight buzz in his head. Before he knew it, he dreamed he was dancing with Nora in a loud, crowded bar. She felt soft and light in her arms as they whirled effortlessly around the floor, his right hand pressed against the small of her back, his left hand caressing her face. Then someone tapped his shoulder to cut in. He snarled and swung an arm to punch the guy. "No you don't, buddy."

He heard an angry yell. Nora slipped from his arms.

"What's your problem, Baran?" Gus shouted. "I'm just trying to get you to roll call."

Walt moaned and pulled his blanket over his head. For a minute, he didn't move. He tried to capture his dream and save it as something real, a precious moment, but when he finally stood, the memory already had slipped from his grasp.

***

Six days later, the clearing company was back in the chase again, this time traveling in trucks. For two weeks the heavy vehicles pushed their way east through northern Algeria. They pitched and rolled in pouring rain that turned the earth to glue. They pursued the Ninth Infantry fighting regiments, which followed the Germans, who seemed to be in retreat. For days, the medics didn't stop anywhere long enough to perform surgery or dispense medical care. All Walt did was set up tents, tear them down and set them up again, day after day after day. Any idiot could do this, he thought.

Then, early one morning before the medics could break camp, an ambulance delivered two wounded men. Two nights later, a few more casualties trickled in. The clearing company began to stay longer at each stop as the number of wounded increased. Walt grew used to the new rhythm.

I know what war is now, he thought. I see its face in every new patient.

Without warning, the infantry sped up again. It moved so rapidly this time that the clearing company couldn't keep up. The front was still a hundred miles away, the staff sergeant said. Walt didn't know whether to be frustrated or skeptical. "If we're so far away from the front, what are those guys doing here?" he asked, pointing to Allied warplanes soaring above.

The planes took off and landed from nearby makeshift airfields day and night, heading for distant battlefields. Their incessant noise rubbed Walt's thoughts raw. He crashed into loneliness like a freefalling paratrooper. Sadness clung to him, even when he wrote Nora.

> Feb. 25, 1943
>
> Dear Nora,
>
> We are a long way from where I last wrote you. There is much I would like to tell you, but it's impossible. Darn this war. It leaves me groping for words. I guess I can say that my days of comparative luxury and peace are temporarily over with. I'm in good shape physically, but you know my appetite. I could use an extra meal most days. By now I hope you received my letter asking for a photo of Junior. Please send a photo as soon as you can. I'm desperate for it...

He tried to remember when he'd first asked for the photo. Time listed off kilter. The tortuous, slow-motion travels of their letters sabotaged every attempt at real communication.

Ink drops fell on the paper with each frustrated stroke of his fountain pen. Censors wouldn't let him say where he was, where he was going next, how many wounded he treated, how many died. Even the tiniest hints might cause his letter to be shredded. So, he wrote trivial things about trivial matters, even on days the sound of the fighter planes made his hands shake.

By the time his letter reached Nora, they would be married two years. Alek would be three months old. Despite her many descriptions, he couldn't imagine what his boy looked like. A photograph would give him something real to cling to.

***

As Company D kept barreling east, Walt marveled at Magnus's unholy enthusiasm for slippery roads and driving rain. "Whoo-eee!" the driver shouted whenever the convoy plowed through fields of foot-deep mud. "All off!" he shouted when they stopped for the night, clearly enjoying the opportunity to utter something resembling an order. Magnus's excitement penetrated a gloom that hung over the company. In the wet, slimy grime of their days, humor found little toehold in Company D.

Walt now shared a tent with Ted, who made it a contest to set up in ten minutes or less when they stopped. Sitting inside their tent in the roaring rain, cupping cigarettes in their hands, they debated their location. "Somewhere, Ted, generals are sitting around a bunch of maps plotting our future. Meanwhile, we aren't even sure what country we're in."

The downpour thundered on the canvas so hard that Walt didn't hear the three ambulances pull up. Ted jumped to his feet. "Let's go!"

Inside the floorless surgery tent every examining table was taken. Walt flinched at the horrific injuries, the deep gashes and dangling limbs. "They stepped on unexploded grenades and minefields," Gus shouted above the relentless storm outside. "The Germans left behind a sea of them." Walt worked nonstop sewing flaps of flesh, setting bones, stanching blood. As the night wore on, the mayhem became something normal.

At daybreak, after two hours of fitful sleep, the men again broke down their tents. They drove like hell to the next stop, passing battered tanks, overturned trucks, graves of British soldiers, and evidence of mines and booby traps. For days, at each stop, Walt faced more wounded, more blood, more broken bones, more torn flesh, and always the rain—a steady, bossy flood of water.

On the night of March 27, his platoon reached Gafsa, in Tunisia, almost 1,200 miles east of where they'd started in Morocco. The city had been wrecked by bombings.

Patients flooded the surgery with different wounds now—flesh punctured by bullets and artillery fire. Walt exchanged a knowing glance with Ted. These men came directly from the battlefield. This was the moment Walt had prepared for ever since he signed up for the medics. Finally, he could help his infantry pals wounded in battle.

A blur of red swept through surgery. Walt cut blood-soaked cotton twill away from wounds and tossed the shreds into a trench he'd dug outside. The trench served one purpose—as burial ground for olive-green fragments that turned black from the dried blood and grit trapped in their weave.

He cleaned patients' wounds, injected morphine and administered blood plasma. He handed compresses and bandages to doctors with sterile forceps. At first, he studied the face of each new patient, checking for features he might recognize—a familiar nose or chin or forehead. One soldier, bleeding heavily from a shot to the chest, reminded him of a guy named Sal Mancuso from the Bronx, a fast-talking jokester from Walt's old infantry company as ill-suited to Army life as Walt was. But when he looked closely, he saw the man's ears were too small, his teeth too even.

Soon, the anguished, grimy faces of the patients all began to look alike. To his exhausted eyes, the same battered soldier was being placed on the operating table over and over. Walt tried to focus on the wounds before him, but soon they, too, became indistinguishable from each other.

Even still, he felt a deep satisfaction.

"God, I'm glad I work in surgery," he confided to Jack Hunter as handed the doctor a scalpel. Their clothing was splattered with blood. They'd had no time to change between patients.

Hunter glanced over to see if he was joking.

"Really, I am," Walt said.

"We're not even supposed to be doing this kind of surgery," said Hunter, who abandoned his practice as an internist when he was drafted. "You're probably better trained for it than I am."

Walt studied the exposed muscle and sinew in the gaping shoulder wound before them. "I doubt that," he murmured. He knew how to patch up torn skin, but Hunter could repair an injured man's insides. Even so, Walt was grateful for the compliment. Other doctors also seemed to rely on his training and skill, but they rarely complimented him.

In theory, Hunter was correct about the clearing company's mission. Its main focus was supposed to be minor wounds and illnesses. Those patients were to be hastily patched up and held temporarily in recovery. Walt winced at the reality of that care. The Army didn't just want those men healthy again. It wanted them returned to battle as quickly as possible.

Patients with serious wounds, however, were supposed to be moved quickly to Army hospitals with full-fledged surgeons. In practice, the clearing company's doctors often had little choice but to operate on major wounds. Such was the case that night. Few of the patients Walt tended could survive a transfer. Their injuries were too serious. Better equipped hospitals were too many miles away.

At the end of each shift, Walt made it a practice to check on patients in recovery. That night, as usual, he heard the men still conscious trade rumors. "I hear the Sixtieth Regiment is at the heart of the American offensive," a private said. "Near Gafsa. Not far away."

"What about the Sixtieth?" Walt said. He knew the Ninth's three regiments had been separated, with each being sent where it was needed most. "I'm looking for word about my buddies in the Sixtieth, Tom Lucas and Frank Hatcher," he said. "They're in G Company."

"Sorry, pal. No idea. We're in the Thirty-Ninth."

Walt held the man's wrist to take his pulse but lost track of the count. He bent close to the patient's ear and said in a slow, even voice: "Tom and Hatch. That's what everyone calls them. If you see them, tell them Walt was asking for them."

***

March 27, 1943

Dear Nora,

Every letter from folks back home tells me how cute my son is. I'm more anxious than ever to get a picture of you both. I've asked for one many times, dear. Just go to your backyard and have your Mom hold the camera. Let her snap away, and then send me a shot. That's all you have to do. I'm a determined fellow and will write others to take pictures if I must. I know you understand...

His lack of control over almost all his life bothered him most. He couldn't work fast enough to handle all the wounded flooding surgery. He couldn't sleep through the night, no matter how exhausted he was. He couldn't convince his wife of his simple need to see photos of their baby.

He finished his letter and tucked it in an envelope. Beside him, his tentmate lay sprawled on his back, his eyes closed. "What a day, huh, Ted? I need some shut-eye badly."

Ted, who usually chattered late into the night, just grunted agreement.

Walt rubbed his temples. The nearer his company came to the front lines, the edgier he became, the edgier every man in the company became. The number of dead and wounded was reaching frightening levels. He capped his pen and lay back, replaying memories of home to calm himself.

When he awoke the next morning, all he remembered were traces of a dark dream, of running, panting, and sticking his hand in a wound as deep as a bucket.

TWENTY-EIGHT

I waved Walt's letter at my mother. "He wants photographs, Mom. He says he's desperate. What do I do?"

"No picture. Is not good."

"But listen to this." I read aloud his postscript: "Don't forget. I need photographs of my big strong boy. Send me some right away. I can't wait another day."

"This is the third time he's asked. I have to do something."

Mother put her hands on her hips. "How you make Alek big boy?"

Her question kept me up that night. By morning, I had a plan. I made an appointment at Simmons Photography Studio on East Jersey Street. Ignoring the dirty laundry and diapers stacked high in the corner of the bathroom, I washed my hair and set it in curlers. When it had dried, I dressed my son in a long-sleeved cotton shirt, thick knit sweater, cable-stitched wool jacket one size too big and matching cap. By three o'clock I was almost ready. I pulled on a snug sweater, combed out my curls and ran my reddest lipstick over my lips. Alek's cheeks flushed as he sat in his many layers, his cap tied under his chin. "I'm sorry, sweetie," I said. "I know it's not that cold outside. But look at you! Aren't you the biggest, handsomest boy!"

***

Max studied the proofs. I held my breath, hoping that showing him the photos would help me stay on his good side. I had yet to figure out a way to change his mind about Alek's extra bills, which I learned were still due.

My father-in-law showed no expression until he spotted the picture I hated most. The photographer had played with the images in the darkroom to disguise the swelling under Alek's eyes. His chubby cheeks made him look almost plump, but his eyes stared blankly at some distant point.

"This one." Max jabbed a stubby forefinger at the photo. "Send him this one. You're a looker in it. That's what your husband wants to see."

"But little Alek's expression, it's so..."

"Smart. Dixie looks really smart, like he's thinking hard. That's what we tell Walt."

***

I lugged a pail of dirty diapers into the kitchen, where my father slumped at the table. He rested his balding head on his folded arms, as he had every morning since he'd slipped on an icy patch the month before.

"Morning, Pop," I mumbled, not expecting a reply. Even before he hurt his back, he rarely spoke in the morning.

I already had rinsed the diapers in the toilet bowl and then in a bucket of clear water. The next steps would take all morning. I scrubbed them in hot tap water and soap flakes; rinsed them twice; put them in a tub of fresh water, and boiled them for five minutes. After they cooled, I'd wring the diapers to get them dry as possible and hang them on a line. My ritual wasn't over until I scrubbed clean every surface of the sink and tubs.

Just before noon, I checked on Alek, fed him a bottle and pinned the last clean diaper on him. A steady rain prevented me from hanging the clean diapers from a second-story clothesline, so I carried them to the third-floor storage room where I strung a web of lines.

Before the clean diapers were dry, Alek soiled his again. I set up the ironing board in the kitchen, turned the iron on high and fetched two damp diapers. Pressing the thick cloths dry was my last resort in my war to keep my baby clean and comfortable.

The moist diapers hissed as I pushed the iron back and forth.

"Aie! Why you make such noise?" My father looked up. His eyes were watery.

His cry startled me. He hadn't made a sound the whole time I'd been working in the small kitchen. "I'm sorry, Dad. I have to get these dry." I turned the diapers over.

He glared at me through thick eyeglasses. "I need quiet, girl!"

"I'm doing the best I can."

"*Jezu Chryste*, Gosia! You only make noise. You only make mess." He gestured toward the ironing board and the dirty baby bottles on the counter, his irritation growing.

His crankiness was nothing new. Right after his accident, I forgave his outbursts, knowing he was in pain and hated being trapped in the apartment. But now I was losing patience. Couldn't he see my dilemma?

"What would you have me do, huh, Pop? Leave the baby in dirty diapers?"

He jerked his head. "You insult me, girl?"

Frowning, I pushed the iron hard against the diapers. An uneasy silence smothered the room until a clammy gust rattled a window and seeped inside. With a loud sigh, he heaved himself up and limped to the windowsill. He pounded it shut before facing me, his lips barely moving as he spoke. "Never talk to me so. *Nigdy!*"

I looked away, avoiding his glare. "Dad, you have to understand. It's hard work caring for Alek. I can barely do it all now that Mom works longer hours." I took a deep breath. "Maybe you could help a little?"

A long, low growl steamed from his lips. "What you say?" My soft-spoken, bookish father was shaking now. He limped back to the table and slammed his open palm on it. "*Nigdy!*"

"I—"

"Nie! Sluchaj!"

I *was* listening. What choice did I have? But his next words were a tangle of Polish and English, of judgment, anger and pain. I tilted the iron on its side and peeled the stiff diapers from the board.

"My baby is crying. I have to go to him." My father's hoarse words collided with Alek's wails. Pressing the diaper to my damp eyes, I rushed to my bedroom and scooped Alek from his crib. If only Walt were here. He would help. He would understand.

***

Five days later, I sat on the front stoop of my parents' house, bouncing Alek on my knee. A crowded bus belched diesel fumes as it rolled by. Few cars traveled the road these days, but they made their presence known with blaring horns. The crowds of pedestrians hurrying past me clutched ration books. How quickly we all learned to use those. The war consumed everything. Even people with money needed ration stamps to buy their share of eggs, butter, gas and other vital things.

The hectic scene around me little resembled the grim silence in my parents' apartment. My mother was getting ready for her hated Saturday shift. My father, who'd barely spoken a word to me since our argument, spoke only when necessary. "What time we eat, Gosia?" "Get me plate, Gosia."

I checked the luggage at my feet one more time: an oversized blue bag filled with Alek's diapers and clothes, a large canvas sack packed with formula and bottles, and my own small case of toiletries and clothing.

My cousin had talked me into this overnight trip to our grandmother's. "Babcia wants to see our babies. We can't deny her, can we?" she argued. I was nervous about being away from Alek's doctors even for a day, but his breathing seemed clearer lately and he fussed less. Milly convinced me our grandmother's farm would be strong medicine for all of us.

Alek needed strong medicine the most, I thought, but the real kind that doctors prescribe. He needed modern cures for his rasping coughs and frequent infections. Babcia was known as a healer, but she worked with herbs and mysterious methods she'd brought with her from Poland. I hugged Alek close and kissed his cheeks, unconvinced Old World medicine was the answer.

A dusty sedan pulled up to the curb, horn blasting. Milly jumped out. "Hey, kiddo! You ready?" She helped me load up her Pontiac. We nestled Alek next to Anna Lee in a cocoon of pillows and blankets in the back seat.

My cousin loved to drive. I wouldn't dream of doing something so foolhardy—not when trains and buses took me almost every place I needed to go—yet I had to admit her big boat of a car made our trip possible. Babies needed so many things. Even a short train ride would be daunting. But we could ride in comfort in my cousin's sedan, a second-hand purchase Milly's family made just before Stan was drafted into the Navy.

My cousin took her husband's departure in stride, the way she dealt with everything in her life. "This war will be over soon. I'm sure of it," she said the day after he left. "Besides, what harm can come to him in a big ship?"

I didn't answer. I admired her pluck, but I could imagine the worst kind of harm. A torpedo. An airstrike.

"Isn't this great?" Milly said as she put the car in gear. "I finally can use this car—*and* my gas rations." From the moment she turned west on Highway 28, she treated the busy road with the same determination she aimed at all life's impediments. I gripped my seat every time she leaned on her horn, passed a long line of trucks or drove inches behind another car. In the back seat, Alek and Anna Lee slept soundly, the rumble of the engine an unexpected sedative.

When I gasped at the speeds we were traveling or the cars we were passing, Milly shouted, "We'll get there in no time, Nor."

I tried to slow my cousin's attack on the highway by talking about our grandmother. Nothing altered Milly's resolve, not even mention of Babcia's crystal ball. "She takes it with her every time she reads people's palms," I said. "What do you make of that?"

Milly shrugged as she barreled past a balky pickup truck. "Babcia is pretty clever. Her customers pay good money to watch her stare into the thing. Why not use it?"

My mother told me that Babcia helped doctors heal patients whom modern medicine failed. I wondered how much money she made doing that. As a child, I watched her mix potions like a pharmacist. She would ladle herbs into her claw-footed bathtub and add water to fill it with her own brown, gooey version of medicine. Her patients soaked for hours in the tub. Many healed quickly. Like magic.

The crystal ball and palm readings were another matter. That seemed like voodoo, even if the ball's mysterious beauty attracted me. "I wonder where she got it," I said. "Did you ever take a really good look at it, Milly? Light seems to sink into its center and disappear."

She stared at me, wide-eyed. "Listen to you. I think you want Babcia to use it for us, don't—" she stopped mid-sentence and smiled mischievously. "Let's do it. Let's have Babcia tell our fortunes." She slapped the horn, and for the rest of the trip—while I held my breath—Milly imagined stories our grandmother might tell us about their futures.

TWENTY-NINE

March 30, 1943

Dear Nora,

Forgive me for not writing for the past few days. This is the busiest we've been, and that's saying a lot. As usual, I can't tell you much about it, but don't worry. Remember, we medics take care of patients. We don't go around looking for trouble. A lot of interesting cases come through our company, so I continue to put to good use everything I learned in Missouri. I admire our soldiers a lot. They're tough young men...

Rommel's tanks growled on the horizon at El Guettar. They were too far away to see, yet close enough for Walt to feel their engines thunder through Tunisia's hard-packed soil. The tanks' constant thrum joined the banshee wail of German dive-bombers. The first time Walt heard the Stukas' scream he pictured demons assembling in the heavens.

This was nothing like Port Lyautey, where most of the shooting stopped before medics came ashore. Here, the clamor of battle seemed in easy reach.

Ever since the clearing company left Morocco, Major Penland had assured his men they would be safe. No matter how violent the fighting, he said, the company would be miles from the front. The large red crosses painted on a white background on each tent alerted the enemy to leave us be.

Walt wanted to believe him, even when the front felt closer than ever.

Badly wounded soldiers from the Ninth Infantry's forty-seventh and thirty-ninth regiments arrived in numbers too great to count. Bitter-cold nights didn't stem the flow. Walt set up IV lines, blotted blood, handed doctors scalpels and made sure supplies kept up with the need. Some of the worst cases had no bloodshed. Patients arrived shaking and crying with what the Army called a "case of nerves." Silently, Walt cursed his powerlessness to be of any use to his friends from G Company. Their regiment, the Sixtieth, was now attached to another unit fighting farther north.

One patient, a hollow-eyed young lieutenant with a shredded arm, described what happened when the wedge-shaped Allied front pushed eastward. "It was horrible," he said. "So many of our men dead. German Panzers blew up our half-tracks. Stukas dove down and unloaded on us."

"I heard the Sixtieth had it even worse," a wounded sergeant chimed in.

Walt turned to the sergeant, his voice demanding, "The Sixtieth? How bad?"

The sergeant shrugged. "They were at Maknassy. Fought like devils, I hear. Lots of guys killed straight out or hurt so bad they died before they could be loaded into an ambulance. Don't know much more than that."

Walt asked the question he'd repeated with each new wave of wounded, shouting loud enough for every patient to hear: "Anyone here know Tom Lucas or Frank Hatcher in the Sixtieth? Tom and Hatch? Anyone?"

No one answered.

***

Walt noticed a smear of carnelian red on the young soldier's lips. He had seen the color before—the dark, deep red caked on some of the corpses at his father's funeral home, more brown than bright. As a boy—he was only fifteen when he started working there—he wiped those bodies with damp rags to remove all trace of the bloody cataclysms that had brought them there. He never felt squeamish about it. He understood the difference between the living and the dead. The bodies at the funeral home were only the shells of men and women, though at times Walt imagined their spirits lingering nearby, obliging him to be careful. The dead deserved a special kindness.

Dried blood caked every crevice of the young soldier's torn uniform. It splattered his face and left his straw-blond hair hard and dark. Walt didn't rush to treat him, as he had been trained to do back at O'Reilly General Hospital. He didn't have to; the boy's face, which looked barely older than seventeen, was another color familiar to Walt—a pale gray. His skin was cold.

"Baran! Get moving!"

He jumped at Captain Chauncey Bradley's order. Not once since they'd landed in Africa had Walt heard the mild-mannered doctor give anything like a sharp command. The war exacted payment from everyone.

"Orderly!" Walt yelled, pointing at the gray-skinned boy. "Tag this patient and move him to the morgue."

He moved to the next patient, already marked as deceased. Walt had no reason to doubt it. A fine mist of sand covered the boy so completely he looked like a stone carving. Northern Africa's soil little resembled the black loamy richness of northern New Jersey. With every bomb, sand pelted soldiers like tiny BB pellets. Walt brushed silt off the soldier's face. It didn't seem right to remove the body without that small dignity. But as his fingers danced on the boy's right cheekbone, Walt felt something unexpected—a trace of warmth. He checked his pulse.

"Doc!" Walt said evenly, taking care not to startle the patient. He bent close to his ear and whispered, "It's okay. You'll be all right."

He tugged at the boy's uniform, searching for wounds. Finding none, he grabbed a small box from the floor and propped up the soldier's legs. As he covered the soldier with a wool blanket, Jack Hunter hurried to his side. "He's in shock," Walt said. He knew that instinctively. He knew how to save lives as well as how to bury them.

***

When the number of patients finally ebbed just before dawn, Walt stumbled outside. Overwhelmed with weariness, he sat on a crate just outside surgery. Confusion and fatigue warped his senses. Sleep beckoned him. Was that his mother's cooking he smelled? What is that grinding noise? I need quiet, he thought, as he slipped off his perch.

Hard ground jolted him awake as a single-engine Stuka plunged earthward. Its dreadful noise seemed to howl, *I'm coming for you, I'm coming for you.* American anti-aircraft guns chattered back.

Suddenly, the wailing stopped. Walt felt a split second of relief before he heard the high-pitched whistle of the Stuka's falling payload. He skittered across the ground, searching for shelter. Time shifted to slow motion. In no rush, the Stuka's bomb whirled, whistled, twisted until it struck ground a hundred yards away. Its fury spewed a heavy shower of debris. Dirt and tree limbs and metal and gravel rained down.

He covered his ears as bigger bombs fell from bigger planes. He wanted to shut his eyes, but he wanted to see it all, too. Explosions at the edges of their encampment looked like a dozen suns bursting. A pungent odor hung in the air, the smell of unknown substances smoldering. He looked around for other medics but saw none. He felt alone on a battlefield, unprotected, with every bomb aimed straight at him. When the barrage finally stopped, a thick haze lingered. He shook his head to stop incessant ringing in his ears.

He was alive. The company's tents still stood. Slowly, medics, techs and patients emerged from nearby foxholes.

Ted rushed to his side. "Hey, Walt. You okay?" His muffled words sounded as if he was speaking behind a heavy mask.

"No thanks to you guys," Walt said. "Why didn't anyone wake me? You had to run right by me to get to that foxhole." A high-pitched droning in his ears made it hard to hear his own voice.

"Jeez, Baran," Big Al said. "You was like a dead man. Like you didn't even hear the commotion."

Ted put a hand on Walt's shoulder. "Sorry, pal. We weren't thinking much, to be honest. Never seen anything like that. Or heard anything like it."

Walt forced a thin, tight smile. "Hope I didn't trip any of you on your way."

His friends laughed with relief while Walt shuddered at his luck. Just one piece of the twisted shrapnel littering the ground around him could have sliced him in two or ripped open his scalp. From the looks of things, the rest of his company was just as lucky.

As the smoke cleared, the men joked like they were brave. They called Walt "The Sleeper." It wasn't until an hour later, as the men cleared out the debris, that they found one of the cooks face down in a pool of blood outside the mess tent. A small piece of shrapnel had sliced his neck, severing his carotid artery. The men called him "Cook," but Walt had chatted with him one night and knew his name was Edgar. He was in his late forties and unmarried. He grew up in Connecticut.

A stranger might think the man's death didn't matter, because almost everyone quickly returned to their duties or crawled into their tents to try to catch a little sleep. Walt knew that wasn't true. The battlefield was like his ship's convoy on its way to Africa. Every death mattered, but the war didn't pause for any man.

***

Bombs continued to fall around the edges of their camp for three days, as dependable as an alarm clock. The rush to foxholes became less hectic. The medics knew what to do now. Steadying their nerves grew harder, though. Some men stopped eating; others grew so edgy even a cough startled them. The patients felt the stress, too. When they heard the bombs, they stared straight ahead, blank and unmoving, until someone led them to a foxhole. Walt stayed calm by yelling and cursing. If we are enduring this onslaught, he thought, the infantry must be living in hell.

The third night, two litter bearers delivered a semiconscious soldier bleeding heavily from a head wound. A temporary lull in bombing made every sound audible, including the man's soft groans.

Capt. Abich, the lone doctor on duty, assumed the proud posture that was his trademark. Chin up, the hint of a smile on his lips, he rubbed his hands together as he gazed at the open wound. Walt guessed it wasn't deep, that any skilled tech could patch it up, but the danger of blood loss, shock and infection made rapid treatment urgent.

"Let's get this done right, okay, gentlemen?" Abich said, sneering slightly at Ted to his left and Walt to his right.

Suddenly, as he touched the wound, a furious explosion ripped the tent's tranquility, startling everyone in it, even the groggy patient. Walt's reflexes told him to seek shelter, but his training ordered him to stay with his patient. Abich answered to no such higher command. The doctor hit the ground and rolled under the examining table, joined quickly by two litter bearers who had just delivered a patient with minor wounds. Walt and Ted gaped at each other.

"Grab the sheet at your end, Ted," Walt said. "I'll take this side." Together, they picked up their patient and carried him to shelter under another operating table. Walt rushed back to their station to retrieve sterile gauze, saline water, forceps and sutures.

Kneeling next to the man, Walt ran sterile water over the injury and looked for signs of a skull fracture. Finding none, he had Ted hold gauze on the wound while he prepared the needle and sutures.

"You ever do this before?" Ted asked.

"Plenty of times. In training. Stitched up a lot of dead bodies in the funeral home, too." His half-conscious patient stared at him in alarm. "Don't worry, pal," Walt said. "You won't fit that category. Might have a concussion though. We'll have to keep an eye on that."

Walt focused intensely on his task. He didn't notice the bombing stop or Abich slowly crawl out from his shelter. The doctor stood over him, brushing dirt from his surgical gown. "What the hell do you think you're doing, Baran" he yelled. "Who authorized you to perform surgery?"

Silently, Walt tied his last stitch with a flourish and wiped the skin clean. Ted placed a large sterile gauze pad over the wound and secured it with a roll of gauze.

"All done!" Walt said. He and Ted lifted the patient onto a litter. Only then did Walt turn toward Abich, hands on his hips. "You have something to say to me, Captain?"

The two men glared at each other. In the background, Ted moved parallel to the space between them, poised to jump in. No one spoke or made a move until Abich turned on one heel and stormed out.

"Unbelievable," Walt muttered, as he tended to the other patient Abich had abandoned. "He's angry at me because he's a coward."

That night, Walt avoided the coffee station, where other techs rehashed the day's triumphs and failures. Alcohol would do a better job. He looked for Magnus. The driver always had extra booze on hand. The man mystified Walt. Cheerful one minute and sullen the next, he seemed unperturbed by war. He scoffed at soldiers in danger who made the sign of the cross and avoided religious services in the field. As far as Walt could tell, liquor was Magnus's god.

THIRTY

Our grandmother huddled over a thick crop of beets in her side yard, clutching her apron, a *babushka* pulled tightly around her head. Fuchsia blossoms cascading from an ancient crab-apple tree clung to her scarf and shoulders.

A few steps away, Tadeusz, her husband, yanked weeds with fierce grunts. His decades-old garden was the reason our family called the land a "farm" even though it stretched only two hundred feet deep and eighty feet wide. For me, it might as well have been a farm; no "Victory Garden" in the city flourished so abundantly.

"Moje kochane!" she called out when Milly and I pulled up. At the sight of our babies, her first great-grandchildren, she released her apron. A dozen dusty red beets tumbled to the ground. *"Moje maluskie!* Give them. *Prosze!"*

"Babcia!" we cried, using the Polish word for grandmother. We placed our babies in her outstretched arms.

As she gazed from one child to the other, I thought I saw a fleeting frown cloud her face. Then she turned and marched inside with hardly a glance at us or her handsome second husband—younger than her by fifteen years. Milly giggled. "Guess we're the second act from now on," she said.

Tadeusz brushed the soil from his hands, a trace of bewilderment on his sunburned face, and patted our backs. *"Czeszcz! Czeszcz!"* he greeted us in his Russian-accented Polish.

"Hi, yourself, Tadeusz!" I replied, giving him a quick hug as Milly playfully rubbed his unshaven cheek. We liked this man our grandmother married when we were just babies. Everyone, even my cousins and I, called him by his first name—the Polish version of Theodore, which sounded like Ta-day-oosh. I wasn't born yet when my real grandfather died in the 1918 flu epidemic, but everything I'd heard about his love of liquor and fighting made me think my grandmother was better off now. I always had to remind myself that Tadeusz was only a little older than my father. He acted younger, despite a leg injury that left him with a limp. He laughed easily and was eager to please. Who wouldn't want a man like that?

By the time we unloaded the car's trunk and unpacked, our grandmother was at work in the kitchen. Even at sixty-two she stayed in perpetual motion. Bending over her gas stove, she held a lit match to a burner. A circle of blue flames burst under a huge pot of vegetable soup. In the corner of the room, the babies lay swaddled side by side in an old wooden cradle. "*Moje maluskie*, my grandbabies," she cooed at them as she stirred the pot. To us, she issued a command: "*Usiandzta!* Sit! Is time for lunch."

It was always mealtime at Babcia's house, where food rations and wartime shortages had little meaning. From early spring to late summer, she harvested root vegetables, greens, and tomatoes from her garden and honey from her beehive. She picked sour cherries from the orchard behind the small barn and apples from a giant crab-apple tree in her front yard. She canned and pickled what couldn't be eaten right away. Each morning she collected fresh eggs from her hen house and tugged at her cow's teats for fresh milk, which became butter, sour cream, buttermilk and cheese.

I couldn't remember a time I wasn't served more food at Babcia's table than an entire family could consume. My grandmother, a shapeless block of muscle and flesh, always looked at my slender frame anxiously and treated me like I was ill. "*Prosze!* You must eat!" she said. Even now, with my waist still plump from my pregnancy, I felt her scrutiny. "Here!" Babcia commanded, placing a glass of whole milk and a basket of warm rolls before me.

While she added spices to her simmering pot, Tadeusz shuffled into the room. Ignoring us, he came up behind her and nestled his body against her squat frame. She looked up at him and winked.

"Is she flirting?" I whispered to Milly. We watched Tadeusz pat our grandmother's broad hip and lift a matchbox from the stove. Pecking her cheek, he slid open the box, pulled out a match and struck it hard against the side. His pipe fumed as he lowered the flame into its barrel, and a great cloud of sweet smoke wafted upward and joined the steaming broth of onions, potatoes and mushrooms. I closed my eyes and inhaled deeply, certain no aroma—not even the most expensive balm—could be more soothing and irresistible.

***

After we ate, our grandmother ordered us to a second-floor bedroom. "You must rest." Reluctant to leave my son, I shook my head, a half-hearted act of defiance my grandmother ignored. "Go!" she said, taking him from me. *"Idz!"*

Upstairs, I collapsed on my cot while Milly took the narrow bed under the window. A dreamless sleep overtook me until an hour later, when I heard my grandmother singing downstairs. Stretching lazily, I tried to remember the last time I'd napped so soundly. "Umm. This is heaven."

Milly, already awake, jumped up and slipped on her shoes. "Come on, Marg, uh, Nora, or whatever you're called! Let's go down to the river!"

Our grandmother wanted the babies left with her, especially Alek, whom she had bundled in an extra blanket. "Thanks, Babcia, but it's a warm spring day," I argued. "The little ones need fresh air." Just to be safe, I dressed Alek in a heavy wool sweater and knit cap.

We carried our babies past the garden and cherry orchard and through a field thick with weeds and green berries. Just ahead was the river where Milly and I had learned to swim as children. I found a sun-warmed boulder and dangled Alek's feet in the cool water. Milly stripped her daughter and dunked Anna Lee neck-deep in a slow-moving pool behind a fallen tree limb.

"If I close my eyes, I can almost imagine everything as it used to be," I said, "back before the war, back when all we knew was our dreams."

Milly nodded. Back home, we had spent many long afternoons wondering what our husbands were doing, where they were, and what would happen to all of us by the time the war was over. Her husband had been shipped to the Pacific, but she knew little more than that, just as I knew little more about Walt than he was in Africa.

A rustling in the bushes interrupted my daydreams. A confident male voice called out: "Hullo there, strangers!" A young man with wild blond hair and ruddy skin strode out of the woods.

"Sam!" I recognized my childhood friend right away, even though I hadn't seen him in more than five years. Swinging Alek to one hip, I rose to greet him.

Sam Wynock stood only a few inches taller than me, but his sturdy build made him seem larger. He studied my face in a way that made me look away. "Wow," he said. "Look at you. More beautiful than ever." He smiled in Milly's direction. "You, too, gorgeous."

Milly, still bobbing her daughter in the river, glanced at him and smirked. "Yup, I'm here, too."

"My grandma said you were drafted, Sam," I said. "You home for a visit?"

"Didn't she tell you? I'm home on emergency leave. My mom's been sick."

"I'm so sorry. My grandmother mentioned she was ill. Is she doing any better?"

"A bit, thanks. I'll be able to go back to my base in Illinois in a few days."

I bit the inside of my cheek. From the moment Sam walked out of the woods, my imagination shifted gears as crazily as Milly drove her car. He was like a mirage—a happy fragment of my past and a painful reminder of the present. While Walt was trapped in the war, Sam walked freely about his hometown, as carefree as he was years earlier. Part of me was excited to see him. The other part begrudged him his freedom, even if it was both necessary and temporary.

"How's Walt?" he asked, pretending he hadn't already heard about Walt from his mother, a cheerful gossip and my grandmother's good friend.

"Fine. He's fine. He's a medic, you know. In Africa." Thinking of Walt made me hug Alek closer.

"I heard. And this"—he rubbed his forefinger against Alek's tiny fist—"this must be your son."

"It is. Walter Aleksander Baran, Jr. We call him Alek."

Sam took my solemn, wide-eyed baby from my arms. "There's a good-looking boy," he said. He gripped my son in his muscular arms but kept his eyes fixed on me. Alek leaned against him contentedly.

Flushing under his gaze, I sat down close to Milly. Sam followed, holding Alek carefully against his chest. He sat crossed-legged next to me in the grass.

I wondered what Walt would think if he happened on this scene. I should be holding my baby, not Sam, I thought. But as I shifted to reach for Alek, I noticed Sam's expression. He was staring intently at my boy. "He's just a little guy, huh?" he asked softly.

"Uh huh," I murmured, overcome by unexpected gratitude for his concern, no matter how lightly he phrased it. No one in Walt's family or mine ever remarked on Alek's appearance any more—not even Milly. Perhaps they wanted to please me or yield to Max. Perhaps they didn't want to cause the baby any more bad luck. Even if they meant well, I needed someone to speak the truth.

As Sam gently stroked Alek's face, I couldn't believe my good fortune. My childhood friend could be an ally.

"Wow! Look at that current!" Milly shouted, ignoring us. "Remember when we used to swing into the river from a rope? What were we thinking?"

Sam grinned. "We were thinking that cold water sure felt good on a hot day."

I listened to Milly and Sam reminisce about summers long gone, when we swam in the river until dark, caught fireflies in jars, and lived each day without worries or responsibilities. When I finally joined in, I made no mention of Sam's and my stolen kisses when we were young teenagers, before Walt entered my life. Those memories seemed to belong to different people. As the three of us chatted, Alek drifted asleep in Sam's arms. I hardly noticed the sun drop low until swarms of mosquitoes buzzed us.

"Ouch!" Milly yelled, slapping her ankle. "We'd better get going."

Sam put Alek in my outstretched arms. "I need to get back to my mom. Will I see you both again before you leave?"

"Sure," my cousin said, her attention on the towels she folded. "Both of us. We'll call."

As soon as Sam was out of sight, she grabbed my arm. "So, what was that about?"

"What?"

"Don't give me that sweet, innocent face. You two looked like you couldn't wait to be alone."

I swatted at her. "You have such a suspicious mind! For goodness sake, we're childhood friends. All of us were." We walked back to the house in silence. Thinking of Sam made me smile. He was a friend worth having, and I felt no guilt about that at all.

***

That night we moved the babies' cradle upstairs and quickly fell asleep. If Anna Lee cried at all, I never heard her, but every faint noise from my boy startled me. I tried to give him a bottle at four o'clock, but he drank barely an ounce. "Oh, baby," I said. "Why can't I make you happy?"

I slept fitfully after that, until glaring sunlight nudged me awake. Reaching down to the cradle, I touched an empty mattress. "Alek!"

Downstairs, I found Milly singing nursery rhymes to Anna Lee in the parlor. In the kitchen, my grandmother sat in a straight-backed chair, holding a baby bottle to Alek's lips. She frowned as he sucked it with lazy tugs.

"Babcia! I didn't hear Alek wake up!"

My grandmother's gaze, usually sweet as the honey in her tea, could not disguise her uneasiness. She was worried about my baby's health, and she didn't even try to hide it.

Why would she, I thought? She wasn't part of Max's circle, any more than Sam was. Babcia knew what was as plain as the baby fretting in her lap: her great-grandson wasn't thriving. At five months he still was not eating right; he was not growing as he should. The doctor told me not to worry, that he would catch up in time. "You may need to give him smaller amounts of formula more frequently during the day," Dr. Wenski said, ignoring my explanations of how I did just that.

I knelt at my grandmother's feet and rested my head in her lap. I don't know how long I sat like that, with my face turned toward the wall. I didn't look up until my tears had dried.

***

An hour passed before Milly finally joined us. "Did you hear the weather report on the radio? Big storm headed this way."

"Soon?" I asked. She nodded.

I wanted time to talk to my grandmother alone. I needed her advice. But Milly's parents needed the car the next day, and if we didn't leave soon, the storm might delay our return. "We'd better get going, Milly."

To my surprise, my cousin shook her head. "Let's do the crystal ball first. Remember?"

Grandma frowned. "*Co?* What you say?"

"We want to see what your crystal ball says, Babcia," I said.

"To tell our futures," Milly said. "Please? We have a little time before the weather turns bad. It would be fun."

Babcia's blue eyes darkened. "Is not for fun." She looked from my cousin to me. *"Nie!"*

***

"Babcia sure acted funny about that crystal ball," Milly said as she backed her car from the driveway. She stared uneasily at the storm clouds churning the western sky. "I guess it's good we're leaving early, but it's too bad we never had a chance to pull it out."

"Or see Sam again," I said, waving good-bye to my grandmother and Tadeusz.

"Oh, right. We were both so desperate to see Sam again."

I rolled my eyes. "You are hopeless, cousin. For the last time, I'm a friend of Sam's, just like you are. It was nice seeing him, wasn't it?"

"You just don't get it, do you, Nor? Guys drool over you and you think they just want to be friends. Married or not, new mother or not, you're still the gal they chase."

We drove in silence for miles. My cousin exaggerated everything, even Sam's kindness. Friendship was one thing and love was another. Love was the way my grandmother and Tadeusz looked at each other like newlyweds. That's how Walt and I looked at each other before he was shipped overseas. That first month he was gone, I studied his photo every day to remember his loving gaze.

Alek's birth changed things, of course. These days, I focused on my son's gaze, an unreliable barometer that wandered in all directions. I stared out the car window, trying to focus on Walt's many assurances before I left him at Bragg. I kept seeing Sam's intense smile.

We didn't reach my parents' house until after dinner. By the time I unpacked, fed Alek and ate the leftovers my mother saved for me, it was almost dark.

April 10, 1943

Dear Walt,

Milly and I had the most wonderful weekend at Grandma's. Her home is so peaceful. The weather was nice enough to take our babies to the river. You would have loved seeing Alek's face when I dipped his toes in the water. I kept thinking about the times you and I went swimming in the river and basked in the sun. I miss you, my darling...

THIRTY-ONE

April 2, 1943

Dear Nora,

Your long-awaited Christmas package at last arrived
this morning. Despite its long journey, it was in perfect
shape. It's a mystery to me where these packages travel
before they reach us soldiers. China? South America?
Every gift was swell, even your card. Thank you for
remembering how much I needed a watch and extra socks,
dearest. They're perfect. It's hard to think of Christmas
when the weather is finally warming. Things are going well
here. Just keep taking care of yourself and baby. Don't
worry about me at all...

Each item was wrapped in red-and-green paper with smiling Santa Claus
faces: thick wool socks, a wristwatch, a dozen cigars, stationery, a fountain
pen and peanut brittle. Walt could almost hear "White Christmas" playing
in the distance of his memory. My wonderful wife, he thought. How normal
her life must be. How crazy my own life is. Here I am, unwrapping
Christmas gifts, while she is probably coloring Easter eggs.

He was glad she couldn't see how scrawny and filthy he was. Their
frequent moves in Tunisia and the busy flood of wounded made proper
showers out of the question. Buckling on the watch, he admired its clean
face, the solid black numbers against a stark white background. He set the
hour and minute and wound the stem tight. Time couldn't play tricks on
him now.

A letter from his father contained gifts of another sort. Besides the five-
dollar bill Max had slipped inside, he dangled a vague promise. "Business is

going pretty good," he wrote. "When you get out of the Army, I may have a job waiting for you."

Walt rolled his eyes. Nothing was guaranteed in Max's universe. He wondered if should consider other jobs when he finally got home to his wife and child. Maybe something in health care. Despite its challenges and heartbreaks, his work as a medic had been more rewarding than he'd ever expected.

Two days later, Walt received the gift he'd wanted most. The photo of Nora and Alek made him whoop with joy. He no longer had to imagine how his boy looked. He could see for himself how handsome and healthy Alek was. What more could a father ask for?

Walt slipped the photo into his pocket but pulled it out again when Ted walked up.

"Did you ever see a better-looking kid, Ted?"

"*That's* your wife, Baran?" Ted grabbed the photo from Walt's hand and gawked. "Boy, what a looker!"

"Hey, stop leering. It's my son I'm showing off. I think he looks a bit like me."

"Hell, no, Baran. Just look at his nose and then look in a mirror. Look at his mouth and eyes. He's the image of your wife and you should be damn happy."

"Lemme see that," Big Al said, crowding close. He let loose a whistle. "Hey, why didn't ya ever show me a picture of your wife before, Baran?"

"Because I knew you'd act just like this. Give me that." Walt swiped the photo back. From then on, whenever he pulled out the photo, he covered Nora's face with his thumb and pointed to Alek, "What a kid, huh?"

At lunch, he found an empty table to study the photo more closely. "What's on your mind, clever boy? Are you thinking about your Pop?" But just like his friends, he couldn't take his eyes off his wife, a woman more beautiful than he deserved.

He was drinking a second cup of coffee when someone yelled, "We're moving out!" He bolted to the medical tents. Packing was as automatic now as hooking up an IV line. One by one, he and Big Al filled empty crates with supplies. Every time his company shifted position, Walt prayed it would take them one step closer to the war's end.

***

May 17, 1943

Dear Nora,

    I can finally tell you about the Tunisia campaign. The Ninth played a big role helping to push Rommel back. My company was about ten miles from the front most of the time. Never was I in real danger, but my old infantry company went through every tough part of it. Tom Lucas and Frank Hatcher are still here, but some guys I knew are not. Tunisia saw wholesale destruction. The city of Bizerte was a wreck. Every building—I mean every one—was gutted. Nothing living could have survived...

He didn't tell Nora how frayed his nerves still were, even after the incessant bombing at Bizerte had stopped. Tom sent word through an ambulance driver that he and Hatch were okay, but in Walt's old G Company, three men had been killed and a dozen wounded.

His duties became mundane. His patients, the victims of truck accidents, malaria, dysentery and the like, argued constantly about where they were headed next. No one mentioned "home," not even Walt. He prayed every night for that destination, even though he knew it asked too much of the war or of God.

For reasons no one understood, the Ninth kept changing its location in northern Africa. In a welcome bit of luck, Walt's old infantry buddies camped nearby at one point. He found Tom and Hatch and took them to an empty recovery tent for privacy.

Crouched on the ground, Hatch chain-smoked cigarettes, grinding the butts in the dirt. Walt couldn't remember him smoking at all when they'd first met in basic training.

Tom folded his arms over his chest like he always did when difficulties arose, but his green eyes, lively and commanding at Bragg, had lost their flecks of gold; they loomed like dark, angry thunderclouds, stripped of their determined optimism.

"We had close calls at Djebel Dardys and Bizerte, Walt," Tom said. "Those Jerries were sneaky as hell. They aimed everything they had at us. We gave it right back."

Stuttering more than ever, Hatch exhaled a stream of smoke "W-w-we showed 'em. We learned to m-m-move like g-ghosts."

His friends grew more animated as they shared their experiences. They were corporals now, a sign they knew what to do on the battlefield. Walt thought back to Fayetteville, when war held no thrill for any of them. He wasn't surprised the battlefield had affected them this way. They were trying to survive. Walt's constant complaints about artillery noise in recent weeks embarrassed him now. He'd been safe while his best friends were risking their lives.

"After all that's happened to G Company, don't you think you guys have earned a trip back to the States?" Walt said.

Tom let loose a brittle laugh. "Doesn't work like that, buddy. Our reward for surviving will be an even tougher battle assignment. Mark my words."

Walt thought he heard a catch in his friend's voice, but in the dim light Tom looked as steady as when they'd practiced target shooting at Bragg. Walt leaned closer. "I'll be honest. I often wish I could be up front with you guys. But the truth is, I want to go home now more than anything."

"L-let's make a p-pact," Hatch said. "After this is over and we finally g-get back home, let's celebrate g-good and hard. You know, really t-tie one on."

"It's a date," Walt said, forcing a smile. He glanced at Tom, remembering when the two of them helped Hatch into bed the first time he sampled some booze.

"You bet, Hatch. We'll get blitzed," Tom said, nodding slowly. Suddenly, his expression changed. He blinked with surprise. "I don't believe it!"

"What?" Walt said.

"We're as close as brothers, but I don't have either of your mailing addresses or phone numbers back home. And you don't have mine!"

Walt laughed at the insanity of it. The war created a new geography. Back at Bragg, they had no reason to write each other. Now, only their platoon's location in the war mattered. "Let's solve that right now," he said. "Write down the address and phone number of someone close to you back home, someone who'll stay put after this war is over, so there's no chance we'll lose touch." They scribbled addresses on scraps of paper and shared them. Tom slipped his into his wallet. Hatch tucked his in his chest pocket. Walt did the same. "One more thing," Walt said. "Let's all promise to call these numbers when we get home. No matter what happens."

His friends nodded wordlessly. Hatch patted his heart. "Don't worry. You g-guys are safe right here."

***

After his friends left, Walt lay on the ground outside his tent, staring at the stars. The front had changed his friends in ways it hurt to see. Yet their short visit reminded him of all that was right in his life—the good men he'd befriended in the Army; his family; his son; and most of all, Nora.

Nora. He imagined her beside him, scented with lilac cologne, the heat of her skin touching his. A tremor of desire passed through him, gone as quickly as it arrived. So much distance separated them—not just the thousands of miles, but the weeks it took for their letters to reach each other. Nora's letters delivered only glimpses of her life. His letters were probably worse for her. Even the one about the Tunisian campaign revealed little. He sat up, determined to fix that omission without breaking censorship rules. For the next hour he wrote in detail about his job, the mystery of their next destination, and his visit with Tom and Hatch.

May 30, 1943

My darling Nora,

A long letter I wrote you yesterday was handed back to me this morning. It seems I mentioned some censorable things. I was told to rewrite it, so here goes. I've been told by my superiors that I do excellent work. In the course of each day, I use every single thing I learned in Missouri. Unfortunately, I won't get a raise any time soon. It's discouraging, but I continue to do the best I can. For reasons I do not understand, I can't say much about my best friends now. You know who they are. They mean a lot to me...

***

It's the Army docs, Walt," Gus said, when Walt told him about his frozen pay. "The Army put them in charge of things like budgets and salaries. Nothing in med school prepared them for it. They don't know how to pay a man what he's worth."

"Maybe you're right," Walt said. "Or maybe the guys in charge don't like the way I stand up for myself."

Gus smiled. Walt knew what the clerk was thinking, but he also knew he was doing his best to play by Army rules. No man with a backbone could tolerate the military's mindless commands any better.

"The Army doesn't make any sense," Walt said in his defense. "Look at these past few weeks. Wandering back and forth along the coast and then stalling at Oran. We're hundreds of miles west of Tunisia and doing nothing at all."

Sometimes they stayed put for days. They passed the time playing baseball and card games and swimming in the Mediterranean. This war business is odd, Walt thought. Unending chaos and blood and din, day after day after day, followed by such maddening boredom he wanted to explode.

Magnus made his life bearable. In the seven months since the reticent loner had driven Walt to Madame L'Amoureux's brothel, Walt had learned how to take advantage of his most amazing talent: An ability to track down booze in the middle of nowhere. Magnus could sneak out of camp on foot at night and return with a bottle before anyone missed him. Walt gladly paid a buck or two for a coffee mug full of hooch. Beer, wine, brandy, it didn't matter, as long as it was alcohol. That was a lot of money, but the drinks kept him out of trouble. They soothed his nerves just enough.

On occasion, Walt tried to make conversation with Magnus, an exercise the driver seemed to find offensive. He shrugged off questions about his life before the Army, about his family, about his birthplace.

***

The day Major General George S. Patton arrived at the clearing company, Walt knew big news would follow. The man was a celebrity. He'd earned his reputation in the invasion of Africa and in Tunisia. Chin held high, Patton stood in his Jeep as his convoy rolled into camp. He looked like he expected applause. "Our fearless leader," Walt muttered.

The general's theatrics impressed a lot of enlisted men. They marveled at his flashy polished helmet, cavalry pants and ivory-handled pistols. Walt thought him a show-off. Rumors buzzed through camp about the reason for Patton's visit. He carried orders for the Ninth's next stop, which, rumor had it, would be a place where many soldiers had relatives.

"Has to be Italy," Walt told a group of soldiers milling about after a ballgame.

"What the fuck d'you care?" a familiar voice bellowed. A stocky corporal strutted into the circle, hands on hips. Walt couldn't believe it. Aiden Leary, the fool from G Company who tried to keep him out of the Medical Corps at Bragg, the loudmouth who called Walt a coward at the brothel. Here he was again, this time sounding like he'd just gulped a large stash of booze.

Walt's tentmate moved in quickly. "Don't start, Cor-por-al." Ted said. "You're ossified."

Walt shook his head. "Ignore him."

Leary stumbled in front of Walt, his eyes swollen and red. "Wassa' matter? Don' like the truth? You don' care where the fuck we go, ya damn coward. Admit it."

Walt glowered. "Do yourself a favor, corporal. Can it!"

Leary stuck out his chin. "Com'on! Admit it, you yella prick! You signed up for the medics cuz you're too fuckin' scared to fight."

Without thinking, Walt grabbed him by the collar and shook him with both hands. The knot of soldiers surrounding them backed up to make room for a brawl. "Shut your mouth, you stupid, drunken Irishman," Walt said through gritted teeth. "Or I'll shut it for you."

Something in the way the man panted made Walt hesitate. Maybe Leary was drunk, or maybe he was cowardly himself, but maybe he was sick. Walt let him go.

Leary sneered and stumbled away, mumbling under his breath.

"Talk about cowards," Ted said. "And a bad egg, to boot."

Walt bit his tongue. He hated to admit his nemesis had touched on a truth. It wasn't fear he felt, but an aching remorse. As much as he wanted to save lives to make up for Cliff's death, he couldn't shake his regret for deserting his infantry buddies.

***

The rumor mill had it wrong. Instead of shipping out right away, the Ninth continued to move about northern Africa before returning to the crushed city of Bizerte. That's my life, Walt thought. Moving in circles.

Then one morning, chaos returned. Unexpectedly, German planes dropped bombs near the clearing company, prompting Allied anti-aircraft weapons to thunder a reply. One enemy bomb almost hit a field hospital. Searchlights swiftly swept the sky to guide the artillery's aim.

Spent casings pattered down on Walt and Ted's pup tent. The metal-fall sounded like gentle rain until it turned into a hail of hot shrapnel. "Let's go!" Ted yelled.

They raced toward a shallow foxhole twenty yards away. For as long as the bombing and antiaircraft fire continued, Walt's body quaked as violently as the ground shook. When the noise finally stopped, he waited for the silence to settle into his bones. His hands still trembled, but the attack revived his purpose. The close call made him more determined than ever to get through the war by saving lives instead of taking them.

He searched the camp for evidence of casualties. Finding none, he went looking for his favorite medicine. He found Magnus crouched behind a truck, a half-filled wine bottle braced between his knees.

"Got any extra, pal?"

"Sure, Baran. How much you want?"

"A liter'll do." Walt handed over one dollar. Magnus jogged toward his pup tent and returned with a dusty, unlabeled bottle, no doubt the product of a local farmer.

Walt cradled the bottle to his chest. "You're a miracle-worker. Don't know how you do it."

Magnus nodded and tapped his forehead. "A gift. I have a gift."

THIRTY-TWO

The only sound in my parents' kitchen that June morning was the Frigidaire's dependable hum. The half-filled coffee pot was cold. My father must have left much earlier, when the streets were dark and buses weren't yet running.

He enjoyed his long, solitary walks to the factory, even when he was in pain. I pictured him grimacing as he limped to his first day back on the job. His bosses didn't have to beg him more than once to return. Such a proud man. So dutiful.

I barely had time to reheat the coffee before Alek's determined cries cut through the silence. He sounded desperately hungry, but I knew better. I heated three ounces of milk over a low flame. Whenever I tried to feed him more, he'd spit out the nipple and waste precious drops.

If only my mother could quit that horrible job at the mattress factory, with its shifts that ended late and started so early she never had time for coffee.

If only I knew how to be a better mother.

Alek's cries shifted into a keening wail. The base of my neck clenched as I poured the warmed milk into a bottle. A week had passed since I'd brought him to the doctor with a nagging cough and sniffles. I touched his forehead with the back of my hand, grateful his skin was no longer hot.

I settled down with him in my father's rocking chair, nudging his mouth open with the nipple. "Here, little one. This will help."

I appreciated the rocker's solid, unadorned construction, despite its stubborn creak at the point just before it rocked forward. Its movement calmed my fretful son. My father kept the chair in the kitchen for reasons I never understood. The kitchen was my mother's domain, and my parents rarely spoke except to quarrel.

159

After Alek ate, I finished my morning chores—the sweeping, the washing, the scrubbing, the folding of clothes. Then I sat at the kitchen table to reread Walt's last letter. His accounts of card games and softball games made his life seem peaceful and mundane.

I craved a sharper memory of my husband. I needed to feel closer to him, but details had blurred—the terrain of his shoulders, the rhythm of his deep voice, the wild waves of his dark hair. Other unsought imaginings kept interrupting my thoughts: the sight of Sam Wynock reaching out to Alek, Sam's lopsided smile, his shock of blond hair, his direct gaze. I pushed them away that morning with memories of my last night with Walt. "We'll have lots of sons," Walt had said. "I hope you don't mind, but the Barans have mostly boys."

"And *I* won't have anything to contribute to this?" I'd said.

He ignored my teasing and described his vision of our first-born. "He'll be big, you can count on it. And fearless, too. Another Baran trait."

I remembered thinking none of that mattered: All I wanted was his child.

Alek whimpered in his crib. He eyed me solemnly as I bent over him. I inhaled his scent, a tangy sweetness that reminded me of salt-water taffy at the Jersey shore.

"How is my precious boy?" I said, smiling with wonder. His serious expression reminded me of a wise old man. At seven months, my baby remained a puzzle. Even though he fretted more than most babies, I could make him laugh if I tried hard enough. I played peek-a-boo and made silly faces and tickled his feet. His smile was worth the effort. It lit up his face and made him look confident and healthy. Two weeks earlier, on a visit to my in-laws, Max grabbed a camera when he saw that look. "That's my Dixie!" he bellowed. "Another photo to send Walt to show him his perfect son."

I had to admit Max's photos made me see my son's perfection, too.

***

June 30, 1943

Dear Walt,

Life here is as usual. I've enclosed another photo of your adorable son. Every time I look at him, I see you. He's smart like you, too. This morning he said "Da." See? He's calling for you. I'm grateful for every sound he makes now that my father is back to work. The apartment is so quiet now. I'm surprised how much I miss Dad each day...

Finding new things to write about was a challenge. Alek consumed my days. On days my boy was cranky and fussy, or congested and feverish, writing was impossible. But if I skipped writing, guilt nagged me. I felt like the rope in a tug of war between my husband and our son.

Walt was far more dutiful. Most of the time, he wrote almost every day. That morning, I received a rare V-mail from him. He hated those tiny bits of paper and rarely sent them. The Army preferred them because they reduced the cost and speed of flying mail overseas. V-mail letters had to be confined to a single page, which then was photographed and greatly shrunk, and, in the process, handled by countless strangers and machines. Walt's imaginative mind loathed those restraints. He preferred to write on both sides of four or five pages, even when raindrops and mud smeared the ink from his fountain pen. Those long letters hardly resembled the stilted tone of his V-mails. I cherished their intimate tone, even though they took weeks longer to arrive. Knowing his hands had touched the same paper I held thrilled me.

The rest of the day's mail held another surprise. As I sifted through it, a thin white envelope drifted to the floor. The unfamiliar handwriting was the opposite of Walt's sturdy, tight penmanship. Its rounded letters slanted slightly to the right. It was addressed to me.

I opened it cautiously. The first words made me gasp.

Sam!

"Dear Nora, thank you so much for spending the afternoon with me in Dunnellon. It meant so much to see you and your cousin and relax a bit before returning to the Great Lakes Naval Station. I may ship out soon, probably to Europe. It would mean a lot if we could write each other while I'm over there. Here's my address..."

I shoved the letter in my apron pocket, then pulled it out again. As glad as I was to hear from Sam, I couldn't believe what he was asking. A chance meeting was one thing. A steady exchange of letters didn't feel right. I hid the letter underneath my clothes in the one dresser drawer I called my own.

As I expected, Walt's short V-mail contained no real news. I pulled out a shoebox filled with his letters and found a longer, more intimate letter from the week before. Settling into my father's rocking chair, I read and re-read the earlier one, especially a line near the end: "I wish this war would end soon, so I could tell you things I can't say now." Some married people claim to know their spouse's thoughts before a word is spoken. I think they lie. Even with my husband's full sentences in front of me, all I knew was that something was bothering him. I saved all his letters, even ones like this, that almost made me cry.

Leaning back, I coaxed the oak rocker into a steady rhythm. My thoughts drifted back to Sam. Should I ignore his letter? If I wrote him, what should I say? How would I ever explain that to Walt?

"Aaai! Aaai." My son's inevitable cries jolted me to my feet.

"Come to mommy. Come to mommy. It's okay, my little man." I scooped him up and carried him to the rocking chair. Stroking his curls, I softly sang my version of a familiar lullaby refrain: *Oh dear, what can the matter be? Dear, dear, what can the matter be? Oh, dear, what can the matter be? Daddy's so long far away.*

THIRTY-THREE

From the top deck, Walt watched North Africa's coastline slowly disappear. His hunch had been right: The Ninth Infantry's next stop would be Sicily. The port of Bizerte little resembled his departure from Norfolk's chaos ten months earlier. No machinery or vehicles clogged its docks. No factories belched in the distance. The battered city's harbor wore a necklace of drab transport ships preparing to depart. The scene mirrored his insides—his bruised determination to survive whatever came next.

In the late afternoon sun, the Mediterranean's blue waters glistened with unnatural brightness. He found a quiet corner to write Nora. Even when he didn't know exactly where the war would take him, he always knew where Nora was. She was his North Star. His almost daily habit of putting her name and address on envelopes grounded him, no matter how little he was allowed to say.

> July 6, 1943
>
> Dear Nora,
>
> You can't imagine how happy it makes me to get pictures of you and baby. I can't imagine Alek ever being cranky. In every photo, he's full of smiles. He's the handsomest little fellow I ever did see and looks so bright and intelligent. I'm glad you're in the pictures, too. You look prettier than ever...

***

Sicily delivered the unexpected. No gunfire greeted Walt's ship in Licata's harbor. No artillery, either. The landing felt almost like coming home.

Southern Sicily's indecently barren, rocky coastline resembled North Africa, but its people didn't stare at him with open hostility or wear long robes and head wrappings. They resembled Walt's neighbors in northern New Jersey. Priests and nuns waved V-for-victory signs. Smiling villagers shouted *"Viva Americano!"*

One old man offered a basket of fresh plums, grapes and melons. Walt picked out a plum and rubbed it on the inside of his shirt. Its thick, golden juice made him picture vitamins coursing through his body. Ted winked at a raven-haired girl handing out bunches of fat, purple grapes. *"Grazie, signorina,"* he cooed, patting her hand as he grabbed a bunch. "Can you believe it, Walt? These people actually like us."

Maybe this will be an easy campaign, Walt thought. He shouted to Gus at the front of the truck, "Where we going?" He'd come to count on the company clerk. He seemed to know more about what was happening than General Patton himself.

"All I know is we're following the Thirty-Ninth Combat Team, and they're following the Germans, who I hear are retreating fast."

The news was a relief, except for the part about following the Thirty-Ninth. Once again, Walt's old friends in the Sixtieth would be treated by another medical company. Once again, rumors would be his only way of keeping track of Tom and Hatch.

"What about Mussolini's Army?"

"Haven't you heard? The Italian soldiers are surrendering as fast as they can rip off their white shirts and wave 'em over their heads."

***

In less than a day, the medics' convoy reached Sicily's barren countryside. Its steep, hilly terrain offered lessons in camouflage. Clusters of earthen homes nestled so discretely amid slate- and rust-colored mountains that Walt often didn't spot them until their inhabitants ran up to the convoy with fruits and vegetables. He never mistook their generosity for bounty. Living conditions clearly were harsh. The people were stick-thin, their clothes ragged. The Sicilians blamed their German occupiers for their poverty, but if Germans were still on the island, Walt saw no evidence of it. There were no land mines, no enemy planes, no distant artillery explosions.

So routine was the company's progress northward that one Sunday the company commander let fifty men hike to the nearest town to attend Catholic Mass with the locals. Walt needed it. He'd been praying as often as ever and attended church services whenever chaplains set up makeshift altars. But no matter how hard he asked God for answers to war's insanity, he received none. Was God even listening? More and more, he found his comfort in a bottle.

Despite the arduous five-mile trek, the men were giddy with their freedom. Walking with Ted near the center of the pack, Walt enjoyed the fast pace, the loud chatter, the raucous laughter. Then, as he rounded a bend, he spotted near the front of the procession a tall soldier with an unmistakable gliding gait. Only one man in the company moved so effortlessly. Magnus.

The man was a loner, a drunk, a rule-breaker who mocked Catholics making the sign of the cross, yet here he was leading a mob of soldiers to church. Walt slowed his pace and nudged Ted. "If he's Catholic, I'm Hindu."

Ted laughed. "Look around, Walt. Every brand of saint and sinner is in this bunch. Jews, Methodists, Catholics, Baptists. Probably atheists, too."

Ted was right. In fact, few soldiers cared who led services in the field, be it a priest, rabbi or minister. Roughnecks and bookworms, brawlers and the pious, they all attended. They just wanted to talk to the Big Guy, as one mechanic called his God.

In town, the men filed into a painted hut that served as a church. Walt preferred the modest setting to his ornate church back home. It helped him focus. All he required from Mass were its familiar Latin chants, the aroma of incense, and its pauses for holy silence. Sitting halfway back from the altar, he wondered if God would choose this day to hear the questions he kept asking: Were his actions in this war enough to redeem him? Would his big brother have approved?

Suddenly, a side door near the altar swung open and a short, wiry priest stepped inside, followed by two altar boys. The priest's vestments—his alb, satin stole and embroidered purple chasuble—were more elaborate than anything else in the hut.

As Mass began, Walt closed his eyes in prayer. When he opened them, he spotted Magnus two rows ahead, listening intently to the priest speak in Latin. Magnus seemed to know the Mass's arcane rituals, too. He stood, kneeled and sat at precisely the right moments. Maybe he really is a baptized Catholic, Walt thought. He shouldn't care—it wasn't his business—but the heathen seemed to enjoy an easier relationship with God than he had known for months.

When the collection basket came around, Walt put in a dollar, as did almost every other soldier moved by the sight of the hungry parishioners. After Mass, the locals returned the favor. They handed out the one thing the town had plenty of: Homemade wine. The men swigged from shared bottles. They laughed and shouted like partygoers. Walt picked up a bottle and sat alone in the shade of an olive tree to enjoy it. On the other side of the square, he saw Magnus do the same.

Slowly, one group after the other returned to camp. Walt waited until most of the men had left and his bottle was drained. His gait was steady as he passed clusters of stumbling stragglers. Halfway back to camp, when he saw Magnus ahead of him, Walt hastened his steps.

"I saw you in church," Walt said when he finally caught up.

"Mm," Magnus responded.

"I didn't know you were Catholic."

"I am not."

"But you knew so—" Walt stopped. Questions put to Magnus rarely worked their way to an answer.

They walked in silence for several minutes. Magnus fixed his gaze straight ahead. When he finally spoke, he said more than Walt had ever heard from him: "I liked being in the church. It was peaceful. It had calm." He paused. "It had mercy."

Now it was Walt's turn to remain silent. How could this man know his most private thoughts?

***

For the next three weeks, Walt didn't tend to a single battle injury. Only when the company neared Mount Etna in late July did ambulances begin to roar into camp. Enemy bombs pounded the earth and artillery guns returned fire.

In the crowded surgery, he raced from one litter to the next. He grabbed a tourniquet for a soldier who'd stepped on a mine and lost half his leg. He stopped the bleeding in a patient peppered with shrapnel and bullet wounds. Doctors and techs yelled for supplies or assistance. Patients screamed in pain and fear. A stranger might mistake the din for chaos.

Amid the clamor, Walt heard a familiar voice. He looked around and heard it again, a weak and scratchy sound. "Baran, help…"

He circled the tent until he tracked the voice to a litter near the tent wall. On it lay a man so covered with blood and shredded flesh that he was unrecognizable. One eye was swollen shut. His jaw looked broken. Walt grabbed sterile wipes and began cleaning the wounds.

"Uh," the patient groaned. "Bad…shape."

The short, red-haired man sprawled on the cot looked vaguely familiar. He could have been any of a thousand men Walt had cared for in recent months. He unbuttoned the man's shirt, fished for dog tags, and wiped off blood obscuring the name. "What the hell?" he said. Pounded into the metal was the name, *Leary, Aidan M.*

God is playing a cruel joke on both of us, Walt thought. How long had he wanted this man gone from his life?

The man moaned, begging for help. Memories flashed in Walt—the grinding sound of metal on metal; his older brother's mangled body; Cliff's weak voice calling his name. He stared at Leary, speechless.

Big Al called out. "Need help, Walt?"

"No. I'm okay," Walt lied. It wasn't that he didn't know what to do. His training made sure of that. He checked for major injuries and found a deep chest wound. "It's just you and me, buster," he said. "Got to stop this bleeding fast."

Leary said something, too, but in a voice so soft Walt had to put his ear close to the man's mouth. The corporal winced as he took a breath. "Can...you?" he exhaled.

Stop the bleeding? Was that what the man tried to say? Or was he mocking him again? Walt didn't care. He placed sterile gauze on the wound and yelled for a doctor. Even after the barely conscious man was stitched up, Walt stayed with him for fifteen minutes—a long time in the busy surgery—to make sure he was stable.

Then he wheeled Leary to recovery.

When Walt returned to surgery, bedlam greeted him. Injuries grew more horrific each moment. He helped a delirious young private gushing blood from a head wound before turning to a gutted lieutenant, whose entrails slipped from a deep cavity in his abdomen. Age and rank made no difference. Ten of his patients that day, including the private and the lieutenant, lasted only minutes. Their final groans and cries echoed inside him long after they died, mocking his motives for joining the medics. A surgical technician could do little to stem the logical consequences of war, no matter how hard he tried.

After his shift, Walt checked on his patients in recovery. He left Leary for last. To his amazement, the corporal slept. His breathing was regular, his vital signs almost normal. A man who routinely brought misery on himself and others had been spared.

God isn't involved in any of this, Walt thought. This war is mankind's work.

***

Walt's jittery nerves wouldn't let him sleep. He took a corner seat in the smoke-filled mess tent. While enemy bombs fell a half mile away, the other medics sipped hot coffee and chatted casually. The pounding reminded him of his first air raid in Tunisia, when Ted and Big Al tripped over him and each other to race to their foxholes. Now, no one even flinched.

The night's injuries unsettled him in ways that furious bombings and past surgery shifts hadn't. He took deep breaths and said silent prayers.

Just as his insides began to calm, the tent's flap flew open. Captain Abich burst in, acting like he was looking for something. The enlisted men scrambled to their feet to salute—all but Walt, who remained hunched over his cup. Abich scanned the tent quickly and left.

Buck let out a low whistle and turned in Walt's direction. "He saw you, ya know. Don't think he didn't."

Walt shrugged. "Don't care."

***

Gus joined Walt at breakfast the next morning. The clerk knew everything that had happened the night before. "Did you really have to do that?" he asked.

Walt grimaced. "We techs had just finished a gruesome ten-hour shift. Dr. Big Shot was probably just waking from a nap."

Gus studied him carefully. "You know, my friend, I hear the doctors talk. You're one of the best techs we have. They all know that. You just have to watch yourself. I know these rules are annoying. But pay attention to them. They're important."

Walt massaged his temples. His raging headache continued to throb. He doubted anyone but Abich cared about pointless salutes. "Saving lives is important, too, Gus."

THIRTY-FOUR

Aug. 18, 1943

Dear Walt,

I'm grateful Milly wanted us to go back to Babcia's again. The heat and smog in Elizabeth have been unbearable this summer. The still night air in the city feels suffocating. Here in Middlesex, Alek sleeps better and so do I. We open all the windows and a cool breeze from the woods blows through the house...

I pulled my hair into a bun and slipped on a gauzy blue-plaid cotton dress that made up for in comfort what it lacked in style. Alek squirmed in his new crib.

Babcia's husband had been eager to show off his handiwork the minute we arrived. Tadeusz shook the two cribs' side rails and beamed. "See, is strong!" Strong and smooth. He'd sanded, stained and varnished the sturdy wood frames. He would do anything to keep my Babcia happy. All she had to do was tell him her great-grandchildren needed bigger beds and he set to work.

Alek groaned in distress. I knew every note on his scale of pain and frustration, his symphony of discontent. "Hush, sweetheart, Momma's here." At the sound of my voice, he moaned more loudly.

I pictured Anna Lee downstairs, crawling at Milly's feet, eager to explore. Though she was a week younger than Alek, at eight months she was taller and at least four pounds heavier. Alek, who had yet to master crawling, usually inched along the floor on his belly. That morning, still weak from another bad cold, he probably wouldn't even do that.

The last time we visited Babcia, everything happened too fast. I blushed at the memory of going down to the river and seeing Sam, of reading the letter he'd sent me after I returned home. He'd written me two more times since then, though I didn't write him back.

This visit would be different. I would use my time wisely. I would be less skeptical about my grandmother's herbs and healing powers. I even would pay attention to the holy shrines she set up in almost every nook and cranny of her home. Holy cards were everywhere of Jesus, Mary and Joseph; of Jesus as a baby, as a young man, and on the cross; of Babcia's favorite saints, of chubby cherubs and brightly colored angels. She put the cards on windowsills, staircase landings, built-in shelving, and even in a corner of the kitchen. Dried palm fronds, votive candles, fresh flowers, and tiny cups of holy water decorated the shrines, which Grandma tended as devotedly as her garden.

Instead of viewing her rituals as Old-World superstitions, I decided to seek strength from them. I'd try anything to make my son healthy. I planned to light a candle at each shrine, dip my finger in the holy water and say the same simple prayer: "Dear Lord, heal my son. Protect my husband. Bring Walt back to me in one piece."

Babcia's house possessed a holy energy. I was sure it would deliver me closer to God than any church could.

That afternoon, I followed my ritual. After I visited all of Babcia's shrines, I returned to the one for Our Lady of Czestochowa. The Black Madonna's healing shrine in Poland was only a few miles from my father's birthplace. I added a special plea: "Mother of God, I beg you, intercede for me. Do this one thing for me and for Alek. He needs his daddy."

As I prayed the "Hail, Mary," Milly yelled from the dining room: "Come here, Nor! You're not going to believe this!"

"Holy Mary, mother of God..."

Milly's voice grew louder. "Come on, girl! You can finish that later!"

"...pray for us sinners, now and at the hour..."

"Do you want me to drag you over here?"

"...of our death. Amen." I crossed myself and rushed downstairs. The crystal ball sat on the dining room table in front of Milly and Babcia. A lit candle flickered next to it, but the globe seemed to glow with its own light.

Slowly, I pulled back a chair. "What's going on?"

My cousin smiled. "I convinced Babcia to tell us our futures. This will be great."

I frowned, remembering my grandmother's resistance on our last visit. "Maybe I don't want to see my future. Are you sure, Babcia?"

My grandmother nodded slightly, a look of resignation on her face. Milly rolled her eyes.

For Milly, the crystal ball was little more than a magic trick. I wasn't so sure. Even sitting next to it, I felt it pulse with energy. I glanced at my grandmother, who emitted her own special power, a full dose of unconditional love.

"*Moja wnuchka,*" the old woman said—my granddaughter. She grasped my hand. "You okay?"

I smiled at her stab at modern English. I loved my Babcia so much. How could I not trust her? "Yes, Babch. I'm okay. Who goes first?"

"I'll go!" Milly sat on the edge of her seat. She propped both elbows on the table.

Babcia probed her with gentle suggestions: What does your heart tell you? What do you need to know most? My cousin giggled. She asked her what color she should paint her bedroom and when Anna Lee would learn to walk. Eyebrows raised, our grandmother stared into the globe before she spoke mostly in Polish. "You see color in roses, yes? You see footsteps on ground. Count them." Her words were a riddle made more difficult by our attempts to translate them.

Milly didn't care. "Okay, Nor. You're next." She acted like we were playing a game of rummy.

I took a deep breath. "My heart wants to know about Walt, Babcia. Will—when will he come home?"

Milly exhaled something unintelligible and exasperated. My question about the real world had crossed her forbidden line.

Babcia stared for the longest time into the crystal ball. Finally, she spoke softly. "*Cierpliwosc,* Gosia." Patience. "He come soon enough."

I sank back in my seat like a chronic invalid who'd received good news about her health. Joy filled me. My silence invited Milly to seize control again. "That's good news, cousin!"

I nodded. "Little Alek will be so happy to see his father."

Babcia turned to me, her piercing blue eyes weary.

"Are you done, Babch?" I asked, touching her arm.

My grandmother shut her eyes. When she opened them again, she seemed at peace. "*Tak, moja wnuchka.* We are done now."

***

The next morning, my Babcia was up before everyone. I found her in the kitchen, furiously beating a dozen eggs in a ceramic bowl. I took a deep breath, summoning my growing determination to trust her healing powers.

"I have a favor to ask, Babch, a big favor." I put on an apron and took the bowl from her. "You see how Alek is. He needs your help."

She grasped my free hand and nodded silently.

After breakfast, she snuggled Alek in her arms and wrapped him in a soft cotton cloth. Then she plunged him into a bathtub filled with warm, moistened herbs and massaged the brown paste all over him. She passed a muddy hand over his face and chanted words in Polish and other languages I didn't recognize. My son lay calmly in the goo, staring intently at her in unexpected and utter contentment.

For the next four days, I visited her shrines twice a day and practiced new prayers. "Dear Lord, protect my son. Keep him well," I prayed. "Holy Mother of God, ask your son to watch over little Alek. He's just a baby, Blessed Mary." If God was listening, He could see I was trying my best.

Every day, Babcia treated Alek with more herbs. Each morning, he awoke with a smile. He drank all his milk and licked oatmeal from a spoon. Was it possible? Were Babcia's treatments working? Were my prayers finally being answered?

THIRTY-FIVE

At the end of yet another grueling shift, Walt cleaned blood, gore and splintered bone fragments off every surface in the surgery tent. He was alone when Gus came looking for him.

"Walt, I just heard news about your old infantry unit. The Sixtieth is in position at the front."

Walt grimaced. The fierce fighting that week had caused the worst casualties so far, and now his friends were in the thick of it.

"Your buddies will be fine," Gus said, anticipating Walt's reaction. "Haven't they done okay so far?"

He didn't answer. The dirt floor of surgery was dark with dried blood these days. He wondered how he had grown accustomed to so much death. Yet Gus might be right. So far, Tom and Hatch had avoided calamity at every turn. They'd survived countless near misses.

Outside, the balmy darkness made his friends' safety seem possible. After a noisy, bloody day of injuries, the soundless night was untouched by slaughter.

Walt decided to check on Aidan Leary. A chorus of faint moans arose from the recovery tent, the sound of pain tamped down by morphine. Lifting the tent flap, he scanned the crowded space.

A wheezy voice called out. "Look who's here...Doc Baran." Leary sneered. Or maybe he just smiled. The man's face was so swollen it was hard to tell.

When Walt had checked on him the day before, Leary gasped what sounded like an insult. "Looks like...you...learned something...in Missouri." Walt ignored him. The hostility between them seemed beside the point. Whether Leary liked it or not, he was just another patient.

Now, a day later, Leary's color was better, his breathing stronger. Walt guessed he'd be transferred the next morning to a hospital further behind the lines. The corporal was living evidence that no matter how unpredictable war was, survival was still possible.

"Tell me something, Leary. How'd you end up wounded? The Sixtieth just got here."

"I ain't with Sixtieth...anymore, that's how...Was transferred to Thirty-Ninth, to the front. Lucky...me, huh?"

***

Days later, the medics moved even closer to Mount Etna and the front. Spewing heavy ash, the ancient volcano seemed to fume at the heavy bloodletting at its feet. Some men viewed the cranky eruptions fearfully. Walt worried more about the unrelenting artillery fire.

The rumor mill said the Sixtieth remained outside the worst battle areas. Even still, he quizzed every new patient, just as he had in northern Africa. "What's happening to the Sixtieth? Any of you know Tom Lucas? Frank Hatcher? Sergeants in G Company."

"You're so fixed on finding your buddies you haven't noticed what's happening on the other side of camp," Big Al said. "A field hospital is going up, Walt. Trained surgeons, fully equipped operating rooms. What'll that leave us to do?"

"A lot. Too much, even," Walt said. Field hospitals were good news. They meant the Army finally realized wounded soldiers needed proper care and that most doctors in the clearing company were general practitioners and internists, like Hector Abich, inexperienced with complicated surgeries. Their hands were full enough treating minor wounds, malaria, flu, dysentery, ulcers and, especially, battle fatigue—all the inevitable result of days without proper food or sleep.

None of Walt's classes in Missouri prepared him for the psychological effects of combat. His first lesson came in Tunisia, when a sweaty young man with a fixed gaze showed up with no visible wounds. "What unit you with, soldier?" Walt asked. The man shrugged, unsure, and collapsed on the ground.

Other soldiers trembled so violently they couldn't put one foot in front of the other. They sobbed and called for their mothers. Some were so bone-tired they couldn't stand. What all needed most was rest and reassurance. Walt put them in recovery tents. He listened to their stories. They needed tending as much as the men wounded by bombs and gunfire.

***

Not until mid-August did men from the Sixtieth Regiment begin to arrive in surgery. Some of their wounds maimed. Some brought patients close to death. As long as Tom and Hatch were not there, Walt assumed the best.

Just when everyone thought the Germans would never yield, they began to retreat across the Strait of Messina. Walt didn't dare write Nora that impossibly good news. Censors in Sicily didn't just cut forbidden information from letters, as they had in Africa. Here, they tossed offending letters into the fire and assigned their authors to KP duty.

When his letters didn't get him in trouble with the censors, they got him in trouble with Nora. Sometimes, he could barely remember the letters that seemed to bother her.

Aug. 17, 1943

Dear Nora,

You are a most understanding wife. I apologize for writing two months ago about seeing American WAACs bathing in the Mediterranean. My "admiration," as you called it, was innocent. Dear wife, there's one thing you need never fear of me. I will never, ever have a thing to do with anyone but you…

Not until Italy unconditionally surrendered a few weeks later did Walt hear news of his buddies.

"Lucas and Hatcher? Yeah, sure, they're okay," said Billy Malone, a private from Company G being treated for dysentery. "Skin and bones, like the rest of us, but they're tough. Good leaders. We'd do anything for them,"

Of course, those infantrymen would, Walt thought. His friends were survivors. Others in G Company had been picked off one by one in Sicily, wounded so badly they couldn't fight. Tom and Hatch could still walk, talk—and lead.

Malone's weak voice droned on. "We had a lot of other casualties in G Company," the private said. "A guy from New Jersey you mighta known. Mike Kowalczyk. Killed by mortar fire at Randazzo."

The news hit Walt like a gunshot. He'd been focusing so hard on his best friends that he hadn't worried about the rest of Company G. He knew Kowalczyk all right. As kids growing up in Elizabeth, they hung out with the same crowd. Everyone called him Kovy. A nice guy, if that had anything to do with who lived or died. The private didn't know for sure how Kovy died, but Gus said the front was so chaotic that G Company took fire from the enemy and Allies alike. He had to tell Nora.

Sept. 26, 1943

Dear Nora,

We're finally allowed to write home about Sicily. We were optimistic when we first landed. The locals were awfully friendly, and we didn't expect the Germans to fight as fiercely as they did at Mount Etna. I have sad news you've probably already heard, dear. Remember Mike Kowalczyk? Kovy from Elizabeth? I know your families know each other. I just got word he was killed in the fighting near Randazzo. He was a good man. Please give my best to his family, would you, dear?

An hour after he dropped the letter in the company mail box, he heard the latest announcement: "Letters home about deaths or injuries in Sicily are strictly forbidden." The Army issued so many orders, Walt couldn't keep up with them.

After dinner, Gus stopped by Walt's table. "The major wants to see you, Walt." He sounded serious, but Walt wasn't worried. He'd been playing by the rules ever since his last encounter with Abich.

"By the way," Gus added, "thought you might want to know. One of your last patients, that little guy Leary, limped out of Penland's office this morning cursing and looking mighty furious. Seems he won't be going to a hospital after all. I hear he's going back to his infantry unit."

Leary. That troublemaker is probably steamed that I took such good care of him that now he's well enough to go back to the front, Walt thought. I never prayed for that, God, but I'm not complaining.

At the CO's tent, Walt found the major sitting behind a make-shift desk. Even reasonable officers like Penland seemed to love having that barricade between them and the men. The major glanced up. "At ease, Private." He tapped a pencil on the desktop. "I'm sure you know why you're here."

"No, sir."

Penland squinted. Slowly, with thumb and forefinger, he lifted a sheet of paper. Walt recognized his own handwriting. "You know what your problem is, Baran? You're so damn independent you think you can write anything you want. The medical corps may not be as strict as the infantry, but that doesn't mean you can get away with shit like this."

"Major, I wrote that before the order came down. It was already in the mail." Walt worked to keep his voice level.

Penland tore Walt's letter into tiny shreds. "Put litter-bearer on your job description this week, Private."

"How could I obey an order not even issued yet, sir? Where's the justice in that?"

"That'll be all, Private."

Good thing the CO's office is a makeshift tent, Walt thought, as he stomped outside. I'd slam a real door so hard it would take the whole wall down.

***

Within days, a new rumor erupted: The Ninth's next stop would be England for a while. No one knew what would happen after that, but Walt, along with every other war-weary soldier, welcomed the respite.

Penland assembled the company. He looked cheerful, as if he was about to give a pep talk. Gus stood at his side, holding a small box.

"I have good-behavior medals to give out, men. When you hear your name, come forward." The medal itself meant little, except to acknowledge a man was doing his best. Walt didn't need praise, but he wouldn't mind a signal that he was edging closer to a promotion. Despite that darned letter about Kovy, he thought, I've been doing my best and more.

One by one, the major called the names of more than half the company, including Gus, Ted and Big Al. Even Magnus got one.

But not Walt.

Afterwards, Gus patted his shoulder. "You okay?"

Walt shrugged him off. "Why wouldn't I be? Who cares about a pointless medal?" He wasn't completely lying. He wanted nothing to do with a medal that ignored a soldier's good work.

THIRTY-SIX

October 15, 1943

Dear Walt,

In less than two months our boy will celebrate his first birthday. I'm so proud of him. He is a happy, healthy boy, and every day he looks more like you. His face has your strength and intelligence. You two will make quite a pair when you come home...

I felt no guilt bragging like that. In that moment, I was telling the truth. Alek was doing much better.

My letter said nothing about Babcia's herbal treatments or my prayers, of course, or that, back home, I continued to soak our boy in her muddy poultices. I also didn't tell Walt about my mother's latest money-making scheme. Any hint of problems with our baby's health or our finances would do Walt no good.

The first time my mother proposed that we sew aprons, purses and pillowcases from fabric scraps, I thought she was joking. Her girdle business had run out of supplies months earlier, she said, but she'd learned that the factory where she worked was throwing away leftover fabrics. "We can use to make things to sell neighbors!"

I doubted she could find scraps pretty enough. I'd forgotten how resourceful she was.

The satchel she carried home from work two days later was stuffed with material. I wondered how she got it. "Who knew mattress scraps could be so attractive?" I said, smoothing my hand over a piece of soft, patterned damask. "I'm surprised the factory let you take so many pieces."

My mother picked up a large pastel cloth. "They just throw in garbage, Gosia."

I rubbed the damask between my fingers. "Hmm. Even this?"

"Not so much pretty things in stores now," Mom said, ignoring my question. "Neighbors will be happy to have something new and different."

We used our own aprons and cloth purses as patterns. After three hours of sewing by both machine and hand, the dining room table was piled high with our handiwork.

"How much do you think we'll sell these for?" I asked. I pictured Dr. Wenski's face as I handed him an envelope stuffed with cash.

"Oh, good money, Gosia. Very good. Two dollar. Maybe three dollar."

"Two...For each?"

Mom laughed. "Two dollar for eight, silly girl."

I computed it in my head. At best, my share for that night's work would be a dollar fifty, more than minimum wage, but I'd need to work four hundred and fifty hours to earn the $225 I still owed Dr. Wenski, and an unimaginable one thousand, five hundred hours to earn the $750 I owed the hospital. Even working seven days a week, it would take me almost two years to raise those amounts. I laughed aloud. Even more ludicrous was the thought of selling that many aprons, purses, pinafores and pillow covers in our poor little neighborhood.

Mom stared at me. "What so funny?"

"Nothing," I replied, my smile slipping away. "Absolutely nothing."

***

I stared at the sheet of unlined paper before me, my mind just as blank. I tapped my capped pen on the table impatiently, searching for the right words.

Even though he had yet to ship out, Sam Wynock wrote me a dozen times begging me to correspond. I thought if I ignored him, he would stop, but his letters kept coming. He asked about Alek's health and mine, about my finances, my parents, my grandmother and even about Walt. He offered words of encouragement. He asked for my prayers. I ripped up most of his letters, but a few touched me so deeply I tied them in neat packets and hid them in my dressing table beneath Walt's letters.

After two months had passed, I finally relented. I sent a few short, harmless notes a sister might write a brother. That was enough, I told myself. But then I found myself composing longer letters in my head. My obsession felt crazy, until I realized what was causing it: I needed to write about Alek. Sam understood my son's fragile health better than anyone. He didn't speak about Alek in code, the way everyone else did. I could tell Sam the whole truth.

"Gosia? Why you up so late? What you doing?" My mother stood at the kitchen door, her arms crossed. There was no escaping her.

Her questions jolted me. Indeed, what was I doing? Why was I still wasting precious time on Sam Wynock? It wasn't right, spending this much time thinking about a man who was not my husband. I tucked my pen in my pocket and stood. "You're right, Mom. I'll finish this later." Writing Sam was foolish, I told myself. Enough is enough.

***

A week later, as I contemplated what to make for supper, the phone rang.

"Hi, Nora, it's me. Can you talk?"

I lowered the phone receiver, wishing I hadn't answered. Sam's voice called out, "Nora? Nora?"

I lifted the receiver to my ear. "Why are you calling here, Sam? Where are you calling from?"

He spoke in a rush. "I'm getting a pass this weekend to visit my mom again. It might be my last before I'm shipped out. I'd like to see you, too, Nora, if I can. I worry about you and Alek. I want to see for myself you're both okay."

"We're fine, Sam. You don't need to worry. Besides, I have no way to get to Middlesex."

"But if I'm in your neighborhood, maybe I could stop by for a quick visit?"

I wondered what made him ask such a thing. "No, Sam, you can't. I'll be busy with Alek. I'll be busy with my family. This weekend Alek and I are going to see Walt's parents."

"I can plan a visit around your schedule."

I should have hung up right away, but before I knew it, he was asking about Alek and telling me about his mother and his naval station in Illinois. This pass would be his first time back to New Jersey since we'd seen each other in Middlesex, he said. He hoped to see friends. "Some of us plan to play poker in Bloomfield, as a matter of fact."

"I didn't know you played cards."

"Poker is my hobby lately," he said.

I knew little about this adult Sam, the Sam I'd met only recently. Now it turned out he liked poker, a game that perplexed me, even though Walt played it, too. The idea of betting hard-earned money on a card game seemed reckless.

"In fact," Sam said, "a friend of one of the guys I play with is from your hometown, Ziggy—uh, gosh, what's his last name? He might join our game this weekend. Dobranowski! That's it. Ziggy Dobranowski."

"You're kidding, Sam! You going to play cards with Ziggy?"

"You know him?"

"He's Walt's cousin! Of course, I know him." Surely Sam knew that. Everyone in our circle knew Ziggy, the crazy jokester who drove like a maniac, even when he drove me to the hospital to give birth to Alek. "We're close to him."

"Nora, you've never mentioned that guy's name. What a coincidence."

"Quite a coincidence."

"So, when can I see you?"

"You can't. It won't be possible. I have to go. Alek's awake." I hung up before he could disagree.

I lingered at a window overlooking our front door, wishing I had objected more strongly. Might Sam try to see me when I was at my in-laws? What if Ziggy gave him directions there? What if Ziggy said something to my father-in-law about Sam? My mind raced, stopping and starting like a misfiring engine until I spotted my mother on the sidewalk below, putting her keys in the front door. I glanced at the clock. Supper hour! I rushed to the kitchen and pulled out pots and pans, pretending I knew what I was doing.

THIRTY-SEVEN

"Listen to this, Walt! I got an invite. A home-c-c-cooked meal. Wanna come?"

Walt peered over the top of his Sunday *London Times*. In the two weeks the Ninth Infantry had been in England, Hatch's offer was the first thing that truly interested him. "Tell me more, Hatch."

Home cooking. That might ease his pesky restlessness. He'd expected England to cure his bad case of nerves, but it hadn't helped a bit, even though he couldn't have asked for more. Camped only seven miles from Winchester, he was in walking distance to his old infantry outfit. He visited often with Tom and Hatch. No sounds of war shattered his sleep. He didn't have to tear down and set up tents every few days. He slept on clean sheets and a thick mattress in a heated building. He ate hearty meals of fresh meat and vegetables.

Yet every day his hands trembled, his head pounded, his stomach churned.

At first, he blamed his state on the reality of his situation: This stay in England was no vacation. Its sole purpose was to prepare him and his buddies for the next ugly stage of the war. Even though he couldn't imagine anything worse than the turmoil of Africa and Sicily, he steeled himself.

His father's letter a few days earlier hadn't helped: "Business is great, son, but I need more help. I'm thinking of bringing in a well-connected guy who knows how to run things. Your cousin is slowly learning the ropes, but you know Ziggy. He's not someone you can count on."

Walt chewed on the news. Someone who can run things? What did that mean for him? Until now, his father seemed willing to wait for him to come home before taking his funeral business to the next step. Again, Walt pondered the idea of doing something else with his life. He had life-saving skills now. Maybe he could go back to school and get more training.

Perched cross-legged at the foot of Walt's bed, Hatch unfolded his invitation. "You listening, Walt? You act like you're in another w-world."

"Sorry, Hatch. What have you got there?"

"I snagged this at the Red C-Cross Club. Some locals want soldiers to spend a day with them. A whole day." Hatch paused, savoring the thought. "Peace and quiet. No rules. A whole day in a B-British home being catered to by some nice folks."

Walt grinned. Hatch had quickly returned to his old self—beaming, trusting, just a trace of a stammer. He wished he could say the same about himself and Tom, whose mood remained as dark and edgy as Walt's. Tom wasn't interested in visiting British families, Hatch said, or becoming too comfortable in their temporary quarters. "He said we infantry can't afford to get soft. Who knows what's c-coming next?"

Leave it to Tom to stay cautious. Guilt creeped back into Walt's thoughts. His medical company faced no such worries. Horrific, sometimes dangerous duty, yes. Close calls and long hours, absolutely. But no combat, no bullets, no direct danger. Not like Tom and Hatch. He could pamper himself now all he wanted; medics could eat too much and sleep too much and pay no price in the next stage of war.

***

The next afternoon, passes in hand, Walt and Hatch took off on foot to a village two miles away. Thick hedges edged the road, as narrow as some American sidewalks.

Hatch buttoned his jacket all the way up in the chill December air. "I guess the locals invited us to thank us, huh? For helping them out?"

Walt shrugged. He doubted this kind of invitation was common. He'd heard tales about Brits cursing "Yanks" for their unruly habits and for dating British women. As he walked, he ran his palm over a row of dormant rose bushes. He tugged off a leaf and rubbed it between his thumb and forefinger. "I tried to start a flower garden for my mother once. Back when I was a kid. Never had much luck." The leaf slipped from his hand and floated to the ground. Up a slight ridge, a patch of bright yellow flowers bloomed in the shade of an ancient oak tree. The vivid color seemed extravagantly out of place in the chill shadow of war.

Hatch grabbed Walt's arm. "Look there. See that old couple waving? I think that's them. The Westbrooks."

The couple stood surrounded by an explosion of flowers—two clay pots overflowing with bright yellow pansies and another containing wisps of pale pink heather. Walt forced his gaze to the Westbrooks. The woman had tight graying curls and a big toothy smile. Her balding husband cinched his pants below a slight paunch.

"Hullo, lads! Welcome. I'm George Westbrook. This is my wife, Ann."

Walt and Hatch introduced themselves as they all shook hands. Only when George stepped aside did Walt see the petite young blond woman standing behind him. She took a step forward, swiping aside a strand of blond hair, and smiled shyly.

"This is my daughter, Beth." George threw an arm around her, beaming. "She's as good a cook as her mum."

Beth nodded at them. "Mr. Baran. Mr. Hatcher." She blushed as she motioned them to follow her parents inside. A thick haze of boiled mutton and potatoes floated over them as they entered. The aroma made Walt drunk with the memory of his mother's Sunday suppers. He shut his eyes to savor the bliss of it. When he opened them again, he took in the tiny cottage, as snug and homey as a fairy tale. Two plump loveseats framed a wood-burning stove in the parlor. Crowding the space between the parlor and kitchen was an oval walnut dining table, already set with rose-trimmed dishes and cloth napkins.

George motioned to the table, beaming. "It's a pleasure to have you boys join us. Have a seat."

Walt took the chair next to Beth, wondering how old she was. Seventeen? Eighteen? He studied the touch of pink on her cheeks, as fine as a porcelain doll's, while George kept the conversation going with questions about their hometowns, their families and their experiences in the war.

"Okay, lads," Ann interrupted, placing a large steaming bowl on the table. "Supper is served."

As soon as he dipped the ladle into the bowl, Walt realized that the meaty aroma that had greeted them at the door was Ann's artful illusion. The stew had plentiful potatoes, peas and carrots but only enough mutton to season the gravy. He didn't care. Every bite made him moan with pleasure. He used a thick piece of fresh-baked bread to wipe his dish clean. Only when he glanced up did he notice the Westbrooks watching him.

"Oh my," Ann Westbrook whispered, wide-eyed. "I should have made more, shouldn't I have? You poor lads are starving."

Beth giggled. Walt tilted his chair back and placed his hands on his belly, smiling with embarrassment. "Sorry, Mrs. Westbrook. I always eat like this. The guys rib me all the time."

Hatch shoved his last morsel of bread crust into his mouth and mumbled agreement. "He's right about that, m-ma'am."

After dinner, while Beth helped her mother clean the dishes, Walt and Hatch shared a pack of Army-issue cigarettes with George. Walt relaxed more than he had in months, until a familiar pain began to throb at his temples. As they had agreed on earlier, he signaled Hatch by ceremoniously checking his wristwatch. "This has been so enjoyable," he said, rising to his feet, "but the Army awaits. I'm afraid we must get going."

Only when Walt took a step toward the door did Hatch reluctantly stand up. He couldn't take his eyes off Beth. "Mrs. Westbrook, B-beth," he finally said, "you're w-wonderful cooks. We can't thank you folks enough."

Beth caught Walt's eye as she shook Hatch's hand. "You two come back soon, okay?"

On the walk back to camp, Hatch chattered about the meal and the Westbrook's daughter, who, after much coaxing, revealed she had just turned seventeen.

"I'd like to get to know her b-better. I wish I could stay here forever."

"She's a sweetheart for sure, Hatch. Enjoy her company while you can. You know the rumors. It's only a matter of time until we invade France."

Hatch shrugged. "Maybe we'll get lucky. Maybe replacements will let us veterans go home."

A thin blade of hope nudged Walt's gut. Immediately he regretted it. He knew as well as Hatch they were both prisoners of the war.

***

As much as he'd enjoyed the lazy afternoon with the Westbrooks, the visit had little long-term effect on Walt's nerves. His shaky hands and pounding head soon returned with a vengeance.

Even worse, five days had passed without a letter from Nora. He understood delays when his unit was speeding from one battlefield to the next, but England was easy to find. Loneliness gnawed at him. He felt adrift.

On the sixth day, he ignored mail call. "Come on, Walt," Ted said. "You'll get letters from someone back home, even if it's not your wife. You always do."

"Doesn't matter," Walt said. "I'm not a kid. I don't need her letters to survive."

Ted wouldn't let up. He kept prodding until Walt joined him at mail call. To Walt's surprise, his only letter wasn't from a family member. "I am quite impressed by your responsibilities in surgery," Otto Brandt wrote. "Your father is lucky to have such a smart, accomplished son."

Walt never expected the Fayetteville businessman to answer his letters as often as he did. The man's sincere praise felt like medicine.

Days later, a letter from Nora written weeks before finally arrived. The one-page note provided little news. "I hope you understand why I don't write more, darling. Our son keeps me so busy."

He didn't understand. How could she not find five minutes a day simply to say all was well?

A second mail delivery that day brought better news—an invitation from the Westbrooks: "We cannot bear the thought of you boys cooped up in those cold Nissen huts the whole holiday. You must join us for dinner on Christmas Eve day. We will expect you at two o'clock."

Walt wondered if the invitation was prompted by his elaborate description of their Nissen shelters. They weren't much, just a large piece of corrugated metal curved to form an upside-down U and fastened to slabs of concrete. Plywood sheets covered each end, with doors and windows cut into them. Pot-bellied stoves kept them warm. The huts had all the charm of makeshift warehouses, but Walt neglected to tell George they were far warmer and roomier than any pup tent.

"I exaggerated a bit," he told Hatch. "Think that got us this invitation?"

THIRTY-EIGHT

Money was tight when we celebrated Alek's first birthday in early December. He had the sniffles that day, but no fever, thank goodness. Walt telegraphed a hand-drawn picture of a birthday cake with a single candle. I gave him a small stuffed bear and my parents gave him a pale blue, hand-knit sweater.

Then Max and Ruth arrived. "You making sure our grandson sees the doctor when he needs to?" Max said before he even took off his coat.

He had his nerve, I gave him that. We glared at each other in a stand-off until Ruth came to my rescue. "Here's our gift, Nora. Let's sing "Happy Birthday" before we open it." Inside the large, gaily wrapped box was a thick, multicolored wool spread.

"Winters can be miserable," she said. "Our grandson needs to be kept warm and healthy. After everything he's been through, this birthday feels like a miracle."

For me, the miracle that day was Max, who eventually calmed down and behaved himself—as much as he was able.

***

Two weeks later, my Babcia's whole family headed to her house for an early Christmas celebration. Clouds of incense stung my nose and eyes as Babcia flung open her front door. Every Advent, she burned dried spices at all her little shrines. She hugged me and Milly but frowned as she reached for Alek.

"Baby okay?" she said, studying his pale face.

"Yes, Babch. Alek is *bardzo dobrze*. Very good!"

I smiled wide to bolster my story, which was so far from the truth that I followed it with a quick, silent prayer of contrition. Alek was recovering from yet another cold that had kept us both awake for nights.

"*Dobrze,* Gosia," she said softly, her blue eyes flickering like opals in the sun. With her free hand, she nudged us in the direction of the kitchen. Moments later, she was issuing orders.

Babcia was back in charge, the commander of her family.

Not until our parents arrived by train that afternoon and claimed Babcia's attention did Milly and I have time alone. I'd pondered the advice I needed the entire ride there, but I didn't have the nerve to ask for it. I sat on the edge of my cot and bit my lower lip. "So, Milly…"

"So, Margaret…" That was my cousin, always with a wisecrack. She grinned at me until she saw my solemn expression. "Okay, Nor. What's up?"

"I have this dilemma. It involves Sam."

"Oh no! You didn't, did you? Don't tell me! I don't—I don't think I want to know."

"Milly, what are you thinking, for heaven's sake? Let me finish."

I told her my concerns about writing Sam.

She had no doubts at all. "Why in heaven's name are you having second thoughts? Just tell him you're not going to write, and then don't! The last thing you need is Sam Wynock in your life."

I sighed. That wasn't the advice I wanted.

***

Tadeusz set a tall, showy pine tree in the corner of the parlor, a room so small it sat only four people comfortably. He'd chopped it down in the woods the day before. Its top branch grazed the ceiling and its lowest branches bumped against the love seat. Brightly wrapped gifts surrounded it.

As tiny as the room was, Babcia's joy drew the family to it like a magnet. Milly and I sat on the floor with our children in our laps. Alek, still sniffling from his cold, solemnly watched Anna Lee grab at a string of popcorn around the tree. Our mothers settled on the love seat; our fathers brought in two chairs from the kitchen. Tadeusz collapsed in his arm chair and patted his lap for Babcia to join him, but she smiled slyly and crouched near her great-grandchildren.

Her eyes glistened as she opened her presents, especially the one from Milly and me. She knew the effort we made amid war-time shortages to find her three large spools of brightly colored silk thread. Then she handed out her presents—hand-knitted sweaters and gloves, hand-embroidered doilies and aprons, homemade jam and candy, and tobacco for the men.

While the men eagerly lit their pipes, we women took over the kitchen. Babcia turned on her oven for the two chickens she'd plucked, cleaned and seasoned. Then she pulled out her homemade mincemeat pie, butter and cherry jam. My mother and aunt prepared a heaping pot of beets, while Milly and I cooked the potatoes and made a salad.

The meal was so different from how we ate at home. Butter, jams, flour and honey all were becoming harder to find, ration tickets or not. My grandmother eked every morsel of food imaginable from her own farm, satisfied with its bounty and wanting little more.

It's a good way to live, I thought, being content with what you have.

December 22, 1943

Dear Walt,

Alek is such a flirt. I wish you could have seen the looks he gave my grandmother at our family celebration at her house. Somehow, we all fit into place for two nights— all ten of us! Everyone asked about you. I told them how glad I am that you're in England now. My mother and I plan to attend Mass on Christmas morning. In the afternoon, Alek and I will go to your parents' house. I got them small gifts. I hope they don't mind I couldn't afford to splurge...

Back in Elizabeth, a frigid wind rattled my parents' windows. I hugged Alek close as wisps of cold forced their way inside. The winter storm alone didn't make me shiver. Newscasts were predicting a major invasion of Europe soon. Walt could end up in the middle of it.

Walt wouldn't be home soon. That much I knew. As long as the war continued, he would be missing from my life. So would my brother, now training in California to fly fighter planes. My parents' apartment ached from Steve's absence. Without him, the simplest chores became drudgery. Without his banter, my parents grew more sharp-tongued with each other. I wished I could add laughter to their tense exchanges like Steve had.

Now, my mother greeted my father after work like an unwelcome guest. "Husband, you home, huh? You ready to eat?" My father would reply in Polish, "Do I look like I'm ready, woman?" Sometimes, he grabbed a dish towel to wipe oily grime from his hands. His defiant glare dared my mother to object.

On Christmas day, I dressed Alek in the tiny navy-blue sweater and pants Milly's parents gave him, his hair slicked to the side. "Are you my handsome boy?" I cooed.

Max picked us up at noon and drove us to his house in silence, which suited me fine. Ruth served lunch, a hearty beef and vegetable soup. As Max slurped noisily, Alek opened his mouth like a baby bird when I gave him a taste. He swallowed two spoonfuls but pushed away the third. "He's excited to be here, Mom. He's not very hungry," I said. "Doesn't he look good? I knew you'd be pleased."

Max frowned. "What do you hear from my son, Maggie?" His voice dropped low. "And what are you writing him back?" That was Max, pushing for control even when he didn't need it. My annoyance made me say something I quickly regretted: "The hospital called about the bill again, Dad."

"What the hell are you talking about?"

"The bill for Alex's extra care after he was born. I've been paying Doctor Wenski as best I can, but the hospital—well, that bill is huge. They just keep calling."

"You really disappoint me, Maggie, you know that? I thought you were smart. Use your head. You can handle this."

"Handle it?" I said. "But you know I have no—"

"That's enough, Maggie!" he shouted.

I turned to brush away tears of frustration. I should have known better. Max had no intention of giving in. My lack of money didn't matter to him.

When it was time to go, Ruth hugged Alek for a long time and slipped me a five-dollar bill. Max tousled Alek's long locks. "There's a big boy, Dixie. Tell your mommy you're too old for those silly, girly curls."

I sighed at the predictability of my visits. Ruth was kind and generous. Max was always—Max. His games wearied me. The burden of the medical bills exhausted me. If only I could share my fears and frustrations with Walt. If only I hadn't already buried them beneath a mountain of lies.

THIRTY-NINE

Walt woke early the day before Christmas so he could get ready to visit the Westbrooks. Special occasions didn't happen often in the Army. He needed time to shave, shine his boots, press his uniform and wrap his and Hatch's gift. He was ready by ten o'clock, hours earlier than he expected. I'll write Nora, he thought. I bet she'll be surprised by what I'm doing today.

> December 24, 1943
>
> Dear Nora,
>
> Tell me everything about your holidays, precious. Does Alek understand how special this time is? You'll never guess what Hatch and I are doing. A British family invited us to a Christmas Eve dinner. It's a small family, just a husband, wife and daughter. We've been there once before and they've treated us like sons. I'm looking forward to attending Christmas Mass at the cathedral in Winchester but I think God hears our prayers just as well in the field...

The more Walt thought about his last visit with the Westbrooks, the more he looked forward to returning. George and Ann were amiable conversationalists, even if they seemed unaware of the world beyond their village. Beth was sweet, if young and a bit shy. He wondered why Hatch hadn't tried to date her yet, but he knew better than to pester him. His friend hated that kind of attention.

Hatch arrived at noon looking like he, too, had spent the morning preparing. "Looking good, pal," Walt said, trying not to grin.

"Gotta be p-polite," Hatch said, smoothing his hair. "The Westbrooks deserve it."

The two men took a long route through the countryside so they wouldn't arrive too early. A few yards from the Westbrook's front door, the scent of roasted duck, baked potatoes, and something sweet greeted them. Beth opened the door, her eyes bright and a smile playing on her lips. "Gentleman," she said in a mock-formal tone. "We await you."

Walt gaped at the tiny parlor, transformed with evergreens, spice balls and red velvet bows. A small pile of neatly wrapped gifts filled a table in a far corner. The effect was as pretty as a Victorian Christmas card, made all the more impressive by the splendor of the dining table. Ann Westbrook had put out her best china, silverware and goblets atop a fancy maroon damask tablecloth. Each place setting had starched white linen napkins.

Walt handed Beth a package wrapped in newspaper and tied with string. "A small gift for your family," he said.

She grabbed Walt's hand when she opened the parcel. "Bananas! Sugar! Oh, my goodness, Walter. You shouldn't have!"

Hatch stood to the side, frowning. Walt's face grew hot. "Uh, it's from both of us. Hatch and I bought it at the base. We thought you might like it."

Ann grabbed the bunch of bananas from her daughter. "We love it! We can't get fruit like this. It's a luxury, truly." She motioned the men to the table.

George poured warm fermented apple cider into the goblets as if it was fine wine. He wore his Sunday best—a white shirt, woolen vest and matching pants. "A toast, lads, to you and your families, to my little family, and to all the soldiers in this dreadful war, may it end soon, God willing." He stressed the last four words to lift the mood, and everyone shouted "Cheers!" and tapped their goblets.

The cider seared Walt's throat. Better than wine, he thought, taking another gulp. More kick. The alcohol warmed his insides. As George sliced the roasted duck, Walt wondered if it had been plucked from the flock the Westbrooks fed at a nearby pond. Ann's generous ladles of vegetables and her thick slices of bread made him suspect the family had scrimped on food for days to prepare the feast.

Walt studied the delicate way Beth held her fork and knife and nibbled her food in tiny bites. He tried to measure his own mouthfuls, slicing small chunks from the duck leg George put on his plate, but hunger soon conquered his resolve. He picked up the leg and gnawed at the meat, skin and sinew until only clean bone remained.

Glancing up, he noticed Beth trying to hide a smile. He cringed. Grease covered his face and hands. Flecks of meat clung to his chin. Still chewing, he placed the naked bone back on his plate and wiped his face and hands with his napkin. Beth giggled. "I'm so glad you're enjoying it, Walter. My mother and I worked on this meal all morning."

"It's terrific," he mumbled. "Wonderful."

"It sure is!" Hatch shouted loudly, leaning toward Beth. "The food is all—it's—it's delicious. Thank you!"

Hatch's unexpected exuberance silenced the table. "You're very welcome, Francis," Ann Westbrook finally said. She had called Hatch by his full first name ever since they were first introduced.

Hatch dropped his head and stabbed at his meat. Beth filled the silence with chatter about her friends in the village and her part-time job at a local bakery. She hardly resembled the shy girl who'd greeted them on their first visit.

When scarcely a scrap of food was left on the table, Beth stood to collect the dirty plates. Walt leaned back to get her attention. "May I help?"

Her eyes met his. "I'm fine, Walter."

Ann Westbrook pushed back her chair. "You and Francis join Mr. Westbrook by the fire, Walter. Make yourselves comfortable. I'll bring a cuppa."

As Walt and Hatch pulled their dining chairs into the parlor, George Westbrook plopped down hard on the loveseat and unbuttoned his vest with a sigh. "What a meal, huh, lads?"

Although the Westbrooks acted as if they had all they needed, Walt knew that three years of war had left the country short of every imaginable supply and apprehensive about every approaching plane. Yet Christmas Eve bestowed a kind of magic on the cottage. Its decorations and crackling fire emitted a deep calm. The simple comfort of a family going about its routines delivered Walt from the past year of mud, sand and grit, of cold showers, of bloody wounds, of sleeping on hard ground.

He wondered what Nora was doing for Alek that night. He pictured them sitting beside a decorated tree. Lost in thought, he didn't notice Beth standing over him.

"Here, Walter. A cup of hot tea, with lots of milk and honey." She blushed, and Walt wondered if he was blushing, too, although he didn't know why he should. Beth handed a second cup to Hatch and sat next to her father on the loveseat.

"The ladies in the village are planning a dance for next week," she said. "Have you heard about it, gentlemen?"

Walt and Hatch shook their heads.

"Well, it's for the soldiers, you see. A little celebration a few days into the new year. I was wondering...I mean it might be nice, that is, if you both might come." She blushed again. "To the dance, that is."

It was Walt's turn to stammer. "Uh, I-I'm not much of a—"

Hatch nodded eagerly. "That would be swell."

January 2, 1943

Dear Nora,

You may not believe this, dear, but I went to sleep early on New Year's Eve. I had no interest in joining the fellows at a pub when even people who rarely drink would be imbibing. They make the worst drunks. Tonight, there's a dance for the soldiers in town. I'll write you about it tomorrow...

***

The way Beth had begged them to attend the dance, Walt expected few soldiers to attend. The only other tech from his company who said he was coming was Ted, who never missed a chance to flirt with the ladies. The last thing he expected to see that night was the long line of men outside the dance hall, all of them scrubbed clean and shaven close. His mind flashed back to the soldiers lining up for the Countess's brothel in Morocco.

"Walter! Francis! You came!" Beth waved from a table outside the front door where she and two older women sold the men dance cards.

"Didn't we say we would?" Walt said.

"You're going to love the band, and we have lots of home-cooked treats." She slipped one arm under Walt's and the other under Hatch's and guided them past the crowd.

As soon as he stepped inside, Walt froze. Most of the ladies were older than the brothel's Countess—mothers and widows forty years old and up. Beth was the youngest by far. At one end of the long room, a five-piece band of white-haired British men played "Chattanooga Choo Choo" while soldiers twirled their partners around the floor like they were teenagers.

Walt leaned close to Hatch's ear, his voice a loud whisper. "Where do you think all the young gals are?"

Hatch shrugged. "P-probably too shy for us GIs."

"Or maybe their families decided to protect them from us," Walt said.

Beth tugged at his arm. "Dance with me, Walter. I can't stand still with that music playing."

He stepped back. "I'm no good at the jitterbug, Beth. How about one of these other guys? How about Hatch?" He looked around for his friend, who had disappeared without warning. All around him, soldiers not already on the dance floor gawked at Beth expectantly. One—a tall lanky soldier—grabbed her hand.

"That's okay," she called out as the GI pulled her to the dance floor. "I'll find you the next slow dance. Get something to eat."

In seconds she was dipping and turning, a tiny swirl of energy amid the crowd of sturdy matrons. One by one, a line of soldiers cut in to dance with her. Walt wished his dance moves could keep up with her, but he knew his feet wouldn't obey the Lindy Hop.

A table crowded with home-made desserts spoke to the local women's considerable imagination given the wartime shortage of sugar. Among the treats were lightly sweetened cookies the Brits called biscuits, crackers spread with home-made carrot jam and an apple-filled coffee cake.

What Walt craved most was a tall bottle of ale, but that treat was nowhere to be found.

"Cuppa tea, lad?" A sweet-faced older woman held up a ceramic teapot and made slight tipping motions.

Walt winced. "Not now, thanks."

He turned back toward the crowded dance floor. Beth's blond hair surfaced here and there like a whitecap in the sea while the band played one fast tune after the other. His sudden desire to hold her made him squirm. How could this little British girl—shy one minute, a flirty burst of exuberance the next—affect him like this? He told himself he was just missing Nora, but guilt quickly intruded on his excuses. He wondered what his wife would say if she saw him there.

He leaned against the wall, struggling with his Catholic conscience, just as the band did something startling. At the very moment it reached for the highest note of a jitterbug tune, it picked up the first note of "Apple Blossom Time," shifted its beat and rhythm, and settled into a slow waltz.

Of all the songs those British musicians could have picked for their first slow dance, they chose his and Nora's favorite.

"Hey, Walter! Did you forget me?" Beth stood before him, flushed and out of breath. She reached up and ran the fingers of both hands through her damp hair. "This is our dance. Remember?"

Energy glowed from her. Obediently, he led her onto the dance floor. Even though his right hand rested only lightly against the small of her back, he felt her hot skin radiate through her blouse.

As they settled into a slow shuffle, a crush of couples pressed against them. Beth settled into his arms, resting her head against his chest. Their closeness sent a thrill through Walt's body. His only defense was to sing to himself the words he and Nora sang to each other the day they were married: *I'll be with you in apple blossom time. I'll be with you to change your name to mine.*

Beth smiled up at him. "You're doing great, Walt. Why did you say you couldn't dance?"

"Uh, because I can't. You're kind, but you know I'm telling the truth."

Rocking from foot to foot, he steered her to the edge of the crowd. That was how his insides felt—on edge. He felt ready to explode, but he couldn't tell if it was with desire or uneasiness. In that moment, he didn't belong anywhere. Not on the dance floor. Not with Beth. Not in the war.

As soon as the song ended, he excused himself and headed for a door. Glancing behind him, to his relief, he saw a soldier grab Beth for the next dance.

Outside, he ducked behind a cluster of bushes and hastily lit a cigarette. Taking deep drags, he wondered what he had been thinking. Slow dancing with that girl was asking for trouble.

"Hey, Walt! Glad I found ya." Ted jogged up, his hand patting a deep pocket in his jacket. "Did you check out the broads inside? Pretty depressing, huh?"

Walt faked a smile.

"Well, I have just the remedy," Ted said. He reached in his pocket and pulled out a pint of whiskey. "Just what the doctor ordered."

Ted took a swig and handed the bottle to Walt. For the next ten minutes, they passed the whiskey back and forth, taking occasional puffs of cigarettes, until the bottle was drained. Walt's edginess began to ease.

Ted headed for the door. "Let's go back in, buddy. Time to face the music."

Walt lingered in the garden's shadows, relishing the alcohol's gentle buzz. "I'll catch up in a minute."

Ted was gone barely a minute when Walt saw her. She walked up slowly, framed by the light behind her.

"So, here's where you've been hiding," Beth said. "It's enough to make a girl think you're avoiding her." She moved close to him and smiled in that surprising way of hers, shyly and then boldly.

Unsure of what to say, he took her outstretched hand. Beth was a mystery. Maybe he had it wrong, he thought. This was no demure country girl.

"You are a funny one, Walter," she said, lifting herself up on tiptoe. She wrapped one hand around his neck, pulled him closer and kissed him softly on the mouth.

Her whisper of a kiss sent shudders through his body. He wanted to push her away but could not move.

She stared determinedly into his eyes. "Don't be so shy, Walt. I know you like me at least as much as I like you."

He groaned softly. If he had one wish that moment, he would split himself in two—one man to kiss her back, the other to do the right thing and walk away. When he finally spoke, his voice was hoarse. "What are you doing, Beth? You know I'm married. I have a child. Why aren't you chasing Hatch?"

"I don't *like* Hatch," she said, her lips forming an enticing pout. Her one hand still clung to his neck; the other patted the front of his Army jacket. She refused to relinquish her hold on him, and he dared not touch her even to offer resistance. In that moment of opportunity, she rested a cheek on his chest and murmured softly. "I want to be with you, Walter. Let's just enjoy our time together, shall we?"

He breathed slowly to steady himself but instead drank deeply of her scent, a whiff of spring with traces of honeysuckle and new mown grass.

She raised herself on her toes again and pressed her lips to his. He pulled her close and kissed her long and deep, her tiny frame a wisp in his arms.

From the doorway, a familiar tenor voice pierced the night air. "Walt! You out here, Walt?"

"Damn!" Walt muttered, pushing Beth away. In a split second she was out of his arms and wiping her smeared lipstick with a hanky.

"Hey! Is that you, buddy?" Hatch called out.

Walt rubbed his face with the back of his hand. "Over here, Hatcher. We were just finishing our cigarettes."

"There you are. Jeez, I was looking—Oh, hi, Beth. I didn't know you were here, too." His eyes surveyed the scene until a glimmer of realization seemed to hit him. "Well, uh, when you two are ready, you and I b-better get going, Walt. It's getting late."

"Yeah, sure. I'm ready now," Walt mumbled. But Hatch had already turned away. Walt nodded awkwardly at Beth before hurrying to catch up with him.

The two men walked in silence until they reached the point where their paths separated. "See ya, Hatch," Walt called out. Hatch waved a hand without looking back.

***

Walt couldn't sleep that night. Shame, lust and guilt claimed pieces of his soul. He couldn't stop thinking of holding Beth, of kissing her. He couldn't forget his promises to his wife.

Nora. The thought of her settled him for a moment. Beneath his wife's quiet demeanor was a steely determination, a strength of character. She had that way of looking at him, clear and hopeful. It reinvented him. He missed her faith in him.

Then the memory of that night returned. What if Hatch hadn't shown up? What might have happened? He pulled his pillow over his face with a low moan, cursing his weakness. "I'll make it up to you, Nora. Trust me."

FORTY

"Thanks so much for this, Ziggy."

"Are you kidding, Nora? You're a Baran. Any time you need a ride, just ask!"

I held on tightly to Alek as Ziggy slammed his brakes, veered and cut off a truck. "Goddam drivers! Sorry, Nor. Hope I'm not a bad influence on the kid."

"Don't worry. Alek won't squeal on you." Squealing was on my mind that morning. I hoped it wasn't on Ziggy's.

I'd asked Walt's crazy cousin for a ride to the doctor's as soon as I scheduled Alek's check-up. The ride had one purpose: To make sure he didn't think Sam and I were more than casual friends.

"Watch out, buddy," he hollered at a bus. He leaned on his horn as he weaved to pass it.

When he wasn't screaming at other drivers, Ziggy hardly made a sound. I tried a few times to start a conversation, but he muttered only one-word answers. Finally, I couldn't stand it any longer.

"Hey, Zig, I hear you played cards with Sam Wynock. That's such a coincidence."

He glanced at me, eyebrow raised. "Yeah, I only just met him at a game. He said he knew you. Sure is a coincidence."

"We don't know each other very well. We were friends when we were kids."

Suddenly, Ziggy wanted to talk. "Yeah? He told me you guys got together in Middlesex a few months ago."

I forced a smile to hide my fear. "More like a chance meeting. My cousin and I ran into him at the river. Completely unexpected."

"I think he's sweet on you, Nora. He couldn't stop talking about you and Alek."

"You're kidding!" This was worse than I feared. Was Sam imagining something that never happened? "That's just leftover kid stuff, Zig. You know how childhood crushes are."

"Me? Nah. I never cared about girls when I was little."

"I guess I was like that with boys when I was young, even with Walt." I smiled, trying to coax him to my point of view. "Then Walt and I got together at his folks' house when we were teenagers. You know the rest of the story."

"A real romance, you and Walt. You guys are lucky."

"We are." I paused. "I miss him a lot."

Ziggy seemed distracted by traffic, but after he pulled up to the doctor's office, he looked at me intently. "So how *is* Sam? Have you heard from him?"

"No," I said, acting surprised. "Not since Middlesex. Have you?"

"Not since we played cards."

"Well, I'm sure he's fine. Maybe he'll end up staying in the States. I feel so lucky that Walt made it into the Medical Corps."

Quickly the conversation shifted—to Walt's job as a medic, his recent letters from England, and the news reports about a possible invasion. It was the most Ziggy had talked all morning.

Maybe my strategy had worked.

***

For the first time, I could write Walt the truth about his doctor visit. Alek was doing well. No new health problems bedeviled him. No fevers. No wheezing. But who knew how long that would stay the truth?

The mail's slow pace drove me mad. If I asked Walt a question in February, I might not receive his reply until April. A white lie told in March could grow into a bold-faced one by June.

At least this one letter would be true, I told myself. Of course, I omitted the fact that Alek remained at the bottom percentile of height and weight. My excuse was that his size might be completely different by the time Walt saw the letter. But other things were left unsaid, too, like how much I owed Dr. Wenksi, who looked as if he was sucking a lemon when he renewed his demands for payments. "Mrs. Baran," he said, making a show of clearing his throat, "the next time you come, it's important you bring the money you owe. We want to keep your son as a patient."

His threat terrified me. All I could do was keep showing my good faith with regular payments in nickels and dimes until Walt came home. Anything to convince Wenski to keep treating my son. But Walt didn't need to know any of that. My money trouble was my business for now.

***

Two more weeks passed without a word from Walt, but two letters came from Sam. He wrote like a casual friend. He didn't mention Ziggy and nothing suggested he misunderstood our relationship. Ziggy's belief that Sam was "sweet" on me must have been his wild imagination.

I wrote Sam a brief reply. My tone mirrored his—a bit distant. But then I sent another letter. I couldn't help myself. This time I held nothing back; the burden of my lies and secrets was growing too heavy. "I worry about Alek," I wrote. "He's still so small. The doctor says he's healthy enough, but you should see him. I'd tell Walt, but that's the last news he needs. Plus, I owe hundreds of dollars in medical bills! Can you imagine? I have no idea where I'll get that kind of money. Walt's father still is no help and he's the one who ordered that care…"

Not until ten o'clock that night did I pull out another piece of stationery. Alek and my parents were asleep. The silence inspired me.

> March 25, 1944
>
> Dearest Walt,
>
> I wish you knew how much I miss you. It's wrong for the Army to keep a husband and wife away from each other this long. Almost two years! Your son misses you, too. I think he already knows you because I talk about you all the time, as if you'll walk in the door any moment. And when you finally do, Walt, I'll hold you so tightly you will hardly be able to breathe. I'll never let you go. It's late, my darling, and I don't have time to write more now. I just wanted you to know how much I want you with me…

FORTY-ONE

Hatch studied his playing cards, his poker face a powerful asset. It hid all manner of emotions. Walt was convinced his friend saw more than he let on the night of the dance, but Hatch still acted like nothing had happened. Walt saw through it. He missed Hatch's trusting, easygoing ways.

"Wanna get a pass to go into Winchester? Grab a drink at a pub?" Walt asked after the game.

"Nah, I'm beat. I'm gonna t-turn in," Hatch said without a trace of anger or resentment.

Walt patted his friend's back. "Sure, buddy. No big deal. See you soon."

Back at his clearing company, Walt found Big Al whittling a woman's face out of a piece of wood. "Nice work, Al, but wouldn't you rather be in town downing a few ales?"

Al looked up. "You are a smart man, Baran."

***

Walt's head throbbed, this time not from nerves. He lost track of the number of ales he and Big Al downed the night before. A series of shouts interrupted his sleep. "The Commanding Officer has news," Gus was yelling. "Everybody up! Attendance is mandatory."

Walt struggled to his feet. He'd been doing his best to stay on good behavior. Dressing quickly, he soaked his hair to tame his wild curls. He fell in line just as Penland began his address.

"First," the Major said, "I want to tell you men how proud I am of your hard work and attention to detail while we've been in England."

Right, Walt thought. We've been stuck here in limbo for weeks, doing nothing but marking time.

"We soon will be entering a new phase of training," the major said. "It'll be tough, but we have to be ready for what's coming next. Now I want to recognize those who have done exemplary work and shown valuable leadership."

***

Jan. 15, 1944

My darling Nora,

I have a little news that affects me. It's not very good news, I warn you. Recently a whole flock of promotions were handed out in our company. Just about every fellow and his brother got one but me. Not so long ago I was the fair-haired boy in charge of surgery. Now it looks like this private will be stuck cleaning bed pans...

Once again, his superiors passed over him. He didn't tell Nora the details. She knew him well enough to suspect the truth anyway.

Back in Sicily, he'd blamed his troubles with his superiors on letters that innocently mentioned forbidden topics, like a location or destination or someone's death. This time he knew there was more. His recent letters home griped about everything. Censors surely saw that bad attitude, yet he couldn't stop himself. Even worse, he couldn't keep his mouth shut when a superior was wrong, like when Abich made him pack up equipment that might be needed again that night.

His father encouraged verbal battles. Max didn't respect men who couldn't stick up for themselves. But even in the notoriously lenient Medical Corps, being headstrong invited trouble.

He was determined to change, he told Tom later. "I'm going to mend my ways. I have to. My pride could cost Nora money she needs for her and the baby."

Tom couldn't hide his amusement. "You always say that, Walt. But as long as I've known you, you've never changed."

"Pay attention, friend. You're about to see a new man."

Tom's grin grew wider.

***

George and Ann Westbrook again invited Walt and Hatch to supper. Walt said he was coming down with a cold. Hatch said he had a training exercise. Without consulting each other, the two men begged off two more invitations. Finally, the Westbrooks stopped calling.

Walt hardly thought about Beth any more, except on lonely nights when the memory of her kisses snuck into his thoughts. Staying away from the Westbrooks was essential, he told himself, and so was writing more letters to his beautiful Nora.

His ward duties dwindled to routine tasks he could finished in a few hours. To escape boredom, he walked to Winchester often to drink ale at quiet pubs or go to the cinema. Sometimes Ted joined him, sometimes Tom or Hatch did. Most of the time he went alone.

Not until late January did Walt get a clue of what lie ahead. A surprise speaker addressed the Ninth Infantry. British General Bernard Montgomery, a wiry, soft-spoken man, quickly got to the point: The Ninth Infantry would soon take part in a major invasion.

"Looks official," Tom said when he caught up with Walt. "We'll be fighting the Jerries on the continent soon."

"But where? When?" Walt's hands shook as he lit a cigarette.

Tom frowned. "You okay?"

"It's nothing. Been feeling this way for a while, actually. Jittery. The way I was in Sicily. It's been going on so long I'm kind of used to it." His match finally took. "Remember when we were in the barracks back at Bragg, Tom? The both of us slept like babies. I remember waking up and seeing you the next bunk over, not moving a muscle. You getting any sleep now?"

"Sometimes."

"Yeah. Me, too."

***

The Ninth Infantry quickly ramped up preparations for the war's next phase. Medics like Walt learned new wound-care techniques and medicines. They also trained as hard as infantrymen. Walt marched miles every day, set up bulky tents and took them down, packed and unpacked gear, polished and sterilized equipment.

On his own, Walt practiced other skills, too, such as sharply saluting officers and saying "Yes, sir" and "No, sir," even to Captain Abich and the few other doctors who sometimes lacked common sense.

If he kept it up, he told himself, he'd soon win a promotion.

In late March, General Dwight D. Eisenhower, General Omar Bradley and British Prime Minister Winston Churchill himself came to review the Ninth's preparedness. Walt no longer needed an invasion date. Clearly, it could be any day. The Ninth would play an important role.

But word to move out didn't come until May. The men packed up quickly and moved in a convoy to southern England's coastline, where they set up camp and waited. And waited. Like most of the men, Walt passed his days playing baseball and cards. But each night, he slept little. He worried about new dangers ahead and cursed the incessant chants of gray, yellow-eyed cuckoos nesting nearby. Their hollow calls repeated like a clock gone amok, alerting everyone in earshot to each minute of each hour.

FORTY-TWO

In an imagined letter I never wrote or mailed, I demanded to know why Walt could not control his temper, why he could not follow simple Army rules for even a few months, why he could not put his wife and son first. I wanted to tell him I stayed up late every night sewing scraps of cloth to pay off Alek's doctor, and that a childhood friend was showing more concern for my welfare than he was. Then I wrote this:

> March 10, 1944
>
> Dear Walt,
>
> Your letter came today about the latest promotions. I know you're upset, but so am I. Not because a promotion would bring us more money, though that would certainly help. I worry more about added danger you might face as a private. Alek and I want you home, Walt. We need you home...

For the first time since those scary months after Alek was born, I begged God for help. Memorized prayers weren't good enough. I didn't kneel, though. God surely understood I wasn't ready to be that submissive. Instead, I sat at my vanity table and let my emotions speak as they had in my imagined letter to Walt: angrily adrift and betrayed. "I'm doing the best I can, God, and it still isn't enough. Where are you when I need you? When will my husband come home?"

***

Days were just starting to turn warmer in late April when Ruth phoned with an invitation. "Max and I would love for you and Alek to join us at Bay View in May. We're going to open up our bungalow for the summer."

To my surprise, I was glad to accept. The trip would do nothing to ease my financial worries, and I might have to spend far too much time with Max. But it offered a respite—a week away from the city, from my parents, from making aprons and purses.

The first thing Max did when we arrived at the two-bedroom bungalow was announce he had to do an "errand" that couldn't wait. The first thing Ruth and I did was raise every shade and open every window. Salty, sun-drenched breezes skimmed across Barnegat Bay and poured inside. A hundred yards from the front door, where Toms River entered the bay, tannic-stained water lapped a narrow stretch of sandy beach.

With Max gone for hours, the house was blissfully quiet. Alek napped, as did Ruth. The balmy air and sea breeze had a tranquilizing effect; I stretched out on a sofa and dozed. I awoke to the soft murmur of Ruth's voice in her bedroom.

"I know. I love the place, too," she said, "but it was Dolores who found it...No, no, he'd *never* admit it, Mable. My husband passes himself off as some sort of genius, but his *a-ssis-tant*, Dolores, is the brains of his businesses."

I'd never heard Ruth speak that way before. Sassy. A bit impudent. Did Max know Ruth talked to her friends about him behind his back? In front of him, she was a mouse. To me, she always sang his praises. "He's a good husband, you'd better believe it," she told me just the day before. "Knew exactly what I liked when he bought our place in Bay View."

Her friend must have been asking lots of questions. "Sure, the place is plenty sturdy," Ruth said. "Max made sure it was." She started giggling, a girlish sound I'd never heard from her before. "Shored up the walls with packing crates. Not him, personally, of course. Had to hire someone. Max never met a tool that made sense to him."

I cupped a hand over my mouth to hide my own laughter. The image of Max hiring someone to do the job was as believable as it was hilarious. But as Ruth continued to mock her husband, my mood shifted. This was serious. Everything I thought I knew about my in-laws' marriage was in question. Ruth had more control in their relationship than I knew, but to keep it, she played a game of compliance. She lived a lie.

My parents danced different steps to a different set of lies. My mother quarreled openly with my father about his attempts to play boss and restrict her weekly allowance. But when he ignored her pleas for more money and kept his own spending secret, she found odd jobs behind his back and hid her savings. She used her secret stash to buy costlier cuts of meat for us, toys for Alek and new clothes and jewelry for herself.

The secrets I kept from Walt seemed innocuous by comparison. The shaded truths I wrote him were for his own good. They would cease when he came home. I could never live the way Ruth and my mother did. Never.

June 1, 1944

Dear Walt,

Alek and I returned from the shore yesterday. My week there was delightful. Your mother and I went down to the pier with Alek in his stroller. A number of people already were on the beach sunning themselves and wading in cool water. Your mom was in a good mood, but just like me, she worries about you. We pray you are safe...

***

I had just tucked Alek in for a nap when the phone rang.

"Hi, Nora. It's me."

I stared at the receiver in disbelief. Why was Sam calling me long-distance? I limited my letters to him now, even though he wrote regularly.

"Nora? Are you there?" The phone line crackled and faded before becoming strong again.

"What is it, Sam?"

"Please, Nora. I need a favor. I'm shipping out soon, I'm sure of it."

"Sam, I have to g—"

"I'm just asking for a few more letters from you, whenever you can," He took a deep breath. "Look, I don't know what's coming next. I don't have anyone else. Only my mom."

His need touched me. Just as before, a wave of connection pulsed between us. "Sam, you know you'll always be my friend. I will try to write. But you mustn't call again. Promise me."

His voice dropped to a whisper. "I promise."

***

Sam's next letter arrived a week later, on the last day of June. He made no mention of his phone call. "I want to thank you for your letters, Nora. Believe me, I know how truly busy you are with Alek and how difficult it is to find the time. You are a dutiful mother, so of course you worry about your son. Your caring will surely make a difference in his life. I could see how much he loved you when we met up in Middlesex..."

He encouraged me to stand up for myself. "Don't be afraid of that doctor, or of Max. Tell them the truth, Nora. The truth always works."

I tucked his letter in the bottom of my drawer with his others. His simple advice possessed a dreadful power. Truth could change everything, but not always for the good.

FORTY-THREE

Sloppy, anxious waves slapped the Higgins landing craft carrying Walt and thirty-five others in his medical team. He double-checked the pouches strapped to his belt that carried medical supplies he needed to keep safe. Most of all, he worried about the damage sea water might do to his most valuable possession—a leather packet filled with photos of Nora and Alek.

Debris bobbed in the water all around them. The chaotic sea matched his nervous insides. For as far back as he could see in the English Channel, hundreds of ships of every size and shape were coming and going, delivering essential goods to the GIs already ashore. Ahead of him, jeeps, trucks, and mounds of supplies and discarded gear crowded the sandy, yellow beach. Meanwhile, American warships and destroyers anchored in deep water blasted bombs at distant German targets further inland.

Walt's company had crossed the Channel that night in a cramped transport ship that made sleep impossible. At dawn, they scrambled down a cargo net into the plywood Higgins boat, which seemed a risky bet. To Walt, the small craft appeared as seaworthy as the rowboat he once fished from in Barnegat Bay.

He steadied himself in anticipation of hitting the beach, but instead the boat jammed into a sandbar fifty yards out. Its ramp clanked down into churning foam.

"Move it!" his staff sergeant yelled. The men rushed single file into waist-deep water. Walt unclipped the packet of photos and held it high. Seven months in England had put flesh on his bones and restored muscles to his legs and arms. He was hungry and tired that morning, and his spirits were tattered and restless, but his body felt whole again. He pushed forward.

Midway to dry land, something bumped against his hip. Glancing around, he spotted a GI's knapsack—debris he felt obligated to rescue. A soldier could be looking for it, he thought. He grabbed a strap with his free hand and tugged hard at unexpected weight. Pulling hard, he tried to free the sack from whatever had it trapped. Beneath the dark surface of the water, something large and shapeless bobbed against the knapsack. "What the...?" he gasped.

A soldier's bloated body slowly floated to the surface. For a split second, Walt's stomach heaved; he almost released his grip. But by instinct, he held on and charged forward. He couldn't save this boy, but at least he could make sure he received a proper burial.

By the time he reached dry ground, Walt was soaked to his chest. He stuffed his photos into his backpack and dropped it on the sand. Using both arms, he dragged the body up the beach to higher ground.

Two litter-bearers rushed over. "Whoa! Where did this one come from?" one asked. They hoisted the corpse onto the litter and took it away—Walt didn't know where.

Gus approached him, shaking his head. "That one's a mystery. Fighting here ended days ago, and this stretch of beach didn't see the worst of it. Maybe he drowned in an earlier landing or got caught up in the barricades the Jerries planted out there."

"Doesn't matter," Walt said. He meant it. To him, the stone-gray body was a hand reaching from the grave, a grisly reminder of the relentless wheel of death that had become part of his life overseas. Not the death of funeral parlors, sanitized and bloodless, with well-dressed, rouged and powdered corpses, stoic prayers and mothers, brothers, fathers and sisters weeping softly into monogrammed handkerchiefs. Here, death wore dirty, torn clothes, its face frozen in contorted pain, limbs torn from sockets, entrails spilling from gashed stomachs, and no one, no one, to grieve properly. No family. No church services. No flower-car processions.

"Move along, Private!" Medics swarmed past him. Gus was gone. Exhausted and famished, his socks and boots soaked through, Walt paused briefly to pray.

For the first time he heard the din all around him, not snipers or machine-gun fire, but the grind of trucks, the crash of waves and soldiers and officers shouting and rushing along the beach. In the distance, bombs crushed earth and forest and brick and flesh. Our bombs, he wondered? Theirs? It made no difference; death itself was too selfish to care. Hungry and exhausted, he clawed up a sandy bank to join his platoon.

For eleven miles they marched with full packs down narrow, dusty, twisting roads. Walt had no way of seeing what was ahead; tall hedgerows lining each farm field blocked their view. Walt had seen smaller, tidier versions of the hedges in England—waist-high earthen banks, matted with roots, from which grew tangled masses of thorny bushes, vines, trees and weeds. These hedgerows reached as high as twenty feet. They seemed to offer safety, until he heard rumors that German snipers used them for cover. They hid in the hedgerows' tangles or in trenches dug beneath them.

Walt eyed the thick green walls as he marched, searching for the glint of a rifle. His wet socks rubbed his ankles like scouring pads until blisters erupted. All the men seemed just as nervous and uncomfortable, but their pace never slackened. A few miles ahead were the fighting men of the Ninth Infantry, including Tom and Hatch. Walt was convinced they had survived the landing. He vowed to do what he could to lengthen their lucky streak.

The medics hurried northwest over rolling hills. In a clearing a few miles behind the front, they set up their six large tents and a dozen smaller ones. Walt was tightening the canvas on a ward tent when Hunter, a captain now, found him. "Get over to the surgery tent, Baran. I need you to set up for wounded."

Walt's easy relationship with Hunter let him say what he was thinking. "Surgery? I thought I only work ward duty now. No promotion, remember?"

The doctor's raised eyebrow revealed his exasperation. "Don't you get anything, Walt? You think the Army is going to waste an experienced surgical tech on ward duty, no matter what his rank? Just behave yourself, okay?"

"Yes *sir*, Captain!" Walt said, saluting sharply.

Hunter shook his head. "Amazing. Even your salutes are sarcastic, you know that?"

Walt swallowed a smile. "I'll get surgery running right away. Sir."

***

June 12, 1944

Dear Nora,

I'm somewhere in France now. You know how strict censorship is. I can't tell you more. To be perfectly honest, you probably know a lot more than I do. That's the odd thing about soldiering. We can see only what our eyes show us. We get a bigger picture from our radios only now and then. Back home, meanwhile, you pick up a newspaper and have the whole story 3,000 miles away. There's no need to feel any concern for me, dear. I'm an old hand at this game...

The wounded became his compass, the only true north he needed. They poured into surgery from the front. Ironically, here on the Cherbourg

Peninsula, half of his patients were enemy soldiers—not the elite Germans fighters Walt had seen in Africa, but young teenagers, some boys barely fourteen years old, as well as Poles, Czechs, Russians and other nationalities. All said they'd been forced into service by threats to their families.

Walt believed them. He'd heard stories of conscripted soldiers bolting toward armed Americans while their German officers shot at their backs. He could only imagine how desperate a man had to be to risk death from two directions.

***

His memories of England dimmed in the days that followed. The hot meals and thick mattresses, the Westbrooks, pretty young Beth, the pubs, the nights in town. He remembered it all vaguely, like a dream that faded each moment he was awake.

Returning to surgery felt like breathing again. He knew which instruments, medications and bandages the doctors needed before they asked. He adjusted tourniquets, administered plasma and sulfa drugs and gave morphine and tetanus shots. He tended wounds and aided soldiers slipping into shock.

His hands were steady and certain. They shook only at night, and then no more than the rest of his body, which he suspected trembled even in his sleep, as it had in Sicily. He'd grown so accustomed to the shaking that it felt like his body's normal function.

For a time, Normandy's smoky chaos seemed no different from what he'd seen in Africa and Sicily. The racket of artillery guns, air raid signals, and strafing enemy planes still sent everyone diving for foxholes. But in past battles, every detail captured Walt's attention; now, all he saw was sweeping, bloody waves of wounded.

June 19, 1944

Dear Nora,

Two letters you sent in early May just arrived. I'm limited to writing quick notes right now. We're forbidden to give any news at all in them. You might try reading the New York Journal-American. Its correspondent writes about our progress. I'm back working in surgery at the jobs I love best. No one has time for such niceties as bathing, shaving and changing clothes. I look crummy but feel fine...

Walt wished he could tell her why he had so little time to write. As the

Ninth Infantry Division chased the Germans along the spine of the Cherbourg Peninsula, the medics had to race at a back-breaking pace to keep up. They tore down tents and set them up again, over and over, sometimes every twenty-four hours.

Casualties were so numerous that an adjacent field hospital filled to overflowing. Walt's company again had to handle serious injuries and complicated surgeries. One afternoon, litter bearers carried in a soldier with muddy curly hair, pleading brown eyes and a gaping bloody hole where his nose and mouth had once been.

The soldier's distant gaze brought back a memory from Walt's childhood, when he was barely nine years old. Someone banged on his parents' front door: "Hurry! There's been an accident." His father grabbed his hand and pulled him down the street to a crowd gathered around a crushed sedan. He and his father and two other men pulled open the mangled car door. When his Uncle Joseph tumbled out, his uncle seemed to stare at him without seeing him at all. As life left him, his uncle peered intensely at something else, somewhere else.

Walt had seen that look in Africa and Sicily when soldiers passed on. "Pass" was the right word, for they seemed to leave life slowly, as if they were moving through to another destination. He shivered at his memory of the second time he saw that look. Walt was trying to stop Cliff's bleeding the night of the accident. He kept calling Cliff's name, but his brother just stared past him.

Was it God his brother saw, or some hellish place unknown to man?

Walt turned from the man with the hole in his face and pleaded with God as he tried to understand Him that moment, a distant Power, all-knowing yet unmoved: "Lord, shield me from those eyes." His next words were like a sigh of pain. "Dear God, please hear me, I cannot bear to see that look again."

***

Five days later, just before dawn, Walt finished his shift and staggered into a foxhole, his bed of choice when artillery fire was nearby. Within seconds he collapsed into a dreamless state more like unconsciousness than slumber. When he awoke hours later, the artillery's massive guns were silent. An acrid haze lingered. In the distance, a bird trilled, a sound reminiscent of normalcy.

He found Big Al and Ted at the mess truck. Al sat on the ground, shoveling soggy crackers into his mouth. Exhaustion dampened Ted's usual exuberance.

"Hey, Baran," Al said. "Didja see that last batch of wounded that came in last night?"

"Nah, I fell asleep soon as my shift ended." Walt stretched and yawned deeply before sitting down. He bent forward and rubbed his hair with both hands until his matted curls pulled away from his scalp.

"I think you knew one of those guys," Al said. He pushed another handful of crackers into his mouth. A spray of crumbs showered his lap.

Walt looked up. "Who?"

"Can't remember the guy's name. Some officer from G Company said a sniper shot the guy while he was on guard duty. One bullet did it. Harrington? Hathaway? Little guy. Didn't last long."

Ted jerked his head toward Walt, his voice low. "Oh, God."

Walt tried to pull in a deep breath, but the air clung damp in his throat. "Hatcher."

"Yeah, yeah. That's the guy. Francis Hatcher. You knew him, didn't ya?"

"Hatch," Walt said evenly.

"Jeez," Ted whispered. "I'm sorry, Walt. I didn't know your buddy came in."

Walt unfolded his limbs, so heavy and stiff they felt detached from his body. He slowly stood and walked to the tent where bodies awaited burial in the French countryside, in soil better suited to growing grapes than hiding death. Like every other medical tent in Company D, the morgue was topped with a huge red cross within a white circle, the same symbol medics wore in miniature on their sleeves and helmets. The crosses conveyed this message: Don't shoot us. Don't bomb us. We aren't trying to kill you. We're here to save lives.

No one questioned putting that symbol atop a tent filled with the dead, or the mystery of why this tent, more than any in the war, had survived countless reckless shellings from enemies and allies alike. Shrapnel and bullets sometimes ripped through other medical tents and even some medics' flesh, but the morgue remained unscathed.

Walt pulled back the tent flap. Gauze covered the face of every corpse. Moving from one stretcher to the next, he checked the tags pinned to each chest. Eight bodies and no one named Hatcher. He visited each stretcher a second time, peeling back the gauze to look at faces. Some faces bore horrid wounds. Some looked as if they were resting. Still others reflected the pain of their last moments. No one even remotely resembled his cheery, boyish, open-hearted friend.

Walt ran to find Gus. He sat at his portable desk with a pen and a pile of papers—a stack that never diminished in size no matter where Company D was or what it was enduring.

"Where is he, Gus?"

Walt knew the company clerk understood his question. Gus knew everything going on in Company D.

"They took him away already, Walt. Too many died last night."

"Dammit. Goddammit." Walt pinched the bridge of his nose and turned aside so Gus could not see his face.

"I'm sorry, Walt. I know you two were close."

Walt snorted. He took a slow, deep breath. "I should have been there when he came in. I could have—" His voice caught. "I might have saved him."

Gus stood and put a hand on Walt's shoulder. "Don't, Walt. The sniper's bullet did its job too well. Nothing anyone could have done."

"*You* don't." Walt pushed away Gus's hand. "Don't tell me what I couldn't have done. I was sleeping when one of my best friends was dying."

Without plan or purpose, he walked north from camp, away from any combat. He needed to be alone. He didn't care who might look for him. His eyes burned. His throat filled with thick phlegm, but tears made no headway.

Three miles from camp, he climbed to the top of a ridge. All he could do was gape. The English Channel glimmered in the distance. "We've only come this far?" he shouted at the horizon. "So much goddamn loss for this?"

FORTY-FOUR

I wasn't sure Sam was right to trust truth. In my house, truth was taking a beating lately. Not just from me in my letters to Walt, but from both my parents. Pained by my brother's absence, they rarely spoke about Steve. They never expressed their fear.

Milly was no better. Her relentless good moods exhausted me. Whenever I tried to talk to her, her forced smiles never reached her eyes. "You worry too much, Nor. It'll all work out. You'll see."

Sometimes I considered revealing my lies to a priest, but that option lacked common sense. What would a priest know about babies and doctor bills and the secrets I kept from my husband? I wasn't sure I trusted those frocked men, even in the hushed darkness of a confessional.

My lies to Walt included our son's fragile health and my rekindled friendship with Sam. Sharing even a shred of those truths seemed cruel right now. How would knowing them help Walt? Eventually, he'd need to hear those things from me, but face to face, in private.

Sam was the only person from whom I kept no secrets. It wasn't right, this taut lifeline that had sprung up between us. It seemed unfaithful to Walt, even though it was far from romantic. There was much I still didn't know about Sam. What I did know was that I absolutely trusted him.

***

July's stifling heat put everyone even more on edge. The putrid odor from nearby oil refineries clung to everything we breathed and smelled and tasted. My mother came to dinner one night possessed by a special fury. "I see fat letter you send nephew, husband. You send money to Poland again, eh?" she said, chopping the air with her hand like a weapon. "We live on pennies, but you family cries for money and you give? You think Germans let them keep?"

My father, his face an impassive barricade, set his jaw.

I knew little about my father's family, except that their town west of Krakow was savaged by the Germans in 1939. I remembered a letter I found the month before on my father's nightstand. "Dear Uncle," it began in Polish in an old-fashioned script. It was difficult to decipher, but I spotted the words for "hungry," "food" and "money."

From what I knew about their income, my parents together barely earned $275 a month. How could my father scrape up more than pennies to send overseas? His family surely needed help, but my mother had a point. What were the odds my father's mail would even reach them?

As their argument grew more heated, I wondered if my father's paycheck was bigger than I thought. Maybe he could help with Alek's medical bills, I thought. Then I remembered the letter from my father's nephew—my cousin—about hunger and food, and I stayed silent.

***

A week later, when Alek woke with sniffles and a temperature of 102, I was grateful I'd paid Dr. Wenski a few dollars of his bill at our last visit. "Bring him right in," Wenski's receptionist said.

The doctor was all business as he listened to Alek's lungs and heart. He sounded like a police detective in a movie as he rattled off question after question.

"He's been doing well lately, doctor. We've even been at the park every day."

He rolled his eyes. "Aha! I assume you let the boy play with other children?"

"Of course."

"And those children were all completely healthy?" Wenski hooked thumbs in his vest, waiting.

"How could I know?" My cheeks burned. How could I have been so careless? "You think one of them gave Alek his cold?"

"Not a cold. The croup. Hear that cough? He needs warm steam to breath, cold compresses for the fever."

"That's what I've been doing."

"Keep doing it. If his breathing gets any worse, call me. He might need to go to the hospital. And be more careful next time." He slapped shut Alek's thick file, tucked it under his arm and left the room.

His words frightened me as much as they infuriated me. I dreaded bringing my son back to the place he'd lingered so long after his birth. Alek's raspy breathing vibrated in my ear as I hurried to the front desk.

"That will be $165," the receptionist said evenly. "Do you want us to send you a bill, or are you paying now?"

"What? For one visit?"

"No, Mrs. Baran. This visit is four dollars. The rest is the money you owe for past treatment." Her lips curled upward in an imitation of a smile. The payment I'd made a few weeks before mattered little. Behind her, the doctor stood next to his file cabinet, engrossed in his next patient's records.

I pulled out four dollars from my wallet—money I kept in reserve for emergencies—and put it on the desk. "I need a word with Dr. Wenski." She shook her head. I ignored her. Slipping behind her, I tapped the doctor on the shoulder.

He looked annoyed. "Mrs. Baran, we went over everything during the boy's exam."

I took a deep breath. "I paid for this visit today, doctor, but the rest of the charges on Alek's account are a mistake. My father-in-law ordered Alek's extra care in the hospital when he was born, remember? He is the one you must bill. The only one."

Before I turned to leave, I planted the same smile on my face the receptionist had displayed earlier. Dr. Wenski stood speechless. "I'm so glad you understand," I said.

That night, I wrote Walt about a visit I'd had with Milly, the weather, and my hopes that I soon would be able to take Alek to Babcia's to escape the heat. Then I wrote Sam about the scare I had about Alek's health, and my confidence he soon would be fine. Sam had shipped out in early July, more quickly than expected, but his letters kept coming at the same pace. Their contents shared one thing in common with Walt's: They both wanted to know how Alek and I were doing.

"You would be so proud of me," I wrote Sam. "I finally stood up to Dr. Wenski. Let him and Max figure out how those bills should be paid."

***

Milly drove us to Babcia's house two weeks later, when Alek's cough was almost gone. As much as my cousin sometimes got under my skin, I appreciated the concrete ways she made my life easier. I felt safe at my grandmother's.

She tapped her horn as she pulled up. The sight of my happy, homely grandmother rushing from her house filled me with joy. With her, just as with Sam, I didn't have to pretend. Truth was all she knew.

"Dzień dobry," Babcia said, arms outstretched. She swooped up Alek first and placed the back of her hand on his forehead. Alek smiled up at her while Milly's daughter chattered short sentences and a few dozen words. I wasn't worry about that. Alek understood me well enough and said his

three most important words: "Mama," "no," and "Baba," the name he gave Babcia.

"He's okay, Babcia. He just has a little cough." I made a coughing sound to make sure she understood. She nodded, a faraway look clouding her expression.

After lunch, Babcia pulled me aside. "I have *nowy przepis.*"

"New recipe? For what? Dinner?"

Her laughter sounded like that of a young girl. "Not food! *Medycyna!* For Alek!"

From her pantry, she pulled out a dozen packages of dried herbs and measured hefty doses from each. From Tadeusz's garden, she cut stalks from two mysterious weedy plants I'd never seen in New Jersey. She shrugged off my questions, as if protecting a trade secret.

She dumped the stems, weeds and seeds into a huge pot of boiling water on the stove and stirred with a long-handled wooden spoon. The recipe looked no different than Babcia's other poultices, but her expressions told me it was something powerful and new. It smelled like rotted weeds.

"Tadeusz!" she called after a half hour of stirring. Her husband lugged the heavy pot to the bathroom and poured its contents into the tub while Babcia stirred in more hot water.

As always, Alek wallowed happily in the warm muck. Babcia rubbed it on his back and arms and legs. He wiped it on his face and into his hair. It took an hour to rinse it all off but when he climbed out of the tub his eyes sparkled. He soaked in the mixture twice a day for the three days we were there. I wondered if he looked healthier simply because he liked to play in the mud, or because he really was being cured. Either way, his cough ebbed each day.

When it was time to leave, I ladled the potion into one of the giant jars Tadeusz used for making pickles. Wrapping the jar in newspaper, I packed it carefully in Milly's trunk.

Back home, I diluted the herbs with warm water almost every day, opening every window to release the nasty fumes. Alek squished the mud through his fingers and smeared it through his hair, face and neck. He smacked the thick goo with the palm of his hand until it splattered the wall, the floor and me. My muddied face sent him into spasms of laughter, a joyous new sound. When it was time to take him out, he struggled to break free.

"Baba! Baba!" he squealed, calling for his great-grandmother. Her healing care lingered in his memory. Most days, I let him stay until the mixture cooled and hardened.

With each soaking, he seemed stronger. His steady progress affected us all. My mother pulled him into her lap as soon as she came home from work, her face bright with wonder. Even my father's face softened when he was around Alek.

I could barely contain my joy when I wrote Walt, though I didn't mention Babcia's potions. Walt would wonder why his son needed my grandmother's powers. That's the way his mind worked, always on the alert.

July 25, 1944

Dear Walt,

Your son is such an imp. His daily bath is now his biggest delight. He splashes and plays like he's never had one before. When you get home, this job will be yours, dear husband. You will love every minute of it. I absolutely believe you'll be home soon. I know you don't want me to put too much faith in that, but I believe it with all my heart...

FORTY-FIVE

The day after he learned of Hatch's death, Walt reported to his shift exactly on time. He clenched and unclenched his fists to stop their shaking, but he kept working. Like the convoy of ships that brought Walt to Africa, the war never slowed its pace for any soldier, even an innocent soul like Frank Hatcher.

"You okay?" Captain Hunter asked as they treated a soldier peppered with bullet wounds.

"Why wouldn't I be?" Walt lied. The doctor no doubt knew about Hatch's death, but Walt didn't want to talk about it.

"Okay, Walt," Hunter said. "Just let me know if you need to be relieved early."

The two men rarely called each other by their first names. They reserved that for the evenings they relaxed with beers and chatted like two human beings, not cogs in the military wheel. Walt didn't realize how much he needed that connection until Hunter spoke his name.

At the end of his shift, exhausted by his effort to disguise every flinch, Walt limped to his tent. He shook violently. Burrowing under his wool blanket made no difference. Finally, he pulled out paper and pen, hoping Nora wouldn't notice his wobbly penmanship. He felt as if he was writing a distant memory, but the letter still calmed him. He didn't tell her about the wounded he'd treated, about the men who died in his arms, about Hatch. He could blame the censors, but the truth was he didn't want to tell her. She didn't deserve to hear such horror.

June 24, 1944

Dear Nora,

Our weather is a bit damp right now. I can't say much

221

about my current situation, except that I've been very busy and my surgery shifts are mostly at night. This work is all I ever wanted to do in the Army. The four or five hours of sleep I grab during the day are enough. There have been challenges. I won't lie. Someday, I will tell you all of it...

***

Walt steadied himself as his convoy truck growled through thick mud. A driving rain splashed the truck's open back end, soaking his hair, shirt, pants and socks.

More than a month had passed since the invasion at Normandy, but the Ninth was still stuck on the Cherbourg Peninsula. The front line shifted snakelike ahead of them as the infantry cleared out stubborn pockets of enemy soldiers. The clearing company tried to keep up. Whenever their drivers glimpsed an armed American soldier ahead, they made a hasty U-turn. That was a sure sign the front was just in front of them.

"Where the hell are we now?" Walt asked no one in particular. "Is the front still close by? Anyone know?"

No one answered. Their nerves wouldn't let them. The convoy proceeded eastward on roads littered with broken German tanks, trucks and even horse-drawn artillery wagons. The horses were dead, their flesh torn and entrails spilling out, their bodies as bloated as the dead Germany soldiers around them. The sickening odor of putrefying flesh made some medics gag. Walt breathed through his mouth and turned away. The horrible death and destruction in Africa and Sicily seemed a minor prelude.

His shifts filled him with sorrow. Often, only he and a single doctor stood between a patient and eternity. Walt helped close their wounds. He gave them whole-blood transfusions and kept them from going into shock. When a soldier opened his eyes to speak, Walt almost cried out with joy. More often, he despaired when patients' eyes fixed on another plane of existence.

"Goddamn it to hell," he muttered each time he saw another hollow stare. "This one damn thing I asked to be spared from, God. Just this one thing."

The medical team drove forty-two miles in pouring rain to reach the French town of Carentan. The men set up camp in a thunderstorm. "You'll run the surgery crew, Baran. First shift," Captain Hunter said. "I expect you'll soon get a field promotion to corporal."

"Uh, thanks, sir," said Walt, grateful for the responsibility again but curious how the other men—all of them already corporals—would react to answering to a private. He'd supervised those surgery techs for more than a year before D-Day, but, ever since, one of the doctors had been in charge. A field promotion couldn't come soon enough.

He didn't ask if the assignment meant a pay raise. He knew Hunter's stock answer: "Just behave yourself."

***

At their next stop, casualties arrived even before the medics could unpack. To Walt's relief, the techs all carried out his directives.

Among the casualties was an infantryman from Walt's old company, a burly Philadelphian named Jimmy Murray who arrived with an enlarged spleen, chills, fever, sweating and nausea. Malaria plagued the troops. Walt pulled out a dose of chloroquine.

"Don't worry, Murray. We'll get you fixed up. How's the gang doing?"

"Eh, you know how it is. We're a bundle of nerves. Burned out. Who wouldn't be, watching our pals die every day? It's a matter of time for the rest of us."

"Luck seems to be on your side so far." Walt paused. "How's Tom Lucas? Bet he's holding up."

Murray shook his head. "He must lead a charmed life to have lasted this long. But he's a wreck. He's in charge of his platoon now. His lieutenant was killed in action. So were the rest of the non-coms." He fell silent, his face filled with regret. "Sorry, Baran. I know Hatcher was your buddy, too."

Walt flinched. Hatch's end hadn't seemed real, especially the way it happened— by a sniper's single bullet in the middle of the night, his body whisked away before Walt could see him. Hearing Murray speak about Hatch in casual past tense reawakened his grief.

Murray shifted the subject. "Don't worry about Tom Lucas. He's a tough one. I just wish he'd listen to advice. The CO keeps telling him to report back here to rest up a few days, but he says he can't."

"Can't? Why not?"

"You know Tom. He's too god-damned worried about the other men. If he left, even for a few days, only new recruits would be left. It's unbelievable up there. A private's in command of the second platoon."

An idea seized Walt, one he'd had before: I should quit the medics and rejoin my old infantry platoon, grab a rifle and stand by Tom's side. Just as quickly, reality sank in. After all this time, he'd perform no better at the front lines than a raw recruit. His best chance to keep Tom safe would be to stay a medic.

"Do me a favor, Murray. When you go back, tell Tom to get his rear end here on the double. I've got a cot waiting for him."

As the last traces of Walt's stoicism began to crumble, he searched for Magnus. He found the driver sprawled under a tree nursing a half-filled wine bottle. Even in the height of battle the man could track down booze.

"Got any for sale?" Walt asked, motioning to the bottle.

"Sure. How much you want?"

"A liter'll do." Walt handed him a dollar fifty. Magnus jogged toward his pup tent and returned a minute later with a dusty, unlabeled bottle.

Walt hugged it. "Mind if I join you?"

Magnus shrugged.

Walt settled on a dusty patch a few feet away and uncorked his bottle. The first vinegary swig made him wince, but he kept on drinking, grateful for Magnus's taciturn ways. Walt didn't want to talk. He just wanted company.

Halfway through the bottle, as Walt settled into the wine's friendly embrace, a memory unexpectedly loosened his tongue. "Do you have any secrets, Magnus?" he asked, without waiting for a reply. "I guess we all do, huh?"

Magnus glanced at him, tilting his head.

"It didn't take much more than this to get my big brother plastered," Walt said, holding his bottle up to the moonlight. "Cliff was a mess that night. Stumbling, slurring, bloodshot eyes. Even he knew he shouldn't be driving."

Magnus frowned. "That night?"

Walt ignored him. "Never seen so many types of booze at one party. I sampled every one. Added up to a lot. A whole lot. But here's the thing"—he frowned—"liquor didn't hit me the way it did Cliff. Didn't touch me. Still doesn't." Walt took a deep swig and stared at his wine bottle.

"I wasn't even seventeen, but I was good behind the wheel. Did a lot of driving for my father back then, you know? I told Cliff I would get us home. Had no choice. How could I have known?" Walt's voice caught.

Magnus put down his bottle. He shifted slightly. "I do not understand."

"The truck came from outta nowhere. Came right at us. I tried—I—tried." Walt opened and closed his mouth to catch his breath. He'd never told anyone these things, not even Nora.

"The truck?" Magnus said.

"I slammed on the brakes. Pulled the wheel hard as I could. A tree, it—it ripped off Cliff's door. Cliff—he flew—he just—it was like a giant hand grabbed him. The truck driver, he kept going."

Walt gasped, feeling the crash once again. He covered his face with both hands. The two men sat in silence.

"Someone must have heard it. The crash," Walt finally said. "The cops showed up minutes later. An ambulance was right behind them. They knew my father. Knew him well. Never asked for my license. Never asked if I'd been drinking. Treated me like a victim."

"And your brother?"

"Oh, God," Walt moaned, as he had that night. "Should've been me. Should've been..."

FORTY-SIX

In mid-August, my mother-in-law phoned with another invitation I couldn't turn down. "We're going to Bay View in two weeks to close the house for winter. Why don't you join us again, Nora? It could be our last chance for warm weather."

"I'd love to!" I blurted. "When are we leaving?" I knew Ruth wanted only a little help with cooking and private time with Alek. Max could be counted on to disappear on business errands.

"Wonderful! I'll let you know." She sounded genuinely pleased. "Can you stay six days? Is that too long?"

Maybe not long enough, I thought. I pictured myself handing Alek over to Ruth, having uninterrupted hours to myself, taking naps, strolling along the beach, writing long letters to Walt.

"That would be perfect," I assured her as Alek fussed in my arms. "Shhh, baby," I whispered, bouncing him on my hip.

In the kitchen, my mother frowned as she gripped and kneaded a mound of dough. "So, you go away again, huh, daughter?" she said in that tone she used with my father.

"Oh, you heard," I said innocently. I suspected she'd been eavesdropping. Despite her show of annoyance, she probably looked forward to my infrequent trips to the shore and to Babcia's house. A vacation for me and Alek meant a break for her, too.

Before Alek was born, my strong-willed mother could come and go as she pleased. His birth changed everything. Now she had little time to join friends at parties and events. Instead, she worked long factory shifts, helped with Alek and sewed aprons to help me pay my bills.

The bills. I shuddered. The thirty dollars my mother and I had made so far on our aprons barely dented the biggest bill—the $750 I still owed the hospital. The amount might as well have been $75,000. In the twenty months since Alek had been born, I'd paid only $70, and most of that had gone to Dr. Wenski to make sure he would keep seeing Alek. Lately, I wasn't optimistic Wenski had settled the rest of his bill with Max. Neither man had said a word about it lately.

My neediness embarrassed me. I should find a job, I thought, then quickly dismissed the idea. It would be impossible without someone to care for Alek.

My mother and I worked silently that night, sewing aprons and purses until my fingertips ached. I gave Alek a sponge bath and put him in his crib.

August 15, 1944

Dear Walt,

Guess what? I plan to take Alek to the shore again in two weeks when your parents close up the bungalow. I can't wait. Your mother treats me and Alek well, and I love to dip his toes into the water. The weather here is still quite warm. I'll be sure to take pictures. Alek is cuter than ever. All he needs is his daddy to carry him to the sand...

By the time I finished my letter to Walt, my father had retreated to his room and my mother was soaking in the bathtub. Blessed with rare privacy, I rummaged through my drawer and slipped out a blank V-mail form.

Writing Sam was easier now. I told him everything about my upcoming trip. "You wouldn't believe how quiet it is there, Sam. Bay View isn't like the rest of the Jersey Shore. Most people are local folks and a delicious breeze blows off Barnegat Bay. I rarely see Max when we're there, but when I do, I finally have a plan to secure his help..."

As I spelled out my strategy, water sloshed in the bathroom. My mother was draining the tub. "...I must close now. I hope you are safe, Sam, wherever your ship is. Best wishes, Nora."

Sam's V-mail reply a week and a half later boosted my morale. "You are a brave gal, Nora," he wrote. "I bet you'll succeed with your father-in-law. How can he turn you down?"

***

Ruth pulled out a package of thick pork chops and three large potatoes. While I shucked fresh peas into a pot, she washed the potatoes and breaded the chops. A store-bought cake sat on the counter for dessert. I wondered how she'd acquired enough ration tickets for such bounty. We would eat more heartily that night than we had at Ruth's house on Christmas Day, or even at my Babcia's.

Only when Ruth placed three plates on the table did I realize why she was going through so much trouble. "Max will be back for dinner tonight?" I asked. When Max wasn't around, I called my father-in-law by his given name. Ruth didn't seem to mind.

"I know, dear. It's unexpected. He called earlier and said to have a hearty dinner ready for him."

"He's so busy when he comes here. Does he ever stop working?"

Ruth shrugged. She lit the pilot light, turned on the oven and greased a heavy cast-iron pan. I didn't mind that she ignored my question. Ever since I'd heard Ruth mock Max to her friend, I'd felt closer to her. Did Max have any inkling of how she spoke of him? Probably not. My father-in-law strutted about as if everyone worshipped him.

"I can finish this," I said. "Why don't you go put your feet up?"

Ruth shook her head. "You're a good daughter-in-law, Nora, but I like to keep busy. Like my husband, huh?"

"Mom, I need advice." For the first time, it felt natural calling Ruth that. She turned, curious.

"There's no easy way to say this." I took a deep breath. "I want to try again to convince Max to help me pay Alek's doctor bills. It's so much money. Too much."

Ruth grimaced. "He's tight with the dollar, Nora. You know that. Especially when he thinks someone is trying to take advantage of him."

"It's just that, he was the one who insisted—"

"That Alek get nothing but the best at the hospital? Of course, he did, Nora. That's my husband for you."

Her honesty startled me. It was one thing for Ruth to speak the truth about Max's character to a friend. But to me?

Outside, Max's tires ground through the sandy driveway. Ruth cast me a warning glance.

Without a nod or a hello, he stomped into the room, opened a narrow low cupboard and pulled out a bottle of whiskey. He poured himself a shot and downed it before turning to Ruth and me.

"Hello, ladies. Having fun, are we?"

"We'll be eating in about an hour, Max," Ruth said.

"An hour? I told you to have dinner ready."

"The potatoes will take that long, dear. Make yourself comfortable and I'll get you some crackers and cheese to tide you over."

Ruth put together a plate for her husband while I stirred the peas. When they were ready, I mashed a spoonful with some potatoes and milk and fed Alek, who already was rubbing his eyes with fatigue. As soon as he took his last bite, I carried him to our bedroom, changed his diaper and tucked him in his crib.

By the time I was finished with Alek, dinner was ready. Max, with a few crackers and three shots of whiskey under his belt, teetered on the edge of something resembling good humor.

"Smells delicious," Max said. "But I guess any husband starving like I am would think so. Right, Ruthie? Right, Maggie?" He patted his belly. "What a day I had, Ruthie. This guy I'm bringing into the business really screwed up. Let a widow pay only half before the funeral. Can you believe it? Now she's stiffing us. Who knows when we'll get the rest!"

Max droned on about his business as he stuffed his mouth, unaffected by Ruth's and my half-hearted attention. I appreciated her more than ever. Thanks to her passive demeanor, the meal went smoothly—more pleasantly than supper at my parents' house. No matter what Ruth felt privately, she never wasted energy confronting Max.

At one point, Max and Ruth even enthusiastically agreed that Walt would be home by Christmas.

"I'm sure of it," Max said. "All anyone has to do is read the Herald's account of how things are going. The Germans can't last long now."

Ruth nodded. "It can't be soon enough, dear. Our son needs some home-cooked meals. Did you see those last photographs he sent?"

I nodded. Walt looked skinnier than ever in those pictures, but he wore a cocky smile and insisted all was well. I wanted to believe him.

After Max finished eating, he settled into his easy chair in the next room while Ruth and I cleaned the kitchen. After she went to her bedroom to say her nightly rosary, I dragged a kitchen chair close to Max and sat down.

"Dad, can we talk?"

He frowned, suspicious.

I'd spent many nights pondering my approach. I knew that my father-in-law liked having his ego fed and thinking he had the upper hand. I decided that if I acted as if I was in his debt, I might stand a chance.

"You've been so good to me, Dad. I can't ever thank you enough for your generosity," I lied. "I feel guilty asking for this, but I need a favor."

His eyes brightened. "Speak up, Maggie," he said, drawing out my hated nickname with a smirk.

Whatever makes you happy, I thought. "Alek is doing much better, but his health is still in question. He may need more care," I said.

"So? Get it for him."

The depths of his deliberate ignorance, his cruel arrogance, momentarily stopped me. I took a deep breath and rushed my next words so he wouldn't interrupt. "If I don't pay their bills, the hospital and its specialists might not give him the same care the next time he's sick. I was hoping to get a bit of money from you." My next words mattered most: "Just a small loan, Dad. I'll pay it back. All of it."

Despite my begging, unfiltered anger darkened Max's face. His smirk was gone. He spoke through gritted teeth.

"You don't listen too good, do you, Maggie?"

True bullies don't have to raise their voices to instill fear. Max knew that. All he had to do was steel his body and fix his glare. But I had an edge that night: I knew what to expect. I stared back. I held my gaze until Max picked up a newspaper and shook it open, a signal he was finished with me. In the bedroom, on cue, Alek whimpered softly.

It was my turn.

"All I'm saying, Dad, is that Alek will need more medical care. Count on it. And he'll need the best."

I stood and left the room, hesitant to push my luck. I had planted the seed. That was a start.

FORTY-SEVEN

"Mail call!" The words always made Walt hope for a letter from Nora, but his only letter that balmy July day bore a lavish script more common in Europe than America. "How are you, dear Walter? And how is sweet Francis? I miss you both terribly and pray you are safe..."

Beth!

"...My parents send their regards. Our little village has escaped the bombing. Life is quiet now that most of you soldiers have left. Please write and let me know you are well. I sent Francis a letter, too, but I haven't heard back."

He hadn't given Beth his address. Hatch must have, in a hasty decision to please her. He scanned the rest of her letter, most of it about townspeople he didn't know. She said nothing about what had happened at the dance, about their kiss, about his abrupt refusal to see her again.

Even after leaving England, his guilt gnawed at him. He'd been unfaithful to Hatch as well as to Nora. If his friend had gone to that dance without him, Hatch might have ended up with Beth. She might have kissed him instead.

Walt crushed her letter but saved the envelope with her address. One day, he decided, when censors allowed it, he would write her about Hatch. Until then, he would ignore her.

***

The clearing company was still mired on the Cherbourg Peninsula when Walt learned Magnus had been transferred to an infantry company. No one knew which one it was. The move happened so quickly Walt had no chance to say good-bye.

Ted cursed at the news. "Gonna be hard to find booze now."

Walt winced. Magnus meant more to him than alcohol. Ever since he'd shared his burden about Cliff's death, the two men had a silent understanding. Whenever they passed each other, Magnus cast him a knowing look or a nod, his usual blank expression softened by kindness. Walt felt unexpected gratitude that another human being knew his guilt and did not judge him. Now he worried for his unexpected friend. As eccentric as Magnus was, he was skilled behind the wheel, but the front was dangerous for everyone, even drivers.

Wherever he went, he carried Walt's secret with him. No one could keep a secret like Magnus.

***

In late July, the unthinkable happened: The Germans took prisoner every doctor, technician and patient in the Third Battalion's medical-aid station. The medics' non-combative status near the front line failed to offer them any protection.

Until then, Walt believed that the crosses on their helmets and tents guarded them from all but accidental enemy barrages. Now he knew otherwise. The Germans couldn't be trusted to spare any innocent person.

"Headquarters wants four of our med techs as replacements," Gus announced in a hastily called meeting.

No one made a sound as Gus called out the first three names. Those men came forward stoically. The clerk took a deep breath before reading the final name, "Corporal Al Lanigan."

"What?" Walt blurted. "Big Al? But he's a surgical tech. We need him here!"

Big Al grinned and held up crossed fingers. "Keep saying those prayers, Walt."

Walt trembled, not from the agitation haunting him after every shift, but from a new mix of fear and adrenaline. He didn't want to die, but he didn't want any more of his buddies to die either.

"Where's Magnus when we need him most?" Ted muttered.

Walt pictured the driver in an easy mechanic's job far away from the front lines, slipping out every night for wine or hard liquor or both.

***

Days later, two techs sent to the front returned by ambulance, so physically and mentally weary they could hardly move. They mumbled incoherent demands for medicines and treatments.

Walt helped one of them to a cot. "He'll be okay," Ted said. "He just needs rest."

Walt knew better, but he didn't argue. Few techs knew how to treat mentally exhausted soldiers.

"At least he's not in as bad shape as Al," Ted said. "Did you hear? They brought the big guy to our field hospital. Took a bullet to his gut."

"No!" Walt blurted. He couldn't speak his fear aloud. A stomach wound could be fatal. He recalled Al's objections to field hospitals when they first appeared in Sicily. Now, a field hospital's skilled surgeons might save his life.

All afternoon, Walt and Ted kept checking with Gus about the big guy's condition. Finally, Gus came looking for them. "He's survived more than three hours of surgery, but the docs say his condition is still grave," the clerk said. "He should be taken by ambulance to an evacuation hospital in a day or two."

"Dammit. Doesn't it make ya want to hit something?" Ted said.

"What?"

"All of it. The injuries. The dead. Big Al. The fact that any minute we could be sent to the front, too."

Walt kept his gaze steady. "I don't think about it."

"You're lyin'."

Walt didn't answer. He hated being called a liar, even when he was one. Despite Big Al's history of bar fights and drunken tirades, his massive presence had a calming effect during surgeries and air raids. Walt missed the big guy and was furious about his injury. But he also felt embarrassing relief that he hadn't called to the front yet. He ducked his feelings like enemy bullets.

"You're one tough fellow to read, Walt, you know that?"

"What do you want me to say, Ted?"

"Whatever you want. I've seen your hands shake. I know you feel something, even though you act so calm sometimes you give me the creeps."

The vein on Walt's temple throbbed. He didn't owe Ted any explanation. He'd felt mostly numb back in Africa and Sicily, where he witnessed crazy extremes—courage and cowardice, misery and elation, camaraderie and resentments. But then came Normandy. Then Hatch was killed. Then Big Al was shot.

When he couldn't tame his whipsawing emotions, Walt tried tricking them instead. He thought about Nora or his son or his home town. If that didn't work, he buried his feelings inside, where only his trembling hands betrayed him.

Walt needed his memories of Nora more than ever, but sometimes they faded like whiffs of cigarette smoke. He studied her photographs every night. He tried to remember kissing her lips and holding her.

Big Al never returned to the clearing company. Gus said he was shipped home. Walt hoped he made it.

***

A torrent of enemy shells jolted Walt and Ted awake. They had pitched their floorless tent over a hole they'd dug next to a thick hedgerow. Two miles from the front line, the ditch provided an illusion of safety without blocking a single decibel of noise.

When the shelling finally stopped, Walt tackled an assignment Hunter had issued the night before: "Repaint that cross on the ward tent, Baran. Don't want the Germans to mistake us for infantry."

Crosses didn't much help the Third Battalion, Walt thought. Setting a ladder as close as possible to the symbols, he climbed up with a can of red paint and braced his thighs against the top rungs. He hated heights. Slowly, he pulled a brush from his waistband and dipped it into the can. The dirty, worn canvas made for slow progress. Its fibers absorbed every drop of his thick, careful layers of paint.

By the time half the can was empty, Walt heard a low rumble in the distance. Bombers, no doubt. He guessed they were American.

Squinting at the horizon, he spotted Allied planes strafing German positions. Just before they veered off, they dropped canisters to mark their targets. The canisters billowed red smoke as soon as they hit the ground.

Without warning, a sharp wind gust jolted him. Leaves and fine dust settled into his paint can and onto his brush. "Dammit!" he cursed. He scraped his brush on the can's edge to remove the gritty debris. Thick clouds of red-tinged dust red drifted past him.

He worked fast to finish another section of the cross before more dust stuck to his brush. Judging from the noise above, bomber planes were drawing close again. He glanced down at the men working calmly beneath him. Ted was picking up trash; Buck bagged it; a cook scrubbed a metal pot; a mechanic tuned a balky truck engine.

Seconds later, when a cluster of heavy payloads landed a mile away, the din was so loud it shook his ladder. Fascinated, he watched the show of force, his paint brush poised in mid-air.

When Walt thought about it later, he couldn't explain why neither he nor any of the other men seemed afraid. Only when German 88 mm anti-aircraft guns roared to life did he notice their proximity. Spent shells landed nearby and kicked up more dust. He couldn't see the edge of camp. Dirt clogged his throat and nose.

Slamming the paint can shut, he scrambled down the ladder to wait for the worst to pass. As he leaned against a large water can to catch his breath, bombs fell on a field of Army engineers fifty yards away. A wall of noise and heat slapped him off balance and pushed him sideways.

Walt heard the chunk of shrapnel pierce the water can before he saw it—a loud *thunk*. He gaped at the water gushing from the exact spot he had stood a half-second earlier. Terror gripped him. Safety anywhere was debatable.

Instinctively, he raced toward the engineers' camp to look for wounded. Before he reached it, a bomb hit a truck packed with crates of TNT. The force of the truck's explosion knocked Walt into a foxhole; another tech landed atop him. Walt was grateful when two other men jumped in to add another layer of protection.

Only after the bombing stopped did the men crawl out. Walt struggled from the hole to find smoke so thick it looked as if the earth itself was burning. Every new noise made him hit the ground again. Moving cautiously, he found two wounded engineers in the rubble. He guided them to surgery, cleaned their wounds and treated them for shock.

Later, Hunter assembled the platoon to give them the unexpected news: It wasn't German artillery that struck the engineer's camp. It was American bombs. Friendly fire. "The thick haze made us invisible. The wind blew that red smoke toward us and the engineers. That's why the bombers missed their target."

"Missed it by a mile," Walt muttered. Two engineers had died in the botched attack; dozens more were seriously wounded.

Like a missing limb, Walt's memory of the mayhem made him wince. He couldn't sleep. If only I had painted that cross earlier, he thought. One hour could have made the difference. Our pilots would have spotted our crosses earlier.

***

The last thing Walt expected after the botched bombing was a Nazi retreat. Yet German prisoners talked of low stocks of food, ammunition and medical supplies. "It's looking sort of good," Gus said cautiously. Surrender seemed a real possibility.

The evening of August 9, casualties were so light that Walt took a break from his shift early for dinner. He was gone no more than an hour. He hated to stay away from surgery too long. Every surgical tech counted.

Gus stopped him on his way back.

"Just the person I'm looking for, Walt. I need to talk to you."

Walt froze. "What's up?" His superiors had a habit of using Gus to deliver him warnings. Maybe his recent letter to Nora revealed too much. Maybe he griped too loudly about staffing the day before. His mind raced through every recent letter he'd written, every conversation he'd had, looking for ways he might have erred.

Gus motioned Walt to follow him to a small tent he used as an office. Standing behind his makeshift desk, the clerk picked up some papers, leafed through them, and put them down again.

"Let's get this over with, Gus. I can't stand the suspense. What rule have I broken now?" What more could the Army do to him. Bust him below private?

"Walt, it's like this, Walt. Tom Lucas came in tonight."

FORTY-EIGHT

August 20, 1944

Dear Walt,

　　Alek is so cute. Right now, he's hanging onto his crib rail watching me write. The weather has been pleasant lately, so he and I often visit a nearby park that has a fountain and benches. Alek always seems happy to see other toddlers. When you finally come home, you will love him as much as I do, my dear husband. Maybe more...

Ever since we'd visited Babcia the month before, Alek seemed to eat more. He seemed stronger and less fretful. My mother bought him wooden blocks and helped him stack them every night. Maybe it was my imagination, but my parents seemed to laugh more, to squabble less.

That happy mood evaporated the day Stephen's letter came.

I found my mother hunched over the dining-room table. She braced her head in both hands. Looking up from the hand-written page, she gave me a wild look filled with fear and fury.

"Read," she said, shoving the paper into my hands.

I recognized my brother's handwriting at once. He had good news, he wrote. He finally had his orders. He would pilot fighter planes in the South Pacific. He would attack ships and drop bombs.

"The men, they are crazy. They do not care about danger. They do not care about mothers' tears." Her eyes welled, but her voice trembled with anger. I'd never seen her talk that way about her son, her favorite. Knowing Stephen's special place in her heart never made me jealous. His soft-spoken, easygoing ways made him everyone's favorite.

I sat next to her and silently rubbed her unyielding shoulders. In the pile of unopened mail on the table, I was grateful to spot Walt's handwriting. His letters used to come every day. Now the war made the length of their journey and their delivery unreliable.

I held his envelope to my face, yearning for a hint of his scent but wary of opening it. If only we could talk to each other. Our letters sometimes just repeated daily routines. Sometimes, his wording sounded so automatic I wondered if he'd lost all memory of me. Every inch of the thousands of miles that separated us weighed on me.

My mother made a low, guttural noise.

"Mom, it'll be all right." I told her about a newspaper article I'd read a few days earlier. American, British and Russian leaders were said to be meeting to decide control of Germany after the war.

"They wouldn't be talking like that if the war wasn't almost over," I said as I ripped open Walt's letter.

She scoffed at my optimism. "No one talks about war with Japan. That is where my Stefan is."

Walt's opening words echoed her skepticism: "Don't believe everything you hear about the war, Nora."

FORTY-NINE

"Tom Lucas is here? Where?"

"He was wounded in the chest, Walt, but still conscious," Gus said, his voice so low Walt could scarcely hear him.

Walt's thoughts misfired like frayed wires in a power surge. Chest wounds could be serious. His thinking stalled, the way his body turned numb during bombings.

"He looked in good shape," Gus said. "They put him in evac so he could be sent to a hospital at the rear."

"I have to see him. Why didn't anyone call me?" He turned toward the door to find his friend. Gus grabbed his arm.

"He came in just after you took a break, Walt. It happened fast."

Walt moved toward Gus. They stood inches apart. "Is he still here? Tell me, goddammit."

Gus sighed. "I'm sorry, Walt. I really am. He—he died in shock minutes after that. They'll transport his body to the rear tomorrow for burial."

"I...you must be...how..." Walt tried to string words together as truth sifted into his unwilling mind. As much as he wanted to cry, his eyes remained dry.

"Have a seat, Walt. Take a minute."

Walt ignored him. He strode quickly through the camp until he came to the gruesome spot where collecting-company vehicles picked up corpses.

In the back of the first truck was the body of a soldier he did not know. His skin was grayish blue, his eyes fixed. Next to him was another GI with deep wounds on his face that made him unrecognizable, except for a dark, two-day beard on his chin. Too dark to be Tom's.

Maybe there was a mistake, Walt thought. Maybe a GI who died of shock was mistaken for Tom.

239

Walt opened the second ambulance door and froze. Inside, Tom lay peacefully, eyes closed. A small piece of shrapnel must have cut his lip, because a thin trail of dried blood made a path down his chin. He looked as calm and tranquil as when he bunked next to Walt at Fort Bragg. Tom rarely tossed or turned. He slept the deep, quiet slumber of an innocent man.

Walt knelt beside him; he wanted to shake his buddy awake. He pressed a fingertip to Tom's cheek but jerked it back when lukewarm flesh gave way to his touch. Did a faint remnant of life remain in his friend's body?

He knew better, but his buddy's soft skin made him wonder. A proper corpse was gray-blue marble, icy cold, like hardened clay. His years working in his father's funeral parlor had taught him that. No matter how many layers of make-up and rouge he put on a corpse's face, the body beneath remained a hard shell of what once was a man or woman or child.

Tom looked like he was taking a nap.

Doubt shredded all his logic and training. He gently touched his friend's shoulder. "Tom, do you hear me?"

He reminded himself that he'd checked the pulse of many a dying soldier only to find no beat of life beneath limp, soft flesh. Not until a doctor checked behind him did an aide take the body away, and usually it hadn't yet cooled. But what if someone made a mistake this time? What if a doctor never took Tom's pulse? What if aides had placed a living soldier in the corpse pile? He placed two fingers on Tom's neck just below the jaw and sat still as stone. There! There it is! I feel something, he thought. He pressed harder. Seconds passed before Walt realized that the faint throb was his own blood coursing in his fingertips.

He cursed silently, his words as intense and sincere as his morning prayers. As certain as he was that God existed, and as easily as he accepted the Church's ways, he struggled with the how and why of it. Why did God play by such unpredictable rules? Why did He let Tom and Hatch die as they had? And Cliff? Why couldn't God let death come softly to those good men late in their lives, like a tap on the shoulder? How could God allow these cosmic mistakes?

Then it came to him—his desperate prayer back on Utah Beach. He'd begged God—demanded, actually—to spare him from having to look into the eyes of any more dying men. He foolishly believed he could endure war's mayhem if he just didn't have to see that vacant, horrific stare any more.

All God did was laugh at him.

Silently, he raged at God: "You're a real jokester, aren't you? You kept sending dying strangers into my surgery tent, and every one of them gave me that cold, lost stare. Each time, it was like death itself taunting me. But when my buddies died, you made sure I wasn't around. No last friendly connection for them. No, sir. You gave me my wish when I least wanted it."

His mind wandered to places it hadn't been since he was a boy—the unyielding wooden pews at St. Adalbert's Church, the slap of Sister Mary Theodore's ruler in catechism class, the forbidden texture of the communion wafer when he bit into it. Where was God in all that bunk?

Shouting outside the ambulance broke his trance, followed by the grinding noise of a rusty door handle. The back door flew open. Two litter bearers hoisted up a body. "What the hell?" one shouted as he pushed the litter inside. "What are you doing in here, Baran?"

Walt scrambled over the litter and jumped to the ground. He ran past the startled soldiers, ignoring their calls. "Why, God," he muttered. "Why?"

***

The medical techs who gathered for coffee that night fell silent when Walt entered the mess tent. Ted finally spoke first. "We didn't know your pal was in such bad shape, Walt. He looked like he would pull through."

Walt tried to muster the strength to speak. When he finally did, his voice was husky. "Most guys would have survived that wound. Tom was too worn out."

A soft chorus of agreement answered him.

"I'm sorry," Ted said. The other men nodded.

A long silence followed. Walt took a deep gulp of coffee. When he spoke again it was in a deadened monotone. "First Hatch. Now Tom. Two of the best friends I ever had. First, I prayed both would be spared. Then I asked God that they'd be wounded so they could get back home."

The techs stared at the ground while he spoke. Only Ted and Gus looked toward him, their gazes understanding. Walt's voice turned hard.

"You know what? For two years I watched my old infantry platoon come through here. Now not one of them is left. They're all dead or wounded so bad they're back in the States. Our job has always been the same: patch them up and send them back to the front—whatever's left of them. Until there was nothing left. Is this the noble war we set out to fight? Does this make us heroes?"

The sorrow he'd fought off filled his chest, his throat, his eyes. He hurried outside. Back in his pup tent, he collapsed on his bedding and pressed a pillow against his mouth. Of all nights, this one was eerily quiet. No artillery barrages, bombs or war planes hid his anguished cries.

Aug. 10, 1944

Dear Nora,

Someday, honey, if you are willing to listen, I will tell

you what war is really like. It seems like we are forever nervous, scared and on edge. It's not enough to tell you that without giving the reasons why. Maybe one day I can do that. I'm not looking for pity, believe me. Compared to an infantryman, I have it easy. The guy right on the front line is the one we all should pray for. He needs that and all the luck in the world, too. Even then, it often isn't enough...

FIFTY

Maybe I jinxed my son by painting Walt rosy pictures of his health. Maybe I expected too much of God and Babcia's healing powers. One night in late October, Alek woke at midnight with raspy breathing and a hot, flushed face. I told myself it was another cold, something common in toddlers. He wasn't quite two.

The next morning, his fierce, dry hacking told me he had more than a cold. I ran hot water in the bathtub until the room was thick with steam, then wrapped a damp washcloth around some ice cubes. Holding him in my lap, I dabbed a cool moist cloth on his head while he breathed in the warm air. His breathing creaked with high-pitched effort. If only my parents hadn't already left for work.

"Baby, baby, baby," I chanted. "There you go. There you go." I undid his shirt and dabbed the cool cloth on his brow, neck and chest. Alek blinked slowly. I took his temperature. One hundred and two!

Dr. Wenski's wife answered my call. He was not expected back from house calls for two hours. "I'll have him call as soon as he returns."

My hand shook as I hung up. Ever since I'd insisted that Wenski charge my father-in-law for Alek's past bills, the doctor sometimes took days to answer my calls. I dialed Milly, praying my busy cousin was home.

She picked up on the first ring. "Halloo."

"Oh my God, Milly, Alek's fever is 102. The doctor isn't in. What do I do?"

"I'll be right there!"

Twenty minutes later, she and I sat on my bed with Alek on his stomach between us, wheezing softly. Milly took his temperature again and exhaled loudly as she rolled the thermometer. "Jeez. Almost one hundred and four. That's bad. You don't have a choice, Margaret Kuchynski. You have to take him to the hospital."

"The hospital? I—not there. I mean…" My voice trailed off. I imagined him back in a room behind thick glass, attached to oxygen, surrounded by other sick children and out of my reach.

Milly calmed me. "It won't be like when he was born, Nor. The doctors can help him."

***

A clammy chill gripped the dimly lit hospital. Nurses hurried from room to room, the click of their sturdy heels echoing in wide corridors smelling of disinfectants.

"Excuse me!" I called out to a nurse laden with clean linens. "Can you help me?"

The nurse paused.

"I've been waiting almost three hours. Is there any word yet about my son? Walter Aleksander Baran Jr.?" Alek was taken from me as soon as I brought him to admitting. What was taking them so long?

Her answer was the same one I'd heard all day: "I'm sure the doctor will be with you shortly."

"Is Dr. Wenski here?" I asked, though I doubted he was. I'd been searching the hallways for him ever since we'd arrived. The nurse sighed impatiently and walked away without a word.

Another half hour passed before a nurse finally lead Milly and me to a large room crowded with rows of cribs and whimpering babies. The sharp odor of antiseptics couldn't hide the lingering stench of soiled diapers. One toddler bawled in distress. The conditions were worse than the room where Alek stayed as a newborn. "I can't believe they put all these sick babies so close to each other," I said.

A young man in a white coat waved to us from a far corner of the room. I hurried to my son, who was still flushed and listless.

"I'm Dr. Samuels, the intern on duty," the young man said, smiling. "Dr. Wenski checked him already. He figured out the problem as soon as he looked in your baby's throat. All that vomiting and crying. A sure sign of streptococcus. Classic symptoms." The intern looked proud. "We've started him on sulfa."

I knew little about medicine, but I knew strep could kill. I'd also heard that sulfa drugs didn't always cure it. After the intern excused himself, Milly hugged me and left for home. I stayed by Alek's side, stroking his damp forehead and holding back tears.

"Don't cry, my big, strong boy. It will be okay, I promise you."

"It will be, Mrs. Baran," a familiar voice behind me said.

"Eleanor!" The sight of Alek's nurse during his first month of life gave me hope.

She beamed with confidence. "I bring good news, Mrs. Baran."

"I need it, Eleanor. How did you know we were here?"

"Luck! I happened to see Alek's name on the new-patient list. My news is the talk of the hospital. We just received a supply of a new drug. Penicillin. It's supposed to work well on strep. But you have to make sure Alek's doctor prescribes it. We didn't get a large supply."

Alek's doctor, I thought. Which man would that be? Dr. Wenski? The young intern? Would a man so new to the profession have the power to prescribe a brand-new drug? Or did I need Dr. Wenski, who may have had his fill of the Baran family by now?

Eleanor didn't seem to notice my hesitation. "I'll check on him every day, Mrs. Baran, I promise. I'm still working with newborns, but I'll look in on him every chance I get."

I hugged her; she surely was an angel in human form. Relieved to have her support, I set off to find the intern—better to deal with the doctor I had than the one who kept giving me the slip. But first I called my mother to tell her why I wasn't coming home yet.

"He needs that medicine, Mom. I'll spend the night making sure he gets it, even if I have to sleep in the waiting room."

Behind me, a man loudly cleared his throat. "You look like hell, Maggie."

"Max! What are you doing here?"

He didn't seem to notice I'd called him by name. "Where the hell else would I be when my grandson's in the hospital?"

"No, I mean, I was just surprised you heard, that's all."

"No thanks to you, Maggie. Good thing I called Milly's father tonight about some business. He filled me in."

"I'm sorry. It took me hours to find out what's wrong with him. It's like I told you at the shore, Dad. Alek isn't strong enough to fight off every germ. They tell me he has strep throat, but this new drug, penicillin, is supposed to work miracles."

Max pulled his lips tight. "You can't just trust 'em to give it to him, Maggie. You have to make sure."

"I was just—"

"I'll take care of it. Wait here." He marched down the length of the corridor to the nurses' station. Even that far away I heard his demands. Leaning over the counter, he poked a stubby forefinger at the nurse on duty. In seconds, she scurried away and returned with Dr. Samuels, who no longer was smiling. Max used the same tone on him he had used on the nurses. I heard only bits and pieces, but I could fill in the blanks. "...my grandson...only the best...you'd better..."

My father-in-law was back to demanding the best for my son. Was he

245

making matters better or worse? Would he pay these bills?

Twenty minutes later, Max was back by my side, his breath wheezy. "My car's parked out on the street. Let's go, Mags. I'll take you home. You need rest."

"No, I want to stay. I want to make sure Alek is all right."

"He will be. I made sure of that." Max nodded toward the nurses' station. "He'll get that new drug. And I hired a private-duty nurse. Gave her strict orders. She'll call me if anything changes."

I shuddered. Even if I couldn't trust Max to pay for this new expense, my son was my biggest worry. I felt unexpected gratitude for my bossy father-in-law. He was making sure Alek would get the care he needed. Max grabbed me by the elbow and led me out a side door. I didn't argue. I would never understand that man. Ever.

For the first time that long day, I no longer was frightened. I climbed into the passenger seat of his bulky sedan. "Thank you, Dad," I whispered.

***

Not until I returned the next morning did I learn Ruth knew how to play boss, too. She had Alek moved to a private room, along with Max's private-duty nurse. At noon, two nurses dragged in a large upholstered chair and an extra pillow for me. "It's no bed, but it's better than sitting in that straight-backed hard chair all day," one said.

Just after lunch, Dr. Wenski himself showed up with the penicillin. He jabbed the needle into Alek quickly and left with a muttered "Good day, Mrs. Baran."

Hours later, Alek still lay listless, his cheeks still flushed with fever, his breath coming in shaky gasps. When he coughed, which was often, his whole body trembled.

I felt hope when his private-duty nurse sponged him with a cool cloth, tented his bed and gave him steam treatments. By early evening, Alek's temperature had dropped to 101 degrees, low enough to please Dr. Samuels, but not me. His breathing still was unsteady. His cough was unrelenting. Dark circles rimmed his eyes.

"He's out of trouble, Mrs. Baran," Dr. Samuels insisted. "All he needs now is rest."

"How can you say that?" I demanded. "He still has a fever. His chest rattles with every breath."

Unlike Dr. Wenski, this doctor didn't scold me like a child. He nodded sympathetically. "We'll keep him here another few days. If his temperature remains stable, I assure you he'll be well enough to go home soon."

After he left, I pulled out the rosary Ruth had given me when Alek was born. Its crystal beads slipped through my fingers whether I uttered a full prayer or not. God surely would forgive my mumbled Hail Marys and Our Fathers.

***

"You must go home, Gosia. You need sleep. I stay with baby." My mother had taken two buses after work to reach the hospital. She stared hard at me. I knew that look. Arguing was pointless.

"Nurse will call you if he get worse. I make sure."

She tapped a foot. I thought about all the sacrifices she'd made for us, the extra jobs she'd taken on, the times she walked Alek when I was too exhausted. The sleep she lost.

"You are a stubborn woman, Mama."

She smiled as if I'd paid her the highest compliment. "There is bottle of port under kitchen sink. Take big glass. You sleep better."

I almost laughed aloud. My mother rarely drank alcohol, but when she did, it was with purpose. One tumbler of port wine or a neat shot of whiskey usually did the trick. I rarely drank alcohol either, but the way I felt at that moment, I might need a whole bottle to calm me. I wouldn't need alcohol to sleep, though. I hadn't dozed for more than a few minutes that day.

I sighed. "You win, Mother. I'll be back first thing in the morning."

***

At my parents' home, a plate of leftovers awaited me atop a pot of hot water. My father sat silently in his rocking chair; a Polish-language newspaper was spread open on his lap.

"*Czesc*, Papa," I said.

"*Jak to moy wnuk?*" he asked, his voice husky.

"Your grandson is a little better," I replied. As I searched for the port wine under the sink, I reassured him. "Mom will call if that changes."

He nodded. "*Tak,*" he said, bracing both feet to still the rocker. "Tomorrow," he said, wagging a finger at me, "you stay here to nine in morning. *Twoja matka* says."

"Nine? That's no good, Pop. I need to get back there as early as possible."

"*Nie.* Is important. You listen to mother."

My mother's directions were as indomitable as her will. I filled a water glass to the brim with port.

In the parlor, I read Walt's latest letter. It was filled with news of prisoners of war, Germany's rain, the cold nights, the damp clothing. The postman that day also delivered bills, magazines, a letter from my grandmother, a letter from a cousin in New York. But nothing from Sam. I hadn't heard from him in more than two weeks. I told myself he was safe. As safe as Walt. A host of reasons could be keeping him from writing.

Overwhelmed by fatigue, I closed my eyes and said a quick prayer for my son, for Walt, for my parents, for Sam, for everyone affected by the war. God must have better answers than this. I finished my wine in a gulp and shuffled to the bedroom. Collapsing on the bed, I pulled the spread up to my chin. Even crying took too much effort.

***

My father's gravelly voice intruded on my dreams. "Gosia! You awake?"

A sliver of daylight trickled into my bedroom from the alley outside my window. I thrashed in the bed, disoriented.

"Gosia?"

The sight of Alek's empty crib jolted me awake. "I'll be right there!"

The clock next to my bed said almost nine o'clock. I had slept eleven hours! I hurriedly dressed and yanked open my bedroom door. My father stood before me, thumping his arthritic foot on the floor. "Hurry," he said, just as the front doorbell blared.

"Answer door, girl," my father ordered. I raced downstairs, unlocked the two padlocks and yanked at the doorknob.

Standing before me was the last person I expected. Tears came. Tears of joy.

"Babcia!" I fell into my grandmother's outspread arms.

FIFTY-ONE

The memory of Tom and Hatch stalked Walt's every waking moment. They haunted his nights. He heard them gab and laugh without a care over bottles of wine and beer.

From habit, Walt still searched for his friends amid each new batch of patients. Sometimes he thought he spotted them: Tom's chiseled chin, high forehead, prominent nose; Hatch's disheveled hair, small frame, dimpled cheeks.

His agitation was matched by the frantic pace his company kept as it traveled through eastern France and Belgium. The convoy raced past the corpses of Germans and Americans, past disabled tanks and machinery. Walt grimaced at the sight of villages reduced to rubble and fields rendered useless by giant craters and shell fragments.

Supply trucks couldn't keep up. Even canned Spam was running low. One night, Walt and one of the cooks came up with a plan to solve their never-ending hunger. They traded cigarettes with local farmers for chickens, milk and eggs. Skulking through unpicked fields, they harvested barely ripe vegetables and green apples. The cook made chicken-vegetable soup for dinner and apple dumplings for dessert. Walt savored each mouthful, pretending he was in his mother's kitchen. The meal tasted that good.

After he swallowed the last bite, Walt crawled into his pup tent, pulled on dry socks and burrowed under his wool blanket. In the heavy dampness, the tent smelled like a barn, or maybe the stench was just his and Ted's unwashed bodies.

In the next tent, a young replacement named Gil laughed so cheerfully he made Walt jealous. Most new men stood out for different reasons. They hogged attention and carried on like experienced soldiers. Gil wasn't like those loudmouths. A farm boy from Kansas, he said "yes, sir" and "no, sir" and showed concern for the other men.

Gil joined Walt one Sunday when the men were allowed to attend Mass at a nearby village. Only a handful of French civilians showed up; the GIs had plenty of room. A soldier stood to the side of the altar, translating the priest's greeting: "Soldiers of America, thank you for the wonderful example you set this morning."

Walt's memory flashed back to the Mass in Sicily more than a year earlier, when he'd marveled at Magnus's knowledge of the ritual. Three months had passed since Walt told the driver about Cliff. He wondered where Magnus was now. He wished they could exchange knowing glances one more time.

***

In mid-September, earlier than Walt expected, the clearing company passed through the Belgian town of Eupen and entered Hitler's homeland. The Ninth's progress felt too easy. Could he be going home this soon?

As the medical convoy bounced along a dirt road through a thick forest of pine and hemlock, he braced himself for the smell of death. He expected to see dead soldiers. To encounter vicious resistance from artillery rounds, bunkers, pillboxes and minefields. He saw none of that. Whenever they came to a clearing, he saw only broad-shouldered women working tidy farms with healthy, chubby children at their feet. The scenery was—there was no other way to describe it—both beautiful and tranquil.

All that was missing were able-bodied men. Walt knew why. For weeks, wounded German soldiers of every age and physical condition had passed through surgery: Fifty-year-old men; thirteen-year-old boys; even the disabled, like the one-eyed young man and the gaunt senior who'd lost three fingers in a previous battle. Any male who could carry a pack was conscripted into Hitler's service. Der Fuhrer wanted them all at the front line.

A few miles into Germany, deep in enemy territory, they set up camp. Walt was staking his pup tent when Captain Hunter found him. "Baran, you're taking guard duty tonight with Gil."

"Are you serious, Jack, uh, sir? I thought MPs and infantrymen were supposed to defend us in Germany," Walt said. "Because, we're not...armed."

Hunter handed him a .45-caliber pistol. "Nothing much going on at the front right now. Use this if you have to. I have one for Gil, too."

"Where did you—?" Walt stopped himself. No point asking. Some higher-up must have decided a medic armed with a lousy pistol was better than nothing. And Walt, yet again, was back to being a private—his punishment a week earlier for ignoring Captain Abich's command to patch

250

the surgery tent after an eleven-hour shift.

Buck overheard the exchange. "I hear you're a crack shot, Baran. Keep us safe, huh?"

"Right, Buck," Walt said, slipping into sarcasm's sing-song cadence. "That's why I'm in the medics. To kill people."

Buck squinted at him. "Sometimes you're one odd bird, Baran, you know that?"

Walt wanted to explain why he dreaded the assignment, but he couldn't bear telling one more person about the night his brother died. Sharing that memory with Magnus had been difficult enough. Cliff's death would always be his burden alone, his punishment for his pride the night his brother died.

He ducked into his pup tent, where Ted sprawled on his blanket reading a magazine. "What the hell is that for?" Ted shouted when he spotted the .45.

"To stop enemy soldiers from attacking us tonight."

"Very funny. Where'd you get it?"

"Not a joke and from Captain Hunter. Gil and I are on guard duty tonight. This is my weapon."

"Know how to fire it?"

"Nope. Never used one before in my life. All I know is a .45 has eight rounds and is great for shooting someone 30 or so yards away. I'm pretty good with a rifle, though." He glanced at Ted. "Feel safe now?"

Ted let loose a long, low whistle. "This war gets crazier every day."

"Actually, I might get lucky," Walt said, placing the pistol down carefully. "It's quiet as a church out there. Unless one of those bulky frauleins decides to attack us, I think we're safe."

He hoped he was right. He held out his hands and spread his fingers wide. He'd grown oddly accustomed to his tremors, which came and went in waves. They never stopped him from doing his job. If he could insert an IV in a vein, he thought, he could hold a pistol.

He just wasn't sure he could shoot it at someone.

At dinner that night, the men bet on how many days would pass before Hitler surrendered. Walt wrote Nora while the men around him wagered. He held on to his money.

Sept. 15, 1944

Dear Nora,

This war may be the greatest drama the world has ever seen, but soldiers live an unnatural life. Ordinary guys like me never had to endure such a gamut of emotions or extremes of living. There are stories to be told of courage, cowardice, suffering and misery, humor and gaiety. After a while, it takes a whole lot to faze us. We become immune to ordinary feelings...

That night, the pistol tucked in his waistband, Walt paced the perimeter of the camp as a passing storm drowned out every other sound. His poncho kept him dry but did nothing to block the chill burrowing into his bones. In the woods, he saw only dense blackness. Deaf and blind, he thought. I make a great guard.

All night long he braced himself, every muscle tensed, his hand resting on the pistol's grip. He prayed nonstop. The wind bent branches and swirled piles of dead leaves. More than once, Walt thought he heard footsteps, but God must have been listening for a change. He saw no sign of the enemy. His wild imaginings of having to shoot someone never came to pass.

"I'll take that pistol, Baran," Captain Spalding said the next morning. "We probably won't need to guard the camp again for a while."

"Probably" wasn't good enough, Walt thought. His nerves couldn't take another night like that.

***

"Goddammit," Ted bellowed, his feet sliding in the mud. He gripped his end of the litter so tightly his knuckles had turned white.

"I got it," Walt yelled above the thundering rainfall. He held his end just as tightly. "Just a few more steps."

The two techs were working as litter bearers out of necessity. Too many wounded flooded surgery. It was hard to keep up. Just days after the medics placed bets on Hitler's quick surrender, the Germans lashed back at Allied troops with the fiercest fighting yet. Casualties—Americans and Germans alike—filled every cot. East of them, Allied troops encountered minefields, bunkers and a deluge of artillery rounds. Like the flow of wounded, the cold rain would not stop.

At least they could set up their station in Roetgen. Walt was grateful that the German town's abandoned buildings provided warm, dry space for surgery, recovery rooms and sleeping quarters. Yet every patient had to stay put, even those needing extensive surgery; ambulances mired in mud couldn't travel anywhere, even to field hospitals or evacuation hospitals

"What's going on?" Walt asked Gus. "I've never seen this many wounded."

"Jerries are pushing back. They aren't giving an inch in the Huertgen Forest," the clerk said. "Damn woods are so thick that Hitler's mortar shells explode above the treetops. Did you see those wounds? That's what human flesh looks like when thick, blazing wood splinters go through it. We can't get replacements here fast enough."

Walt's shifts lasted ten hours and more. He never complained. He took pride in his newfound determination to work well with every doctor, even Captain Abich.

"Gauze!" Abich yelled at Walt during one late afternoon shift. "Saline!"

The young soldier before him writhed in pain. The left side of his face sagged like molten lava. His screams sounded like a towel had been stuffed in his mouth. Walt searched a crowded storage crate for a bottle of saline.

"Goddammit, Baran. Now! Not next week!"

Walt silently handed over a bottle. Abich had learned a lot in the last two years. No matter what the injury, the man now seemed to know what to do. He was still a first-class jackass, however, the kind of guy destined eventually to feel another man's fist in his face. "Please, help me not be that man," Walt prayed to the God he no longer fully trusted. "Give me patience. Lots of it."

The next morning, Walt stood at attention before Major Penland, wondering what trouble he was in this time. He had been summoned without explanation. Had Abich complained about his work the night before? Had one of his letters again gone too far? He wondered what damage the Army could do to a tech already busted to private.

"Private, I've been watching you the last few weeks."

Walt braced himself.

"I saw you last night with Abich."

Heart thumping, he opened his mouth to defend himself, but instinct took over. Don't say a word, he thought, you'll only make things worse.

Penland leaned forward, his hands clasped in front of him. "You have quite a colorful track record for conduct, but you continue to do high-quality work. You're a natural leader."

"I—Thank you, sir,"

"Even more important, you handled Abich professionally last night. For once, you acted like the Army taught you. That's why I'm putting you in for a field promotion. To Corporal. Again."

Walt's mind raced. Here was a chance to let the Major know more about Abich. "Sir, I think you—"

"That will be all, corporal," Penland interrupted. He stared at Walt. "Do not make me regret this decision. Do you understand?"

Walt snapped a smart salute. "Yes, sir!"

He had stopped telling Nora about these field promotions, which came and went as easily as Europe's bad weather. The title was helpful when he occasionally needed to issue an order, but it was of little importance to wife and son. Field promotions didn't result in more money, and inevitably were rescinded when circumstances changed or Walt's behavior again was deemed unacceptable.

Days later, to his surprise, he held onto the promotion after he found a way to alert Nora of his whereabouts. He let the Army talk for him in Stars and Stripes newspaper articles.

Oct. 17, 1944

Dear Nora,

Enclosed is an article with summaries of the Ninth's battles. Fighting goes on all the time, actually, and one battle merges into another without anybody half realizing it. There's been a hell of a lot of combat since we landed in France, but things are quieter now. Our medical battalion motto, "Where you lead, we follow," tells the whole story. The infantry goes in first and we are on its heels. Theoretically, we're considered within the front line, but in fact we can be two to fifteen miles from where an infantryman's life isn't worth a plugged nickel...

After days of fierce combat, each day more intense than the one before, the fighting near Roetgen unexpectedly stalled. Both sides dug deep trenches resembling scenes from World War I. They seemed ready to spend a cold winter at Germany's Siegfried Line.

Few patients arrived in surgery now; Walt's duties were light. The small number of wounded who did arrive were mostly German soldiers. He gave them care as good as any GI got, no matter how uncooperative they were.

"What next, Gus? This lull is unnerving."

"The Rhine River, I hear," the clerk said. "If we cross it this winter, we can move deeper into Germany."

As Walt's third Christmas abroad neared, the only gift he yearned for was the war's end. He clung to a fragile hope. Germany's best fighting units had been decimated. Der Fuhrer surely would realize that it was time to surrender.

But on December 16, the enemy mocked his longing. On that snowy, overcast day, the Nazis did something no one expected. They hurled their toughest soldiers at a poorly defended section of the Allied front in Belgium, about twenty miles south of the clearing company. The Ninth Infantry was sent to attack the bulge. For all of them, it was a return to familiar territory. The western edge of the Ardennes Forest was the same rough, hilly region they had passed through three months earlier.

Walt's patients spoke of fierce fighting in the dense forest, with its steep-sided valleys and high ridges. Winter's brutal weather and the war didn't choose sides. German and American soldiers alike showed up in Walt's surgery with wounds, frostbite, trench foot, combat fatigue and pneumonia.

December 20, 1944

Dear Nora,

You probably shouldn't expect any Christmas gifts from me this year. Things have been awful busy. Although the recovery ward is eerily quiet right now, every cot is taken. Usually, our patients chatter like magpies about everything but the war. Not these guys. If they do speak at all, it's only about the war, and they don't tell tall tales...

FIFTY-TWO

The mere sight of my grandmother relieved me. She would make sure things would be all right. I settled her at our kitchen table, poured hot tea and told her what had happened so far.

As I relayed Alek's treatment, an unsettling realization hit me. Babcia's deep connection to her farm and her husband meant she rarely traveled to the city. We always went to her. For her to pack a bag and take a two-hour train ride, she had to think something awful was happening. "Why are you here, Babcia?" I chose my words in Polish carefully. "Tell me the truth."

Her fierce blue eyes softened. "I love you, Gosia. I love Alek. That is truth," she said.

I felt no peace as Babcia and I hurried to the hospital, even though love should explain everything, should heal everything.

People turned and stared as she strode through the children's wing. I suspected it was her odd peasant clothing—her long woolen skirt, high-topped leather shoes and *babushka* tied back so tightly it hid her hair. But when she entered Alek's room, the hospital nurse and Max's private nurse both nodded respectfully. Maybe it was the confident way she carried herself, like the hospital was her second home, or the purposeful way she took Alek from my mother's arms.

My mother looked exhausted. She must have been awake with Alek all night. Her wary gaze seemed to ask, Is it okay I call for your Babcia? I nodded. I was frightened but grateful.

Speaking in her mix of Polish and English, Babcia asked the nurses about Alek's condition and his medicines. Sometimes my mother interrupted with translations, but it wasn't always necessary. The nurses and my grandmother seemed to understand each other.

All the while, my son gazed at Babcia serenely. His sunken eyes were as tired as my mother's, but for the first time since he'd been in the hospital, he looked calm.

"Alek, Alek," she whispered as she touched his forehead and pressed her ear tightly against his chest. I knew her ways by now. I held my breath as she listened to his lungs and heart, convinced she heard more than any doctor could with a stethoscope.

She took so long with her exam that I turned to my mother for reassurance, but she already had slipped away. "Your mother went home to rest," a nurse said.

My grandmother stroked Alek's hair and kissed his cheeks until his eyes closed. Then she motioned me toward the hall. "We go." Outside the room, she reached for my hands. "Fever almost gone," she said, pumping my hands up and down with each word. "It is okay."

Poor Babcia. Her magnetic blue eyes, the very feature that attracted people to her powers, were also her lie detector. They flashed with fear.

In an instant, she turned and hurried downstairs to the exit. I followed close behind. "Where are you going?" Ignoring my question, she rushed toward the bus stop. She was breathing hard. "Alek must stay in hospital now. You not worry. We come back with herbs. I fix."

"Herbs, Babcia?"

Did I hear her right, or was she mangling her English again? Was she really planning to treat Alek with her Old-World mud baths?

She smiled knowingly as she boarded the bus. For all I knew, she was planning to smuggle in candles and holy water, too.

I couldn't imagine her getting away with it. As respectful as the nurses and doctors had been, they surely wouldn't let her slather a sick baby with mud. Ancient superstitions had no place in an antiseptic hospital stocked with modern medicines and equipment.

The bus wheezed as it lumbered past tall buildings, English-language signs, traffic lights and impatient automobiles. Like the hospital we had just left, everything I saw outside made sense to me. Modern, busy, purposeful. So unlike my grandmother.

Babcia touched my arm. "Gosia? You okay?" She looked worried. I slipped an arm through hers and nodded. She touched my face.

For a split second, I stepped outside my pride and saw myself—a full-fledged American girl—pressed against an old woman in a *babushka*. I relied mightily on her. She'd brought with her to America every custom, recipe, language and prayer of the Old World, even the way she walked and tied back her hair. Ready for the plow. Her ancient healing rituals might just save both my son and me. I laughed aloud at the irony. Babcia gave me the oddest look, which made me laugh harder. Despite her confusion, she soon was laughing, too.

Only later did I learn that our shared moment on the bus, in my grandmother's mind, meant everything was settled; I would be her accomplice.

***

Back at my parents' home, Babcia plundered the pantry and refrigerator and added new ingredients to the herbs she carried in her satchel.

We returned to the hospital early the next morning. Babcia carried a cloth satchel bulging with clean diapers, more pouches of herbs, some juice from my mother's kitchen, and a clean ceramic cup. We arrived an hour before shift change when the nurses were busy finishing their duties. No one seemed to notice us.

My job was simple: Distract Alek's nurses so that Babcia had time alone with him. I cornered Max's private-duty nurse first, sending her to the cafeteria for snacks. Then I quizzed the ward nurse with a dozen questions about Alek's condition.

Babcia's job was more complicated. She told me later she made a poultice in the ceramic cup by mixing her herbs with warm water. Next, she spread most of it on Alek's chest. Her last step was the real miracle. She left a spoonful of the mix in the cup, added juice and sugar, and gave it to Alek to drink.

"He drank it? All of it? Really?" I asked, imagining the gritty, muddy concoction. My son's picky appetite surely wouldn't have allowed it.

Babcia nodded.

"How does it work?" I asked.

"Like magic."

***

We followed the same routine the next morning, even though the ward nurse seemed exasperated by my endless questions. The third morning, she tried to avoid me by ducking into a storage closet. I acted surprised when she finally emerged. "Oh, hello! I'm so glad I found you. I need your help. What's that report I saw at the nurses' station?"

She frowned. "Report?"

"Something about a release schedule. I thought I saw Alek's name on it."

She glanced warily toward the nurses' station at the other end of the hall. "I haven't heard anything like that," she said.

I walked steadily in that direction, chatting amiably to move her along with me. When we got to the station, and no one knew about any report, I switched quickly to my latest list of questions: "Did my son eat all his dinner? What was his temperature that morning? Was that low enough?

Shouldn't he get a different medicine for his congestion?"

Glancing at the clock over the nurse's shoulder, I saw I had sidetracked her for only four minutes. I switched to personal questions. How long had she worked at the hospital? Was she a mother, too? Did she grow up in Union County? That's when she held up a hand and stopped me. "I must go, Mrs. Baran." She excused herself just as Babcia slipped out of Alek's room.

"Let's go home, Babcia," I whispered when I caught up to her. "I am exhausted."

***

My grandmother's formidable powers did more than spark Alek's slow recovery. They even worked on Max. He stomped into the hospital room a few days later the same way he entered every room, itching to take over. "Step aside," he ordered the nurse.

Only when the nurse backed up did Max spot my tiny Babcia hunched over Alek. His voice dropped. "Eh, hello, Mrs. Petin. I didn't know you were here. How's my grandson?" His polite tone was akin to a miracle. Almost as startling was hearing him speak my grandmother's last name. To her family, she always was just Babcia.

She smiled broadly. "Alek is perfect, Max. Most perfect little boy."

Max glanced at my boy and nodded.

"Hi there," I said, not waiting for Max to greet me first.

"Ah, Maggie. So, what's going on here?"

Babcia wasn't ready to cede control. She jumped in, speaking in rapid Polish. Max hung on each word, sometimes nodding, sometimes frowning, more often looking shocked. After she finished, my father-in-law looked intently at Alek, then turned back to my grandmother.

"Let me know if you need anything," he said, and he left.

Babcia's presence had a different effect on my mother-in-law. It fortified Ruth's natural good-heartedness. Their combined affection for Alek worked almost as well as the hospital's fancy modern medicine. Whenever they both were in the room, he beamed at them, a happy smile crinkling his eyes.

***

During those long, trying days at Alek's side, I felt guilty every time I thought of Walt. What would he think if he knew what was happening? His son was in the hospital, so sick Max again had to get involved, so sick my mother summoned her own mother, the mightiest healer any of us knew.

At last, I knew what I had to do. Walt deserved the truth—or at least a bigger piece of it.

November 18, 1944

Dear Walt,

News reports say the war is nearing an end. I pray every night they are right. When you come home, dear, our life will be grand. Our worst times will be behind us. Right now, I have some important news, but please don't worry. Little Alek was sick enough recently to spend some time in the hospital. He's already on the mend. He is getting the latest medicines. My Babcia is helping, too. He is very brave, just like his daddy…

My grandmother visited Alek every day in the two weeks she stayed with us. Her determination seemed to bolster the efforts of his doctors and nurses. Her presence at home steadied our household. I grew so accustomed to her presence that I was shocked when I found her folding her clothes and stuffing them into her satchel.

"You're packing, Babcia? Shouldn't Alek have more treatments?"

"*Tak*. You give," she said. "Tomorrow I take train. Here." She handed me a pouch of her herbs. She carefully reviewed with me how to prepare them and how much to give Alek in the hospital and after he came home.

Whether or not her dried powders could cure Alek, she believed they would. For the first time, I saw the source of her powers. It was nothing less than her unshakeable inner strength.

I wanted that faith, too.

FIFTY-THREE

December 24, 1944

Dear Nora,

    Your November 18 letter came today with news of Alek's stay in the hospital. I admit the news shook me a bit. Our letters take too long to reach us. How is our boy now? What did the doctors decide? Does he need any special treatment? If only I could just pick up a phone and get answers. The decisions about our son's care are in your hands. I have faith in you...

He chose his words carefully to disguise his fear. Babcia had written him, too, and he knew enough Polish to understand she was watching Alek closely. That worried him but made him hopeful, too. He'd witnessed the old woman's healing skills countless times. He knew they were more than superstitious luck.

Censors wouldn't let him tell Nora that his company was headed back to Germany again. The day before, it retraced its earlier eastward trek for almost thirty-five miles. On their return to Eupen, the medics were forced to dive into ditches three times. Enemy planes strafed the road before them, aiming at the 240-mm artillery gun leading the way. The planes dove so low that machine-gun bullets sang over the medics' heads. Walt wasn't sure if the bullets missed them because of the crosses on their helmets or dumb luck.

In Eupen, thousands of GIs rested—if rest was possible so close to the front line. Patrols prowled its narrow streets; booming heavy artillery weapons aimed at German bomber planes. During one flurry of artillery, Walt sought refuge in a brick building that seemed secure, even though its foundations shook every time a weapon was fired. Acrid clouds of dirt and debris filled the air. Walt braced himself. Mindful of the date, he said a hasty prayer. No matter how much his faith had faltered in recent months, he was determined to squelch his pessimism.

The clearing company set up its wards in a two-story abandoned building that night. Just before midnight, Ted shouted welcome news: "Hey guys, the Christmas service starts in five minutes." Midnight Mass was an answered prayer.

The stillness of the hour settled Walt's spirit. He hurried to join a cluster of men singing familiar Christmas carols. They sat cross-legged on the floor before a makeshift altar. Midway through the service, when the chaplain placed communion wafers on their tongues, Walt accepted his gratefully. For the first time in months, he thought God could see him.

Walt and Ted were certain that the war's end would be their Christmas present, but days later they learned that fierce fighting had erupted again in the Ardennes forest. The Germans weren't ready to walk away. The combat continued for weeks. For just as long, Walt heard no more news about Alek's health.

At one point, the medics had to move into a former sausage factory to make room for other units. Then, in advance of a new Allied offensive in late January, they moved into an abandoned restaurant on a deserted road that led to the front. *"Gaststatte Shumacher"* read the worn sign out front.

Outside, howling wind whipped falling snow into eight-foot drifts. At night, an army of rats scurrying behind the walls made a muffled racket. "They're probably just trying to stay warm," Walt said, rubbing his hands near a hot stove.

Ted cupped his hand to one ear. "Who cares about the rats? Listen to that! Damn artillery bombs and machine guns surround us. We're unprotected. All the Jerries have to do is shift their sites an inch and we're done for."

Ted was right. The restaurant, the only building in a flat open area, was surrounded by German observation posts atop nearby hills. The front was a mere two miles away. Walt rubbed steam off a window for a better look, but falling snow draped everything in a white haze.

He checked on a dark-haired young private in recovery named Heaney. He'd been knocked unconscious by a bullet fragment that ricocheted off his helmet and into his scalp. Blood oozed through the thick gauze on his wound. Heaney needed experienced surgeons, but no ambulances could get through the snow to take him to a field hospital.

The man's unconsciousness was probably a gift, Walt thought. The eyes of the dozen other immobilized soldiers in the room registered terror. Heaney looked like he was sleeping, the way his friend Tom Lucas looked the night his body was taken away. Walt took Heaney's pulse and blood pressure, aware of how death had tricked him before. Was stillness a chance for the body to rest, or a step toward death? Was sleep itself just the body's way of getting used to its eventual fate? Walt gazed around the room. They all were at God's mercy. If Germans attacked them, he and every other unarmed medic could do little to save the vulnerable patients, much less themselves.

It wasn't smart to let war become habit, he decided. Too much stoicism left a soldier unprepared for fresh pain.

***

Ted drew deeply on a cigarette as he and Walt sat at a dusty table, finishing their morning coffee. Outside, wind stirred up the snow so violently it was hard to tell if new snow was falling. They'd been stuck in the restaurant for a week.

"Did ya hear the news about Magnus?" Ted asked.

It was the first time in weeks Walt had heard the driver's name. "What about him?"

"A casualty from the 39th told me. Magnus snuck out of camp one night to get hooch. You know how he used to do."

"Nothing new about that," Walt said.

"He got shot trying to sneak back in, Walt. A guy on guard duty thought he was the enemy. He's dead."

Walt's temples throbbed. Magnus's death, like so many others, should have been expected. The loss should have been easier to swallow. But the news gutted him. Magnus alone knew an elemental fact of Walt's life, a truth only he now possessed.

***

When the Germans finally began to retreat in February, the clearing company followed in the infantry's footsteps. A letter from Nora, postmarked in late December, found him at their next stop, the German town of Monschau. Alek was out of the hospital, she wrote. She made it sound like his release was expected. She wrote nothing about her Babcia.

He took it as good news. The war's mayhem distracted him too much to think otherwise. His company was following the infantry through the Huertgen Forest, where deep woods were filthy with mines and booby traps. Wounded GIs again filled every cot. Gruesome injuries and heartbreaking losses were routine.

Near the German border town of Remagen, the medics reunited with the Ninth Infantry and Armored Division. Walt gaped at the town's battered wooden bridge, one of the last crossing the Rhine River still standing. He wondered if it would hold up long enough to let them cross.

According to Gus, German forces had done their best to destroy the bridge ever since it was captured by U.S. Forces on March 7. They used howitzers, mortars, floating mines, mined boats, a railroad gun and more. The punished span still stood, thanks to the U.S. Army engineers. The bridge, like the Ninth Infantry itself, seemed determined to hold on.

Even Gus was caught up in the anticipation of crossing. The night of March 16, the usually steadfast clerk ran into Walt's ward shouting, "We're moving out tomorrow! Let's get packing."

"Wooey!" Ted shouted. "Time to eat some wiener schnitzel."

Walt found himself smiling, an unfamiliar expression for him ever since Normandy. He could see war's end. Soon, he thought. Very soon.

He packed equipment and personal items, a routine he now performed as effortlessly as tying a surgical knot or applying a splint. The next afternoon, seated in a truck near the front of the convoy, he waited impatiently for the driver to turn the key. Nearby huddled a cluster of officers. Finally, Hunter approached the driver. "Change of plans," he said. "The bridge is gone."

"What?" several medics yelled at once.

"Collapsed just a little while ago. We'll be crossing on a pontoon bridge."

"Casualties?" Walt asked.

"More than thirty engineers dead. Twice that number wounded. The field hospital will handle them."

Walt and Ted exchanged a glance. No bombs or explosions had sounded that day. The bridge had fallen apart after days of furious attacks. Like some battle fatigued soldiers at the front, the aged structure had seen too much action. It had no strength to carry on.

***

The further east the medics moved, the more Germany reminded Walt of a Seaside Heights' funhouse—all illusion and sleight of hand. Behind the quiet façade of the countryside, a determined disorder stalked. Shadows flitted in the woods. Noises erupted where they did not belong.

Every time Walt heard twigs break or footsteps thump, he thought he saw movement, too. It was impossible to know if his ghosts were friend or foe. The front line no longer existed. All over Germany, America's First, Ninth and Third Armies were running wild.

Some of the sounds came from wounded Allied soldiers searching for their units. But some sounds came from captured men in Nazi uniforms who moved in every imaginable direction and told every imaginable story. Some were German soldiers separated from their units. Others claimed to be foreigners conscripted by Hitler's Army. "We were forced to fight for them against our will," they said. "We just want to go home to our families." No one knew who spoke the truth.

One night, Walt traced the sound of muffled voices to a group of women and children. They told him German soldiers had taken them from their homes months earlier. They were trying to return.

"They looked terrified, starved," he told Ted as they gulped mugs of coffee on a break. "That could explain some of the other civilians we've spotted in the woods."

A litter-bearer nearby interrupted. "The sounds you hear could be something else."

The man's explanation was so disturbing Walt refused to believe it. "They're the walking dead," the man said. "Rail-thin, heads shaved, filthy clothes, covered with sores. Escaped from prison camps. Or labor camps. The Nazis starved, tortured and slaughtered too many to count in those camps."

Walt shook his head. "You sure they got that right?"

"I heard it from a soldier I drove to an evac hospital, who heard it from an artillery soldier in another division," the litter bearer said. "Who would make that up?"

Ted interrupted. "I heard similar stuff from one of my patients. The goddam Jerries skinned some of them prisoners alive, he said. Killed babies with their mothers standing right there. Hard to believe."

Buck wandered over, frowning. "I heard they lined up Jews and shot them dead--women and children."

"I wouldn't believe everything you hear," Walt said. He didn't want to believe it. The stories didn't seem possible.

Accounts of German torture, like every other rumor, burned through the ranks of enlisted men more quickly than a telegram. After all these months of war, medical companies remained the hub of the delivery system. Each new patient brought a new tale or a variation of a previous story; each patient returned to his unit fueled with new rumors.

Early in the war, anxiety clouded Walt's natural skepticism. Back then, he tended to believe every tale that hinted of Allied success and German failure. He was different now. He clung to hard-nosed logic, no matter how much the others mocked him. Most often he was right. The "sure thing" heard at nine a.m. emerged as little more than a half-baked notion by noon.

In this part of rural Germany, the medics passed carnage Walt already had seen in a half dozen other countries: fields ripped apart; buildings leveled; hastily dug trenches; decaying corpses of livestock and even men and women. He tried to feel compassion, even if Germany had brought the ruin on itself.

The medics pillaged abandoned houses, factories and shops once used as Nazi quarters, Walt felt no guilt scrounging supplies other soldiers had left behind—food, socks, scarves, knives, cameras, stationery. In one cottage, he grabbed a thick stack of writing paper with German lettering at the top. The large sheets left plenty of room for his longer letters.

"Don't get any ideas, Walt," Hunter said when he spotted Walt carrying the paper to his tent.

"Ideas?"

"Don't try that innocent look on me. I know you. Remember orders about letters home."

"Right, Captain. Say nothing about where we are, who or what we see, where we're going."

"And nothing about those concentration camps rumors. Nothing."

"Why not? Everyone's talking about it now. Shouldn't folks back home know, too?"

Hunter sighed, just as he did every time Walt challenged a censorship order.

Walt was tempted to keep arguing. He knew his friendly relationship with the captain let him get away with things other officers might call insubordination. But the urge quickly disappeared. He had little fight left in him. The reality of the situation was clear: Hunter had no more control over the Army's mystifying rules than he did.

Hunter motioned him closer and dropped his voice. "You know how the Army is about rumors, Walt. They can ruin us. Especially something that big."

Even if the argument was less than persuasive, Walt appreciated his friend's attempt to explain. "Okay, Jack. I hear you."

He tore up several drafts before handing Hunter the final version in an unsealed envelope. "Just making sure, Captain. Before I get in trouble again with whoever is on censor duty. This pass muster?"

"I wish I didn't know you so well, Walt," the captain said, pulling out the letter. He read it quickly, his face registering faint surprise and then impatience. "You walked pretty close to the line, you know."

"I didn't say a word about concentration camps. Kept it vague. Is it okay? Sir?"

Hunter laughed softly. "Yeah, it's okay. Barely." He pulled out his pen and initialed the envelope.

Walt felt victorious. He finally won a censorship battle. But by afternoon, he wished he could get that letter back. Nora was better off knowing nothing about these things.

March 29, 1945

Dear Nora,

I never thought my miserable knowledge of Polish

would be of use here, but it helps me talk to Russians and Poles who the Jerries forced into labor. I heard stories about their treatment that I'm not allowed to describe in my letters. That's just as well. The details are almost enough to make a person lose faith. One Pole said he was abducted from his farm ten months ago and forced to work in a German factory. He was a mess by the time he arrived in our station. When I get home, we can finally talk. I'll tell you everything...

FIFTY-FOUR

To my amazement, Max made me grateful again. Thanks to his watchful eye on Dr. Wenski, the doctor kept Alek in the hospital until his fever was gone and his strength was back.

I meticulously obeyed Babcia's directions. Every morning, I mixed a teaspoon of her greenish powder in a small jar of water and snuck it into the hospital. I was unconvinced the unappetizing concoction would help, but Alek gulped it down like sweetened milk.

To my amazement, my boy's breathing cleared. His cheeks regained color. Even so, I stuck to our daily ritual. If I delayed his dose for even a minute, he fussed and strained for his cup. His cries for his great-grandmother sounded like an incantation: "Ba-chee, ba-chee." My doubts didn't matter. My grandmother believed in the cure. My son did, too. All I could do was act on their belief.

Faith must work like that, I thought. Not through any sleight of hand. Not through study, the way my Babcia memorized her ancient texts on herbal healing. Not through begging or hoping either. It worked through action.

Mysteriously, faith began to enter the rest of my life. I came to believe that Babcia's herbs would work, without knowing how. I believed Alek soon would come home from the hospital and Walt would come home from the war, without knowing when. I trusted I would have enough money to pay the doctor, without knowing where it would come from. My newfound acceptance of the unknowable brought me to Mass every Sunday and even on some weekdays. My crystal rosary beads slipped through my fingers as I murmured its chants.

On some days, I confess, my doubt returned tenfold. On those days, I worried faith might never be enough. I feared that Alek might relapse and

Walt might be injured. But surrender was the only power I had left. I clung to it. My clever husband, the man who scorned superstition and questioned every rule, *he* never gave up faith. Even when he entered the Army and every force moved against him, even when the war separated us for years, he believed his God would see us through.

> December 10, 1944
>
> Dear Walt,
>
> Good news, dearest. The penicillin worked well on our boy. Alek is home from the hospital. He eats everything I put in front of him. He gets stronger every day and is walking now. I'll send you a photo as soon as I can...

As sparse as my letter was, it contained more truth than almost anything I'd written Walt since our son was born. The day I mailed it, the postman delivered a V-mail from Sam written in early November.

"You were right to bring Alek to the hospital right away, Nora" he wrote. "It sounds like that new medicine will help. Give Alek a hug for me, would you? He is lucky to have such a devoted mother and family. I'll bet even Max may surprise you."

I smiled at Sam's words, so full of faith. But just as quickly, regret replaced my cheer. I wished our mail moved more quickly so that Walt and Sam would already know about Alek's progress. I regretted that Sam knew more about Alek's health than my husband might ever know.

***

As Alek's second birthday approached, I expected a bill from Max's private-duty nurse to arrive any day. I emptied my spare change into a giant pickling jar, hoping the coins eventually would add up to enough for a payment. I refused to scrimp on my son's birthday, though. I bought him a wooden truck and a picture book. I splurged on sugar to make him a chocolate cake. I beamed when Walt's gift arrived: a sketch of a puppy holding two balloons, with "Happy Birthday, Son" printed in large block letters.

No medical bills came that month to darken our holiday preparations, thank goodness. I memorized a half dozen tunes on the piano—from "Silent Night" to "White Christmas"—and sang along as I played them for my family and my son throughout the holidays.

By the middle of January, I began to wonder if my father-in-law had paid the medical bills without telling me. I couldn't imagine it. The hospital bill alone would be enormous.

Another mystery haunted me even more. Sam's V-mail in early

November was the last I'd received from him. Something was interrupting his usually prompt correspondence, and I had no way of checking on him. I wasn't sure exactly what Sam did in the Navy. He couldn't tell me those details, he once wrote, and I let it go, just as I did Walt's battles with censors.

I'd hoped for the war's end countless times since Walt left us more than two years earlier. For the longest time, I avoided news reports from Europe, knowing my overactive imagination would fill in the missing pieces and feed my worries. Now I did the same with the war in the Pacific. Sam was there. My brother was there. I assumed the best for both of them.

FIFTY-FIVE

A hint of warm air grazed the first few days of April. After months of cold rain, sleet and snow, the spring thaw fanned Walt's optimism. Two years, five months and God-knew-how-many days after he'd landed in Africa, Germany's forces at last seemed to be crumbling.

Even if he was sent to the Pacific after this, he thought, he surely could first go home to see Nora and Alek. He missed his son, this child he had never met, as much as he missed Nora. Letters from home—from Nora, his parents, his uncles, aunts and cousins—painted images of the boy. Alek was well again, and an imp—funny and smart, by Nora's description. He and his son would be quite a pair.

He felt no danger as his convoy drove through Germany's Harz Mountains, whose rolling hills and deep green forests reminded him of rural New Jersey. By the time they set up camp on April 12, he was more hopeful than ever.

Not until late that night did a buzz of shocked voices startle him from his tent. He hurried to the mess tent, where a radio was turned to full volume. "We repeat: The United States is in mourning," the announcer said. "President Franklin Delano Roosevelt died this afternoon at his retreat in Warm Springs, Georgia. He was 63."

Shock reverberated among the men, followed by grief and fear. Walt understood it. As much as he had suspected FDR's motives for wanting to enter the war, his long months overseas had left him with a grudging respect for the man. During his twelve years as president, FDR had led the nation through the Depression and into the final days of the war. Now a hat salesman from Missouri was president. Could a guy like Harry Truman get the job done?

The men debated the question for hours over countless pots of coffee.

Walt left just after midnight. The answer was a mystery, and even prayer couldn't solve it.

***

Captain Hunter looked tense. He stood before his platoon with his hands on his hips. "You men better remember one thing: This war isn't over. The Germans are determined as ever to keep our troops under fire. Stay alert. Watch out for snipers. A guy hiding in the bushes might not see that red cross on your helmet before he fires."

"There's no way I'm going to get nailed by some gun-happy Nazi," Walt whispered to Ted, "not with home so clear in my sights."

Ted shrugged, still too cocky for his own good. "We got nothing to worry about."

Two hours later, it wasn't snipers that stopped the company cold, but a railroad yard filled with flat cars and large rocket components. A short distance away, a string of lights illuminated the entrance to a poorly camouflaged mountain tunnel. No one was in sight. Walt nudged Ted. "What the hell is that?"

The convoy slowed to a stop. One by one, the medics warily left their vehicles. They followed a dirt road to what looked like a burned-out warehouse. Behind it, a handful of bombed-out buildings stood stacked as closely as tombstones in a cemetery.

"Wonder what those guys are doing here," Gus said, pointing to a cluster of American first-aid men. "I didn't hear anything about this."

A single man knelt beside a body on the ground. A crowd of aid men encircled them. The scene, so far from any battlefield, spoke of something wrong. Walt ran to the side of the kneeling man, who turned out to be a doctor. Walt wanted to help, but he saw no blood or wounds, just an emaciated, motionless man with skin as gray as his ragged, soiled clothing.

Without warning, the man's bony left hand gripped the doctor's wrist, like a limb trying to escape a grave. A gasp escaped the group, a shudder of disbelief. The living corpse turned its skeletal face toward Walt. Leathery skin coated high cheekbones; strands of greasy hair dangled over eye sockets; a gaping mouth opened and closed, trying to speak.

The aid workers stepped back like an awkward drill team. One by one they shifted positions, until only Walt, the doctor and a single aid worker remained close to the body.

"What's he saying?" Walt asked the doctor. "Can you make it out?"

The doctor stared at the hand still holding his wrist. Almost imperceptibly, he shook his head.

The corpse aimed pleading eyes at them.

"Help....me," he whispered.

A hush replied, the disorientation of weary men hearing an apparition speak. The doctor shook the group into action with shouted orders for plasma, saline infusions and more blankets.

Walt looked on in shock. The skeletal body was a grisly reminder of death's relentless appetite. Ted nudged him. "Come on, Walt. Let these guys do their jobs. Let's find Gus. He'll know what's going on here."

They entered a one-story building nearby apparently damaged by shelling. Gus was inside, jotting down notes as he inspected a make-shift ward for men and women who looked like prisoners. Like the skeletal man outside, the patients wore striped uniforms that hung loosely on bony frames. Their mouths hung open, but they made no sound. Even a groan seemed to take too much energy.

"This is a slave labor camp. These are the lucky ones," Gus said, his voice low. "The 104th Infantry found thousands of corpses when they came across this place a few days ago. A lot of the bodies stacked like cordwood. Dozens of men and women almost dead."

Walt couldn't comprehend what Gus was saying. "What is this place?"

"Mittelbau-Dora. The Nazis made V-1 and V-2 rockets in underground tunnels here. You know—the same bombs that hit Paris and London and The Hague a few months back." Gus's voice cracked. "They worked their prisoners to death, goddammit. If they were too sick or weak to work, they were left to die in those hangars. No food, no medical care."

"And the man outside? The one on the litter?" Walt asked.

For a second, Gus closed his eyes. Walt wondered if the clerk had heard him. When Gus finally spoke, his voice sounded hard as gravel. "They found him yesterday in a pile of corpses in one of the hangars. They tried to save him, but this morning the medics had a hard time finding a pulse. When we drove up, they were thinking he was a goner."

"Maybe he still is."

"Probably so."

Walt's stomach churned with disgust. Of all the evils the war had produced, this was the worst. He couldn't just stand there, watching in horror. He had to help.

A low-pitched rattle from a corner of the room launched him into action. He cleansed his hands with rubbing alcohol and examined what looked like an elderly man covered in sores. As Walt wiped layers of dirt from the wounds and wrapped them in bandages, he realized his patient was barely middle-aged. Next to the man hunched a skeletal woman, her dry, cracked lips bloody from the urge to speak. Her pinched face and sunken eyes hinted at unspeakable pain. Walt fetched morphine and fresh water from his medical supplies. After he treated her, he moved on to the other patients until he had checked every one.

Back at his truck, he grabbed a camera and film he'd found in an abandoned cottage two days earlier. He had to record what he was seeing. Who would believe him otherwise?

He snapped photos of the tunnel, the demolished buildings, and, finally, the piles of naked and half-dressed corpses. He tried to hold his camera steady but he couldn't still his shaking hands. It makes no difference if the pictures are blurry or not, he told himself. They're proof. In the makeshift recovery ward, he aimed the camera at a woman in bloody rags, her matted hair clinging to her scalp, her right arm dangling uselessly at her side. As he brought her into focus, the horror of the day overtook him. He fell to his knees and took deep, slow breaths to steady himself. He didn't know how long he'd been there when Captain Hunter found him.

"You okay, Walt?"

"I'm trying, Jack."

"This might help. Some of us officers are going to the town just south of here, a place called Nordhausen, to round up the locals. Both men and women. We plan to order every one of them to bring back a shovel. They're going to dig deep holes for each and every dead person in this camp. Want to join us?"

"Try and stop me," Walt said, teeth gritted. "Let's see how the Germans like hard labor."

***

Walt had hoped the mass burials would release his anger, but they infuriated him even more. The people of Nordhausen denied all knowledge of what had happened in the camp. Part of him wanted to shove them into graves, too. They surely had done business with the Nazi overseers; they must have delivered goods and services to the camp. They had to know.

He found a medic from the 104th. "You know the worst part of this?" the medic said. "Our Air Force caused most of this destruction. They screwed up. Thought this was a munitions depot and bombed the hell out of it."

The medic's face darkened. "A survivor told me what happened when the bombs hit the dormitories. Damn Nazis locked the doors so no one could escape. People inside burned alive."

Walt imagined prisoners screaming and banging on locked doors as flames and fumes slowly killed them. "Why would any human being do such a thing?"

"There's more," the medic said. "On Easter Sunday, the Nazis rounded up prisoners who still could walk and led them away. Those poor souls probably thought they were being taken someplace better. Before they got two miles, the Nazis sprayed them with machine-gun fire."

"And the prisoners here?" Walt said. "How did they survive?"

"I guess the Nazis thought they were dead or couldn't possibly survive. If you look at them, you can see why. We're just trying to keep them stable."

Walt shuddered. Until that day, all he wanted as a medic was to save lives. As much as the deaths of Tom and Hatch had shredded that desire, he'd still clung to the belief that he could control a small corner of his world. If he tried his best, he thought, he could make that corner right. He could make amends for his dead brother. He could make sure his buddies didn't die in vain. God would answer his prayers.

Now, he wasn't sure. What was the point of these last three years, of the battles, the blood, the bombs; of Tom and Hatch and all the rest? He possessed no power, not a scrap. Surrounding him was a state worse than death. A painful lingering neither here nor gone. Limbo in its most wretched imagining. Where was God in all this?

Standing in the middle of the ward, he couldn't shake the notion he was standing in a graveyard, charged with caring for the decaying remains of the dead. If their ghoulish eyes weren't locked on him, he would try to walk away.

He imagined finding this labor camp weeks earlier, when German soldiers still were torturing their captives. He closed his fists so hard his fingernails dug into calloused palms.

He looked for Gus. He passed medics and soldiers whose faces mirrored his fury. He found the clerk carrying a box of sulfa drugs to the recovery area. "Where are the assholes who did this?" he shouted. "Forget the townspeople. What are we doing to find the people in charge?"

Gus shifted the box to one arm and grabbed Walt. "We will. We will."

"Goddamn cowards," Walt said. "They're animals. They deserve no mercy."

April 17, 1945

Dear Nora,

All the horror I have seen in this war cannot match the horror I've witnessed these last few days. The Germans have violated every law of decency toward mankind. For years, I never believed the stories of German atrocities, but there is no doubt they are true. The whole German nation is involved in these crimes. They all must be punished. If only half of what took place reaches America, you will agree with me. Already the guilty are placing the blame on Hitler, the Gestapo, whomever they can. Nobody wants to be blamed, when all are to be blamed...

Walt had no desire to disguise his fury. He mailed the letter that night. This time, no censor stopped him.

FIFTY-SIX

As Alek splashed half-heartedly in his herbal mud bath, our telephone rang. "Can you get that, Mom?" I called.

Two months had passed since Christmas, but still I had no word from Sam or sign of a medical bill for Alek's care. I mixed up one of Babcia's concoctions that morning when my boy woke cranky and lethargic.

My mother picked up the phone on the third ring. "I wash Alek, Gosia," she called out. "Call for you."

"Nora?" a woman said. "Is that you? This is Mrs. Wynock, Sam's mother." I barely recognized her voice. We had spoken only once before on the phone and never met in person.

"It is," I said warily. The only reason I could imagine her calling was to share news that Sam himself couldn't.

"Have you heard from Sam, dear? I know you two keep in touch. Did you get a letter recently?" Her voice caught at the last word.

"I haven't, Mrs. Wynock. Not for a couple of months." I tried to sound calm. "He's probably been too busy to write."

For a moment, she was silent. "That's how long I've gone without a letter, too," she said. "It's not like him. He usually writes me every few days."

Her fear echoed my dread, but I pushed it from my mind. "Please don't worry. Things happen overseas the men can't always share with us. We'll hear from Sam soon, I'm sure of it. I promise to call you the minute I do. Let me know if you hear from him first, okay?"

My false bravado seemed to satisfy her but did nothing for me. Two months was too long to receive nothing from Sam. Even Steve wrote us at least every two weeks.

I didn't hear from Mrs. Wynock again that week, or for weeks after that.

She never called me, not even when a Western Union messenger bicycled to her front door on the tenth day of March. I had to learn the heartbreaking news from my grandmother, whose voice shook as she spoke. Babcia had known good, decent Sam from the time he was a little boy. Now he was gone, and neither she nor I knew how or why. Without a story attached to his death, a horrible weight burdened me.

I should have been as good a friend to him as he was to me, I told myself. I should have written him more often or found other ways to thank him for being so kind.

His sudden death forced me to consider a truth I'd been avoiding for months. If Sam could be killed so close to the war's end, how safe was my husband? What difference did it make that the Allied troops now were advancing into Germany? All it would take was one crazed Nazi soldier refusing to surrender, the way Japanese pilots were doing, and Walt's life could be in danger.

Milly alone understood my fears, yet I barely spoke my feelings to her. On our phone calls, I sat with silent tears as she prattled on about her parents, her husband, her daughter, herself. She was doing me a kindness, really. She understood my pain.

***

Sam again invaded my dreams. In almost every one, he reassured me everything would be all right: "Just tell the truth. The truth always works." I argued with him: "But it doesn't, Sam. I've tried and you're wrong."

My dreams at night exhausted me. My imagination during the day did not help. I couldn't stop picturing how Sam might have died.

"You've got to let him go, Nora," my cousin said. "Those thoughts do you no good."

"You talk like I want them."

She frowned. She was losing patience with me again. I stopped talking to her about Sam. Our relationship worked better that way.

Nine days after I learned of Sam's death, an unexpected letter arrived.

March 19, 1945

Dear Mrs. Baran,

You don't know me, but I served with your friend, Sam Wynock, aboard the USS Abner Read and we became close friends. I was a gunner's mate. Sam was a torpedoman's mate. He often spoke of you, so I know you must be grieving as much as I am. Please accept my condolences. I've already visited Sam's mother, and she gave me your address. If it's okay with you, I'd like to talk to you in person. Please call and let me know where we can meet.

Sincerely,

Joe McConnell

That afternoon, I called the phone number he penciled at the bottom, hoping that information about Sam's last days might release me from imagination's grip. We decided to meet at an Italian restaurant on Jersey Street on a day Milly could watch Alek.

I had to angle my umbrella against a blustery rainfall as I made my way from the bus stop. A damp blast of air joined me as I stepped inside the restaurant, which smelled of garlic and spices even in the middle of the afternoon. I gazed around the room for a booth far from the front door.

I didn't have to wait for Joe McConnell long. I spotted him the moment he opened the door. He was young for a veteran, but his body was lean and his face worn. I raised a hand.

"Nora Baran? I appreciate you meeting me," he said, sliding into the booth. He fingered the menu absentmindedly. "Did you order?"

"Just this cup of coffee. I'm not hungry."

He ordered coffee and a plate of focaccia rolls, then sat in silence until the waitress brought them. "Talking about Sam helps me," he said, stirring his coffee slowly. "I hope it does you."

"To be honest, Mr. McConnell, it hurts even to speak his name." I needed to get to the point of our meeting. Small talk was too hard. "Please tell me what happened. I need to know."

He nodded and without pause began his story. The USS Abner Read was a large destroyer, he said, equipped with big guns and deck-mounted torpedoes and about 250 officers and men. The morning of November 1, it was taking part in the Battle of Leyte in the Philippines.

"Our ship was built for war, able to sink submarines and knock out aircraft. No one was worried. We blew a wing off this one enemy plane. Never expected the pilot to turn kamikaze. Aimed his plane right at us." He paused, breathing hard, experiencing the danger anew. "There was a horrible explosion. I found out later the Jap dropped a bomb into one of our stacks as his plane went down. Set everything on fire."

I shuddered. The sailors had to choose between the flames and the sea.

"The ship sank fast. Most of us were lucky, me included. We made it to lifeboats or clung to floating debris until other ships moved in and rescued us. I looked for Sam, but the smoke was too thick. The water was too stirred up. I couldn't see a thing." His youthful voice cracked.

"More than 200 men were rescued." He pushed his plate back and forth and took slow, deep breaths. "Twenty-two were unaccounted for, including Sam. Those missing in action were presumed dead."

Presumed dead—callous words. What if Sam was still missing? What if he had made his way to a nearby island or was picked up by an enemy ship?

"It was a rough out there. No one could survive for long," McConnell said, reading my thoughts.

"There's more, Mrs. Baran. The main reason I'm here—to pass along things Sam always wanted to tell you."

Lingering guilt flickered inside me. Had Sam died clinging to a misunderstanding of our friendship?

"He told me what a loyal friend you were, how important your friendship was to him. He often said that if anything happened to him, he hoped you would stay in touch with his mother and comfort her the way you did him."

I considered how isolated and lonely Sam must have been to entrust something so important to me. One chance meeting and a dozen or so letters had forged an unbreakable link in his mind. His thoughtfulness to his mother filled me with fresh grief. Kind-hearted Sam, right to the end. "Yes, of course I will."

"There's one more thing. He said you didn't need to worry about Alek. 'He'll be all right,' he said. Is Alek your son?"

From the way he asked the question, I suspected McConnell knew my story. "Yes, it is. Sam has been—he was very kind to Alek. He gave me such good advice. Like a devoted uncle." I fought back tears. Sam's honest wisdom did more than help Alek. It helped me through some of my hardest days as a mother.

***

Milly tried to find out every detail of my conversation with the sailor, but I hurried her out the door. I needed the house to myself before my parents came home.

I dreaded calling Sam's mother. I didn't want to talk about him in the past tense. Despite Joe McConnell's certainty that Sam had died, I clung to the words, "presumed dead."

"Mrs. Wynock? It's me. Nora Baran. I'm sorry I haven't called sooner. I am so very sorry about Sam. How—how are you?" I bit my lip, embarrassed by the emptiness of my condolences.

"I'm all right, dear," she said.

"Sam is—was a good friend, Mrs. Wynock, and a kind one. The next time I go to my grandmother's, I'd like to visit you. To talk about Sam. To remember him. May I do that?"

"Certainly, dear." I could hear her weeping softly. "I would like that."

FIFTY-SEVEN

"You're on guard duty again tonight, Baran. And tomorrow. You, too, D'Amico. We're doubling up on lookouts. Snipers in the area."

Captain Hunter's order made no sense to Walt. Since leaving Nordhausen, they'd heard rumors about snipers but seen no sign of them. The war was all but over.

But Ted D'Amico looked relieved. He wasn't ready for the war to end any time soon. Ever since seeing the labor camp, all he talked about was killing Nazis.

Hunter handed them M1 Carbines, lightweight rifles more deadly and effective than the handgun Walt was given the last time he stood guard. He tried to imagine using it on a human being.

Being armed again brought Walt no pleasure, even though his anger toward every German man, woman and child left him tangled in his bedding at night. His emotional state was nothing like the rage he'd felt toward the unknown sniper who'd killed Hatch, or the cold grief that shackled him after Tom died. This was a fierce agitation spawned by brutal imaginings of walking skeletons, mass graves, beatings, starvation and torture.

"Don't looks so miserable, Walt." Ted aimed his forefinger at Walt like a gun. "With a little luck, we'll nail a Jerry or two."

Ted was all bluster. He was a lousy shot. Chances were good he'd miss whatever he aimed at. Carrying a weapon was no game to Walt; his aim was too good. He hadn't shot a rifle for a long time, but his sharpshooting skills remained part of him. His keen vision was an ironic curse for someone who couldn't even bring himself to shoot a deer.

He was twelve when his father first took him and Cliff hunting in a deep forest in northern New Jersey, if stalking deer at a salt lick could be called hunting. Before long, a hefty eight-point white-tailed buck ambled up. It stared at Walt through the thick morning fog, almost daring him to shoot.

"Pull the trigger, goddammit," Max hissed at both of them. "What the fuck's the matter with you two?"

Cliff fired and hit a tree. Walt's bullet skittered through the dirt. He and Cliff exchanged knowing looks just before their father grabbed Walt's Winchester and took out the buck with one shot. Afterwards, Max ordered them to skin and butcher the beast. The three of them silently ate a thick slab of its meat for dinner.

Clutching his M1, Walt coughed up phlegm. He spit out the memory of the venison, of its earthy seasonings of shoots, twigs and grass.

***

Positioning himself in dense woods just east of his company, Walt studied the tight cluster of medical tents. A blackout had been ordered, but the walls of the floorless tents didn't reach the ground. Low trails of flashlights flickering inside the recovery tent revealed each surgical tech as he checked on patients.

In the forest, a faint breeze tugged at low-hanging branches, pushing the spindly limbs to the ground. They scratched the soil like small, hungry animals.

One hour into his shift, Walt thought he heard a sound that had no place in the woods—a thud, like a heavy object being dropped. He lifted his rifle and aimed at the silent blackness. Thick, cloudy skies obscured the moon and any natural light. Holding his breath, he wiped sweat from his face with his shirtsleeve.

He saw nothing, heard nothing.

***

The next morning, soldiers assigned to detail the camp checked its perimeter. In a clump of bushes twenty yards from a tent, they found two cellophane candy wrappers with German wording.

"They look fresh, like someone just dropped them," Ted said, eyeing them closely.

"Bullshit," Walt said. "Are you trying to make me a wreck?"

Ted smirked. "We'll get another chance tonight."

That night, a full moon and clear sky mocked all attempts at blackouts. The moon hung so low and large that the silvery bark of scattered birch trees glowed like lanterns. Walt saw everything around him and heard even more. The woods wheezed and crunched and whistled. Something pushed its way through a pile of dried leaves. A weasel? A fox?

He pressed his body against the smooth gray trunk of a beech tree, hoping to make himself invisible. Something deep in the woods reflected a shard of moonlight. Walt lifted his rifle to his shoulder and held his breath. He froze his stance until his right arm grew numb. When he felt sure nothing moved, he eased the weapon down.

He scanned the woods until he knew every limb and twig. He did this for an hour, two hours, three hours, until the night noises grew softer and less frequent. Leaning on his rifle, he crouched down, not daring to close his eyes. To fend off fatigue, he counted trees. When he realized he could see their outlines as far as a hundred yards away, he scrambled back to his feet.

If I can see that well, he thought, anyone out there can see me just as clearly.

Moments later, he heard them. Not a single thud, but something quieter, repeated again and again.

Footsteps.

He pulled the M1 to his shoulder and studied the forest. Nothing. He heard the steps again. The closer the steady plodding came, the more it sounded like a person walking. Walt's eyes burned. Why can't I see him? Why isn't that moon helping?

Heart pounding, he shifted his gaze back and forth, scanning the darkness for what seemed like minutes.

There! That must be it! A dark shape emerged at least eighty yards away. Slowly, it took form. A man, he was sure. A solitary man, head slightly bowed, walking slowly in his direction.

Walt wondered if sleeplessness and tension were causing him to hallucinate. But as the man moved closer, he made out a uniform. It looked like the field-gray wool of German uniforms, but he couldn't swear to it. Moonlight and distance played tricks on colors.

He took in a long, slow breath and stepped out from the beech tree's shadow. "Halten zie!" he shouted. "Stop!" he yelled for good measure, remembering how a GI guard had shot Magnus dead when he tried to sneak back into his camp.

Images ricocheted inside him, some imagined, some too real: Max slaying the buck; the nameless, faceless Germans drowning inside that submarine off Africa's coast; Magnus taking a bullet in his heart; Hatch felled by a German sniper; Tom shot in battle; Nordhausen's prisoners howling and hammering on locked doors as they burned alive. Then came the worst images and sounds of all, the squealing tires, the crash of glass and metal, his brother's bloody body. If only...if only.

He drew in a deep, shaky breath. Stop this, he commanded himself. Think! This man could be a deserter. He could be trying to surrender. He could be wounded and needing help.

He could be a sniper.

He could have abused prisoners in that labor camp.

He could have aimed his rifle at American soldiers.

The footsteps stopped. A full second of silence followed. When the man moved again, he no longer moved straight toward Walt but ducked into moon shadows every few feet. He came so close that Walt heard the clear crunch of his boots on the forest floor.

The next time the man stepped into view, Walt stepped out and screamed, "Halten zie!" as he aimed his M1 at the man's shirt pocket, just above the heart.

What happened next, he did not know. Sitting on the ground seconds later, he had no memory of pulling the trigger. He wondered if he had shouted that second warning or whispered it or even spoken it aloud. He remembered only blackness.

Ted ran over, rifle in hand. "You got the sonuvabitch! You fuckin' dropped him, you lucky dog!"

Lights came on. Officers shouted orders. Techs rushed over. His friends told him a single shot had ripped the still night air, a blast that left their ears ringing.

The German lay motionless in a bed of leaves. Ted picked up the man's rifle before pressing fingers to his neck. He quickly yanked them back, "Dammit! He's alive!"

"What happened?" Walt muttered, more to himself than the men gathering around him.

Captain Hunter pushed to the front of the crowd. "Get that man to surgery," he ordered.

The men rumbled like angry hornets, their fury from Nordhausen unsated. No one moved.

"Surgery! Now!" Hunter bellowed.

Everyone but Walt obeyed. Numbness, more than anger, held him fast. He couldn't touch a wound he himself had inflicted.

He needed to reclaim the moment he'd squeezed the trigger. He reviewed his every move leading up to it. He remembered his memories, his anger, taking aim. But not the shot itself.

The one soldier unafraid of Walt's dark moods walked up. For six months, Gil had served without complaint as litter bearer, a lowly job that nevertheless exposed him to war's horrors. In every conversation with the young replacement, Walt recognized himself. They shared the bond of loners trying to make their way.

Gil held two empty coffee mugs and a bottle of schnapps he'd found in an abandoned *gasthaus*. He sat down without waiting for an invitation and filled the mugs. "I thought you could use this."

Walt took a deep gulp. As the liquor settled inside, it clicked into action.

His shaking stopped.

Gil waited. "You okay?" he finally asked.

"Sure," Walt said, with forced bravado. "I just...I wish..."

The young soldier frowned. Walt could see he wanted to help. No one could. No amount of booze could. Instead of unlocking what had happened that night, the schnapps ignited thoughts Walt wanted to bury forever—details of the night Cliff died. Not just what he'd told Magnus.

"I'm okay, Gil. You don't have to stay."

He didn't want to burden the boy. He wasn't sure why he'd decided to shoot that German, but he did know exactly why his brother died. His own reckless bravado killed Cliff. His ego. Walt hadn't just had too much to drink that night. He hadn't just driven with too little experience. He had punched the gas and sped down that narrow, tree-lined road like it was a wide, paved highway. He had howled with delight as trees blurred in his side-view vision. He drove so fast he didn't see the truck edge out of a driveway until it was too late. He had no time to stop.

"Should have been me," he murmured. "Should have been me."

***

When Hunter finally pushed back the heavy canvas flap of surgery, his face was unreadable. "I did all I could," he said. "We'll see if he makes it through the night."

The captain's words ripped loose a stray memory that clung to Walt like gauze stuck to a wound. In it, Walt's forefinger was lightly touching the trigger when an unexpected emotion intruded—a furious desire to strangle the intruder instead. A bullet would be too fast, he thought, too kind. He checked his aim. He squeezed the trigger.

Walt rubbed his temples. His aim was too reliable. If he'd wanted that Nazi dead, he would be. What stopped me from killing that man? God? Cowardice? Revenge? He prayed to a God he no longer relied on. "Answer me. You know the last thing I wanted when I joined the Army was to cause another man's death. What happened out there?"

He sat cross-legged on the ground, wrestling with his conscience, until he decided on a wisp of truth. The only reason his conscience would accept for shooting the Nazi was to stop him, not kill him. I wanted to protect the camp, he thought. I was doing my job. This war has hardened my heart, but it hasn't beaten me. I am not a killer.

FIFTY-EIGHT

An early spring invigorated Babcia's garden. She picked herbs, dried them in the sun and mailed me weekly packages in case Alek needed them. I gave him daily treatments whether he needed them or not. As long as Babcia sent her herbs, I kept it up. I had faith.

I saw changes in my son. He toddled around my parents' apartment and explored every surface. He gained three pounds and learned a handful of new words, like "mine," "Mommy" and "dog." I couldn't wait for Walt to come home and hold him. He would never guess how much Alek had been through.

A sunny day invited us outside. I dressed my boy in a thick wool sweater and knit cap. "Let's go, little one. Let's see what spring has to offer."

Even in the middle of a crowded, concrete-covered city, nature can surprise. Bright green buds erupted from a spindly linden tree at the end of our block. Fooled by days of mild weather, three tiny yellow flowers on a high branch bloomed in full sunlight. A pair of robins nested nearby. I lifted Alek from his carriage and pointed to them.

He gurgled and flapped his arms. "I know," I said, laughing. "I want to fly, too."

A memory of Sam holding Alek at his most frail interrupted my thoughts. How delighted he would have been to see my son thriving like this, I thought. As quickly as the thought arose, a wave of grief followed it.

I kissed Alek's cheek. "See the pretty bird, Alek? See him fly? Can you say 'fly'?"

***

Three days before Easter, I boiled a half-dozen eggs and added vinegar and water to pots of beets and carrots. I ladled the colored liquid into teacups. Alek's eyes widened when the egg I dipped into beet water turned rosy pink.

The dyed eggs were part of our dinner that Easter, a holy day that fell on April 1. It seemed sacrilegious to celebrate it on April Fool's Day, but my mother was convinced the war was about to end. She wanted to celebrate. She even invited Max and Ruth. I sliced a ham and kielbasa for the centerpiece and surrounded it with bowls of mashed potatoes, green beans, beet salad, cucumber salad, stuffed cabbage and the boiled eggs.

Max strolled around the table, eyeing each dish. "Well, well, nice job," he said to my mother. His tone mimicked how he spoke to customers— unctuous and condescending—but he redeemed himself during dinner by taking extra helpings of everything. My mother saw his appetite as the highest compliment.

As we passed the serving bowls around, my mother gushed about a new clothing shop in downtown Elizabeth. We women saw it as a bold bet on the future.

Max snorted. "Not much risk if the war is almost done. You been reading the papers, Maggie? They're calling the Allied push a rout. The Jerries are on their last legs!"

I wasn't sure I believed the papers. They'd hardly said anything about the battle that killed Sam. I didn't trust Walt and Steve's letters either. My brother sounded like he was on vacation, but as an Army Air Force pilot in the Pacific, he could be anywhere—on some landing field on a remote island, on a base in Australia, or even on an aircraft carrier.

After dinner, while Max and my father smoked cigars in the living room, I helped my mother and Ruth in the kitchen. As soon as my mother stepped out on the back porch to shake the tablecloth, I pulled Ruth aside. "The strangest thing is happening, Mom," I whispered. "It's been six months since Alek was in the hospital and I haven't received a single bill, not even the old bills we owed from after Alek was born. And when I took him in for a checkup with Dr. Wenski last week, the nurse said our bill had been handled. That was her exact word: 'handled'."

Ruth smiled and took my hand. "I know."

"Then Max did pay for it? I can't believe it! What came over him?"

"Not Max, dear. Me."

"What?" I frowned, confused. Ruth lived on whatever money Max gave her.

"I know what you're thinking," she said, lifting one eyebrow, a hint of a smile on her lips. "Where did Ruth Baran get that kind of money?"

"Well..."

"It was easier than you can imagine, Nora. For all his fondness for money, your father-in-law never keeps proper track of his cash. Small bills stuff his wallet every night. He never misses ten dollars here, twenty dollars there."

I stared, dumbstruck. I couldn't imagine pious Ruth stealing from her husband. I couldn't believe she was sharing her deceit so boldly.

"I started saving for those bills after your mother mentioned your dilemma months ago. I called the hospital to find out how much you owed. I knew I could cover it if I also sold the pricy jewelry Max buys me on his business trips. Have you ever seen me wear those fancy things?"

I glanced at her cheap clasped earrings with their tiny clusters of white beads.

"My favorites," she said, fingering the beads. "Max never notices I don't wear the ruby rings and gold necklaces he gave me. They fetched a pretty penny."

I couldn't help it. I grabbed her in a hug and burst out laughing. In seconds, Ruth was giggling along with me.

"What are you two girls up to?" Mother stood at the door to the porch, eyebrows raised.

"Oh nothing, Mom," I said, swallowing my laughter. "Just how funny people can be about money."

Ruth shot me a look, a signal to keep her secret.

***

Max was right. News about the war in Europe grew more positive every day. Walt almost certainly would come home soon. All my troubles seemed behind me until the night of April 12, when news bulletins announced the death of our president at Warm Springs. We had lost our commander in chief. What if the Germans took advantage of that? Reporters gave scant information about the little man who was now our president, except that he once owned a men's clothing shop.

"Don't worry," Milly said. "All those smart generals are still there. They know more about war than any politician."

My mother said the same thing, but what did she know? She and my father still received most of their news from Polish-language radio stations. "You worry too much, Gosia," my mother scolded.

For three days I peppered God with prayers. I even said the rosary aloud twice a day, a routine that made my mother roll her eyes and my father snort disapproval. I wondered if God was paying attention. I would do anything to reach Him, even if I had to go to Babcia's to use her crystal ball again. My faith worked more easily when things were going my way.

FIFTY-NINE

Walt eyed the quaint German homes surrounding him, their tidy yards, their clusters of shade trees. Their charm mocked all the devastation he'd witnessed in the war. He knelt, his emotions too heavy to bear. The war—the fighting part of it, at least—was over.

Just that morning, on a sunny, balmy day in late April, he learned that his old infantry regiment had encountered Russian soldiers near Dessau. The Eastern and Western fronts soon would meld into one. Germany would be forced to surrender.

On May 7, Major Penland made it official. He stood before the medics and read General Eisenhower's order in a calm monotone. "All hostilities in Europe will cease."

No raucous celebration erupted at his words. The men were too fresh from war for that. Walt observed the moment by shaking hands with every tech and officer in his company, from Gil to Captain Abich. For the first time in almost three years, he was certain he would see Nora again. His thoughts were a jumble of joy, grief, relief and anger.

He hunched over, head in hand. Out of nowhere, someone thumped hard on his back. Walt swung around, fists up, the edginess of more than three years of war ruling his reflexes.

Aidan Leary hooted. "Look at your face, Baran! Do ya think I'm a ghost? Didja think ya got rid of me when ya sent me back to the front. Too bad, bud!"

Walt sighed. "Unbelievable," he muttered. "I wish I had that kind of power." But he never wanted his nemesis dead. He never wanted anyone dead. He just longed for a sign that God – or some grand cosmic order – was still in charge of the universe. Now here was Leary, wearing his usual smirk, pretty much the same self-absorbed bully he always was. And alive.

As alive as that German soldier Walt shot on guard duty, who somehow had survived his emergency surgery.

Walt's hands shook worse than ever. I'm alive, too, he consoled himself, even if I'm not the person who signed up for the medics three years ago. He frowned at the corporal, wishing Big Al was still there to intercede. "If you're smart, Leary, you'll get your ass out of here. Pronto."

Leary stayed put until Walt slowly rose to his feet. In seconds, the corporal vanished in a crowd of passing soldiers.

He sure acts like a ghost, Walt thought. He wished he could disappear like that. He needed time to blend into the background, time to recover.

***

Weeks later, Walt stood on a transport ship's top deck. He didn't need to brace himself. The solitary ship plowed westward through calm Atlantic seas. This trip was nothing like the one that delivered Walt to the war three years earlier. No convoy accompanied the ship. No fighter planes kept watch.

Danger was behind them. Home was ahead.

To his relief and astonishment, he would be home in two days—to hold his son, to embrace his beloved wife. He wanted Nora more than anything, and just the thought of his little boy made him smile. Yet a crushing melancholy weighed on him. His every movement required effort. The emotion wasn't the grief he'd felt for all the losses and deaths he experienced. This was a new depth of sadness. Even calm seas and brilliant sunshine didn't help.

What had he lost now that the war was over, he asked himself, except daily dangers, the Army's rigid rules and the companionship of men as miserable as he was?

He shared his misery with Ted D'Amico during a card game, after his former tentmate ribbed him about his glum mood.

"There's not enough booze on this tub, that's the problem," said Ted, who with Walt and Buck were the only medics from Company D aboard. The Army's point system for deciding which men went home first had split their clearing company apart.

"Booze won't fix this," Walt said, inhaling deeply from a cigarette. "I tried that back in Germany. It didn't make a dent. You know how a wound itches like hell when it's trying to heal? That's what I feel inside—an agonizing itch I can't scratch without making it worse."

Ted nodded. "Maybe because four months ago we were still ducking Nazi snipers. You gotta shake that stuff out of your head, Walt. We're going home to our families, to our own beds, to home-cooked meals."

"It sure will be different, won't it, Ted? No Army swill. No reports from

Gus. None of your smelly socks. And all the baths we want!" He laughed feebly, running his fingers through his tangled hair. He wondered what Nora would think when she saw him. His clothes hung loosely on his scrawny frame. He'd tried to get a haircut before he boarded the ship, but every other soldier and sailor seemed to have the same idea at the same time.

Maybe exercise will help, he thought. He followed the routine he practiced aboard the *Florence Nightingale*, but no matter how many times he walked the top deck or inhaled the bracing sea air, he couldn't erase his blood-soaked memories.

The first time Walt encountered Buck on one of his walks, his friend grabbed his arm. "What are we doing up here, Baran? That rogue wave on the *Nightingale* should have kept both of us off top decks for good."

"That wave feels like a lifetime ago, doesn't it?" Walt said.

Lowering his head, Buck grimaced. "More like an eternity."

Buck understood. Ted did, too, even if he wasn't ready to acknowledge it. The men who served with him through the blood, gore, bombings and close calls—they all knew. They had lived a lifetime in their three years together. Now everything they experienced was over —the camaraderie as well as the brutality.

Walt lingered at the railing long after Buck left him, staring out at the sea. Soon, his relationships with his fellow medics would slip into memory. All would eventually return to their hometowns. The Ninth Infantry's Clearing Company would be no more.

***

Walt grinned at the battered blue car that pulled up for him at Fort Dix. The sight of Ziggy's heap was a relief. He hadn't been sure who would pick him up. He dared not hope Nora would be in the car, too. Better his eccentric cousin at the wheel than his father or some powerless employee his father had just hired.

True to form, Ziggy sped along highways and back roads faster than any truck had carried Walt in the war. The drive overwhelmed him. Nothing looked familiar. Trees loomed larger, roads spread wider, traffic seemed heavier.

"Almost there, Walt," Ziggy said, as they passed by the town of Linden. "Recognize anything?"

"Sure," Walt lied. The old neighborhoods looked foreign. Were their houses always so close together?

"Nora really missed you, Walt. I got to know her better while you were gone. A real sweet gal. And your boy—he's something. Looks a lot like you, I think," Ziggy said, glancing at Walt.

"I can't wait to see them. They'll be at my dad's house, won't they?"

"That's a helluva question. Of course, they'll be there! Didya think they'd skip it?"

Walt barely heard his cousin's chatter. He imagined holding Nora in his arms.

"Wait 'til all your family sees you, Walt. They're gonna jump and holler," he said as they turned onto his father's street. "Your folks have a feast waiting for you."

"All my family? A feast?"

"Sure. Everyone's gonna be there. Aunts, uncles, cousins, in-laws, even friends. They're all waiting for ya."

Panic seized him. He didn't want a crowd of people. He didn't want a celebration. He wanted only his wife, his child.

***

Ziggy opened Max's front door with a flourish. "After you, pal."

The bright morning sunlight left Walt blinded in the dim parlor. He squinted at indistinct shapes and flashing cameras. Boisterous shouts greeted him. Max pumped his hand. "Good to have you back, son. Real good." Walt's mother gently hugged him, her expression trapped between tears and a smile. "Oh, Walter, I am so happy you're finally home."

A crowd of family and friends surged forward. Everyone but Nora. They wanted to hug him, shake his hand, touch him. With each greeting, he grew more anxious. As his eyes became accustomed to the light, he glimpsed his wife on a sofa in a far corner. She was struggling to calm a small child, who whined and pulled from her grasp, his unhappiness growing. The two of them were like the mirages he'd seen at the edge of the Sahara Desert, shimmering pools of hope. That is Nora, isn't it? He no longer trusted any of his senses.

"Nora? Alek?" He spoke their names softly.

Ziggy rescued him. Clearing a path with one arm, he led the way. "'Scuse me, 'scuse me," he called out. "The man wants to see his wife. Move it, Uncle Charlie. Move it, John."

Nora rose to her feet and took a step toward him. The boy clung to her dress, whimpering. Patting his head with one hand, she pushed back her long, golden hair with the other. The crowded room grew quiet as he reached her side. She seemed to take forever to move her gaze from the boy to him. In her eyes he saw what he was feeling—disbelief, longing, hesitation, emotions so deep she was close to tears.

Wrapping his arms around her, he whispered in her ear, "You're really here, Nora, you're here."

She felt soft and yielding. He kissed her lightly, aware of the many eyes watching them. He couldn't take his eyes from hers.

Within seconds, curious relatives encircled him again.

"Yes, I did see Patton and Churchill. General Eisenhower, too," Walt answered an uncle. "If you'll excuse me a min—"

The questions kept coming. "No, we didn't get to Rome or Paris." He bit his tongue. Did they think he had been on a vacation?

Someone brought him a plate of food. When he took it to Nora, Alek ducked behind her. "Hi there, big boy," Walt said. Kneeling down, he held out both arms. "I'm your Daddy. Can you give me a hug?"

The boy shoved his thumb in his mouth, eyeing him suspiciously. Walt studied his tired eyes and pale skin. His son looked small, frightened, overwhelmed, nothing like the child Walt had conjured up in his years overseas.

"Looks like the little guy didn't get much sleep last night," he said, glancing up at Nora. He leaned back on his heels and lowered his arms. "Don't worry, son. We'll have time to get to know each other."

Behind him, Ziggy issued a new command. "Come on, folks. Let's eat." Rising to his feet, Walt smiled at his cousin's repeated rescue attempts. He reached gratefully for Nora's hand just as Max bullied to his side

"I'll bet you could use some rest, Butchie," Max said, clenching Walt's arm and pulling him away.

"Yeah, Pop. And time alone with my family."

"All taken care of. Your mother has a room upstairs all fixed up for you and Nora. We'll have Nora's folks watch Alek for a few days so you two can, you know, get some rest." Max winked slyly. "Come Monday, I want you at my office to talk about your future with the company. That'll give you three whole days of rest and relaxation."

Before he could reply, Max slipped away. "Three days?" Walt said, glancing toward Nora. He could tell by her expression she had heard every word.

SIXTY

The moment Walt stepped through Max's front door, the room exploded with chaotic cheers. All I could make out was a dark shadow surrounded by the sun's glare. Little by little, a scruffy, wild-haired man came into view— as skinny and ragged as the homeless men who sometimes wandered through town.

The commotion frightened Alek, who grabbed me and whimpered. I rubbed his back and whispered, "Shh, darling boy, that's your daddy. Remember his pictures? Dada?" Alek stared at me.

Though my husband stood barely ten feet from me, he still seemed an ocean away.

Ziggy took charge. "Move it," I heard him order over and over as he moved in my direction.

My son clung to me fiercely. "Shh, love, it's okay."

Walt and I faced each for what felt like minutes but was only seconds. His sunken cheeks and weary eyes troubled me. When we embraced, his bony body felt like a stranger's.

As much as I longed for this moment, I feared it, too, knowing how much had changed for me while he was gone. With Walt gone, I had to face frightening challenges alone, the worst being our son's illnesses. I found unexpected sources of strength.

Walt had to have changed, too. That much time in war would change anyone. I wondered what he would think when he met his son. Would Alek be the child he expected?

Friends and relatives pushed close, desperate for Walt to tell them about the war. Milly, whose own husband had yet to return from the Pacific, filled a plate of cheese, bread and fruit for him. "Eat, soldier. You need some flesh on those bones."

While Walt fended off the crowd's attention, Ziggy limped close to me and whispered, "Don't worry about Walt. He'll be okay. And he knows nothing about Sam. Trust me on that."

His words both startled me and reassured me. What was Walt's rambunctious cousin thinking? Could I trust his wild imagination? Ziggy must have seen my uncertainty. He smiled kindly. "I'm serious," he said. "Don't worry."

I looked back to Walt, whose panicked glances begged for help. Once again, Ziggy was smarter than I gave him credit for. Spreading his arms wide, he scooped everyone toward the dining room. "Look at all this food, folks. Please! Help yourself!"

Relief softened Walt's expression. I bent down to encourage Alek, who watched his father intently, "Say hi to your daddy, Alek."

Walt crouched low and opened his arms. "Can you give your daddy a hug?"

For years I'd imagined our boy falling happily into his father's embrace at a moment like that, but it was not to be. Alek's lower lip quivered. He stepped back.

There was no mistaking Walt's confusion and worry. I wished he understood that little children needed time to warm to strangers. That's what Walt was to both of us, a stranger.

As soon as Walt stood again, Max grabbed him by the elbow. I overheard my father-in-law's plan, one he hadn't shared with either me or my parents. I couldn't believe it. Max wanted us to be away from our son? He wanted Walt back at work already? Only Max could expect us to bridge our three-year separation in three days. Only Max would separate a toddler from his parents. Only Max wouldn't notice that his skinny, haggard son needed time to heal.

Anyone could see Walt's wounds were not the visible kind. Anyone but Max.

SIXTY-ONE

The guests lingered, hungry for war stories, until Max and Ziggy finally sent them on their way. Ruth took Alek by the hand and led him to a box of toys she kept for his visits.

Walt glanced at Nora. She smiled and nodded. Without a word, they quickly sought the privacy of a rear bedroom.

Cupping his hand behind her head, he pulled her into a deep, lingering kiss. He held her tightly against him. "I can't believe I'm home," he murmured. "I can't believe we're together."

Nora spoke in a whisper. "We have to talk, Walt. What your father said…"

"What?"

Her voice turned firm. "Our son isn't even three years old. He's never been separated from me for more than a few hours. You barely had time to say hello to him. We simply cannot leave him this weekend."

Her resolve was unmistakable. Could Max have met his match while he was gone, Walt wondered? "What do you want to do instead, my love?" he said. Anything you want, he thought.

"We'll go to my parents' house. My mother already fixed up the third-floor bedroom for us. Alek will sleep with her downstairs. It's all arranged."

He grinned. "You're perfect in so many ways."

She squinted at him, still serious. "There's one more thing. You don't really plan to go to work on Monday, do you?"

"I don't want to, Nora, but I have no choice."

"Why? You don't have to. Wait a few weeks. Get your strength back." She ran her hand up and down his bony arm and squeezed.

That I can't do, he thought, even if she begged. "I know my father, Nora. We don't have to stay here this weekend, but I do have to show up

Monday if I want a job to support us."

Disappointment clouded her face. There was so much she did not know. When he was a medic, he often thought of pursuing a medical career after he got home. He was that good at healing. By war's end, he knew he couldn't bear it. Too many memories would haunt his every action. Like it or not, his father was his best chance to support his family.

***

Walt didn't know what to expect when he walked into his father's office that Monday morning. It was one thing to greet his father as a soldier coming home from war. It was another to report to the man who was both his father and his boss.

Max glanced up from the pile of papers. He looked satisfied with himself.

"Well, well. Look at you, Butchie. Still a bit ragged around the edges, but nothing a haircut and close shave can't fix."

Walt nodded, self-conscious. The last thing on his mind during his precious few days with Nora was visiting a barber. "Ragged but ready, Pop."

"The important thing is that you survived, Butchie. Good thing my conversations with Brandt landed you in the Medics. You might never have come out alive otherwise."

He pondered the irony of his father's ego. He'd long suspected that Otto Brandt played some role in the Medic's offer to him. It came too soon after his ride in Brandt's yacht. But the Fayetteville businessman was an altruist who loved to help soldiers, no matter what strings others might ask him to pull. Besides, no amount of Brandt's help would have made him a surgical technician if he himself hadn't passed those tough medical classes. Let the old man believe what he wants, Walt thought. I know the truth.

***

Nora had been right. He'd needed more time to recover. He moved like a zombie at work that first week. At least the blessed routine of his job, embedded in his memory from before the Army, guided him through each day. No horrors or grim surprises awaited him in the cool basement of his father's funeral home. There, the constant presence of death scarcely fazed him. The corpses were mostly of older persons reaching a logical end to life. Their deaths made sense.

At home, simple chores overwhelmed him. Unpacking his duffle bag, stuffed only with his meager Army possessions, should have taken minutes, but he ignored the job for weeks. Just the thought of pulling out

297

everything—his shabby khaki pants, shirts and jacket, his well-worn boots, a small packet of photographs and papers—filled him with an angry sorrow.

Three shots of whiskey finally gave him the nerve one Saturday morning. He unwrapped the packet of papers first. On top were photos from the war he decided to stash away for now. Maybe one day he would want to see the faces of Tom Lucas and Frank Hatcher and his fellow medics. Maybe one day he could stomach the photos from Nordhausen. Not yet, though.

Below the photos were his Army certificates, discharge papers and the telegram announcing his son's birth, a document that brought him the most joy despite the long time it took to reach him. He would definitely save all those, as well as the photographs of Nora and Alek he carried with him throughout the war. An officer once urged him to toss those photos away. "Your bag is heavy enough, Baran. You'll be sorry you're hanging onto them." He was never sorry.

Last in the packet was the empty envelope he'd saved with Beth's return address on its front. It weighed down his bag like a brick. When he'd first read her letter, he was amazed it contained no hint of what had happened between them. Now he understood that it reflected her youth. He copied her address to a blank envelope, then carried the original to the basement and tossed it in the furnace.

Then he stuffed his Army clothing into paper sacks, determined to throw it all away. "When does the trash go out?" he asked Nora.

"Tomorrow. Are you getting rid of all that? Don't you want to save some of it?"

He snorted. "Not one stitch."

"Are you sure you emptied all your pockets?"

The question struck him as odd, implying he'd led such a normal existence for the past three years that he'd nonchalantly stuffed his pockets with odds and ends. But he didn't argue. Nora might be right. He did laundry so rarely in the latter months of the war that anything was possible. At the kitchen table, one by one, he turned every pocket inside out. At the bottom was a shirt he'd worn mostly as a second layer; its collar's rough binding chafed his neck. It wasn't in bad shape compared to the other pieces, he noticed, but he had no interest in keeping it. He yanked out its chest pocket, relieved to be finished. A small scrap of paper floated to the floor.

Two names were printed on it in faded ink, followed by addresses and phone numbers.

Tom.

Hatch.

***

July 30, 1945

Dear Beth,

The letter you sent me in Europe arrived only a few weeks after I learned Frank Hatcher had been killed by a sniper. It happened when he was on guard duty in Normandy. You probably knew he was sweet on you. He should have told you himself, but he was too shy. I am relieved to be home now with my wife and son. Please give my regards to your parents. They were very kind to me and Hatch. We both appreciated it.

Walt Baran

Walt felt an obligation to let Beth and her parents know about Hatch. He mailed it with no return address, though he didn't worry she would try to pursue him. By now, Beth surely had found another man.

***

He postponed the phone calls for days. He wasn't ready. He mentally rehearsed what to say, unsure if he'd picked the right words. Finally, on a day his father agreed to let him go home early, he settled next to the phone in his in-law's parlor. Nora's parents were at work. Nora was outside walking Alek in his stroller.

"Mrs. Hatcher? My name is Walter Baran."

"Walter Baran?" She paused. Her next words came slowly. "Yes, I recognize your name. My son wrote about you often. Francis said you were his best friend and the smartest medic in the whole army."

For a fraction of a second, her words resurrected his friend. Walt swallowed hard.

"Walter? Are you there?"

He inhaled deeply. "Yes, ma'am."

"It's nice of you to call." Her voice trembled slightly.

You can do this, he told himself. "I'm privileged to, ma'am." He paused and took another breath. "I want to tell you what you already know. Frank was the best. I was lucky to call him my friend. Always cheerful. Always kind. A good soldier, too."

She was silent.

"I'm calling to make sure you are all right. And your family, too. I live in New Jersey. Not close, but if you need anything, anything at all, call me and I'll come." He gave her his parents' phone number and his father's work number. "They will pass along any message, okay?"

"That's very kind of you. I assure you I am fine."

"I wish I could do more," he said. "A year before D-Day, while we were still in Africa, Frank and I and another pal named Tom Lucas all made a promise to each other. If anything happened to any of us, we would contact the families back home. We'd take care of them."

"I recognize Tom's name, too. Is he all right?"

Walt inhaled sharply, wondering why he hadn't anticipated that question. "No, ma'am. I'm—sorry to say he, he didn't make it either. I, I'm the only one of the three of us who did."

A cry escaped her, a wounded sound that echoed his. "Oh my," she finally whispered. "I'm so sorry."

He wanted to offer solace but his anguish interfered. "I have to go, Mrs. Hatcher. Please stay in touch."

He sat very still for a long time, mouth dry, head pounding, until Nora's footsteps on the stairway jolted him to action. Picking up the receiver, he dialed another number.

A young woman's soft voice sounded expectant. "Hello?"

"Hello, my name is Walt Baran," he said, waving to Nora as she entered the apartment. "Is this Bernadette?"

"I'm sorry, who is calling?" Unlike Hatch's mother, Tom Lucas's widow acted like she'd never heard his name before. He remembered her well, a strikingly beautiful woman with sleek black hair and long eyelashes. She and Tom seemed to love each other the way he and Nora did.

"Walter Baran," he repeated. "I was a close friend of your husband. We trained together in the infantry."

He wished he could speak to her in person and not through a crackling long-distance telephone line. "I met you in Fayetteville once when my wife was staying there. Nora." Walt glanced up at Nora, who sat opposite him in her father's chair, holding Alek in her lap.

"Walt! Of course. I remember now. I, I'm sorry. This has been a difficult..." Her voice grew softer. "I just need time. You know?"

"I do." He couldn't tell if she was crying. If she was, she smothered it well. "I want you to know I treasured your husband's friendship. He was smart and brave, a born leader. I wished I could have..." He stopped. She didn't need to hear his guilt. That wasn't why he called. "I wished he didn't have to be in the infantry."

"Thank you, Walt."

He told her about the promise he and Tom and Frank had made in Africa. He offered to help her, just as he had Frank's mother. "I—I'll keep your phone numbers," she said, her voice so soft he could barely hear her. "I'm sorry, I really must go." With that, she hung up.

He stared into the telephone receiver, stunned by its silence. Nora set

Alek on the floor and came to his side. He could tell by the way she searched his face that she saw his sadness. They reached for each other and held on tightly. He never wanted to let her go.

***

"Come here, you!" Walt grabbed at his son as he toddled past. The boy screeched and pulled away. Was he playing or frightened? Walt couldn't tell.

"He's not used to roughhousing after having so many women in his life," Nora said. "Me, my mother, your mom, my Babcia, Milly. We don't tussle with him."

She had spoiled him. It made sense, given all the time that had passed. She and Alek were bound as one. He vowed to become part of his son's life, no matter how long it took.

***

The heat of late August made his in-law's tiny parlor seem even smaller. As soon as Walt came home from work, he gave Nora and Alek quick hugs and opened every window. He was glad Ben and Janka weren't home yet, so he could tune the radio to an English-language news broadcast. A week had passed since Emperor Hirohito's surrender, but news reports still buzzed with speculation on how the Allies would finish the war with Japan. Walt leaned close to the radio to hear every word.

Unexpectedly, the doorbell rang over and over. Someone pounded on the building's front door. "I'd better get that," Walt said, jumping to his feet. He bounded downstairs and warily opened the door. Before him stood Nora's brother, grinning broadly, arms crossed. "I had orders to fly some big wigs to the East Coast," Steve said. "Thought I'd take a slight detour before heading back."

As soon as she heard her brother's voice, Nora rushed down, too. She nudged Walt aside and grabbed Steve in a hug. "You could have let us know you were coming!" she scolded. "We don't have enough food in the house to feed the likes of you."

That night, Steve told tales about his years as a pilot. His bombing raids were so accurate they stalled even mighty ships, he bragged. As soon as his hitch was up, he planned to take advantage of the GI Bill and go to college.

Walt envied his brother-in-law's unbroken spirit. A man who views warfare from miles overhead sees no anguished faces, no bloody bodies, no mangled flesh, he thought. He sees billowing smoke and abstract patterns of civilization. War must seem hypothetical.

SIXTY-TWO

Not until the three of us had spent weeks together did my husband stumble into the reality of our years apart. Sitting at my parents' kitchen table, he watched Alek silently run a tiny toy truck across the floor.

"He doesn't talk much, does he?" he asked.

I knew that moment would come, the moment my husband would need to know why our son was not what he expected. A pang of sadness clutched me. If I could write the story of my life, it would have only happy endings. God would answer my every prayer.

"Not yet," I said "Every baby is different."

I waited until Alek was asleep that night to tell Walt more. Sitting on the edge of our double bed in our snug, third-floor room, I revealed some of Alek's first few months—his difficult birth, his hospitalization, his fragile health. But not his constant fretting and crying, and not what Eleanor said about his sensitive nature. Walt didn't need to hear all that.

He listened silently. A frown never left his face. "I wanted to tell you, Walt. I did. But Max convinced me it would only add to your worries in the war."

His frown twisted into a scowl. "What made him think he knew what I needed? All I wanted was the truth."

His words felt like a reproach. We sat in silence for a moment, holding hands. I wondered how much truth was possible.

When he finally spoke again, his voice turned tender. "I know that must have been hard for you, Nora. Having to leave our boy in the hospital, having to take care of him when he came home."

"I had my Babcia and my mother and Milly, too, and...friends. Your mom, too. They all made it easier." One day I might tell him about Sam, I thought, but not now, not when my heart still aches from Sam's death, not when Walt appears as fragile as our son.

"And God helped. I prayed like you taught me, even when God didn't seem to answer my prayers." I reached for his hand. "How about you, Walt? God must have been a comfort to you. I'm sure my difficulties hardly compared to yours."

Walt winced. Bombarded by volleys of loss and inhumanity, his own faith barely clung to life now. Gathering Nora in his arms, he struggled to find the right words answer her. "Not tonight, Nora. It will take a long time to tell it all and I'm beat. We'll talk about it soon, though. I promise."

A week passed without him keeping his promise, then two. He lacked the strength. He lacked the words.

At night, Nora anchored him. She fed him and held him and never pried, even when nightmares of artillery fire, bombs and incoming wounded jolted him awake.

***

Walt sat across from me at our kitchen table, chain-smoking cigarettes. I pulled my sweater close around me. Our tiny radiator was working hard to protect us against November's dropping temperatures, but I still had a chill. Our apartment was small and worn, furnished as it was with second-hand tables, chairs and a sofa. But it was all ours. Its blessed privacy made it seem like a castle.

Yet again, I was grateful to Max, who let us live in the third-floor unit above his funeral home. We had to pay a small fee for utilities and serve as the building's caretakers in exchange, but we couldn't afford better.

"You don't mind living here, do you, Nora?"

"Of course not! I don't need anything fancy."

"As soon as we can afford it," Walt said, "we'll get a house. With a big yard where Alek can play. And grow stronger." His son needed fresh air, he thought, a place to learn how to throw a ball and play tag. As hard as Walt tried to get close to him, Alek still shied away.

"This place is fine for now," Nora said. "All in good time."

She smiled in that lopsided way of hers that made his heart jump. He reached over and took her hand. "Do you have a few minutes? I'd like to talk to you about something."

"What? Is something the matter?"

"No, no. It's just about the Army, that's all." Each time he shared a small piece of his life overseas, he realized how much he could never say. "You know how I was when I was at Bragg, Nora. I hated Roosevelt and the Army and the war. When we got into the war, I even thought about running away with you, going AWOL. Remember?"

"I do. We were both so frightened."

"Well, near the end of the war, I learned FDR knew what he was talking about. Hitler's Germany was an evil place, Nora. Evil beyond anything you can imagine. Hatred ruled them. They acted like they had lost all knowledge of right and wrong."

He could tell by her expression that she wanted to know what he meant. He avoided her gaze. He couldn't go into detail. He himself wasn't sure he understood all that had happened. Only six months earlier, he had aimed a rifle at a Nazi soldier's chest and pulled the trigger. I did the right thing, he told himself daily. But every day he asked himself, was I truly right?

"Getting into the Medics saved my life, Nora. And I was able to save many other lives. I'll always be grateful for that. But—and I don't know if this makes any sense—I wonder if saving lives was enough."

***

St. Adalbert's Church was so crowded that chilly Sunday morning that my shoulders touched Walt's as we knelt two rows from the altar. Many of the young men sitting in the pews near us looked like they, too, had just returned from war. Their eyes echoed the frightening darkness I'd seen in Walt's.

I glanced at my husband's bowed head, in awe of his steadfast faith. I might never achieve it myself, but I was grateful for what I did possess. The women in my life bolstered my faith. Whether they were skeptics, healers, pious churchgoers or casual churchgoers, they all gave me hope. Did Walt have hope? He hid so much from me. Silently, I begged God to restore my husband to joy.

Midway through Mass, I followed my husband to the altar. The priest placed a paper-thin wafer on my tongue and declared it the body of Christ. I heard my Babcia's words: "Be patient, dear Gosia. Your husband will return."

Walt bowed his head and pretended to pray. The communion wafer clung to the roof of his mouth, dissolving slowly. The Medical Corps was supposed to be my salvation, he thought. My chance to survive the war. My chance to keep my best friends safe. My chance to make amends to Cliff.

He survived all right. He even saved many lives. But he couldn't save his friends, and he almost killed a man. He wondered if he had even come close to atoning for Cliff.

A musky aroma of incense lingered in the church, blessedly milder than the acrid artillery smoke that drifted into camp on the war's darkest days. Back then, he helped to set up makeshift altars on the backs of Jeeps, never caring if a priest or minister or rabbi would lead the service. Even with artillery rounds exploding all around them, even when he couldn't hear God's answers, he rarely doubted God was there.

Where was God now?

He joined Nora at Mass every Sunday. Her faith amazed him, a depth of belief she had not possessed three years earlier. He'd had that once. As a child, and even as a young man, he always felt God's presence in church. Now, he waited impatiently for faith to return. He waited for God.

He stared at his folded hands. Weeks after returning home, they still trembled. Invisible wounds and memories shook them. In the hushed darkness of the church, he heard Tom's voice: "Don't forget how hard you tried to get in the Medics. Don't forget why you did. For Nora, for your child."

I didn't do it just for my wife and son, he thought. I did it for peace to return to my soul. He glanced at Nora gratefully. If the war gave him little else, it gave him a thankful heart. Maybe that was a step toward healing.

Gratitude was no equal to faith—a mere ember where once a flame burned. Yet it gave him a measure of hope. It was a beginning.

ACKNOWLEDGMENTS

I greatly appreciate the advice, moral support and encouragement of the numerous individuals who contributed to the completion of my novel.

Had my father not given me his letters and journals from World War II before he died, I might never have started this book. His papers revealed early opposition to the war in the U.S., the struggles Americans endured even far from the front lines, and the fragility of truth. What I discovered about my father's two best friends in the Ninth Infantry Division, Eddie Hutchinson and Fred Harvey, compelled me to write.

I am grateful to the members of the Ninth Infantry Division Association, whose shared memories and stories at annual reunions informed my book. The map of the Ninth's movements through Africa and Europe, generously sent to me by member Bill Mizell, was an invaluable aid.

Many, many thanks to my favorite veteran, Herb Stern, an association member whom I met at a reunion in Orlando years ago and whose personal story is remarkable enough for its own book. Herb, who turns 102 this year, served in the same medical company as my father. When I needed to check a fact, he was the one I called. I deeply value his wit, his friendship and his remarkable family.

I am indebted to the many talented individuals who critiqued my work during its evolution from essay to historic fiction. Among those generous with their time and talents were Linda Dunlap, Connie May Fowler, Pat Matthews, Terri Chastain, Julie Compton, Jamie Morris and Bruce Aufhammer. I thank them and all the friends and family members who coaxed me to the finish line of this book.

A special thank you to Margaret Reyes Dempsey. I cannot thank her enough for her unfailing assistance in all things creative and technical.

Finally, my deepest gratitude to my talented and supportive children, Michele and Ryan, and to my loving and patient husband, Ray. I am incredibly lucky to have them in my life.

ABOUT THE AUTHOR

Geri Throne was born and raised in New Jersey. A graduate of Syracuse University, she had a career as a journalist at the Orlando Sentinel before turning to creative writing and fiction. She lives in Winter Park, Florida, with her husband. To learn more about her, see her website www.GeriThrone.com or follow her on Facebook at facebook.com/gerithroneauthor.

Thank you for reading *Secret Battles*. If you enjoy it, please let others know. Tell your friends, spread the word on social media and post an online review.

Made in the USA
Columbia, SC
16 August 2021